Bravo! Brava!

Jet Mykles, JP Bowie, and Kimberly Gardner

mlrpress

MLR Press Authors

Featuring a roll call of some of the best writers of gay erotica and mysteries today!

Maura Anderson	LB Gregg
Victor J. Banis	Drewey Wayne Gunn
Jeanne Barrack	Samantha Kane
Laura Baumbach	Kiernan Kelly
Alex Beecroft	JL Langley
Sarah Black	Josh Lanyon
Ally Blue	Clare London
J.P. Bowie	William Maltese
P.A. Brown	Gary Martine
James Buchanan	ZA Maxfield
Jordan Castillo Price	Jet Mykles
Kit Cheng	L. Picaro
Kirby Crow	Neil Plakcy
Dick D.	Luisa Prieto
Jason Edding	AM Riley
Angela Fiddler	George Seaton
Dakota Flint	Jardonn Smith
Kimberly Gardner	Caro Soles
Storm Grant	Richard Stevenson
Amber Green	Claire Thompson

Check out titles, both available and forthcoming, at www.mlrpress.com

Bravo! Brava!

Jet Mykles, J.P. Bowie, and Kimberly Gardner

mlrpress

This book is a work of fiction. Names, characters, places, and incidents either are products of the author's imagination or are used fictitiously. Any resemblance to actual events or locales or persons, living or dead, is entirely coincidental.

Copyright 2009 by Jet Mykles
Copyright 2009 by Kimberly Gardner
Copyright 2009 by J.P. Bowie

All rights reserved, including the right of reproduction in whole or in part in any form.

Published by
MLR Press, LLC
3052 Gaines Waterport Rd.
Albion, NY 14411

Visit ManLoveRomance Press, LLC on the Internet:
www.mlrpress.com

Edited by Kris Jacen
Cover Art by Deana C. Jamroz
Printed in the United States of America.

ISBN# 978-1-60820-000-9

First Edition 2009

TABLE OF CONTENTS

About Something by Jet Mykles 1

Sometime Life's a Drag by J.P. Bowie 71

Woman's Weeds by Kimberly Gardner 173

About Something

Jet Mykles

Bonnie snapped her fingers and turned from Shawn as she read from her script, "*You always end with a jade's trick: I know you of old.*"

"Stop."

All scripts came down and all eyes turned to their director, who sat behind a folding table before the playing area in the small rehearsal space. He eyed them over the rims of his glasses. "Shawn and Bonnie, switch."

"What?"

"You heard me."

Shawn blinked, script nearly falling from nerveless hands. "Switch? Switch what?"

Bonnie laughed. "You don't mean switch *roles* do you?"

Roscoe raised one smooth brow. "I do, in fact."

Shawn stared. Three weeks into rehearsals and Roscoe was still playing games? "Uh... why?"

"Because I said so." That strong, square jaw tilted up, causing some of that wayward black silk he had for hair to fall back from Roscoe's high forehead. Behind his black horn rims, he blinked as though he didn't understand. "Is there a problem?"

Shawn opened his mouth, then wisely snapped it shut. After a semester and a half of Roscoe's acting class and another year before that hearing the stories about the hip young director, he knew better than to question. Doing so would only result in some far more embarrassing activity than what was asked. Besides, Roscoe was adept at coaxing magic out of an actor, sometimes when they didn't realize it. But Roscoe was asking him to play a *girl* here.

Bewildered, he looked at Bonnie. Her blue eyes went wide and she shrugged. Gritting his teeth, decidedly *not* looking Roscoe's way, he flipped his script back a few pages. "Ooo-kay then. Top of the scene?"

"Yes."

Heaving a breath, Shawn scanned the script as he joined the four other cast members on the opposite side of the playing area from where he'd entered as Benedick. He had a good handle on his lines already but he hadn't paid that much attention to detail on Bonnie's yet, and certainly not the ones when Benedick wasn't on stage. *It's just an exercise,* he told himself. Roscoe was testing him, making him see his own role from another angle. It made sense. In *Much Ado About Nothing,* Benedick and Beatrice were at each other's throats constantly until they finally admitted their love for one another. This little role reversal could be good. Maybe this way he could show Bonnie what he wished she'd give him to react on. As he listened to the beginning of the scene, he got himself into character. Damn it, if Roscoe wanted him to do this, he'd *do* it! Besides, Beatrice was a righteous bitch. She'd be fun to play for a bit. He'd show Roscoe he could act! Without any of that stupid acting like a girl crap too. He'd just play the character as he knew her, screw the gender stuff.

When his first line came, he cocked a hip, placed his free hand on it and adopted a tone dripping with sarcastic scorn: *"I pray you, is Signor Mountanto returned from the wars or no?"*

He bandied lines with Tony, the guy playing the messenger, and had fun with it. There was more in Beatrice's lines than he'd realized. When Bonnie strutted into the play area with Dustin and Gavin and delivered Benedick's lines, Shawn realized Beatrice's lines were *better.* She got all the good jabs. *That's okay. I've got more scenes.* They traded insults, comfortable in the adversary after three weeks even if they had switched roles. They'd done plenty of talking about their roles already so he used a lot of what he'd heard and seen from Bonnie. Shawn even made Trina, who was playing Beatrice's cousin Hero, giggle. Okay, the character was supposed to giggle, but he was pretty sure the laugh was real.

When it was his cue, he exited with the rest then turned in the wings to watch Bonnie finish the scene with Gavin and Dustin. She was a terrific actor and he enjoyed watching her play with the words. Admittedly, Benedick was hands-down his favorite character in Shakespeare. He'd been stoked when Roscoe had ignored the odds and cast the short, cute kid in the lead. Hell, even Bonnie was a little taller than him—maybe an inch or so, more if she wore heels. He'd been afraid he'd have to play one of the constables and do a Marx Brothers parody. The most he'd hoped for was Claudio, the starry-eyed romantic lead.

When the scene was done, he stood with Trina at the back of the room, facing Roscoe, waiting the lord's judgment on how they'd done.

How the hell did a theater geek turned college professor look so put together anyway? He was supposed to be the typical scruffy, distracted director with wild eyes and hair sticking up like Albert Einstein's thanks to his shoving his hands through it too much. He was supposed to have a corduroy jacket with fake leather patches on the elbows and horn rim glasses. But Roscoe Schroeder was nothing if he wasn't contrary. The only thing he had to the stereotype was the glasses, and fuck if he didn't make the thick black horn rims look *good*. His piercing black eyes and equally dark, ridiculously expressive brows just somehow made the nerdy glasses work. The corduroy jacket was replaced with a sweet black leather bomber jacket with a custom roaring white tiger blazoned across the back. When he wasn't wearing the jacket, he had on one of many crisply ironed dress shirts that he wore open at the collar to expose the thick silver chain that always rested on his sharp collar bone. In the warmer months, he'd roll up the sleeves to expose long, toned forearms dusted with a thin layer of sparse hair. Shawn had never seen the flesh of his shoulders and biceps, but he could very well see how slim muscles filled out those shirts. His black hair was always impeccable, in an Ivy League cut, short on the sides and back and a little bit longer on top and front. He far more looked the part of a leading man than a director.

Roscoe sat with his fingers laced over his belly, his feet propped up on the table before him. Shawn was a little unsettled to find those sharp black eyes on him. He wasn't sure he liked Roscoe's smile. "Well. That was quite interesting. What do you think?"

Shawn shrugged. He'd no idea what Roscoe was fishing for and he knew better than to put forth his opinion if he could help it. Personally, he thought he'd rocked, but he'd been wrong before. He didn't relish the dressing down if Roscoe thought it had sucked.

"Bonnie?"

She laughed. "I don't know. It was kind of fun."

"You did very well."

She nodded but didn't say more.

"Dustin, what did you think?"

Shawn groaned silently. Dustin was as self important as the prince he was playing and certainly the most outspoken in the cast. He would put forth an opinion on *any*thing. Too bad he didn't have enough brains to put forth many *good* opinions. "Bonnie makes a better Benedick."

Shawn shot Dustin a glare, which was returned with a grin and a shrug. Matching the grin, Shawn responded by flipping Dustin the bird, which produced laughs all around.

Roscoe ignored the laughter, still looking to Dustin. "Why do you say that?"

True to form, Dustin had run out of words. Now he just shrugged. "She's got more... bravado."

"You trying to say she's got bigger balls than me?" Shawn quipped.

Again Roscoe ignored the laughter, turning to the tall man playing Don John. "Juan?"

John looked up from his script, then shrugged. "They did pretty good." He went back to reading.

"Trina?"

She giggled, pushing blonde sprays of hair from her round face. "Shawn's a much bitchier Beatrice."

"Why *thank* you, darling," Shawn mushed, throwing his arm around the only person shorter than him in the cast—even if it was barely an inch—and laying a big kiss on her round cheek.

This time Roscoe did join in the genial laughter. "I agree. On all counts" Roscoe carefully lifted his black cowboy boots from the table and set them on the floor, then leaned forward to fold his arms where his feet had just been. He set his square chin on the backs of his hands, his smile pure evil. "What would be the general consensus if I made the switch permanent?"

"What?" His wasn't the only exclamation, but Shawn's was certainly the loudest.

The bastard director/teacher didn't look at him. Instead, he focused on Bonnie. "What would you say to that?"

Shawn glanced up to see Bonnie's wide eyes on him. "I, uh..." She looked back at Roscoe. "Why?"

"I think you're both better in the other roles. The rest of the cast agrees."

"The whole cast hasn't said shit," Shawn piped in.

Finally, those black eyes turned back to him, full of amusement at his expense. "Shall we ask?"

"No. They're all gonna agree with you." Of course they would. Roscoe was... well, *Roscoe*. He was *the* acting teacher at school. The dean and other teachers catered to him. His picture and list of popular credits was on the front of the brochure that advertised the school. Every student wanted to be in his class and in his productions. All the girls—and some of the guys—lusted after him. Shawn had never been to New York so he'd never seen any of the plays that Roscoe had directed both on and off Broadway, but he'd heard plenty about them. He *had* seen the indie movie Roscoe had been in and was suitably impressed.

Roscoe tilted his head. "I take it you don't agree?"

"No!"

"May I ask why?"

Shawn glanced around and saw absolutely no support from his fellow cast members. Not even Bonnie. She was staring at the toes of her sneakers. Snorting, he returned his attention to Roscoe, slapping his script against his thigh. "Why the hell would I want to play a girl? And don't give me any of that shit about how men used to play all the girls' roles in Shakespeare. I don't see you asking Trina or Gayle to play Don Pedro or Claudio."

Roscoe extended one thumb upward, lifting his chin to rest it with the cleft just above the tip. That was one of Roscoe's classic 'thoughtful' poses. *Shit*. "No. I think it would be interesting just to change the two notable roles."

"What the hell for?"

"You make a wonderful Beatrice."

Why did his heart have to swell at the praise? "You saying Bonnie doesn't?"

"No. But she does make a wonderful Benedick."

Panic started to set in. He laughed. "Oh come on. You're just yanking my chain, right? We were just doing an acting exercise."

"Which you seemed to enjoy."

"You are fucking kidding me?"

The steady look in those laughing black eyes told him he wasn't. "The play on gender roles would be very interesting. And," he tilted his head to run the side of that thumb against the edge of his jaw, "you'd look rather fetching in a dress."

Everyone laughed but Shawn.

Roscoe stared at him until the laughter died down, then a little longer. Shawn gave as good as he got and was gratified when it was Roscoe who broke the stare. He sat up and shot back the cuffs of his blue striped dress shirt to check his watch. "That's enough for today, folks. Shawn, Bonnie, perhaps we should discuss this." He glanced around. "And anyone else who might have an issue with the switching of roles."

Predictably, no one else did. Shawn endured the snide jokes and slaps on his back as his fellow cast members filed out of the rehearsal space. Roscoe stood and came around to the near side of the table and sat on it. Shawn dropped into one of the folding chairs along the perimeter of the open space. Bonnie pulled up a chair beside him.

Roscoe spoke briefly with Ted, the stage manager, before the other man left the three of them alone. Then he gave his two stars his full attention. "So. I take it you don't like my idea, Shawn."

"I think it sucks."

"Because you'd be playing a woman?"

"That about sums it up."

"Beatrice is one of Shakespeare's finest female leads."

"Agreed. Bonnie'll do a great job at it."

"With all due respect to Bonnie, I think you'd do a better job."

The flimsy seat creaked under Shawn's shifting. "Why the hell are you riding me about this? I don't want to play a girl."

Roscoe leaned forward, all amusement draining into one of those scary, intense expressions. "I'm riding you because I think this would be a good thing for you. Personally. You are far too comfortable in your schtick."

Shawn reeled against the back of the chair. "My 'schtick'?"

"Yes. You could play Benedick and you'd do it beautifully, of that I have no doubt. But it wouldn't challenge you. You could do it in your sleep, even in iambic pentameter."

"Flattery will get you nowhere."

"It's not flattery. It's fact." He glanced at Bonnie. "You two are the best actors in your class. I'm not afraid to tell you this because everyone knows it. I wouldn't ask this of any of the others. But I think you two *could* do this and I think you could make it interesting." He held up a hand, stalling Shawn's protest. "Stop for a moment. Put aside the fact that the role is female. Think of the scene you just played. You had *fun* with it. There was more expression in your face and more animation in your body than I've seen outside of a few isolated moments in class. And you hadn't even memorized the lines yet. That's because it was different. It was outside your known scope, so you could play with it." He was talking to both of them, his piercing gaze flitting back and forth. Then he took the glasses off and the intensity magnified. "We could do it the traditional way. And if you truly object, fine, we'll do it. But I think we could have a more lively, more *interesting* performance if you'd do it my way."

Fucker. Roscoe was known for taking quirky chances in his plays. They usually made it better. He'd seen Roscoe's version of *Romeo and Juliet* when he'd been in high school and was enchanted. He'd seen last year's *Midsummer Night's Dream* and nearly busted a gut laughing. He'd been determined to make it into Roscoe's Shakespeare production this year.

Roscoe put his glasses back on. "Let's not make any final decisions now." He stood. "Go home. Sleep on it. We'll talk about it tomorrow."

Shawn grimaced as he went to retrieve his backpack, knowing he was doomed.

✦✦✦✦✦

"Maybe he likes you," Gavin mused, then leered at Shawn. "You know he's gay, right?"

"No! Really?" Shawn snorted and shot him a look. "Everyone knows he's gay, dipshit."

Gavin folded his arms on the plastic table, his cropped blond hair shining in the sunlight. "So that's probably why he wants you to play Beatrice."

"Yeah, right, because secretly what all gay men want is just a chick with a dick. Are you a fucking moron?"

The others laughed.

Gavin sat back, wrapping his hand around his bottle of Coke. "You're just scared I'm right."

"Fuck you." He shot up from the table, grabbed his backpack and stormed off.

Bonnie called after him as he walked away. "Shawn! Come on."

He kept walking, hands in fists, muttering at the pavement.

He heard the slap of her sneakers behind him so he knew when her hand was going to grab his arm to turn him around, making him stop. She fixed earnest baby blues on him, her sunglasses on top of her head to keep her short, sandy blond hair from her squarish face. Damn it! With the right makeup and costume, she'd look more like a guy than he did. A good looking guy, but still. *Shit!*

She tried a smile. "Don't let Gavin get to you."

"I'm not. He's an idiot. It's just..." He grumbled.

"Dude, is it so bad?"

"Yes."

"Talk to me."

"Why?" He glanced back to their two friends still seated at the round patio table, a grimy plastic umbrella mostly shielding them from the California sun. "Everyone's decided." He'd spent morning classes hearing hearty congratulations on his new role. Seemed his helpful friends in the cast had made some calls last night. UofC was a big college, but the drama department was pretty insular. He'd heard everything from genuine excitement to sarcastic derision. Three guys had already jokingly asked him out on a date, as long as he dressed in drag. Oh yeah, he was having fun. Not!

She smoothed a hand up and down his arm. "We haven't talked to Roscoe yet. You can still say no."

"I said no last night."

"Yeah, well, I'm sure if you're really uncomfortable with it, he'd respect that."

Shawn frowned at her, watching the cast aside eyes and the shuffle of feet. Bonnie was a good friend. She and Shawn had already spent time over cafeteria dinners discussing the relationship between their characters. Beatrice and Benedick had some unknown past that had caused an animosity between them. He and Bonnie had broken it down and made up their own version of a sordid affair that had ended badly. They had given each other plenty of juicy background for the continued sniping between the two characters. He'd looked forward to working with her, to building the romance, to reaching that crucial scene where they finally couldn't take it any more and had to confess their love. Could he really do this from the other side?

He could tell by her body language that she did. "You want to do it."

She took a little breath, then looked at him again. "Yes."

"Shit."

"Come on, it'll be fun."

"For *you* maybe."

"Oh please, I'm going to get just as many dyke jokes. That's nothing new. So why can't we both just have fun with it? You're good enough to pull it off. They're right, you'd make a better girl than me."

He shut his eyes tight, matching the move with his fists at his side. There it was again. At a mere five foot five with his mom's wavy, glossy mahogany hair, his dad's big brown eyes and too long lashes, and someone else's pert little nose and far too lippy mouth, all in and around an oval face, he'd been mistaken for a girl countless times, Adam's apple and breastlessness aside. He used to get in fights in school all the time when he was really little, and learned to cope later through sheer bravado. That's where his acting had come in. But he wanted the leading man roles, not the leading *lady* roles!

"Oh Shawn." She squeezed his arm. "You know I know how you feel."

Only partially. While she could look kind of masculine, Bonnie was rarely mistaken for a guy. Her main problem was that people kept labeling her a lesbian when she wasn't. "It's not the same."

Another squeeze then she let her hand drop. "Let's go see if Roscoe's available now. We'll tell him no."

He opened his eyes. She stood before him with her hands dug into the back pocket of her jeans, her face full of nothing but sincerity. "You serious?"

"Sure. Beatrice, Benedick, I'm thrilled to play either one. And it's not going to help anyone if you're miserable. Even

Roscoe won't be able to coax a good performance out of you if you really don't want to do it."

"There's that…"

She turned, waving for him to follow. "Come on, let's go."

He caught up to her. "Don't you have class?"

"Yeah, but I can blow it off."

He frowned as they neared the building and the table with their friends. "You know what, why don't I go find Roscoe?"

She stopped. "You sure?"

"Yeah. I'm the one with the problem. We can talk it out. You don't need to come."

"Well, okay, if you're sure." The hand was back on his shoulder. "I'm good with either way you decide to go."

Smiling, he pulled her into a hug. "Thanks."

A whistle sounded somewhere behind him. "You two get a room!"

✣ ✣ ✣ ✣ ✣

Shawn didn't find Roscoe in the little office he shared with Mr. Banks, the voice teacher, but he did find him behind the rehearsal hall that doubled as a classroom for acting classes. Roscoe sat on the manicured lawn underneath a spreading oak tree, back propped against the tree trunk, reading a book. His long jeans-clad legs were stretched straight in front of him, the ankles of his black cowboy boots crossed. The horn rims were perched up on top of his head, holding back his wealth of curls.

He looked up when Shawn approached, that obsidian gaze was unfettered. "Mr. Finnemore." He set a bookmark into the hardback and set it aside. "I thought I might see you sometime soon."

"You got a minute?"

Roscoe spread his hand to indicate the grass beside him. "Take two."

Shawn dropped to the grass, folding his legs and setting his backpack beside him. Since the oak gave a lot of shade, he pulled off his sunglasses and tucked one earpiece into the collar of his t-shirt as he met Roscoe's patiently waiting gaze. "What the hell are you doing to me, man?"

Roscoe chuckled, low and deep, not unlike a big cat's purr. "I take it you're referring to my suggestion of switching roles?"

"You know I am."

Long fingers folded over Roscoe's flat belly. "What am I doing to you?"

"You want me to play a girl."

"Yes."

"Do you know the ribbing I've been getting already?"

Roscoe blinked. "Has word already spread?"

"You knew it would."

"Actually, I didn't. How?"

"Dude, actors are worse gossips than bored housewives."

"I suppose that's true." He frowned. "Is that's what's bothering you?"

"Tch, yeah."

"And what bothers you about it?"

"Dude, look at me."

His words stopped as Roscoe's dark gaze raked him up and down, distracting him. Oh man, he wanted to be able to do that to people. To make them *feel* his looks.

"Yes?"

Shawn leaned back on his arms, spreading his legs in the most masculine pose he could muster at the moment. "Has it escaped your notice that I'm little and girly looking?"

Roscoe's generous mouth kicked up into a smile. "No."

"Right. I've been dealing with it my whole life. People *still*, to this day, sometimes mistake me for a girl. And now you want me to play one?"

"What is wrong with playing to your assets?"

"Huh?"

"I've had you in acting class for nearly a year now. I've spoken to your instructors from last year and the year before. I've seen the last three productions you were in, and I've looked at your pre-school resume. You've always gone for parts that were exceedingly masculine. While I can understand your desire to do so, you're doomed to fail in those parts."

Shawn scowled, not sure how he felt about Roscoe doing research on him. Did he do that for all of his students? Or only the ones that he wanted to screw with one of his strange decisions? "I've done just fine, thank you very much."

"The acting itself has been exemplary." Said so matter-of-fact, it meant more. "You're very talented. However, in the real world, if you were to make a living from acting, you would never be cast in such roles."

Shawn opened his mouth to protest, but Roscoe kept talking.

"Acting is a business of perception. More people are going to hire on your looks rather than your ability." He gestured to indicate Shawn's face and body. "I am sorry, my friend, but you are beyond cute. You could star in a live action anime. If you do play a male, you'll be playing high school kids well into your late twenties. *Those* are the roles you'll get and those are the roles in which you will be believable."

Shawn scowled, his thoughts had hiccupped on hearing Roscoe call him 'beyond cute' so he was having trouble coming up with a rebuttal.

"I'm offering you a chance to *use* your visible assets. You could not only play a female, you could play a female without anyone suspecting you're male. You can showcase your talent to the extreme. The opportunity I offer you is something that none of the other boys in the class could possibly accomplish. They couldn't look the part."

"Looking like a girl and acting like a girl are two different things," Shawn grumbled.

"I have faith that you could pull it off. Spectacularly." The man spoke like every line he delivered was scripted but with a spontaneity of a good performance.

Shawn grimaced at him. "You're not just blowing smoke up my ass?"

"Now why would I do that?"

"To get me to do what you want."

Roscoe laughed. "I find the truth is quite effective in doing that for me. I'm rarely wrong." Unfortunately, the last was true.

Shawn sat up, brushing grass from his palms as he folded his legs. "Anyone ever tell you you're an egotistical bastard?"

"Occasionally, yes."

They both shared a laugh.

Shawn took a deep breath, gazing up into the leaf canopy above them. "You think it'll be good?"

"I know it will."

A shiver of delight shot up Shawn's spine on hearing the dark promise in that voice. "Okay."

"Okay?"
"Okay. I'll do it."

✤✤✤✤✤

Shawn got a laughing ovation when he walked into the rehearsal room in a corset and skirt. So maybe his sneakers didn't match and he wasn't supposed to wear the t-shirt underneath the corset, but he was playing along, right?

Gavin circled around him, lifting up the side of his skirt. "Digging into the back of your closet, man?"

Shawn snatched the skirt away and slapped Gavin's arm. "This old thing? I only wear it because it's dusty in here." He batted his eyes. "Wait until you see my *real* dress. Gloria promises it'll be gorgeous."

Arms surrounded him from behind and Bonnie kissed his cheek. "You're looking good, m'love."

He arched a brow at her. "Watch it, you." But he smiled and kissed her back.

"My, my, my," drawled a very familiar voice. Shawn turned to see Roscoe entering. "Don't you look lovely?"

Shawn pulled from Bonnie and dropped into a curtsey. He'd been practicing all night and he thought he did pretty well. "Thank you, sir." Rising, he was cheered to see Roscoe's raised eyebrows and broad smile.

"We'll have to work on the curtsey, but you'll do for now." Chuckling, he headed for his table and chair. "All right, people, act two, scene one. Beatrice, Leonato, Antonio, and Hero onstage."

✤✤✤✤✤

Bonnie held Shawn's upper arms, staring down into his eyes. "*With no sauce that can be devised to it. I protest / I love thee.*"

Shawn clutched at her elbows, lowering his gaze and twisting his head to the side, facing the audience. "*Why, then, God forgive me!*"

Bonnie cupped Shawn's jaw with her palm, urging his face upward. "*What offence, sweet Beatrice?*"

"*You have stayed me in a happy hour: I was about to / protest I loved you.*" Shawn let his voice go breathy just before raising his eyes to meet Bonnie's.

She put her arms around him, pulling him closer. "*And do it with all thy heart.*"

He put his arms around her, smiling. "*I love you with so much of my heart that none is / left to protest.*"

Bonnie leaned down, tilting her head for the kiss.

"Stop."

They both froze at the sound of Roscoe's voice.

Sighing, Shawn shared a suffering look with Bonnie, then stepped out of her embrace to face Roscoe.

He scowled over the table at them. "Do it again."

Ted sat behind him but wasn't paying much attention, his head bent over the student desk, probably doing his homework. No one else was present to witness the incessant tries of the two actors to attain the satisfaction of their director. They'd repeated this particular bit at least seven times so far by Shawn's count. That was in addition to the emotion exercises Roscoe had put them through for the first hour of rehearsal. The scene was the emotional apex of the play, the moment when Beatrice and Benedick break through years of rivalry to take a chance and bare their souls. Both Bonnie and Shawn were putting their hearts into it, wanting to get it right. But that wasn't enough for Roscoe.

Shawn grimaced, scrambling for the cool he'd lost about a half hour ago. "You gonna let us finish this time?"

"Are you going to put some feeling into it this time?"

He crushed handfuls of his long blue rehearsal skirt in his fists. "What the hell do you think I was doing?"

Roscoe crossed his arms, pique showing through his usual calm. "That's a good question. Care to answer it?"

"Fuck you, man. I'm doing my best."

"Bullshit. I've seen you do better when you're jerking off in class."

Shawn turned to face the blinded windows to the side of the room rather than face Roscoe. "What the hell am I doing wrong *this* time?" Because it seemed to be him. Roscoe had a few notes for Bonnie but not nearly the criticism he had for Shawn.

"You haven't corrected anything so my answer would be the same."

"I was softer," Shawn growled around gritted teeth.

"That's not what I asked for."

"I didn't bite her head off."

"Slight improvement."

"What do you want from me?"

Roscoe's eyes narrowed. "Are you afraid of him?" He pointed to Bonnie.

Shawn sighed, a hand raised to cover his eyes. "Not this again."

"Yes. This again."

"Why would I be afraid?"

"You should be."

Shawn spun, starting to pace. "What the hell for?"

Bonnie scooted to the back of the open area, watching.

Roscoe stood, rounding the table to stand beside it. "He's a man."

Since reason had deserted him an hour ago, Shawn blurted what he really thought. "He's not much bigger than me. I'll kick his ass."

"That's a man's argument, not a woman's."

"This is Beatrice. She'd totally kick ass."

"Beatrice talks a good game. Yes, she'd *say* she'd kick Benedick's ass, but he's a veteran of wars. *He hath done good service, lady, in these wars… a good soldier too… a lord to a lord, a man to a man; stuffed with all honorable virtues.*" Words spilled out in that trained voice, impossible to ignore. "But she knows she's not up to the task. *O God, that I were a man! I would eat his heart / in the market-place.* She knows she can't do what a man can."

A chair at the side of the open area rattled away from him. He'd kicked it. He kind of realized that after it happened. "Yeah, I know, but Beatrice isn't scared of him. He's never hurt her. As much as he's done, he's never hurt her."

"But he *can*. Beatrice would deny it, but she is a woman of her times. A *woman*. And a woman of her times, like it or not, rail against it or not, would be at least a little afraid of a veteran soldier." Roscoe took off his glasses and set them on the table then turned to approach Shawn. "She would have to respect that he had fought in wars. She would have to respect that he is a soldier and a lord."

A frustrated cry burst from Shawn's throat. "I don't *get* it." He kicked at another chair, frustration and confusion flaming behind his eyelids as his fists pulled at the sturdy fabric of his skirt. "You don't want me to cower, do you?"

"No. I want you to use all that anger you're feeling right now."

"*Fuck* you!" Shawn whirled on him, dropping his handfuls of cloth to curl his fingers into claws. "You told me not to bite her head off."

Roscoe's eyes blazed as he faced Shawn from just a few paces away. "You're a woman and she's a soldier."

Shawn thumped his own chest. "This is *Beatrice*. She's one of Shakespeare's biggest bitches. Soldier or not, she'd kick him in the balls."

"Not true." Roscoe advanced, shoulders hunched slightly like a stalking predator. "She'd kick another man in the balls. She wouldn't kick Benedick. She loves him. You're about to say that."

Shawn set his feet apart, skirt whirling as he snapped his hands up to his head and let out a loud, frustrated scream. "I don't get what you want!" He tore at his hair. "First you tell me to be softer, then you tell me to be angry, what the fuck…?"

Strong hands gripped his arms. Instinctively, he reared back, lashing out, but Roscoe was a lot quicker than Shawn would have suspected. With humiliating ease, Roscoe spun Shawn around, pinning back to chest, steely arms banded around Shawn's chest and arms, restraining him. Holy shit, he'd never realized just how *big* Roscoe was.

"I want you to feel helpless," Roscoe hissed in his ear, pressing his weight against Shawn's back, straining the smaller man's knees.

Shawn froze, staring blindly at the dusty floor beneath his feet, overcome by Roscoe's heat. The man stood more than a head taller and he was far more muscular than he looked.

"I want you to know deep in your heart that no matter what you do, no matter how hard you fight—" he gave Shawn a hard shake for emphasis, "—no matter how much you rant, you're *never* going to win. You're *never* going to overcome. You *can't*. You're helpless. You're physically ineffectual. *That's* Beatrice's tragedy and that's her burden to bear. She has the will of a lion in the body of a lamb."

To his horror, Shawn realized he was shaking. He wasn't scared. Not exactly. But Roscoe had him trapped. It was as exhilarating as it was frightening. He let his body sag a little, making himself heavy. Roscoe tightened his grip, fully supporting Shawn's weight. *Easily* supporting him.

Roscoe spoke into his ear, tone harsh as a leather belt closing around Shawn's neck. "She knows Benedick probably won't hurt her, but they both know he *can*. And without much effort on his part. She knows that if he did, he'd probably get away with it." Leaving one arm around Shawn's torso to support him, Roscoe slid the other hand up and around to the back of Shawn's head to grip a handful of hair. Ruthlessly, he tore at it, twisting Shawn's head around so they were almost face-to-face. The muscles of Shawn's neck strained. "You. Are. Helpless. And you *hate* it. You *will* rail against it. But it's a fundamental fact that you *must* accept."

Shawn swallowed, overwhelmed by Roscoe's strength, his nearness. The man's dark, spicy scent surrounded him, as tangible as his arms and grip. Roscoe was all around him, pressed against him.

Black eyes bore into his from underneath half-lowered lids. "You get it now?"

Shawn nodded.

Abruptly, Roscoe released him.

Unprepared, Shawn crumbled to the floor, his rehearsal skirt spreading around him on the floor. He caught himself on braced arms, staring at the blue fabric, panting. The actor in him clicked in, storing the sensations, memorizing the cold race of his blood through his limbs, cataloging the feel and smell of the bigger man before he could forget it. He didn't know if that's how all women felt, but he could see the reasoning that this could be how *this* woman felt. It was an echo of what he'd gone through himself when he was much younger and had pissed off the wrong bully. Roscoe was right. He could use this. If he could just stop shaking.

Roscoe left him like that for a few minutes, standing over him. There was no sound from Bonnie or Ted, nor any from the world beyond the off white walls of the rehearsal room.

Then Roscoe was kneeling in front of Shawn, close but not touching him. The rolled up cuffs of his shirt were so white against the dark tan of his skin and the darker spray of hair over his skin. "Shawn?"

Slowly, Shawn looked up.

Roscoe's expression was back to normal. No, it wasn't. It was softer. Kinder. He smiled a little and slowly reached out to draw the pads of his fingers over Shawn's cheek. Watching Shawn, he turned his hand around so the younger man could see the fingertips.

They were wet. Shawn blinked and a fat tear fell down his cheek.

Roscoe turned the hand again and cupped Shawn's cheek. His voice was soft. "You all right?"

Shawn swallowed. Nodded.

"Should I apologize for frightening you?"

Shawn smiled. A small laugh escaped him, a little shaky. "No." He cleared his throat. "I get what you mean now."

Roscoe nodded, his thumb caressing the curve of Shawn's cheekbone. "I never doubted you."

A few smart replies to that skittered through Shawn's brain but none made it to his lips. He was far too interested in the intense, hot look in Roscoe's black eyes. If Shawn didn't know any better, he'd think…

Roscoe dropped his hand, sitting back on his heels. "All right. Why don't you take a few minutes to collect yourself." He pushed to his feet, turning to face Bonnie. "As for you…"

✤✤✤✤✤

"So does this mean you're gay now?"

Shawn sat back in the corner of the couch and took a swig of his beer as he studied Matt. "Why? You wanna fuck me?"

Laughter burst out all around them but Matt just grimaced. "Ha ha, pretty boy."

"Oooo, he finds me pretty." Shawn jumped forward and rubbed his shoulder against Matt's. "Wanna take me back to your room?"

Matt jumped off the couch as everyone around them continued to laugh. "What is it with you actors?"

Shawn stuck out his lower lip in an exaggerated pout and gave Matt puppy dog eyes. "Awww, you don't like me anymore."

"Fuck you, fag boy."

Shawn flipped him off and sat back on the couch, dropping the act. "Fuck you." He'd never liked Matt in the first place.

Matt rolled his eyes and moved on to another side of the common room with his friend. *Fuck 'em.* This is why he far preferred theater group parties over regular college parties. Shawn only knew the people at this party through his dorm buddies, of which Matt was not, even if they did live in the same building. Matt and his friend had just gotten drunk enough to confront Shawn, which he found ridiculous. Maybe the hulking homophobe *did* have a crush on him. How funny would that be?

Another body dropped down to take Matt's place beside Shawn. "*I* for one would be happy to find out you were gay." Ian swung an arm around Shawn's shoulders to haul him close. "Then I'd have someone to troll the bars with."

Shawn laughed, barely managing to not tumble into Ian's lap. Ian was the one openly gay guy that Shawn knew in the dorm. He also knew Ian from the drama department since the taller man was a junior in the tech department.

"I didn't say I was gay, Ian."

Ian snorted and nuzzled behind Shawn's ear. "They *all* say that at one time or another."

"I mean it," Shawn laughed, struggling to sit up. "Let go of me, freak."

Chuckling, Ian held him. Ian did *not* look gay. Or, at least, any gay man that a homophobe would imagine. He was built like a football player and looked like the boy next door. Well, except for the tattoo of a dragon snaking around his left bicep. His blond hair was buzzed short and his blue eyes were big and soulful. Plenty of girls had tested whether he was actually gay or not, but his roommate Ben would confirm it even as he assured whomever he was talking to that *he* was *not* gay. "I'd be happy to give you a tutorial in the ways of buttsex."

Laughing, Shawn pushed at Ian's chest. "I'll just bet you would. Let go."

The bigger man hesitated. Shawn had a moment's flash of worry, reminiscent of the fear/excitement he'd felt in Roscoe's arms a few days ago. But then Ian snorted and lifted his arm.

"All right, but you let me know if you change your mind." The grumble was good natured.

Not surprisingly, most of the guys at the impromptu party had chosen to drift away, pointedly ignoring Shawn and Ian's antics. Shawn chuckled. "Looks like we scared them off."

"Fuck 'em." Ian tilted his head back, upending the last of his beer down his throat. Lowering the empty, he exploded with a belch and slammed the bottle on the littered table before them. He grinned at Shawn. "I need another beer. You?"

Shawn took a look at his drink, then copied Ian's move and finished it off. "Yep."

They made their way back to the three coolers full of drinks around the back of the house. That spot was, predictably, crowded and they got separated. Shawn started talking to a few friends, but found his eyes tracking Ian's whereabouts. Ian was the only guy at the party he knew for a fact was gay, and he was fascinated by how Ian didn't let that fact single him out. Ian just kind of stayed away from the overt homophobes, who had learned to keep their distance from him as well. As for everyone else, no one seemed to care.

As Shawn got progressively drunker, his musings expanded. What was it like to be gay? No, that question was a bit too esoteric for his inebriated state so he settled on something more basic. What was it like to have sex with a guy? He ended up in a shady corner of the relatively deserted side yard of the house, watching the stars through the sparse hanging of trees above, contemplating the feel of a male body. He'd been in enough tousles to get an idea what it was like to be held and pinned down. He'd even been hit on once by a guy during his freshman year, but he hadn't let that get to any sort of touching. Strangely enough, that guy and he were now friends. What if Shawn had let it progress? But, no, that guy wasn't his type. Neither was Ian. Too big and beefy. *Roscoe* on the other hand... Roscoe was that perfect balance of big without being bulky, strong without being an ox. In looks and manner he was the ideal leading man, and Shawn could easily imagine enjoying his embrace, his kiss, his naked body...

Shawn blinked, then looked down at himself and laughed. Well hot damn! He was hard. Carefully, he set his mostly empty bottle on a short wall beside him then started to untuck and arrange his button-down to cover the bulge. As he did so, he let himself imagine Roscoe on his knees. Roscoe opening his fly and wrapping those long, elegant hands around his dick. Shawn swallowed and swayed, clutching his crotch as his imagination got the better of him and he damn near felt the wet warmth of Roscoe's mouth sinking down on him.

Arms closed around him from behind.

He jumped with a terribly undignified squeak, twisting and clearing the arms.

Margo, a friend and one-time bedmate, at first looked shocked, then burst out in laughter. "Jesus, Shawn, what's eating you?"

Shawn shook his head in a desperate attempt to clear his mind of very vivid images of Roscoe's wet lips surrounding his shaft. "Nothing."

She cocked her hip and crossed her arms over her beautifully shaped chest. "Oh?" She tossed her dyed-red curls from her heart-shaped face then let her gaze stray below his waistline. "You got something in there you need help with?"

He stared at her, recognizing the blatant invitation. He also recognized that he wasn't particularly interested. Which was stupid. Margo was a knock-out and a fun lover. They'd never be more than fuck buddies, but a buddy like that was good to have sometimes. "Uh…"

Smirking, Margo stepped forward to slide her arms around his neck. They were exactly the same height, which made the eye contact way too intimate for Shawn's current liking. "You sure?" she asked, lips just a breath away from his.

Instinct kicked in. He was, after all, a virile, unattached young man. His hands found her hips, warm and soft underneath the stretchy fabric of her skirt. His head tilted and his lips found hers. The kiss was nice, no doubt about it. Trouble was, he kept wondering what it'd be like if she was at least a head taller than him, a lot stronger and a lot… harder.

Finally, he pulled away. "Sorry, sweetheart," he whispered, rubbing her sides, "I don't think I'm up for this."

"Too much to drink?"

He nodded, taking her excuse. It wasn't entirely a lie. If he was more sober, he could probably control his wayward thoughts better.

"Okay." Brushing her lips against his in a friendly peck, she stepped away. "You need a ride home?"

He was going to say no, then realized that his ride was probably far from ready to leave. "You leaving now?"

"Yeah. I stopped drinking a few hours ago when Kevin…" She grimaced.

Shawn's eyebrows rose. *Aha! Someone else's problem.* He stepped in and put his arm around her as he turned her toward the house. "Come on, doll. You can tell Uncle Shawn all about it."

✥ ✥ ✥ ✥ ✥

Gavin turned around and his jaw dropped. "You've got to be kidding."

Bonnie laughed and gave Shawn a wolf-whistle as he sauntered up.

Shawn grinned at her then gave Gavin an innocent look. "What?"

Gavin raised one eyebrow high and made a big deal of looking Shawn up and down. Gloria, his friend majoring in costumes, assured him that the mid-thigh black pleated skirt looked very cute on him, especially with his green Converse. "You like?"

"Do you?"

"I dunno, I'm starting to like the skirt thing." He tugged at the hem and wiggled his hips. "The breeze is kinda sexy."

Bonnie bleated out a laugh. "You've *got* to be kidding. Skirts are the devil's work." She made the sign of the cross with her fingers.

Gavin was still shaking his head. "You're starting to scare me, man."

Shawn patted his arm. "Gotta keep 'em on their toes, right?" With that, he led the way into their classroom.

And there was the main *them* to which Shawn referred. Roscoe looked up and raised his eyebrows, a lazy panther grin taking over those generous lips. "A skirt for class too, Finnemore? The girls don't even wear them that much."

Shawn stopped, blocking the door to pose, holding his arms out and popping one hip out to the side. "I'm starting to like 'em." Laughing when one of his classmates pushed him out of the way with a whistle, he walked right up to Roscoe and put his foot up on the metal folding chair beside his teacher. "I shaved my legs too."

Score! Even if Shawn hadn't been looking for it, he was pretty sure he'd have seen the hungry look in Roscoe's black eyes. That alone was worth wearing skirts outside of rehearsal, despite getting razzed by his dorm mates.

Probably to cover the look, Roscoe took off his horn rims and leaned in closer to inspect Shawn's smooth shin. "Very nice." He chuckled as he sat back. He'd recovered his control by the time he looked back up at Shawn. "You sure you're not taking this too far? Women in Beatrice's time didn't shave their legs."

He batted his eyelashes coyly. "But this way I feel more feminine."

"I never suspected you were that much of a method actor."

Shawn shrugged, lowering his foot so he could sit in the chair and get out of the way of the others who were taking their seats for the beginning of class. "It's no biggie. I used to shave all over back in high school." He dropped his backpack at his feet then gave Roscoe a winning smile. "I was on the swim team."

Roscoe nodded, eyes tracking Shawn's hands as they smoothed the skirt over his thighs. "Distance or sprint?"

"Sprint."

Looked like Roscoe realized he was staring because he shook himself slightly then looked away as he stood. "All right, class, let's get started…"

Shawn sat back in his seat, spreading his bare legs out before him and crossing his ankles. He tried not to smile but it wasn't easy. He'd been teasing Roscoe for nearly two weeks, both in class and in rehearsal, and the man couldn't resist him. Which, to Shawn's thinking, was a good thing. He wanted Roscoe to be obsessed with him. It was only fair, since *he* was obsessed with the older man. Ever since that damn party he'd lain awake nights picturing every aspect of Roscoe's body. He'd gone way beyond kisses and blow jobs in his imagination, progressing to full on, hot sweaty sex. He'd even gone so far as to find some gay porno to watch. It'd taken awhile and a tip from his new best friend Ian, but he'd finally found a site with pay-per-minute that he liked and had done his research on at least what gay sex *looked* like. He liked what he saw. He liked it even more when he substituted himself and Roscoe in his imaginings.

It needed to happen.

He managed to mostly control the boner in his briefs, calm enough to get up to participate in the acting exercises during class. A good jerk off at his dorm that morning helped with that. He didn't think anyone suspected he was trying to drive their teacher to distraction, and he'd rather keep it that way.

✥ ✥ ✥ ✥ ✥

"You coming?" Bonnie asked as everyone was drifting off on their way home as rehearsal broke off.

"No. I need to talk to Roscoe."

Bonnie paused, giving him a speculative look.

He just gave her blank back.

"Ooookay. See you in voice tomorrow?"

He nodded and grinned at her.

She leaned in to give his cheek a kiss then left.

Roscoe was seated on the edge of the stage, talking to Ted. They'd finally moved into the main theater a week ago, to rehearse on what existed of the actual sets. The college only supported a two-hundred seater, but it was nice. A center section and two side sections of seats all in comfy dark blue. The stage was large enough to support respectable scenery, complete with curtain, backstage and wings.

Shawn waited in an aisle seat in the third row until the two men finished their conversation. Roscoe said something about locking the main door then the stage manager headed up the aisle. He shut off the house lights, which just left the stage work lights, then walked to and out the main double doors, shutting them behind him.

Roscoe couldn't miss Shawn's presence. "You need to talk to me, Finnemore?"

Shawn stood, surreptitiously wiped sweaty palms on his almost knee-length skirt and started toward him. "Yep."

The older man leaned back, his green pullover stretching over his broad chest as he braced both hands on the stage behind him. "What's on your mind?"

Shawn stopped two steps in front of him. "The kiss."

Roscoe clicked his tongue. "Oh?" He sat up, dusting his hands off.

Shawn took another step. "Yeah. I've been thinking about that time, you know? When you told me you wanted me to feel helpless?" Just thinking about it made Shawn want to squirm but he managed to suppress it.

He didn't move, but Roscoe's expression changed. Maybe his nostril's flared. Maybe his eyes narrowed a little behind the glasses. Shawn wasn't quite sure but he was suddenly more intent. "You've done very well with that."

"Have I?"

Roscoe nodded, reaching up to scratch the side of his long nose with one fingernail. "I think you've settled in just fine."

Shawn shook his head, frowning. "I think something's missing."

"What's that?"

"I don't know what it's like to kiss a guy."

Black eyes raked him up and down. "I'd be willing to bet you could easily find someone to help you with that."

Shawn placed his hands on Roscoe's spread knees as he stepped between them. "How about you?"

Strong fingers snapped around his wrists and lifted his hands away. The frown on Roscoe's face was not encouraging. "Stop it."

"Stop what?"

"I don't appreciate being toyed with."

"No?"

Still holding his wrists, Roscoe hopped off the stage to his feet so that he could look down at Shawn from his full height. "No." A black curl brushed the top rim of his glasses.

Anxious to keep him there, Shawn stepped into him, chest to chest—mostly, given the height difference—forcing the taller man to stumbled back into the stage's rim. "I'm not playing."

Roscoe scowled. "No?"

"No."

Roscoe dropped their hands to their sides but kept hold of Shawn's wrists. He didn't move his body, however, so Shawn felt the growing interest in his slacks. "What do you want?"

"I want you to kiss me, like Benedick would kiss Beatrice."

"Why?"

"So I know how it feels." He cocked his head to the side, a hunk of his glossy brown bangs falling over one eye. "You said you wanted me to feel helpless. Bonnie can't do that."

"Why me?"

"You showed me before. I figured you'd be the best to show me this."

Fingers dug into Shawn's wrists. Shawn fought not to grin. *He so wants me.*

"This is rather inappropriate, don't you think?"

"What? It's for the play. I won't tell if you don't."

"For the play?"

"For the play."

Whoa. Shawn stared, helplessly mesmerized as Roscoe's expression melted. His lips curled up into a sexy-as-sin smile, the frown lines smoothed from his brow and his eyes dropped to half-mast. He released one of Shawn's wrists to reach up and pull off his glasses, the better to reveal the seductive eyes. The glasses clicked softly, set unseen on the stage behind Roscoe, then the taller man's hand was back, fingers lightly stroking the curve of Shawn's cheek. "For the play."

Yeah, sure. Whatever. Shawn probably should have answered. His lips parted but the only sound that emerged was a sigh as Roscoe dipped his head.

The first brush of lips was soft, the gentle sharing of a barely spoken secret. Sweet and subtle, Roscoe shared breath with Shawn as he brought his other hand up so he could frame Shawn's face with both hands. Barely hearing his own greedy little moan, Shawn leaned into Roscoe, placing his hands on the other man's ribs, pressing his rigid cock into Roscoe's thigh. Fingers delving into Shawn's hair, Roscoe used the hold to tilt Shawn's head back and hold it steady as he opened his mouth and slid his tongue between Shawn's teeth. Shawn held on tight, sucking on the invader, drinking in the heady combination of mocha coffee and Roscoe spice. *Shit!* He fumbled as Roscoe continued to press, holding fast as their teeth clashed. A whimper bled from his throat before he could help it.

Taking the sound for a sign, Roscoe tore his lips away and spun Shawn around in the same movement. Dizzy, Shawn clutched at Roscoe's hips as his back came up against the side of the stage where Roscoe had just stood. Roscoe still held his head, black eyes boring into his as he pinned Shawn against the stage. At that moment, Roscoe was every dark and dangerous sex god who had ever graced the silver screen. "Helpless," he murmured before delving back in to take control of Shawn's mouth, swallowing Shawn's helpless cry.

All hesitation sizzled away, falling at their feet. One of Roscoe's hands remained in his hair with a punishing hold as his other arm slipped down to encircle Shawn's torso. Once more, Shawn was caught, trapped, with one of Roscoe's legs shoved between his, the steely hard thigh pressing up against Shawn's balls. Shawn slid his arms around to dig fingers in Roscoe's back, clutching at the meat of his shoulders, anchoring to the only solid thing in his life at that moment. His jaw hurt from being forced open, his tongue couldn't hide. Roscoe released his hair and circled that arm around Shawn's neck so that his other hand could slip down to palm Shawn's ass, yanking him close and up on his toes so that his cock pressed hard and aching into Roscoe's lower belly.

Rocking. His hips were rocking, urged on by Roscoe's hand. His cock rubbed Roscoe's through skirt, slacks and underwear. He growled, climbing Roscoe as best he could to facilitate the friction, wrapping his leg partway around the other man's hips so they could…

He gasped when Roscoe pulled his mouth away.

"Stop." With both hands, Roscoe stilled the motion of Shawn's hips, clasping Shawn to his body. He tucked Shawn's head underneath his chin, pressing his face to his chest. "Stop."

Shawn struggled, pounding the back of Roscoe's shoulder. "No!" It was no use, Roscoe was stronger. Shawn could barely move.

"Damn it, I said stop. If we do anymore, I'll…" His harsh tone drifted off but the slight twitch of his hips made his meaning evident.

Shawn squirmed, still trying to catch his breath. The seductive scent of Roscoe underneath the fading smell of laundry detergent in the pullover was driving him nuts. "It's okay."

"No. It's not."

Shawn dropped his hand and made so bold as to cup the meat of Roscoe's ass. *Holy shit, you could bounce a quarter off that!* "Yeah. It is."

Roscoe ripped out of his arms, stepping back and thrusting Shawn out of reach. Shawn stumbled, knees entirely unprepared to support his weight. He caught himself on the edge of the stage, well aware that his skirt had ridden up high on one of his thighs. No doubt his boner was obvious, tenting the fabric.

Roscoe took it all in and fell another step back, breathing hard. "What game are you playing?"

Off guard at the feral nature of Roscoe's kiss—if one could just call that a kiss—it was Shawn's turn to scowl. "Don't tell me you didn't enjoy it."

"Not the point. You *shouldn't* have enjoyed it."

"Fuck." Because he simply couldn't stand, Shawn hitched himself up to sit on the edge of the stage. "I think I'd have to be dead not to enjoy that. Where the hell did you learn to kiss like that?"

Roscoe still glared, sexy as hell with his tanned face all flushed and his black eyes aflame. "You're not gay."

"Don't be so sure of that."

"You can't put on a skirt, kiss one man and claim to be gay."

"How about if I put on a skirt and all I can think about lately is getting into your pants?" Shawn cocked his head to the side. "That qualify?"

Roscoe was caught somewhere between floored and pissed off. "You don't know what you're talking about."

Shawn grabbed the hem of his skirt and lifted it, spreading his legs a little so Roscoe could get a good look. "How about this?"

"Oh my God, are those panties?"

"Yeah, brand new. Like 'em?"

"No." Roscoe may not have known that he licked his lips. He did figure out that he was staring, though, because he tore his gaze away, trying to act disgusted. "Put that away."

"You sure?"

"Yes! Damn it."

Shawn wasn't sure if he knew where this was going, but he did know for damn sure that he liked seeing Roscoe all riled up. The calm, collected professor turned into a wildcat. Roscoe couldn't stay still. He paced a little, then spun to face the back of the hall, hands on hips, chest heaving as he breathed deep. Shawn stayed very still, unsure what to do. Afraid that if he pushed the point, he'd push Roscoe away. There was a chance to lure the other man back to him. He just had to figure it out what it was. Maybe he should ditch the skirt. The panties looked like they were working…

But when Roscoe finally turned around, the controlled professor was back. Almost. He was still flushed but his expression was back to normal. "You need to go home."

"No." Shawn hopped down and started for Roscoe, but had to stop when the other man put out a hand.

"Forget it. This didn't happen."

"The fuck it didn't…"

"No. It didn't. Neither one of us can afford this."

"You *want* me."

To his surprise, Roscoe heaved in a deep breath and took a long, longing look down Shawn's body and back up. "Yes. I do. But!" His pointing finger stopped Shawn in his tracks again. "I'm not going to let you trick me again."

"Why not? I won't tell anyone. I swear."

Roscoe shook his head. "It's a bad idea."

"It was the fucking best idea in the world a little while ago."

"No. I'm the adult here and I say what goes."

"Fuck you! I'm an adult!"

"Only just. And I will *not* be your toy as you play at being gay."

Shawn's heart deflated a little. "I'm not playing, man. I really do think about you all the time."

"Have you ever kissed another man?"

"No."

"Which stands to reason you've never had sex with a man?"

"No. But I've been watching porn." He'd meant it to be a joke but his smile faded when Roscoe didn't match it.

"No. Not me. I've had my time of flings. I'm only interested in adults." He turned and found his script and his keys on a board that had been placed over a few of the front row seats. "If you really think you're gay, then I suggest you find a boy your own age."

Fingers curled into fists, Shawn watched Roscoe slip further and further away from him, even though the man stood not three paces away. "Coward," he sneered.

Finally, Roscoe smiled. Shawn didn't think he was wrong to think it was a little sad. "Perhaps." He licked his lips and gave Shawn another once-over. "But my decision stills stands. This didn't happen." He gestured up the main aisle. "Now, let's go. I need to lock up."

Shawn snatched up his script and keys and stomped up the main aisle. He was at the main doors before he realized the stomping bit just proved Roscoe's point about him being a kid. Disgusted with himself, disgusted with Roscoe, he kept right on stomping out of the theater and down walkways to his dorm.

✦ ✦ ✦ ✦ ✦

Well of *course* it happened! Did Roscoe think he could melt Shawn's mind like that and he'd just *forget* it? No way in hell! But, okay, Shawn was an adult. He wasn't stupid. Roscoe was right that anything between them could spell trouble for him. For both of them. Shawn didn't want to be known as the twink who got Roscoe fired.

So he backed off. At least, he tried. But the first time he saw Roscoe at rehearsal over the weekend was torture. The anger and longing that surged up into his throat was unexpected and it just got worse when Roscoe acted like nothing had happened. True, it was tech weekend so things were beyond chaotic, and since Roscoe was the director a lot of his time was spent with the tech crew, ironing out the details of the sets, lighting and sound, but he barely spoke to Shawn at all beyond the curt stage directions he gave all the cast. He joked around with the others, but not with Shawn. He spent an enormous amount of time working on the constable scenes. Shawn he pretty much ignored, which was a pretty big feat considering Shawn was one of the lead characters. He declared that Bonnie and Shawn were doing fine and concentrated on helping everyone else.

Maybe, for Roscoe, nothing really *had* happened between them. Maybe he kissed guys like that all the time. Business as usual. But the experience was never far from Shawn's thoughts and made his skin tingle. Maybe he was right calling Shawn a kid and pointing out his inexperience.

And maybe you're thinking like a girl, idiot!

So what the hell. As long as he was thinking like a girl, he'd channel it into his acting. He was playing one, after all. He poured over his script, seeing his lines in a new light. His Beatrice got some subtext to her anger. If Benedick had pulled a stunt akin to Roscoe's, if the soldier had left the woman and as much as denied what had happened between them... Oh yeah, Shawn now had rock solid identification with his character!

✤ ✤ ✤ ✤ ✤

The next week flew by, as it always did the week before opening night. Too many last minute things went haywire for Roscoe to focus on much else. All of the cast and crew sank into that barely-alive lethargy during the daylight hours which turned into frantic clarity once they reached the chaotic ruins of the theater stage during its metamorphosis. Tempers ran high right alongside levity. All of the cast was suddenly one unit, a solidified group against the world, almost ready to give birth to a collective creation. It was Shawn's second favorite part about being in a play and he lost himself in it to try as best he could to not think about tackling Roscoe and riding him to heaven.

Roscoe gave a traditional pep talk right before the curtain went up on opening night. The cast and crew sat in the empty theater while early arrivals milled outside waiting to come in and take their seats. Roscoe thanked the crew and spoke of a long journey to get there. He praised the cast for their talent and their efforts and proclaimed that everyone had worked hard.

"And special thanks to two people who completely transformed themselves for this."

All eyes turned to Shawn and Bonnie. Bonnie sat on the edge of the stage in her silver-trimmed blue doublet, her hand comfortable on the hilt of the sword at her hip. She even had a fake beard glued to her chin. Shawn thought she looked great. He thought he looked pretty damn good too. His dress was a deep, rich wine color with black embroidery along the edges. He was the only one in the play to wear red. His hair was done up and braided in this weird but stylish circle thing on the top of his head. The girls who'd decided how to do him up had told him what it was called but he couldn't ever remember it. He had fake rubies in his newly pierced ears—he'd figured what the hell—and an awesome necklace that set off the v-neckline of his dress. All in all, he felt rather feminine and beautiful, and was surprised at just how neat that felt.

Surprised how it affected Roscoe too. He hadn't missed Roscoe's appreciation of his costume the first time he'd shown up in it. That appreciation showed now in the admiring look he gave Shawn across the circle of actors. "Bonnie and Shawn deserve kudos for being great sports and marvelous actors. They've taken huge chances and I think you've both done a fabulous job." He led a round of applause.

Because Bonnie was Bonnie and couldn't have accolades pointed her way for very long, she turned right around and gave kudos right back to Roscoe. Shawn sort of heard her but he missed the details. The look Roscoe dropped on him was full of promise that Shawn was trying not to see. Roscoe had said it didn't happen, he's said that was it. So why was he giving Shawn *that* look?

He was still puzzling it out when Roscoe dismissed the cast so they could open the house. Shawn turned to head backstage, but a hand about his upper arm stopped him just after he passed into the darkened wing to stage right.

Roscoe stood over him, looking edible all in black except for the pristine white collar that folded neatly over the collar of his sweater. He smiled down at Shawn, his eyes shadowed behind the lenses of his glasses. "I just wanted to tell you to break a leg."

Shawn managed a smile but it stuttered when Roscoe pulled him into a hug. Against his will, his body responded and melted into that warm embrace, the sense-memory of Roscoe's kiss washing over him.

Roscoe brushed his lips over Shawn's heavily made up cheek, then he straightened with a grin. "You look beautiful."

Shawn could only manage a soft "thank you" before Roscoe patted his shoulder then left.

At first he was elated. Then the warmth of the hug evaporated and he was left stunned and confused. *What the hell was that?* Roscoe had carefully kept his distance for over a week then he comes through with a hug like that? And just a hug? What the fuck?

Growling, Shawn stomped off, ready to do battle, morphing his ire and confusion into Beatrice's.

✦ ✦ ✦ ✦ ✦

Shawn spent a lot of time after the show talking to friends who'd been in the audience, as well as cast members. The first night had been a rousing success and he rode the high of it. As a consequence, he didn't get back to the single dressing room that all the male cast members shared until well after the others had changed back into their street clothes.

Gavin came up behind Shawn, looking at him in the mirror. "You need any help?"

Shawn was down to his shift and hose but had chosen to take off his makeup before slipping into his clothes for the party. "Nah." He rubbed cold cream all over his face, used to the colorful muck it made of his makeup. "I'm good."

Gavin shouldered his backpack. "You need a ride to the party?"

"Bonnie said she'd take me."

Gavin nodded. "Okay. See you there."

Shawn waved him off, grabbing for the tissues to wipe the makeup and cream. With Gavin gone, he was alone with the brightly lit mirrors over the back-to-back dressing tables, his costumes hanging on a rail in the open front closet behind him.

"These are beautiful."

Shawn froze, eyes closed and gunked up. But he knew that voice. Quickly, he wiped off the rest of the cold cream from his eyes and opened them.

Roscoe sat on the chair beside him, fingering a leaf of one of the red roses in the bouquet his sister and her husband had brought Shawn. Cellophane crackled as he lifted the flowers to his nose and inhaled. "And very appropriate." He smiled at Shawn as he set the roses down.

"Thanks." Shawn continued to wipe tissues over his face, anxious to get all the cold cream off. Strangely, he wished Roscoe had waited to see him until he had the makeup on again. He wanted to be pretty for him, which was kind of absurd. *Obviously, I'm letting the dress thing get to me.*

"I just wanted to come back and tell you how wonderful you were tonight."

Shawn smiled before he could completely recall he was kind of mad at Roscoe. "Thanks." Roscoe *really* needed to stop looking at him like that. Self conscious, Shawn reached up to start unpinning the fake braids from his hair. "It went well."

"It went more than well. You and Bonnie were spectacular."

"Thanks." Roscoe was *still* looking at him with that half-lidded expression. It made things low in Shawn's belly sizzle. He was wearing normal underwear underneath his shift but the skirt was still going to tent if Roscoe kept on. "You going to the party?"

"Yes. For awhile." Roscoe took a deep breath as he rose to his feet. "We've earned it after all."

"Damn straight."

Roscoe's hand squeezed Shawn's mostly bare shoulder. "See you there."

Shawn had snatched hold of Roscoe's wrist before he really thought about the move. Startled, Roscoe paused and their eyes met in the mirror. Some of Shawn's loose curls tumbled down but it failed to hide the stark need even he saw in his face. Roscoe's expression went from bemused to wary in an instant, fingers digging in Shawn's shoulder. Shawn stood and spun, keeping hold of Roscoe's arm.

Roscoe stepped back, coming up against the edge of the open closet behind him. "Shawn."

Shawn moved into him, sliding his free hand up to curl around Roscoe's neck. He pulled.

Roscoe resisted. "Shawn."

"Kiss me."

"No."

"The door's closed."

"I shouldn't…"

He pulled harder with less resistance. "Take a chance." He went up on tip toes to meet Roscoe's lips when they were in reach.

A small, breathy moan leaked out of the taller man as his free hand crept around Shawn's waist. His mouth opened over Shawn's and his tongue snaked inside. Freeing Roscoe's wrist, Shawn wrapped both arms around the taller man's neck and used the leverage to practically climb him. Both of Roscoe's hands gripped Shawn's ass, supporting him, lifting him closer.

Straddling Roscoe's thigh, Shawn's thin skirt was tangled in their legs. Desperate, they ate at each other, clutching, giving in to a moment of recklessness.

It was Roscoe who broke the spell. He released Shawn's ass, letting the shorter man drop back to his feet.

"No."

Shawn tried to hold on, tried to reclaim him, but Roscoe caught his hands and unwrapped them from his neck. "Stop it. We can't do this. Not here."

"Then where?"

He pushed his glasses back up on his nose. "Nowhere."

"Damn it, Roscoe..."

Roscoe pushed Shawn back into his chair, holding his wrists between them. He glared at Shawn through smudged lenses. "You listen to me. This is not something either of us should want."

Shawn noted the careful wording. *Should* want, meaning he *did* want it. "But we do."

"That is unfortunate." He stood up, loosing Shawn's hands. "But it's not a chance either of us should take."

Shawn sank against the back of his chair, watching Roscoe as he took of his glasses to clean them with a tissue. "You're always telling us to take chances in class."

"This is completely different and you know it."

"Why does it have to be?"

"I could lose my job."

"You're wasted as an acting teacher anyway."

That stopped him. Roscoe froze, staring at Shawn, his mouth slightly open in surprise.

Shawn wasn't really sure why he'd said that but now that he had, he went with it. "What? Everyone says it. We love being in your class but no one can figure out why you're here. You were a big deal for awhile."

"That's all behind me now."

"And I'm sure there are reasons for it, but you're wasted on us."

Roscoe shook himself and finished wiping off his glasses in a huff. "I happen to like teaching."

"But you were a fucking brilliant actor. Bet you were an even better director."

"Not everyone seemed to think so." The words were muttered but Roscoe's enunciation was just too damn good for Shawn not to understand him. "Regardless, that has nothing to do with what just happened between us."

Shawn stood. "Sure it does. If you weren't my teacher, we could…"

"Hey, Shawn, you almost ready to…" The dressing room door opened and Bonnie walked in, dressed in a pair of baby doll tanks and jeans with her backpack over her shoulder. She stopped on seeing the two of them. "Whoa, I'm sorry."

Roscoe switched gears in an instant. "Nothing to be sorry about." He put his glasses back on as he crossed over to pull her into a hug. "You were magnificent tonight, sweetheart."

Shawn saw her close her eyes to enjoy the squeeze. He couldn't blame her in the least. "Thank you." She pulled away. "You coming to the party?"

"Actually, I think not." He glanced briefly at Shawn. "I'm not sure I'm up for it."

Shawn dropped back into his chair, barely managing to suppress an indignant huff of breath.

Bonnie didn't seem to notice. "Oh no. Are you feeling okay?"

"I'm fine. Just a little tired. I suppose I was more worried about tonight than I'd thought." He stroked her hair. "But I needn't have worried. You and Shawn pulled it off brilliantly."

Shawn opted to finish unwinding his hair rather than watch Bonnie simper. She wasn't one of the worst ones, but she had a crush on Roscoe just the same as most of the women in the drama school.

"All right, my dears, I shall leave you to get ready. Be careful tonight. Don't drink too much. You have a matinee tomorrow."

Shawn heard him leave.

Bonnie sank down in the chair beside Shawn. "Man, that bites. Roscoe should go to the party."

Shawn stood, gathering up his skirt so he could pull the shift up and over his head. "Yeah, well, it's his choice."

"You okay?"

He tossed the shift onto the floor of the closet and grabbed up his jeans. "Yeah, sure." The last thing he felt like doing right now was partying, but he wasn't going to let Roscoe rain on his parade. *Maybe I'll pick up some guy.* That would show Roscoe!

✚ ✚ ✚ ✚ ✚

Shawn was just as ignorant of gay sex on closing night as he had been on opening night. Four parties in between and he hadn't met one man who he'd even wanted to make out with. Of course, it didn't help that he kept thinking of Roscoe and his magic tongue. So Shawn gave up on the idea. At least for the time being. He gave himself to the play and lost himself in the ordeal of it.

The true tragedy of school performances, in his humble opinion, was that the runs were so short. Two small weekends of three performances each and then months' worth of agonizing preparation was over. Not for the first time, he gave serious consideration to moving to New York and trying his hand at a part in a real show to see what it was like to have to play a part practically every night for months.

But not yet. For now, he had two weekends. Despite his frustration with a certain acting teacher, they flew by. All too soon, he and Bonnie were taking their final bows with the cast on their set. It was both his favorite and his least favorite part about the run of a show. Depressing to think that it was over.

✚ ✚ ✚ ✚ ✚

Shawn held his skirts as he stepped over a puddle of spilled Coke, litter being one of the perils of taking the outside way around to the backstage door. But there were way too many people still milling around in the audience chamber and this time he wanted to try and get changed out of his costume before everyone else left.

"Shawn!"

He stopped at the sound of his name, turning away from the door. Two older men stood across the way. One of them was Dean Travis Wurther, the head of the drama department. It was the dean who'd called his name and was now waving him over. "Could you come here for a moment?"

The other man was someone Shawn didn't recognize. He wore a dark suit and striped tie. His frosted hair was trimmed short and he had a broad smile fixed on Shawn as he approached.

The dean gestured at the man. "Shawn, I'd like you to meet Dennis Connor."

Holy shit! Shawn managed not to shout as he shook the hand of one of the better known talent agents in the Los Angeles area. "Nice to meet you."

"Nice to meet you." The man tilted his head, studying Shawn in the light of the outside lighting, grinning. "Wow, even up close I'd be hard pressed to say you were a man."

Keeping in character, Shawn spread a hand over his padded bosom and dipped his head. "Thank you."

"You're a mighty talented actor."

"That's an honor coming from you."

Connor held a rolled program in one hand, tapping it against the other palm. "Roscoe Schroeder's a good friend of mine. He told me I should come and see you."

Roscoe was looking out for him. Or rather, all of the cast. Everyone knew Roscoe had a friend who was an agent, but no one Shawn knew had ever met him or even knew his name. Certainly no one thought it was *the* Dennis Connor from the Connor Agency. Roscoe claimed not to want to take advantage of the friendship, but he was known to invite his friend to performances and that friend was known to make up his own mind and as a result to call one or more of Roscoe's students.

Like maybe Shawn. "I'm glad you liked it."

The rolled up program pointed at him. "I liked *you*." He winked. "I think you and I should talk sometime." He reached into his jacket and pulled out a shiny business card case. "Dean Wurther's given me one of your headshots with your vitals. Call my assistant and he'll set up an appointment." Connor held out a card, grinning. "I think there's something coming up that might be right up your alley."

Shawn blinked, taking the card. Was this happening? "I'll be sure to call."

"You do that." He tapped the program to his open palm again. "Now, I've got to get going and I'm sure you'd rather get out of that dress." He laughed as he turned to clap the dean on the shoulder. "Good to see you Travis." He shook Shawn's hand again. "Shawn."

Shawn watched the man's back as he faded into the darkness beyond the light.

Dean Wurther patted his shoulder. "Congratulations, young man. That right there was a first step."

Another pat and the older man was gone.

Shawn stood there, staring at the card in his hand.

✢ ✢ ✢ ✢ ✢

Par-tay! Shawn had every reason to celebrate and then some. He chose not to tell anyone about his meeting Dennis Connor tonight. He knew his classmates. They'd be happy for him, sure, but they wouldn't be able to help the envy. He'd feel the same way in their shoes. So for tonight, at least, he'd keep it to himself and enjoy the high of closing night with his friends.

It was tradition for Dean Wurther to host the closing night party of both the fall musical and the spring production. He lived up in the hills on three acres of land surrounded by lush greenery and sporting a tremendous view of the valley. Dean Wurther, it was said, came from money, and the house led credence to that rumor. True or not, it gave them a fabulous spot for a party, especially since the teachers in the drama department tended to get as wild and crazy as their students.

On nights like this, Shawn *loved* his life. There was one thing—one person—who could make it better for him, but even without Roscoe's attentions, Shawn was flying high.

There were a lot more gay men at this party than the others and they all found Shawn. It could have something to do with the tight black mini-skirt that showed off his legs or the frilly white half shirt that showed off his flat belly. He hadn't even chosen to wear the padded bra or the high heels, but his flat chest and Keds seemed to work just fine. His hair was loose and curled about his made up face, and he loved the fact that even he couldn't quite decide if he looked more like a girl or a boy.

A few hours into the party found him in the middle of the dance floor with two girls and at least a dozen guys. He'd lost track of which were gay and which were not because it didn't seem to matter. After enough alcohol and other mind-altering substances, sexual preferences were becoming very flexible.

As one thumping song morphed into another, Shawn gave up and threw his arms around his current partner's shoulders. "I'm dying of thirst," he yelled in the man's ear then pecked him on the cheek and slid away.

When he got to the kitchen to grab a plastic cup, the guy was still with him. Shawn sized him up again. Taller than Shawn but not what other people would call especially tall. He had nice dusky skin, silky black hair and sweet brown eyes. Pretty good looking. But he didn't have that wicked quality that seemed to get Shawn's blood racing.

"Hey," he said, grabbing the spout for the keg and holding it over Shawn's cup. His eyes were big and brown and really rather pretty, as was his smile. "Are you really gay?"

Shawn stared at him, trying to remember his name. He was one of the sound crew, right? Or was he one of the backstage crew? Greg? Gary? "I don't know," he said with a smile. He watched beer fill his cup. "I'm still figuring it out."

"Well, when you figure it out, maybe I can give you a call?"

Shawn blinked at him and couldn't help the warm feeling in his chest at the offer. "Maybe. Yeah." *Grady? Grant?*

The guy grinned again and filled his own cup. "Or if you need help making up your mind...?"

Graham! "Thanks, but not tonight. 'Kay?"

Graham nodded, gracing Shawn with that shy little smile again. "Sure. I understand."

They drifted apart and Shawn spoke with some of his friends as he finished his beer. They were still riding high on the closing night experience, rehashing the highlights and bemoaning missed opportunities. The normal stuff. But Shawn's mind had moved on to other things. He didn't know how excited he should be about Dennis Connor's offer. Just getting interest from an agent didn't mean he was going to be an overnight sensation. That's not the way the game worked. Still, it was something and certainly a step in the right direction. All because of Roscoe. It was Roscoe who'd pushed Shawn into the role, Roscoe who'd invited his friend to see the performance, and it was probably Roscoe who'd talked him up to Connor.

Where is *Roscoe?* He scanned the heads at the party but he hadn't seen their tall, dashing director since shortly after he'd arrived.

"Hello, Shawn."

Shawn blinked at the hand waving in front of his face. Startled, he twisted his head to look at the girl standing beside him.

Trina grinned, leaning drunkenly against the wall by which they stood. "Where were you?"

"Huh? Oh, nothing."

"Sure. You scoping out your next conquest?"

"My next what?"

She snorted. "Please. How many guys have your turned down already tonight?"

"Just one."

"Yeah, right." She sipped her drink, unsuccessfully hiding a grimace. "So, are you really gay now?"

He stared at the little blonde who had played his cousin. She'd had a thing for him in the past, but they'd sorted that out last year. "I think it's a possibility."

"You can't just put on a skirt and decide you're into guys, you know." Trina was not what you'd call a pretty drunk.

"I know. But I'm not so sure I wasn't into guys before." Perhaps not the best thing to say, given the fooling around they'd done.

But then a small smile dawned on her and he thought maybe it was a good thing to say. "So you think that's why you never stayed with a girl?"

He shrugged, realizing that he hadn't, in fact, settled with one girl since... well, ever. Even in high school his brief flings had always been just that. It was fun but not something that held his interest for long. Certainly nothing all consuming like what he felt for Roscoe. "Maybe so." Again his eyes scanned the crowd for a head of dark, satiny curls and horn rimmed glasses.

"So," Trina propped herself on the wall beside him, watching the crowd. "Is there anyone you're interested in now?"

He shrugged. No way was he telling anyone about what happened with Roscoe. If it got out, that'd just prove to the older man that he'd been right to nip things in the bud.

Dustin came along soon after that to sweep Trina away. Shawn hoped that Trina would finally give in to the guy since he'd been after her since auditions for *Much Ado*. Not feeling a particular need to dance, Shawn ended up in the little breakfast nook attached the kitchen, watching a bunch of idiots play quarters.

That's where Roscoe found him.

He suddenly felt a large, warm presence brushing up behind him. Looking up over his shoulder, he'd expected one of his dancing partners from earlier had found him. His breath left him when black eyes met his through thick rimmed glasses. Roscoe's smile melted that thing in Shawn's belly that made his thighs tingle.

The waistband of his stretchy skirt snapped. "I approve," Roscoe murmured.

"Thanks."

Roscoe glanced at the game, which was barely a game anymore since the players had switched to downing tequila shots instead of beer. When his gaze met Shawn's again, he nodded briefly toward the door into the side yard. A hand on the small of Shawn's back made his request that Shawn join him obvious.

Shawn wasn't even conscious of his feet obeying. Roscoe dropped his hand from Shawn's back, but it was like the touch had created an invisible tether, allowing Roscoe to lead with ease.

There you go, thinking like a girl again.

Outside, the night air was brisk from late spring. The moon shone through a line of pine trees that guarded the side yard, and music spilled through the open door to provide a soundtrack for the few people quietly talking in the cemented courtyard.

Roscoe led Shawn closer to the open gate that led to the front yard, stopping beside a covered, unused barbeque. "You seem to be rather popular tonight."

"Am I?"

"I saw you dancing."

"Oh."

"I also talked to Dennis. Congratulations."

Shawn shrugged but he did smile. "Yeah, that was cool. Thanks."

"No need to thank me. It was all you."

"But you asked him here. You made me play Beatrice."

Roscoe chuckled. "It seems to have been a good choice."

"Yeah."

There was that stare again. Like the one from opening night. Like Roscoe was trying to memorize what Shawn looked like. "Well, I just wanted to say goodbye."

Shawn took the hand that Roscoe extended but gripped it tight, not willing to let go. "You're leaving."

"Yes."

"Wait." Shawn jerked at the hand that Roscoe tried to retrieve. He searched that handsome face, wondering at the strange calm there. It made him anxious. "I'll walk you to your car."

"No, that's not necessary."

But Shawn had already released his hand and walked through the gate toward the street. "Where are you parked?"

"Shawn, you should go back inside."

"Don't want to." He reached the street and turned to face the other man. "Which way?"

Roscoe wanted to ditch him. It was obvious. But there wasn't much he could do to keep Shawn from following. Muttering something about 'obstinate child' he turned to his left and began walking, Shawn at his side.

At first they didn't speak as they walked down the street, leaving the noise of the party behind. It was a gorgeous part of town. Nice big houses set back from the street and fronted with trees and bushes. Made everything quiet and quaint. The streetlights were sparse so he and Roscoe walked mostly in shadow and muted moonlight. It was still relatively early so soon they just had the cars as company.

Roscoe stopped by the driver's door of his silver Camero.

Shawn wasn't an expert but he knew enough about cars to be impressed. He whistled. "This is yours?"

"Yes."

"What year?"

"'98."

Shawn trailed his fingers over the trunk then the tiny back window on the driver's side. "Sweet."

"Thank you." Roscoe leaned his butt against the car, hooking his thumbs into the pockets of his black slacks. Made him look very GQ, very hot.

Either the alcohol he'd consumed or the general high of the night made Shawn bold. "Give me a ride home?"

"Don't you have a ride?"

Shawn stopped in front of Roscoe. "I didn't mean *my* home."

Roscoe sighed, shaking his head. "Shawn..."

"I know, I know. We shouldn't do this. You could get fired. I'm too young. I'm too inexperienced. But—" he took a step closer to the car, to the man. "I've been thinking."

Roscoe raised one eyebrow. "An ominous occurrence."

"About what you said the first night you kissed me."

A brief exhale of air that might have been a half chuckle. "The night you asked me to kiss you." His voice was heavy and sort of slow.

"About finding someone my own age."

Roscoe glanced quickly back up the street the way they came, but other than cars and maybe a few squirrels overhead, they were completely alone. "And have you?"

"I don't think I should."

"No?"

One last step placed Shawn with the toes of his Keds almost touching the toes of Roscoe's shiny black boots. The breeze caressed the bared skin of his belly and thighs, reminding him of his attire. Strange how the feminine clothing made him feel more attractive, more daring. "No. I think it'd be a lot better for me if you—as an older, experienced adult—fucked me first."

That startled him. Roscoe's head raised up a bit, his eyes boring into Shawn's through the lenses of the horn rims. But then his smile grew. "How did you arrive to this conclusion?"

Score! Shawn edged closer. He placed one foot in between Roscoe's, putting him just a handspan away from touching the man. He imagined all that hard muscled warmth reaching out to surround him. "If I find a young guy for my first time, he's more likely to hurt me." Coyly, Shawn tilted his head and batted his eyes. He was sure Roscoe could see his face clearly even in the half-light. He'd removed the thick cake makeup from the performance but he'd reapplied eye shadow, mascara, eyeliner, blush and lipstick for the party, after he'd shaved to make sure his skin was still smooth. Lifting one hand, he spread it over the middle of Roscoe's chest. "You wouldn't want me to get hurt, would you?"

The deep rumble of the older man's soft laugh sizzled the blood in Shawn's veins. "You're playing a dangerous game, Finnemore." He reached up to grasp Shawn's wrist to lift it away. "I'm honored but I'm afraid I must decline."

"Don't."

"We're not…"

"Just once."

Roscoe dropped his gaze to their feet. "That's not fair to you. To either of us."

Interesting answer. "Come on, man, you've admitted you want me. I want you. Oh, man, do I want you."

Roscoe caught his shoulders to keep him from leaning in further. His gaze snapped back to Shawn's face, scowling. "Quit it."

Shawn leaned into the hands that held him away. "I wake up picturing your mouth on my dick."

Roscoe breathed in sharply.

"I want to know what you taste like."

Roscoe groaned, shaking his head. "Don't do this to me."

"Please. I want you inside me." Saying the words sent a shiver down his spine. He meant it, but the thought was still ominous.

The grip on his shoulders tightened, the hands shaking just a little. "Do you even know what you're asking?"

"Yes."

"I shouldn't."

"No one will know."

"Famous last words." He pushed as he straightened, pushing away from the car and forcing Shawn back a few steps.

"I'll quit school."

Roscoe turned and pulled his keys out of his pocket. "Don't talk crazy." The car blipped when he pushed the button to unlock the driver's side.

"Who knows what Dennis Connor will do for me?"

Roscoe glared at him briefly as he opened the door. "Don't be stupid. You know that's not a sure thing. Certainly nothing to quit school over. Not yet."

Desperate, Shawn inserted himself between the man and the driver's seat. "Come on, Roscoe. Maybe you'll get lucky. Maybe I'll hate it. Then I'll never bug you again."

Surprised laughter tipped back Roscoe's head.

Shawn took his chance and snatched the keys from Roscoe's hand.

"Hey!"

Before the bigger man could grab him, he scampered out of reach and circled around to the passenger side.

Two presses on the key fob opened the passenger door for Shawn to slide in. He grinned at Roscoe, who glared at him over the driver's seat. "Come on, Roscoe. Take me home."

The shadows didn't allow him to get a good look at the black eyes behind the rims of those ridiculous glasses. *Don't say no!* Shawn willed, knowing he was going to. Knowing this wasn't going to happen but refusing to give up. *You want to fuck me, damn it.* He dangled the keys.

Roscoe sank into the driver's seat and snatched them. "Buckle up."

✞✞✞✞✞

"I've gone out of my mind," Roscoe grumbled once they got on the road.

Shawn settled back in his seat. "Yeah, but in a *good* way." He slid his cell phone out of the little slot in the waistband of his skirt and flipped it open.

"What are you doing?"

"Texting Ian to let him know that I got another ride home."

"Who's Ian?"

Jealous? Shawn could only hope. "A friend of mine who lives in my building."

"Gay?"

"Yes, in fact."

"Why aren't you plaguing him?"

Shawn grinned at the martyred tone. After finishing his text, he flipped his phone closed. "I told you. I think I'm better off with an older man for the first time." And *boy* was his stomach doing flips. Was there a trampoline in there or something?

Roscoe sighed, combing the fingers of his far hand through his hair. The curls bounced back around his face when he released them. "What am I doing? You're so young."

"I'm not so young. You're not even thirty yet."

"How did you know that?"

His phone buzzed. "All the girls know exactly how old you are." Ian had texted back an 'ok' so Shawn tucked the phone away again.

Roscoe snorted. "Have they not heard that I'm gay?"

"They know, but hope springs eternal." He chuckled. "When you're fantasizing, it doesn't matter. Sometimes I think they purposely pick the guys they have zero chance with to go ga-ga over."

"And you are an authority on this?"

"I have three older sisters and a single mom. Yes, I'm an authority."

Roscoe laughed. It was so much nicer when he laughed freely like that. His face, when calm and relaxed, was simply stunning. Of course, he was stunning when he was angry too so that negated that argument. "And what will be their reaction, do you think, if they find out what's about to happen?"

Shawn's cock took notice that Roscoe spoke in the affirmative for the near future. *Ah! He's committed now.* "They already know, kinda. I told my mom I was starting to think about other men. She thought it was cool and told me to go for it."

Roscoe chuckled. "Lucky you."

"Yeah, she's cool. Her parents were really strict and she got married young, so she didn't get to do much when she was younger, so she's always encouraged us." He studied Roscoe's profile. "Your parents weren't so understanding?"

Roscoe shrugged, eyes fixed on the road ahead. "They've accepted but they aren't happy. I'm the only boy so I ruined my father's chances of a grandson."

"Family name crap?"

"Something like that. Although, he's never quite approved of my chosen profession either. However, my sister has since supplied him with three boys and one of those out of wedlock so she let my nephew carry on dad's name."

"Nice of her."

"She's my last ally in my family." The melancholy in his voice sounded old and comfortable. It tugged at Shawn's heart.

"I never knew my dad. He died right before I was born. My sisters think the world of him, though." He laughed. "People will probably blame my being gay on being brought up without a male influence in the family."

"Are you gay?"

Shawn watched Roscoe in the flashing lights of passing traffic. The other man kept his eyes on the road and wouldn't even glance his way. "Growing evidence seems to support that."

"Wearing a dress doesn't mean anything."

"Wanting to suck your dick does."

Roscoe swallowed, his grip on the steering wheel tightening briefly. "You don't have to talk like that. I'm already taking you home."

Shawn turned as best he could in the restraints of his seatbelt to face Roscoe. "I'm telling you the truth."

"You don't even know if you like sucking dick."

"I really want to find out."

"You could have easily found that out with a number of willing test subjects."

"None of them are you."

Roscoe scowled. "Why me?"

"You're the sexiest thing I've ever seen. Male or female."

"Looks aren't everything."

"I'm not just talking about looks."

He was silent for a few streets. Shawn knew Roscoe lived somewhere in the area so this couldn't be a very long drive. He hoped not. Roscoe was fully capable of talking himself out of this.

Roscoe turned into a complex of condominiums, then into a narrow driveway not long after that. The Camero's engine rumbled to a halt. Roscoe switched off the lights then finally turned to face Shawn. A strange look of wonder and confusion marked his features. "Why can't I resist you?" It was a whispered question that Shawn wasn't sure he was expected to answer.

Still, he gave Roscoe what he hoped was a sexy smile. "You find my talent and charm unbearably sexy? Or—" he fingered the hem of the skirt that rode high on his shaved legs, "—you like my new wardrobe."

Roscoe smiled, turning his keys over in his hand. "There is that." He stared at Shawn as though trying to figure him out.

The *last* thing Shawn wanted Roscoe doing was thinking. He unlatched his seatbelt. "Come on, Roscoe. Make a man out of me." He opened his door with Roscoe's soft laughter following him out into the night air. He led the way to the front door, refusing to glance behind him. If he put a little bit of a swing in his step, was that bad? He had a nice butt. He wanted Roscoe to notice.

Roscoe crowded him up onto the miniscule porch, trapping him bodily up against the door. "Are you truly as fearless as you seem to be, or is it an act?"

"Can't you tell?"

Roscoe's arm snaked around him, hand hot on his bare belly as the other hand managed the keys in the door's lock. "No."

The press of Roscoe's erection into the small of Shawn's back was unbearably exciting. "Some kind of acting teacher *you* are."

Roscoe walked him through the door, keeping his hold. "Mmm, perhaps someone should fire me."

Not liking where that line of joking could lead, Shawn spun so he could wrap his arms around Roscoe's neck. He reached up to deftly pluck Roscoe's glasses from his nose. "Perhaps you should shut up and kiss me."

Roscoe growled his approval and rushed Shawn up against a wall. Shawn barely managed a surprised squeak before Roscoe devoured him. Happily, he succumbed, wrapping his arms around Roscoe's neck as the taller man hitched him higher. The toes of his Keds barely scraping the carpet, Shawn's entire weight rested on the thigh Roscoe shoved between his legs. He didn't know how long they stayed there, mouths fused together, playing tongue tag. He was too aware of Roscoe's hands exploring, sliding over his bare belly, slipping down to his thighs, pushing the hem of his skirt well up and over his waist to expose the new thong panties he wore underneath.

It seemed to be the last that brought Roscoe out of the kiss. He pulled away and looked down, snapping the band. "Where the hell did you find these?" The gruff rumble in his voice made Shawn lightheaded. Or was it the fingers that traced the lacy edges of the scraps of fabric?

"Amazing what you can find online," he breathed, the back of his skull thudding against the wall as Roscoe nuzzled his neck.

Roscoe hummed, teeth sinking into the meat of Shawn's neck, just enough to be thrilling. Shawn responded with a whimper, digging his fingers into the back of Roscoe's shoulders, almost dropping the glasses. "Sh-shouldn't we move to a bed or something?"

A wet tongue drew a line up Shawn's neck to circle the shell of his ear. "Are you sure? I could still take you home."

Shawn punched Roscoe's back. "Fuck you. You're not backing out now."

Roscoe laughed, tilting his head to recapture Shawn's lips in a far gentler kiss than before. "All right. Can't say I didn't give you a chance."

"Don't want it."

Roscoe nodded, kissed him again, then slowly pulled back. He held Shawn's arms as the shorter man found his balance. The only light came from a single lamp lit in the main room to Shawn's left, the shadows letting him get an unaccustomed view of just one of Roscoe's eyes, unfettered by the glasses. The pupil and iris were indistinguishable and huge, black and hypnotic beneath a fringe of thick lashes. The other eye was far too deep in shadow. That dark gaze dropped down to Shawn's crotch and his smile grew. "Lace, even?"

Shawn shrugged. "What the hell, right?"

Winding his fingers with Shawn's, he plucked his glasses from Shawn's other hand as he led the shorter man from the door. As he followed to the darkness of a short hall leading to an open door at the end of it, Shawn got a glimpse at a big empty room to the right. The only furniture was a couch and a table amongst a slew of boxes. More boxes were stacked on the counter of the kitchen to the other side. Yet more boxes lined the wall of the bedroom Roscoe revealed by turning on a lamp by the bed.

Shawn was thrown enough to turn his back on his imminent lover, frowning at the boxes. "Did you just move in?"

Roscoe spun him so his shins came up against the edge of the unmade bed. He didn't answer, choosing instead to reach up to cup Shawn's jaw, aiming him for another kiss. Shawn let it distract him, sliding his open palms up the front of Roscoe's sweater as Roscoe's hands drifted south to find his bare ass. Massively amped by Roscoe's massage of his cheeks, Shawn tore the hem of Roscoe's sweater and shirt from his slacks, eager to find some bare skin himself. Warm, smooth satin it was when he finally touched and he was immediately addicted.

Roscoe laughed, breaking away when Shawn had his clothing bunched up under his armpits and continued to push. "Okay, okay. Hold on." He stepped back to pull off the sweater, but the dress shirt needed unbuttoning.

Shawn sat, toeing out of his Keds as he pulled the frilly shirt up and over his head.

"Leave the rest," Roscoe ordered when he started to hook his thumbs in his waist band.

Shawn grinned, glancing down at the bunched up skirt and panties. "Okay." Still, he pulled his cell, ID and cash out the waistband and put them on the nightstand. Which brought his attention back to the boxes. There were more by the bed and there were only a few clothes hanging in the half-open closet. *What gives?*

He didn't manage to ask the question before Roscoe short-circuited his brain by taking off the dress shirt. Toned and perfect, his chest sported a light spatter of dark hair over his pecs and a truly beautiful trail down the center of his body to gather around his navel. Shawn had seen and appreciated male bodies before—he'd been on the swim team after all—so it still confused him why *this* man affected him so much more. Was it because he was a teacher? Was it because Shawn happened to think he was brilliant? Did the brain turn Shawn on more than the body? And wouldn't his sisters just crack up if that were true?

"What are you smiling at?" Roscoe's hands fiddled with the buckle of his belt.

Shawn watched, clutching the edge of the bed rather than reach between his legs to caress his cock. "What do you think?"

Quickly, Roscoe leaned down to pull of his socks. His low boots were already discarded by the nearly empty closet. Barefoot, belt undone, he stepped close to Shawn. "Scared?"

Shawn slid his hands up the soft fabric of Roscoe's slacks. Impulsively, he leaned forward to press his lips to the bare skin right beside Roscoe's navel. "Not at all." Not really a lie. The fluttering low in his gut was excitement, not fear.

The flesh beneath his lips quivered, prompting Shawn to open up and let his tongue swipe it. Roscoe smelled so good, deeper and darker than a woman and the texture of his skin was silkier. Shawn gripped Roscoe's thighs and thoroughly explored the skin he could reach, including a nuzzle and taste of the dark trail that stopped at Roscoe's waistband.

Roscoe's fingers threaded in his hair, just caressing. He didn't move to stop Shawn when he unbuttoned the slacks or pulled down the zipper. The boxer briefs inside were dark and full, Roscoe's erection straining the stretchy fabric. *Whoa.* He'd been prepared, but Roscoe looked really *big* to him. He glanced up to find Roscoe watching him patiently, still stroking his hair. His hesitation had to be clear so Roscoe must be letting him take it at his own pace.

So he did. He let the slacks fall into a puddle around Roscoe's ankles then reached up to palm Roscoe's cock. Encouraged by the man's groan, Shawn leaned in to touch his tongue to the damp spot where the head was.

"God, you're going to kill me," Roscoe muttered softly.

Smiling, Shawn took another taste, intrigued by the salt and spice mingled with musky fabric. Roscoe's hips rocked gently into him, the man's fingers cupping the back of his head. Bold now, Shawn hooked his fingers in the top of the boxers and pulled them down. He caught the cock that sprang out at him, leaving the boxers only partway down Roscoe's thighs. Eagerly, he opened his mouth and, with his eyes rolled up to watch Roscoe, he took the head past his lips. He missed Roscoe's reaction, though, his own eyes closing as he was overcome by the texture and flavor of what filled his mouth. It was both exhilarating and scary as hell at the same time. He closed his lips securely around the shaft and pulled his head back, letting his tongue drag the vein underneath. A few creamy drops of pre-cum oozed on his tongue as reward. Hey! That was cool. He leaned in to take as much of Roscoe back into his mouth as he could—and he couldn't get it all—then pulled back again. The fact that he was sucking cock struck him and he nearly laughed at the weird wash of relief that sluiced through his body. He'd given it so much thought over the past few weeks that he was nearly giddy to finally be *doing* it.

"God." Roscoe's whispered curse brought him back to the task at hand. He stole a peek up at Roscoe to find those dark eyes mostly closed and focused down on Shawn. His hips flexed underneath Shawn's hands, gently guiding himself in and out of Shawn's mouth. Shawn had to give him credit. He knew he couldn't be that calm when getting a blow job.

It didn't last long. Shawn had just started to suck in earnest when Roscoe pulled away. "Enough." He paused a moment, breathing. Then his eyes reopened and he grinned down at Shawn. "You sure you've never done that before?"

Shawn matched the grin as Roscoe pushed him onto his back among the dark, rumpled sheets. "I did okay?"

"Fabulous." Roscoe trailed his fingers down Shawn's chest, gaze tracking their progress. "But now it's my turn." He stepped out of the rest of his clothes and urged Shawn closer to the middle of the bed, then crawled up to kneel over him. Smiling, he lowered himself for a kiss, then another. Soft and sweet, unlike the all-consuming kisses Shawn craved, but intense in their own way. Shawn relaxed into the sheets, his focus zeroing on the brush of their lips and lightly tapping tongues. When Shawn was suitably hypnotized, Roscoe trailed away from his mouth to trace his jaw with equally soft kisses. Down his neck and over his collarbone, Roscoe took his time, igniting a sizzle that burned pleasantly under every inch of Shawn's skin. Part of Shawn was anxious for Roscoe to get on with the good stuff already, but a larger part of him was starting to get the opinion that this was a damn fine ramp up to the good stuff. He felt wonderfully alive. The only similar expansive feeling he could think of would be when he was acting and he knew it was going well. But Roscoe was his only audience now, or was he Roscoe's audience? Didn't matter. Roscoe's lips found his nipple and the electric feel forced Shawn's back to arch. Damn, he'd been missing out on *this*? None of the girls he'd ever been with had been this attentive. Of course, they'd all been his age or younger. Perhaps there really was something to this older man deal.

Shawn did start to get antsy as Roscoe took his time exploring with lips, teeth and tongue, so he started a little exploring of his own. Roscoe's soft, silky hair slipped through his fingers and the smooth skin of Roscoe's back was just too amazing. Hot, velvety satin over firm muscle. He bent his knees to let the inside of his thighs rub against Roscoe's sides. His cock strained against the hold of his panties, the thong rubbing his anus.

Roscoe chuckled. "Anxious?" A warm hand caressed Shawn's shaft through the fabric.

He cried out. "Unh, yeah."

Laughing softly, Roscoe stroked as he readjusted to lie between Shawn's thighs. Shawn heard a drawer open and saw the bottle of lube that Roscoe took out to toss on the bed by his hip. Then the black eyes locked with his as Roscoe rolled Shawn's skirt until it was a band at his navel. "Relax." Warm fingers carefully pulled the side of the panties, freeing Shawn's cock without removing the scraps of fabric and elastic. Roscoe bent his head and stuck out his tongue to trace just the point against the tip of Shawn's cock. Moaning, Shawn bucked but Roscoe's hands kept him pinned. Thankfully, Roscoe must have decided that he'd teased enough. He spread his lips over the head of Shawn's cock and plunged down, sliding his tongue along the shaft until the head bumped the back of his throat.

Shawn clutched at the sheets, moaning loudly as Roscoe pulled up and plunged back, again and again. He must have missed the click of the bottle of lube opening or shutting because then there were wet fingers nudging aside the strap of the thong, rubbing behind his balls, skimming their way down into the crack of his ass. He thrashed, trying to hold out and let this last, but his hips had other ideas. They started to rock, seeking those fingers, trying to bring them where they wanted them.

Roscoe dipped down to tongue Shawn's balls as he circled Shawn's anus with one finger. His other hand stayed wrapped around Shawn's shaft, his thumb toying with that sensitive spot just underneath the head.

"Fuck!" Shawn slapped both of his palms over his face, knowing he was losing the battle. It felt *too* good. Then Roscoe's finger popped just inside him. "Oh, fuck, man, Roscoe, I'm gonna come."

"Go ahead," came the purred reply.

"But..."

"I'm not done with you." He squeezed Shawn's shaft and pushed his finger in a little farther. "Come for me." Then his mouth closed around Shawn's cock and he sucked.

"Jesus, fuck shit!" That was it. Shawn lost it. His body locked in a spasm and fire shot down his spine and out of his cock. Roscoe rode through it, swallowing him down, massaging, coaxing and sucking until Shawn settled back in the sheets, exhausted.

It took a minute for Shawn's brain to kick back into gear. When it did, he realized that Roscoe had released his cock to nuzzle his balls again. At least two, maybe three wet fingers massaged gently inside Shawn's ass. Shawn swallowed, trying to reconcile that full feeling. He pushed up on his elbows and tried to get his eyes to focus on Roscoe.

Who peeked up at him over his bunched up skirt and spent cock, smiling. "You all right?"

"I'm..." Shawn groaned, head falling back a little when Roscoe twisted his fingers and found something inside there that felt *really* good. "Whoa."

"Want me to stop?"

"God no." He licked his lips, rocking his hips to move Roscoe's fingers just a little... *Oh yeah!* "But I don't think... I can... come again soon."

Roscoe chuckled, shifting up to his knees without removing his hand. "And here I thought you were a virile young man."

"Fuck you." Shawn glared at him but it was somewhat ruined when his gaze got sidetracked by the sight of Roscoe's cock at full mast, jutting up from that dark nest of hair.

Roscoe laughed, reaching for the lube. "I think I will. Do you mind?"

Shawn bit his lip.

Roscoe paused. "I'll stop if you tell me to."

Shawn swallowed. "No. Don't stop."

Roscoe twisted his fingers again and Shawn moaned, sinking off of his elbows to his back. The lube bottle popped and Roscoe poured more on the hand that was still deep inside Shawn. "I'll go as slow as I can." He dropped the lube back onto the mattress then something small and light plopped onto Shawn's chest. "Mind opening that for me?"

Shawn picked up the condom packet. *Damn, we're really going to do this.* He tore it open and took out the lubricated ring of latex. "You need me to put this on you?" When had his voice gone all husky?

Roscoe plucked it from his fingers. "No." Watching Shawn's face, he slowly pulled his fingers out of Shawn's ass. Shawn couldn't help a little moan. "God, you *are* beautiful."

Shawn wasn't sure he was supposed to hear that murmur and he wasn't sure how Roscoe could think that. The skirt was a wrinkled band of fabric at his navel and the thong panties were pushed aside and stretched out of proportion. He was sure that his makeup had smudged thanks to the light sheen of sweat that had broken out all over his body. His cock was tingling like it wanted to get hard but it still couldn't quite manage it yet. He was sure he probably looked a wreck, but then that might have been part of it. Shawn had felt a certain sense of satisfaction to muss the girls he'd been with before. The same probably went for Roscoe.

Roscoe stared at him, drinking him in as he rolled on the condom, then patted his thigh. "Turn over. On your knees."

"But…"

"It's easier the first time. Trust me."

Not like he had much choice. He didn't want to spoil the moment. Shawn twisted to his belly and pulled his knees under him. He hissed when the panties pressed awkwardly at the base of his cock.

A warm hand smoothed over his back. "You okay?"

"Yeah." He reached down to tug at the offending band of elastic. "Can we take these off?"

A finger tucked underneath the band in the back then slid down the center of Shawn's ass to pull it up and away. "I'd rather not. Is it that uncomfortable?"

He likes it. Shawn imagined his ass with that little bit of white bisecting it. Yeah, that was probably sexy. He arched back when Roscoe rubbed a finger on his opening. "No."

"Good." Something wet and much larger than a finger rubbed Shawn's hole. "Relax." A hand wrapped in the back of the thong, holding it aside as that something bigger started to press inside.

Shawn wanted this more than anything, but that didn't stop him from being a little scared. He held onto an armful of sheets and bedspread and listened to his own breathy little whimper as his opening stretched and took in the first little bit of Roscoe.

"You all right?"

Roscoe. He closed his eyes, letting the man's voice, the scent of him soothe the weird stretching sensation. "Yeah."

A damp hand smoothed over his back. "Push back into me. Slow."

Shawn obeyed, taking his time, letting himself adjust. It wasn't nearly as painful as he'd thought it would be, but Roscoe had taken lots of time to get him amped up and ready. *Roscoe.* Always looking out for him.

When Shawn had as much of him as he could take—and he couldn't tell how much—Roscoe bent over him to press chest to back. One hand braced on the mattress beside Shawn's head while the other palm slid under his chest, holding him. "God, you feel good." Roscoe nuzzled the back of his neck. "Still okay?"

Shawn twisted his hips and gasped. "Oh yeah."

"That's my boy."

Roscoe's cock started its retreat and twin moans bled from both men. Electricity sizzled in Shawn's spine, shorting out the pain of the unfamiliar stretch in his anus. He rocked back when Roscoe pushed in, anxious to feel his lover, his teacher, his idol deep inside of him again. When Roscoe found a good pace for deep, grunting thrusts, Shawn was right there with him. Roscoe fell onto his elbow beside Shawn's shoulder, his weight forcing Shawn's knees further apart. Shawn's cock rubbed into the sheets, still soft even with that exciting tingle stirring in his balls. Blindly, Shawn's fingers sought Roscoe's, holding the other man's arm under his neck as he was pounded into the mattress. Roscoe's other hand now twisted in Shawn's thong, making the bands bite cruelly into Shawn's skin. Oddly, that little bit of pain only added fuel to the fire, helping to coax great, gulping moans from deep within Shawn's chest. He cried Roscoe's name, heard his own in a grunted echo. Roscoe's sweat smeared with his all along Shawn's back. When Roscoe's pounding rhythm faltered, his thrusts locking as he came, Shawn succumbed to an answering pulse that burst deep inside him and sent a thrilling buzz throughout his limbs.

Roscoe braced above him as they both tried to breathe. Then, slowly, he unraveled his fingers from Shawn's thong to slide his palm up Shawn's side to his shoulder. Which he kissed, softly. Reverently. "You're all right?"

A weak laugh burst from Shawn's lips. He still held Roscoe's fingers, the man's arm underneath his cheek, and he refused to let go. "I'm great."

Roscoe chuckled, nuzzling the back of his neck. "I'm going to have to get up in a minute."

Shawn took stock of their legs tangled together, of his ass pressed into the bend of Roscoe's hips. The position kept Roscoe's softening cock inside him and he rather liked the sensation. "In a minute," he murmured, turning his head to kiss Roscoe's arm. "But not just yet."

✥ ✥ ✥ ✥ ✥

Shawn woke with his face pressed in an unfamiliar pillow that smelled heavenly. Half-conscious, he sighed and rolled into it, reaching up to wrap his arms under it. He was just drifting back to Slumberland when the mattress shifted behind him. It was an odd enough occurrence that it jarred his brain back to wakefulness. Gradually, the events of the previous night resurfaced, melting away the clouds of sleep and urging a morning woody. Eyes still closed, he edged back until his butt and back collided with warm flesh, still hugging the pillow he now knew smelled like Roscoe. The body behind him moved, turning so that one arm could snake around Shawn's waist and snug him up into the curve of Roscoe's body. The continued heavy breathing assured Shawn that Roscoe was still asleep.

Shawn let his eyes drift shut. The dark gray light assured him that it was still early. Roscoe was warm and the bed was quite comfortable. Happily ensconced, he skated on the edge of wakefulness, not letting his mind settle on any thought too much. But he was doomed. No matter how much he liked lying there, Shawn simply wasn't capable of getting back to sleep once he'd passed a certain point of consciousness. Gradually his thoughts solidified, so he mulled over the explosive sexual awakening he'd experienced the previous night. The excitement of closing night, alcohol from the party and exhaustion from the sex had wiped both of them out. Shawn remembered a trip to the bathroom and a half-hearted attempt by both of them to try a second round, but they must have fallen asleep in the midst of it because that's all Shawn remembered.

The first round, though... He grinned into his pillow. Man, that'd been hot! If that was sex with guys, he was *so* done with women. Of course, he had a feeling that sex with Roscoe wasn't like sex with all men. Certainly Ian had relayed some horror stories to Shawn when asked. Roscoe had been gentle and patient, and had coaxed feelings out of Shawn the younger man hadn't imagined. Just like when he was directing, he'd used whatever means necessary to get the result he wanted, and Roscoe had wanted Shawn to enjoy.

But would he want to do it again? That jarring thought opened Shawn's eyes. Pale yellow sunlight now painted the wall opposite the bed, shedding light on the cardboard boxes sitting there. Roscoe was going to want to fuck him again, wasn't he? This wasn't it?

Carefully, Shawn turned onto his back. Roscoe's arm lifted and fell with his body, a heavy weight. A look at the man's face assured Shawn that he was far from awake. Those generous lips were parted for breath and tousled black curls threatened to hide his closed eyes. Shawn reached up to gently trace his stubbled jaw. He'd never seen Roscoe with a shadow before. It made him look different, less collected and more rugged. Shawn liked it. He very much wanted to see it again. Often.

Wide awake now, Shawn slipped out of bed. He was a little surprised to find his skirt still wound about his waist, but the thong was long gone. Yawning, he padded across the carpet to the bathroom, frowning at the mostly empty top of the single dresser. The bathroom was scaled way back too. Nothing in the medicine cabinet at all except a bottle of Listerine. All of Roscoe's necessities sat on the white tiled counter by the sink.

Shawn wondered at that as he used the facilities, availed himself of the mouthwash and washed the smudged remnants of makeup from his face.

Shimmying out of the ruined skirt, he returned to the bedroom. The only serviceable piece of clothing he had left was the frilly little top. Shrugging, he dropped the skirt on the floor by his top and shoes and left naked for the kitchen. Roscoe had already seen him and then some so what did it matter?

Shawn found the coffee maker and the pre-packaged coffee packet to put in it. There were three mugs in the entire kitchen and all of them were sitting in the dish drainer by the sink. Four plates, four bowls and two glasses were the only other dishes Shawn could find after looking through all of the cupboards. No food in the cupboards other than sugar, salt and pepper. The contents of the refrigerator consisted mostly of drinks: water, soda, fruit juice and beer. The freezer was the only thing stocked, filled with frozen entrees.

"He lives like a college student," Shawn laughed to himself as he waited for the coffee to percolate. Looking over the counter at the main room of the condo, he was struck again by the boxes and the lack of furniture. There wasn't even a television. "Okay, scratch that. He lives like a monk."

It must have been the smell of coffee that woke Roscoe. Shawn heard him in the bathroom just as the coffee beeped ready. The man himself shuffled naked into the room as Shawn was pouring creamer in his coffee.

"'Morning," he gruffed, kissing the back of Shawn's head as he passed behind him to get another mug.

"'Morning. I found the coffee."

"Mmmm. Bless you."

Obviously, Roscoe wasn't much of a morning conversationalist. The brief kiss made Shawn happy though. Cradling his mug, he left the kitchen to Roscoe and wandered into the main room. Eventually Roscoe joined him on the couch.

"Don't like television?"

Roscoe glanced at the table with the non-faded mark on top of the table where one probably had sat. "I got rid of it."

Shawn nodded, turning a pointed look around the room. "Yeah. That and a lot of other things. What gives?"

Roscoe didn't meet his gaze, which wasn't a good sign. "I'm moving."

Shawn's warm fuzzy started to shed. "What?"

"I'm moving."

"To a bigger place?"

"No." Roscoe sighed, taking a big sip of his coffee. "I wasn't going to tell any of you students until a later."

"Later when?"

"Later after finals."

What could wait four weeks? "Tell what?"

The black gaze met his, stark and unfettered by glasses. "I'm moving back to New York."

Shawn gaped. "New York? When did this happen?"

Roscoe leaned back into the corner of the couch, folding one leg up in front of him so he could balance his mug on his knee. "Last week."

"What?"

"Last month I received an offer to direct a play off Broadway. I put off making a decision because of *Much Ado* but then, last week..." He shrugged. "It's an opportunity I should probably take."

Shawn stared, dumbfounded. His heart thudded in his throat and a cold wash of dread crept over him. While he realized that Roscoe was right, that he shouldn't let the opportunity pass, he couldn't help an inner whine: *What about us?* He wanted to ask, but he didn't. Clearly, there was no *us*. At least not to Roscoe. "What about teaching?"

"It's like you said. I don't belong teaching."

"Did you make your decision before or after I said that?"

Roscoe met his gaze levelly. "After."

Shawn stared into his coffee. "Well. Fuck."

"I'm sorry."

"What for?" Something broke in around his heart and he was dangerously close to tears. He fought them. "That's great news." He stood up, turning back to the kitchen despite the fact he had a half mug of coffee left. "Off Broadway. Shit, yeah. What play?"

"A new one. The author's an acquaintance of mine from school. She asked me to come and direct it."

"That's great." *Fuck!* This shouldn't hurt this much. He set his mug on the counter and stared at it. New York was where Roscoe belonged. It was where he made his name in the first place and the only place to make a real living doing theater. But it was so far away. Shawn just connected with him and now he was leaving?

He didn't realize how long he'd been standing there, thoughts whirling as he desperately tried to breathe over the lump in his throat. But it must have been awhile. Another mug appeared on the counter beside his just before warm hands slid over the back of his shoulders and down his arms. "You okay?"

The question echoed the gentle question from their lovemaking too closely, spoken in the same soft tone. Shawn closed his eyes and bit his lip over a sob.

"Shawn?"

It had to be the emotional build-up from the stress of the play. He always felt a letdown after a run ended. Add that to the best sex he'd ever had then the fact that the person who'd shared that sex with him—who also happened to be his idol and mentor—was about to leave, and it was understandable that he was cracking up. Right?

"Shawn?"

"Don't go."

Hands appeared beside his on the counter as Roscoe stepped into him, trapping him between warm body and unyielding counter. Roscoe sighed, leaning his forehead against the back of Shawn's skull. "I have to."

"Why?"

"I told Lisa I would."

"That's not the reason."

Pause. "What do you want me to say?"

"Why did you all of a sudden decide to move across country?"

"I don't belong here."

"Because of what I said?"

"What you said helped me see the truth of the matter."

"What about what I did?"

No answer. Shawn hung his head, in control of the tears now but still cracking inside. "If I hadn't come on to you, would you be leaving?"

Roscoe paused too long, then replied: "If I can give in that easily to a student, I shouldn't be teaching."

"Well. Fuck."

They stood there for a few moments more but both of them were out of words. At length, Roscoe stepped back, trailing his hands over Shawn's back. "I've got some sweats and a t-shirt you can borrow. Why don't I take you home?"

Part of Shawn wanted to protest, to throw Roscoe on the couch and fuck him into next week. Instead, he just nodded.

✞ ✞ ✞ ✞ ✞

They were halfway into the twenty minute ride to campus before Shawn exploded.

"You know what? Fuck you." He glared at Roscoe's profile, noting the way the man's grip on the steering wheel tightened because it was the only outward sign of emotion. "What the hell did you sleep with me for if you knew you were running away?"

"I'm not running away."

"Fine, 'moving' away."

Roscoe's eyes were hidden behind pitch black sunglasses rather than his normal horn rims. Somehow, being denied the sight of his eyes pissed Shawn off more. "Sleeping with you was not my idea."

"But you sure as hell went with it."

Roscoe sighed. "I knew this was a bad idea."

"You could have filled me in."

"You're right. I should have."

"So why didn't you?"

Roscoe paused long enough that Shawn doubted he'd answer, but then he did: "I wanted you." He sighed, scratching at the stubble he had yet to shave off. "It's hard to deny when a gorgeous young man wants to sleep with you."

Shawn was somewhat mollified but not enough. "So what now?"

Roscoe shook his head. "Nothing. We can't do this again."

"Why not?"

"I should think that would be obvious."

"So you're pulling the teacher thing again?"

Roscoe's lips pressed into a line to show he was starting to get pissed. "It's not a good idea. For either of us."

But Shawn was way ahead of him. It was all he could do to keep from punching the man while he was driving. "I can't sleep with you again while you're my teacher, but you're moving away just as soon as you're not my teacher again. Terrific." He faced forward, aware he was pouting but unable to stop. "Was I that bad?"

"No. Of course not. I made the decision about New York before last night. And it wasn't my idea…"

"…To sleep with me, yeah I know." He *did* know, but logic was not on his side at the moment. He glared at the campus clock tower as it got closer and closer. "It's not right, man. It's not. I just had the best sex of my life and you're telling me I can't have it again."

"There is no way in this world that *you* could lack for partners."

"But I want *you*, damn it." Shit, he was close to tears again. Manfully, he did his best to swallow them behind a hollow laugh. "You don't get what you did to me. No one else can do that."

An echo of Shawn's laugh spilled from Roscoe. "I'm sure you're wrong."

"I'm sure I'm *not*."

"You haven't slept with enough men to make that call."

Which meant that Roscoe had, implying that last night wasn't special to him. Shawn should know that. He hadn't gone into this wearing rose-colored glasses, but something *had* happened to him last night and he refused to believe it was just losing his gay cherry. He hadn't felt like this the first time he'd slept with a girl. "And you have?"

"You're talented, young and gorgeous. Men will be falling over themselves to have you once you make your interest known."

"Just not you."

"If circumstances were different…"

"Then don't move. You won't be my teacher in a few weeks."

Roscoe shook his head. "It's not right. You have a lot of growing up to do. I've already gone through that phase of my life."

"Oh come on…"

"No! I am past wanting one night stands. I want something with meaning. Not just sex."

Shawn opened his mouth, ready to promise that he could provide that. But words didn't come. He was far too honest to admit that he was ready for any kind of commitment.

They rode in silence, then Roscoe turned past the gate officially leading onto campus. Shawn wondered that he seemed to know where he was going but had more important things on his mind. "I won't tell anyone," he assured the older man. The least he could do was prove that he wasn't a child.

"Thank you."

There was more he should say, but it wouldn't come out. Wouldn't make a difference. Roscoe had made up his mind. And maybe he was right. His only lapse had been taking Shawn home last night.

The Camero stopped on the street closest to his building.

"How did you know which dorm I'm in?"

"Lucky guess."

Shawn doubted it, but then he didn't care. He opened his door.

"Shawn."

"What?"

"What we shared last night was amazing." The words spilled out, like Roscoe was saying them before he could stop himself. "*You* were amazing. I don't want you to think that I didn't feel it too. But…"

Shawn peeked over. Roscoe was twisted in his seat as far as the cramped space and seatbelt would allow. His elbow was propped on the steering wheel and that hand held the sunglasses so that Shawn could see the truth in those black eyes.

"Yeah. But." Like back in Roscoe's condo, they ran out of words.

Clutching the small bundle of his skirt and top to his chest, Shawn stepped out of the car and closed the door. He headed for his dorm building without looking back.

✤ ✤ ✤ ✤ ✤

One year later…

Shawn adjusted his cap on his head, made sure the tassel was visible, then moved into Gavin, making sure that his skintight, bright red dress was fully visible for the picture. Surprisingly, Gavin turned to face him and caught Shawn's knee, holding it up at hip level as he snaked his other arm around Shawn's shoulders. Delighted, Shawn broke into laughter just as Gavin's brother snapped the picture.

He slapped Gavin's shoulder after the flash. "You naughty boy, you!"

Gavin grinned at him, letting go of his knee. "I figured what the hell, right? Besides, you look damn good in that dress."

Shawn batted heavily made up eyes at him. "You sweet talker." Before Gavin could protest, he bounced up on his toes to brush his lips against the other man's. "You sure you're not gay?"

Gavin flushed, immediately reaching up to thumb bright red lipstick from his mouth. But he was smiling. "Yeah, I'm pretty sure."

Bonnie insinuated herself in between Shawn and Gavin and bonked Shawn on the head with her cap, knocking his askew. "*I'm* sure," she asserted, winding her arm with Gavin's. The two of them had developed a surprise fling over the past few months. She mock glared at Shawn. "Stay away from him, you slut."

"Well!" Shawn snatched his cap off his head in mock indignation, letting his mahogany curls tumble about his face. "I never."

"And you never will. Not with him anyway." Bonnie grinned, then reached to put her arm around Shawn to bring him close. "Come on, I need a picture with both of you."

Graduation. Shawn was enjoying the hell out of the moment but he was ambivalent about the whole thing. He'd barely earned the right to his diploma, just sneaking by in passing his classes despite of all the time he'd missed during his senior year. Dennis Connor sent him out on a lot of auditions and a few had actually paid off. One of these days he was going to start seeing royalties off the national snack food commercial he'd done last fall.

The photo with Bonnie and Gavin became a group one with five other classmates, which veered off into other individual pics. Then Shawn decided that he should probably get outside and look for his family. His mother, sister and her husband were out there somewhere. He headed up the aisle between the padded audience seats, a little torn that this would probably be the last time he'd be in the theater. Oh, he might come back to see a play or two, but it wouldn't be the same. He wouldn't be a student. Of course, he hadn't actually performed in this space since *Much Ado About Nothing*. Paying work had kept him from committing to any but his required class performances, both of which had been held in the smaller on-campus venues. It seemed rather fitting that *Much Ado* was his crowning glory during college, even if it was also the prelude to a crushing time in his life.

Those last few weeks of his junior year had been hellish. He'd ditched two weeks of acting classes before Bonnie finally convinced him to come back. She didn't know why he'd stopped—no one but Roscoe did—but she'd been asked by the assistant dean to talk to him before his grades started to suffer. He'd gone back reluctantly. Roscoe didn't give him grief, didn't say much to him at all. They'd kept their interaction at a minimum and strictly on the student/teacher level. When asked about it outside of class, Shawn had refused to acknowledge that anything was wrong. The summer had proven both better and worse. Better that a steady stream of auditions and call backs as well as a part time job in his sister's shop had kept him busy. Worse that he knew Roscoe was gone. He hadn't been able to decide if it was better to know he was close and not talk to him or to know he was far away and not talk to him. But he'd persevered and grown.

Sexually speaking, he'd done some exploring in the last year as well. He couldn't be called promiscuous, but he had slept with four different men and even tried something of a relationship for a few months. While the encounters had confirmed for him that he did like sex with men more than he liked sex with women, not one of his lovers could hold a candle to that one night with Roscoe. It was sad. One of the men had even been a few years older than Roscoe and insanely turned on by Shawn's tendency to cross-dress. But his maturity hadn't been Roscoe's and his obsession had turned out to be a little creepy. It just proved to Shawn that Roscoe was one of a kind.

The cross-dressing had turned out to be one of the better things in his life. His sister loved the fact that he wore the dresses she sold in her shop and many of her customers couldn't even tell that he was a guy. Predictably, his mother and other sisters had embraced the news of his sexuality and his mother was on a crusade to find just the right man for him. She remained the only person he'd told about Roscoe and she guarded his secret religiously.

He stepped out of the theater's front doors into the blazing afternoon sun. Momentarily blinded, he stepped aside and got sidetracked by another friend wanting a picture.

"What's going on over there?" she wondered after hearing an excited squeal.

Shawn shielded his eyes to look in the direction she was looking. There was a cluster of their classmates over by the fountain but Shawn couldn't tell what the fuss was about. "Let's go see."

On his way, he caught sight of his family talking with Dean Wurther and waved. Since they seemed to be doing okay, he kept on toward the commotion.

He was almost there when a few people stepped aside and he finally saw who was in the middle of the cluster.

Roscoe.

Damn he looked good! Clean shaven, with his glossy black curls cut much shorter than the last time Shawn had seen him. The horn rims had been replaced with stylish wire rims, with the lenses that tint darker in the sunlight. He wore a smooth ivory button down over light brown slacks and low boots in darker brown. He hadn't lost his tan back in New York.

Smiling, he was commenting on something one of the others said, but his words died off when he caught sight of Shawn. No joke. His eyes locked on the younger man and his sentence stopped. Everyone looked to see who had his attention.

Lapping it up, Shawn closed the distance between them with his cap in hand and his gown open to show off his dress. Yes, he put a swing in his step and, yes, he did thrust his padded chest out a bit. Yes, he was showing off. Roscoe didn't even try to hide sizing him up, even raising his hand up to tilt his glasses down so he could see over the rims.

"Hey, stranger," Shawn greeted, unable to smother the grin that possessed his mouth. Last he saw Roscoe he'd been pissed off and he hadn't heard from the man since junior year finals. Despite that, this was the man who'd introduced him to a new chapter of his life, who'd taught him a hell of a lot about acting. Without Roscoe, Shawn may never have made that leap into who he now was, and he rather *liked* himself now.

"Finnemore," Roscoe set his glasses back properly on his nose, "still wearing dresses I see?"

"I've discovered that I like them."

"You look beautiful."

"Awwww." Shawn raised a hand to his chest and turned his head aside in a practiced blush. "You're too kind."

He was blown away when Roscoe stepped even closer and plucked his hand up to raise it to his lips. "You are."

Shawn stared, aware that things had suddenly gone very quiet around them. He tried to come up with a joke but the serious look in Roscoe's eyes threw him off. "What are you doing here?"

The warmth in Roscoe's smile melted his toes. "I came to see you."

"To see graduation?"

"That too."

Shawn blinked. *What are you doing?* "How long are you in town?"

"That depends on you."

"On me?"

"Yes."

"What are you talking about?"

Roscoe smiled and Shawn realized the man still had his hand, holding it against his heart. "Have dinner with me and I'll explain."

A female someone to Shawn's right squealed but was immediately hushed.

Laughter bubbled past Shawn's lips as he searched Roscoe's face. "Are you serious?"

"Yes."

"Are you asking me out on a *date*?"

Roscoe's smile grew. "Yes."

"I knew it!" that outburst definitely came from Bonnie but Shawn couldn't spare her a look, caught by sexy black eyes.

"How do you know I'm not still pissed at you?"

"I don't."

"What if I am?"

"Then my trip is going to be very short."

"And if I'm not?" He had no idea really what he was saying, but it was sure fun.

Even more fun when Roscoe raised his hand to kiss the back of his knuckles. "Let's discuss that."

Shawn cocked his head, considering, eating up the moment and the attention for all they were worth. "All right. On one condition."

"Name it."

"Kiss me."

"With pleasure."

Roscoe reached up to snake his free hand around Shawn's neck to pull him closer. Shawn went gladly, steadying himself with a palm on the warmth of Roscoe's chest as he presented his lips for Roscoe's. *Oh yes.* That was the kiss he remembered, the kiss he craved. Happily, he freed his hand so he could wind both arms around Roscoe's neck, delighted to feel those strong arms sweep him close. He heard the cries and yells from his fellow graduates around him but chose to tune them out. Roscoe was here and Roscoe had shown open interest in front of people they both knew. That meant something, and Shawn had a good feeling that it meant something very special.

Sometimes, Life's a Drag

J.P. Bowie

CHAPTER ONE

London, England.

Patrick Farland grimaced as he dashed from the shelter of Selfridges's storefront out onto the drizzle slicked pavements of Oxford Street.

"What a pisser," he muttered, feeling his hair curl immediately in the damp air. *It bloody well would have to rain today*, he thought, half running to the Underground station. He'd wanted to get to the nightclub at least in decent condition, but now he'd be soaked by the time he got there. He'd heard that Kenny LaFontaine, the star and the owner of the nightclub, was a stickler for presentation, expecting anyone who auditioned for him to look like they were ready to perform—no jeans, no tennis shoes, no unshaven chins, and if a girl showed up without makeup, it was the door right away.

He was meeting his friend Lawrence there, and after the audition they'd go to the nearest pub and have a late lunch. No way would they dance and sing on full stomachs! As he rushed through the station toward the escalator, Patrick caught a glimpse of himself reflected in one of the glass mounted advertisement panels that lined the station walls.

"Oh, *Gawd.*" His hair was a mess of black curls. So much for spending a fortune at Selfridges's hair salon. Well, he daren't touch it now. He'd just make a bigger mess of it.

Lawrence was waiting inside KENNY'S THEATRE CLUB doorway when Patrick finally arrived, out of breath and sweaty.

"I'm a mess," he moaned in greeting.

"The hair's lovely," Lawrence said, laughing. "Where have you been?"

"Would you believe, the hairdresser's?"

Lawrence patted his own light brown perfectly cut hair and smiled. "I told you to get it cut shorter. Bangs are out, dear."

"Oh shut up, and let's see what's happening inside. They might make concessions because of the rain."

"They might suggest an umbrella!"

Patrick gave his friend a push and they both fell into the stage door entrance, giggling. An older, gray haired man gave them a baleful look that said, without words being necessary, 'Bloody poufters.' Patrick cast him a look of disdain. After all, the old geezer was working for Kenny LaFontaine, one of the biggest 'poufters' in the business.

"We're here for the audition," Lawrence said.

"No need to tell *me* that," said the old man. He pointed down the hall. "All the way down, then left turn."

"Thanks." They set off, hand in hand, just to annoy the old fart. "Bloody cheeky old git," Patrick whispered. "I bet he doesn't look at *Miss LaFontaine* that way." They turned left at the end of the hall and found themselves backstage where about twenty young men and women were standing about. "Gawd, look at them all. And he only needs one singer."

"But six dancers," Lawrence reminded him. "And you can do both."

"Right, but I prefer to sing. It's what I really want to do. Oh look, there's Maggie." Patrick pointed to a pretty young girl doing stretching exercises off to the side. "Let's go say hello."

Lawrence followed Patrick over to where Maggie sat, intently stretching her leg muscles.

"Maggie..." Patrick knelt by her side. "Hello."

Maggie smiled up at the two friends. "Hi... I thought I might see you here." She jerked her thumb toward the stage where a young man was pacing around. "He's just waiting for the diva to arrive. Always late apparently." She got to her feet gracefully. "I'm just going to run to the loo, be right back."

No sooner had she gone than a strident voice sounded from the front of the club. "Ralph, let's get started shall we? I haven't got all day."

The man on the stage sprang into action, clapping his hands for attention and calling all dancers on stage immediately. Patrick looked around for Maggie, but there was so sign of her coming back.

"Shit," he muttered, wondering if he should run to get her. "Lawrence..." He pushed his friend toward the stage. "Stall them, somehow."

"What?" Lawrence looked at him in amazement. "How the bloody hell can I do that?"

"Think of something," Patrick hissed. "Maggie's not back!"

"Come along, you two!" The man called Ralph yelled at them. "Let's not keep Mr. LaFontaine waiting. He's a very busy man."

"Shit," Patrick muttered again, walking on stage with Lawrence. He looked back into the wings. Still no sign of Maggie.

"All right," Ralph said, clapping his hands again. "Just going to show you a *very* simple routine to begin with, then we'll see how fast you can pick it up. Okay?" Ralph smiled sweetly but Patrick could see the bitch underneath. He and Lawrence exchanged glances, then he saw Maggie sidle onstage, joining the end of the line. He was just going to breathe a sigh of relief when that strident voice rang out again.

"You there! Yes you... the pretty one with the ponytail. You're late coming onstage." Kenny LaFontaine swept down toward the stage, his face grim. Patrick had seen Kenny several times on TV but never up close or out of drag, so he was surprised at how young he appeared. Young—and full of himself.

"If I can be here on time," Kenny snapped, "then so can you, young lady."

"But you weren't here on time, I'm afraid," Maggie said matter-of-factly. "You were a good fifteen minutes late."

"Excuse me?" Kenny gasped, placing his hands on his hips.

"I said, you were fifteen minutes late," Maggie repeated. "I was here on time, but had to go to the loo just as you deigned to show up."

"That's quite enough," Ralph yelled, marching up to Maggie and glaring at her. "You can go!"

Maggie shrugged, and Patrick stepped to her side. "There's no need to shout at her," he said quietly. "She couldn't help going to the loo."

"You can go, too," Ralph said, sniffing. He turned to Kenny. "Honestly, who do these kids think they are?"

"Ralph..." Kenny was tapping his foot and looked as if he were about to implode. "When I want you to interrupt me, I'll let you know. I'll say who stays and who goes, not you."

Someone, somewhere, tittered and Kenny's eyes narrowed to slits. "All right, we're not getting off to a very good start here. Young lady, what's your name?"

"Maggie Roberts."

"Don't be late again, Maggie. And you..." He stared at Patrick. "You with the hair, who're you?"

"Patrick Farland, Mr. LaFontaine."

"Right. Don't go butting in when it's not necessary. Now let's get on shall we?" He made a big show of examining the diamond watch on his wrist. "I have a very important business meeting to attend. Ralph, get a move on!"

Ralph, after shooting dirty looks at Maggie and Patrick, flounced to the center of the stage. "Like I was saying," he hissed, his eyes blazing with anger, "this is very *simple*. Now, follow me—and one and two, and one and two..."

And off they went.

"No, no, no!" Ralph screamed at Patrick. "That's not it at all."

"Well, I'm really a singer," Patrick said.

"I don't care if you're Placido Domingo—which I'm sure you're not—if you want to be in this show, you have to do these steps properly."

"I thought I was doing them properly..."

"Ralph dear, move on," Kenny called out. "The kid looked fine to me. Let's get this bit over with."

Patrick could almost hear Ralph grinding his teeth. *This is not the way to get on his good side,* he thought. *If he has a good side.*

For the next hour or so they galloped about the stage following Ralph's lead, then Kenny sashayed down to the front of the stage again.

"Okay, boys and girls," he said. "Thanks for coming. I can only take seven of you, so we'll be phoning those we want. Oh, you with the hair. I'd like to hear you sing. What's your name again?"

"Patrick."

"Right. Did you bring your music?"

"Yes, I did."

"Well, go get it and take it over to Tom there at the piano. Just one song, then I have to go."

Patrick shot off to where he'd left his bag and pulled out his sheet music, getting the thumbs up from Maggie and Lawrence as he hurried back onstage. Kenny was in deep conversation with Ralph, who didn't look at all happy. No doubt about it, he was getting it in the neck from Kenny. They looked up as Patrick approached them.

"What are you singing?" Kenny asked, dismissing Ralph with a flick of his fingers.

"Uh… 'Somethin's Coming' from West Side Story."

"Ooh, ambitious, aren't we?" Kenny's smile was superficial at best. "Let's hear it then."

Tom at the piano was better than most accompanists Patrick had sung with, and inspired by the solid chords and driving rhythm behind him, Patrick gave the song everything he had.

"Not bad… not bad at all," Kenny cooed when Patrick had belted out the top notes at the end. "Now, what's happening with your hair?"

"It was the rain," Patrick said, trying to chuckle. "It curls up in the rain."

"Well dear, I can't have you in competition with some of my wigs," the drag star told him with what Patrick hoped was some humour. "So if you want the job you'll have to have it shorn. That a problem?" he added sweetly.

"Oh, no." Patrick felt a prickle of excitement at Kenny's words. "Does that mean…?"

"You've got the job? Yes, it does, but get yourself a haircut, love. Butch it up a little, you know…" He pumped his pelvis forward in a parody of humping someone. "Show 'em you've got balls!"

✥✥✥✥✥

Lawrence and Maggie were waiting for Patrick when he exited the stage door.

"Well?" they demanded in unison.

"I got it!" Patrick yelled, jumping up and down, and hugging both his friends at the same time. "All I have to do is get a haircut."

"No loss there, love," Lawrence remarked without sounding bitchy. "Let's head over to the King's Arms and have a celebratory pint—or two."

"Lovely," Maggie said. "And lunch, I'm starving."

"Did they take your phone numbers?" Patrick asked as they walked quickly together toward Charing Cross Road.

Maggie chuckled. "Yes, although I think it was killing Ralph to be nice to us—me especially."

"He's a wanker, that one," Patrick said, putting his arm around Maggie. "But he's not so far in with Kenny as he likes to think. Did you see the way *Miss* LaFontaine put him in his place?"

"I could almost hear his blood boiling," Lawrence said, laughing. "He's got to be pissed off that Kenny hired you as the lead singer. Rehearsals should be very interesting. I only hope I'm there to see the goings-on!"

Chapter Two

Kenny sat opposite the two police detectives who had arranged themselves on one side of his dining room table and were taking copious notes. Well, one of them was, Kenny noticed. The other was either staring at Kenny or looking around the sumptuous flat Kenny had just had redecorated, paid for from the proceeds of his latest television appearances.

The one who wasn't writing anything down asked, "So, when did you first notice you were being stalked?"

"Oh, some months ago," Kenny replied, looking at the detective's mouth. *God, but I'd like to plant one on those luscious lips*, he thought. He cleared his throat and continued. "The blighter seemed to be shy at first, just hanging around the stage door, that kind of thing, you know... I wasn't very worried about it—didn't even notice 'til someone pointed him out, saying he always seemed to be there, you know. Then he started showing up here—outside the flat."

"Did he ever talk to you?"

Kenny shrugged. "Well, yes... he'd sort of mumble things, you know. Things I couldn't quite hear—but his intentions were quite clear."

"What d'you mean?"

"Well, you know... I'm presuming he wanted to get into my pants."

The two detectives exchanged looks. The one with the nice mouth frowned. "Why would you presume that?" he asked gruffly. "It's been our experience that stalkers generally are just that, stalkers. They very rarely indulge in intimacy with the person they're stalking—unless they're invited to do so."

"Well, you know... *I* certainly wasn't going to invite him in. Not my type at all... I mean, I couldn't really see what he looked like, but honestly... a *stalker*."

Detective Ian Bannister shifted in his seat, wishing this interview was over. He already couldn't stand Kenny LaFontaine, had actually disliked him on the TV, thinking him just another no-talent drag queen—but one who'd got lucky. No doubt about that. He looked at his partner, Detective Ernest Holloway, silently willing him to stop writing so many damned notes and call it a day.

Kenny smiled coquettishly at Ian. "So, what did he have to say when you arrested him?"

"He said he wanted a job at your club."

"*What?* He must be mad."

Ian shook his head. "No, he's quite sane, decent enough bloke really, just a bit down on his luck, and looking for work. He thought if he hung around a bit he might get a chance to ask you if you needed some help at the club. His name's Bert Halford. He's an electrician by trade."

"Is he, now? Well, you know, that's too bad. I've already had an electrician, and a plumber, and…"

"Mr. LaFontaine," Ian interrupted abruptly. "We're not your audience. No need to crack jokes for our benefit."

Kenny laughed. "Who said I was joking?"

Ernest cleared his throat noisily. "Well, I think that's all we need." He looked at Ian for agreement. Ian nodded and the two detectives stood up ready to leave. "Thank you for your time, Mr. LaFontaine," Ernest added.

"But what are you going to do with… with Bert, the stalker?"

"He's already been released," Ian said. "Nothing to hold him on really…"

"But what if he keeps pestering me?"

"You've already said all he does is mumble," Ian replied patiently. "He's probably mumbling about needing a job. He's harmless really."

"Well, you know—I don't want him hanging about everywhere I go."

"We've told him to be a good boy and keep his distance," Ian said. "I don't think you'll see him again."

"Well, you know…" Kenny put on his most winsome smile. "I'd feel a lot better if you'd stop by now and then, just to make sure."

Ernest changed his laugh to a cough as he barked into his hand. He glanced at Ian from the corner of his eye. His partner was staring at Kenny, a polite smile painted on his face.

"I don't think that will be necessary." Ian was the model of politeness. "However, if Mr. Halford does show up again, please let us know immediately."

Kenny watched the detectives leave, a sour expression on his face.

Outside Kenny's flat, Ernest gave vent to a fit of the giggles. "Blimey," he spluttered. "All that stuff in the papers about him being as straight as a die, and he's a bloody poufter if ever I saw one."

Ian grimaced. "He's enough to give poufters a bad name. And that incessant use of 'Well, you know' drove me mad."

"He liked you," Ernest teased him. "Give him one and you'd be set for life."

"And bored every day for life," Ian said, laughing.

From his vantage point behind a parked van, Bert Halford watched the two detectives leave Kenny's flat. *Woops*, he thought, just as well he'd seen them before they spotted him. He waited patiently while the men climbed into their car and drove away, then he crossed the street and waited outside Kenny's front door.

✤✤✤✤✤

Patrick, Maggie and Lawrence were having their pub lunch when Lawrence directed Patrick and Maggie's attention to the television over the bar.

"There's Kenny LaFontaine on the news," he remarked. "Blimey... look, he's surrounded by coppers. Wonder what happened."

"Can you turn up the sound please," Patrick called across to the bartender, who obliged by picking up the remote and raising the volume.

"Earlier today," a reporter's voice was exclaiming, "London's Metro Police were called to the home of Kenny LaFontaine, the well known female impersonator. Apparently Mr. LaFontaine was accosted as he left his Bloomsbury flat by a man who reportedly has been stalking the drag star for several weeks."

A close up of Kenny followed. "I just don't know why this man was released," Kenny was saying, his voice bordering on the hysterical. "Well, you know, I complained to the police before. Only today I had detectives here telling me this pervert wouldn't be bothering me anymore, and look at this, I can't even step outside without him pouncing on me! It's nerve shattering..."

"That was Kenny LaFontaine telling reporters what had occurred earlier today. In other news..."

The three friends stared at one another for a few seconds before chuckling loudly. "Can you believe him?" Patrick shook his head. "He obviously loved every moment of that."

"He didn't look like he'd been accosted," Lawrence said, still laughing.

"Probably ran inside to make repairs before going in front of the cameras," Maggie suggested.

"I hope this doesn't mean he'll delay rehearsals for his new show," Lawrence remarked.

"I doubt it," Patrick said, swallowing the last of his pint. "Want another?"

"No thanks." Maggie was gathering her gear together. "I have dance class in half an hour."

"You're so dedicated." Patrick smiled at her

"I'll have a half," Lawrence said, pushing his glass toward Patrick.

Maggie gave them both a kiss on the cheek. "Toodles, then. I'll phone you if I get the job at Kenny's Club."

"So, what d'you suppose all that with Kenny was about?" Lawrence asked after Maggie had gone and Patrick had ordered a couple of half pints.

"Could be some ex-boyfriend or something," Patrick suggested.

"Does he have a boyfriend right now?"

"Not sure. If he does, he keeps him out of sight."

"Right, can't sully the straight image he's worked so hard to project," Lawrence chortled.

"I don't know why he bothers, really," Patrick said. "I mean people expect drag queens to be just that—queens. It surely couldn't surprise most of his fans."

"Yes, but the 'blue hair set' haven't a clue he likes to suck cock, Patrick. They think he's just a lovely man—and a lovelier woman."

"He is good at what he does," Patrick remarked. "I've never seen a better looking drag. Those gowns he wears must cost a fortune."

"Yes, I'll give him that," Lawrence agreed. "And if I get the job I'm going to ask him what cream he uses on his face. There's not a line on that skin, and he must be, what, forty?"

"He looks younger even close up. Well..." Patrick grinned at his friend. "I'm sure all will be revealed when we start rehearsals!"

✝ ✝ ✝ ✝ ✝

Kenny stood seething in front of his bedroom full length mirror. Those bloody stupid policemen, and those even more bloody stupid reporters all laughing at him behind his back. Well, he was going to show them! On Saturday night he was going to be a guest on Chris Gorman's live chat show, and he was going to rip those coppers new ones.

"They'll be sorry they didn't take me a bit more seriously," he said to his reflection. "Kenny LaFontaine is a star—and will be treated accordingly! No fucking copper, no matter how good looking, is going to get away with making me look stupid! Bastard... I'll have his bloody job before I'm through with him."

He was reliving the aftermath of his confrontation with Bert Halford outside his flat. The fool had approached him, *again*, as he tried to walk to his car, and Kenny had punched him on the nose, then screamed at the top of his voice that he had been viciously attacked by the man who had been stalking him for weeks.

Meanwhile, of course, Bert had fled the scene, holding his bloody nose. When the police had finally shown up, they had been skeptical of Kenny's story, seeing no evidence of a 'vicious attack,' and that good looking arsehole, *Ian*, had more or less accused him of lying about what had taken place. No amount of indignation on Kenny's part had served to sway Ian's opinion that Bert, if he'd even been there, had not actually accosted Kenny, but was merely trying to ask for employment.

"I know it's causing you a nuisance factor," Ian had said in that oh, so suave way he had of speaking that made Kenny's heart race, "But he's really quite harmless."

Be that as it may, Kenny thought. *If that's the only way I can get that copper near me, I'll punch that silly bugger Bert's light's out every time I see him come close to me. Poor bastard will have no teeth and a broken nose by the time I've finished with him.*

Kenny was nothing if not tough. Born Kenneth Plunkett, and raised in the East End of London, he'd had to be tough to survive. Being a *pansy*, as his mother had called him, he'd learned fast that defending one's self effectively was paramount if he was to live through his teens without getting his face mashed and his arse plundered. Not that the latter hadn't happened—but that had been on his terms only.

And now, Kenny was determined that Detective Ian Bannister too would come to him on Kenny LaFontaine's terms. That he would get down on his knees and suck Kenny's cock—gladly, and enjoy every minute of it. Because Kenny's street intuition told him something about Detective Bannister that not many other people knew—and he was going to use that knowledge to get what he wanted. Kenny struck a pose in front of the mirror, his arms held high above his head, his hips thrust forward in a provocative fashion.

"Oh yes, Detective Bannister, *sweetie*," he crowed. "You just don't know *yet* what's in store for you."

CHAPTER THREE

Patrick waved happily as Lawrence and Maggie walked into the rehearsal hall. He'd been thrilled when they had phoned to say they'd both got the job at Kenny's Club. He had been called for rehearsal earlier than the dancers to learn some original songs written especially for the new show, and he and Tom, the rehearsal pianist, had already struck up an easy going camaraderie. Patrick was getting a very good feeling about the success of the new show. The music had a good vibe to it, and if all the dancers were of Maggie and Lawrence's standard and ability, it should rake in good reviews—and a nightly audience. After Tom had told him to take a break, he ran over to where Lawrence and Maggie were warming up.

The three friends exchanged hugs. "I'm so glad you guys are in this too," he said sincerely.

"Like your haircut," Maggie remarked, running her hand over the top of Patrick's head.

"Takes years off you, dear," Lawrence teased.

"Thanks," Patrick said, chuckling. "D'you know any of the other dancers? I thought I spotted Penny Danvers earlier."

Lawrence nodded. "She's in, and I saw Albert Goring going into the loo when I arrived. He's so dishy, but he thinks he's too good to say hello, that one."

"I think he's just shy, Lawrence," Maggie said.

"Shy?" Lawrence scoffed. "I mean, look at him…" Lawrence jerked his head in the direction of a tall, slender young man with a mop of golden hair. Lawrence groaned. "Gawd, look at that beautiful bum. What I'd give to have a go at him. Too bad he's so stuck up."

"You are such a romantic," Maggie sighed. "Have a go at him? I don't think he'd fall for that line somehow."

Patrick chuckled. "Lawrence always has a way with words. Anyway, you've got lots of opportunities to get to know him better, Lawrence. We should all be working together for quite a long time."

As the room filled up with more dancers arriving, Ralph, the choreographer, called for their attention. "All right kids," he yelled, clapping his hands loudly. "Gather round. I want to get heights sorted out—let me have a line, boy, girl, boy, girl..."

Maggie ended up standing between Lawrence and Albert, and flashed quick smiles at them both. Albert gave her a nervous smile and Maggie nudged Lawrence.

"*Shy*," she hissed at him between her teeth.

Lawrence glanced at Albert and smiled, but received a blank look in return. "*Stuck up*," he hissed back at Maggie.

"All right boys and girls," Ralph was saying, "Kenny will be here in a couple of hours and I want him to see a good representation of the opening number. I'll also be looking at your individual strengths for some of the solo spots, so give me your best!" He looked around the room. "Where's the singer?"

Patrick jumped to his feet. "I'm right here."

"Oh well, please join us," Ralph said, with a slight sneer. "As you're opening the show and introducing Kenny you should be aware of what's going on."

Patrick nodded and bit his tongue. If Ralph wanted to be the bitch of all seasons he'd let him, as long as he didn't get in his face too many times.

Apart from that slight confrontation the morning's rehearsals went smoothly, and by the time Kenny arrived, Ralph was feeling confident that there was enough of the opening routine ready to give him a good idea of how it would look.

Kenny, wearing the tightest white jeans Patrick had ever seen on any living human, summoned him over with an imperious wave.

"Well," he said, hands on hips and looking Patrick up and down. "The haircut certainly improves you, you know. Short hair always makes a man look younger. What are you, late twenties?"

"Twenty six," Patrick replied, resisting the urge to ask 'And you are?'

"Well, I can give you two or three years," Kenny said, touching his blond hair high-lighted with silver. "And see what short hair does for me. You'd never know I was over thirty, would you?"

Patrick smiled. *Over forty, you mean.* "No, I wouldn't have thought that at all."

Ralph bustled over, flapping his hands. "Are you ready to see the opening number, Kenny? I've really worked hard on it this morning, but want your opinion before I go any further..."

"Well, you know, you are the bloody choreographer," Kenny told him, his top lip curling. "What am I paying you for if you need me to supervise everything? Honestly..." He looked at Patrick and rolled his eyes. "The help these days..."

From the look on Ralph's face, Patrick thought it a good idea to beat a hasty retreat at that moment. "I'll just get in position," he muttered, and fled. *Oh, Ralph is going to be on a rampage this afternoon,* he thought as he hurried over to where Ralph had positioned him for the opening of the show. He choked down the chuckle that threatened to burst from his lips as Ralph swept toward him, his face like a block of granite. Patrick's eyes widened with surprise as Ralph hissed in his ear, "That fucking bitch! That's the last time she insults me like that!" Patrick wiped Ralph's spittle from the side of his face and looked straight ahead, saying nothing.

Ralph yelled at Tom the pianist, "Right, Tom, opening routine, from the top!" And they were off. Kenny sat with a sphinx-like expression on his face throughout the entire routine, then when it was over he rose from his seat and walked slowly over to where Ralph stood, still fuming from his earlier exchange with Kenny.

"Not *bad*," Kenny said, with a patronizing air. "Not bad for a first run through, though I do think you could make more use of those two tall boys." He waved a hand at Lawrence and Albert. "They stand out, and the ladies will love them. Have them do a routine with the girl who was late at the audition. What's your name again, dear?"

Maggie grinned at him. "Maggie."

"Right, Maggie. So, Ralph, somewhere in the middle of all of this, have the three of them alone on the stage—Patrick will sing something sweet and sexy, and they'll do some lovely adagio or something—you know what I mean, don't you?"

Ralph blinked rapidly several times. "But... but that's going to make the opening routine very long, Kenny."

"So? It builds up the anticipation of my first appearance," Kenny said. "Just do it, Ralph. It's what I want. God..." He threw up his hands as he walked away. "Do I have to think of everything?"

If Ralph had had a knife in his hand, Patrick reckoned he would have plunged it between Kenny's shoulder blades at that moment. His face dark with anger, Ralph swung round and glared at the dancers. "You three," he snapped. "Over here—the rest of you take lunch. Be back in an hour."

"You need me, Ralph?" Patrick asked quietly.

"Of course, *you're* to sing something *sweet and sexy*... didn't you hear Kenny?"

Any sympathy Patrick might have been feeling for Ralph dissipated quickly. He really was too much of a bitch to be likeable. It was Patrick's opinion that Ralph and Kenny were cut from the same cloth—only Kenny had the power to make Ralph look, and feel, like shit.

"So what does sweet and sexy mean to you?" Ralph asked Patrick cattily.

Not you. "How about 'The Look of Love?'" Patrick suggested.

"Oh, that's good," Tom the pianist, said. "I have the music here, Ralph."

"Let me hear it then," Ralph muttered. He glared at Patrick. "Sing it."

Patrick sighed and glanced at Lawrence, who looked as though he was about to explode with laughter. His shoulders were shaking from the effort of stifling his amusement. Maggie glared at him and poked him in the ribs, while Albert looked down at the floor. *Was he smiling?* Patrick wondered, standing by Tom as he played the intro.

"The Look of Love is in your eyes, a look that time can't disguise..."

While Patrick sang, Ralph moved pensively across the floor, trying out different steps, before calling Maggie, Lawrence and Albert over. "Try this," he muttered, and the dancers followed him through the intricate steps. "Okay, then we'll have a lift here..." They rehearsed for the best part of an hour while Kenny sat watching, then Ralph called for a break.

"That's good, Ralph," Kenny sang out. "See? I told you my idea would work just lovely."

✦ ✦ ✦ ✦ ✦

A week later, and the show had evolved to Ralph's satisfaction. Patrick could tell he was still smarting from the verbal abuse he'd taken from Kenny, but Patrick felt this was probably something the man was quite used to, having worked with the drag star for several years. At any rate, a kind of truce had been reached and Kenny seemed content to let Ralph do his thing. Then came the day when Kenny himself was to be a part of the rehearsals.

Kenny's routines were pretty standard, more or less the same wherever he appeared. He would come on stage between dance routines, wearing one fabulous gown and wig after another, crack a few jokes, do a few impersonations, kibitz with the audience, get someone up on stage and embarrass the hell out of him or her, crack a few more jokes, and get off—usually to tumultuous applause.

However in this new show, Kenny wanted to sing two songs that he had written himself, and he was going to sing them out of drag, wearing a man's evening suit. No one could persuade him that this was not a good idea. The fact that his audiences paid good money to see him dressed in high fashion drag, and for an hour or so live the illusion with him, didn't bother Kenny.

"Frankly, I'm tired of the drag routine," he told Patrick and Lawrence one day over a drink at the back of his club. "It's time I went legit. I've got a CD coming out in about a month. It's going to launch a whole new career for me."

Patrick couldn't believe his ears. Was the man mad? He couldn't sing a note. God knows, they'd all been subjected to Kenny's off-key warbling for the past three days, ever since he'd been in rehearsal. Patrick hoped that Kenny's ego was strong enough to disregard the horrible reviews his singing was bound to garner.

✦ ✦ ✦ ✦ ✦

Opening night and the club was packed with an invited audience of Kenny's friends, acquaintances, talk show hosts, some minor celebrities and of course, critics. Before he got changed for the show, Patrick stood on one side of the club, casting a nervous eye over the assemblage. First night jitters was nothing new to him, but he would have felt better if the dress rehearsal hadn't been such a catastrophe, with Kenny screaming the place down and firing Ralph at least a half dozen times. Patrick had actually felt some sympathy for the bitchy choreographer, who'd looked as though he would burst into tears at any second.

But it wasn't just Ralph that Kenny had vented his spleen upon. Everyone came under fire as the drag queen stormed about in a senseless rage, talking to himself when he wasn't screaming at the top of his lungs about how useless everyone was and how horrendous his life had recently become. Nothing and no one could appease him, and after one particularly bad attempt to struggle through one of his own songs, he had headed for the door, threatening everyone with the sack—and was not seen again that night.

As Patrick's gaze swept the room, he became aware of a man standing at the back of the club who appeared to be staring at him. The man was tall, wide shouldered, good looking in a rugged sort of way, and his gaze made Patrick's skin tingle with a kind of anticipation. As they locked eyes, Patrick smiled tentatively, and the man nodded slightly in acknowledgement.

Who are you? Patrick mused. *And how do I get to meet you?*

Before he could make a move, Lawrence was at his side, whispering they'd called the fifteen and he should really get changed. Sighing, Patrick followed Lawrence backstage. He would much rather have sauntered over to the bar where the tall man had been standing and struck up a friendly conversation. Backstage was in chaos, with Alfred, Kenny's dresser, suicidal, Ralph really in tears and the band leader and Kenny going at it toe-to-toe.

The gist of it, as far as Patrick could tell from the shouting, was that the musicians couldn't come to grips with Kenny's arrangements, and without more rehearsal the band leader wanted to cut the songs from tonight's performance.

"No!" Kenny screamed. "You will not cut any fucking thing without my say-so. The songs stay—or *you* go!"

Lawrence stared at Patrick with big eyes. "And you said we were all set for a long run!"

Patrick laughed. "It's just first night nerves. Everyone's on edge. Just wait—tomorrow night it'll be as though we've been doing it for ages." As he slipped into his black silk evening suit he asked, "How's it going with Albert? Are you friends yet?"

Lawrence pouted. "He ignores me except when we're doing the adagio with Maggie. She still maintains he's shy, but Patrick, I have tried everything in my charm arsenal to get him to just smile at me, and nothing. He's so lovely, though. I'd love to put my lips on his and suck his tongue."

"I saw someone tonight I'd like to put my lips on," Patrick said, straightening his bow tie. "Chap standing out there by the bar. Tall, dark and 'has some,' I bet."

Lawrence giggled. "Maybe he'll be at the party afterwards. You can point him out to me."

"The party," Patrick murmured. "I'd forgotten about that. He might very well be there." He smiled at his friend. "Well, chukkas for tonight, Lawrence."

Lawrence kissed his cheek. "Chukkas, love. You look super in that suit. Your tall dark and 'has some' will fall in love at first sight when you step on that stage."

"Thanks—and you look very haveable in what almost is a costume."

Lawrence giggled again. "My mum wants to come see this. She'll faint when she sees what I'm wearing—or not wearing, I should say. When Maggie pulls off my harem pants, does my arse look all right?"

"Lovely. Most delectable, like twin peaches bouncing around," Patrick said, chuckling. "And don't think I haven't seen Albert giving it the once or twice over!"

"*Really?*"

"Really, so give him some encouragement, why don't you?"

"Overture and beginners, please!"

The call caused Lawrence and Patrick to shiver with apprehension and hug one another. "You'll be swell," Patrick sang to Lawrence. "You'll be great—gonna have the whole world on a plate!" Laughing, the two friends made their way to the wings where Maggie was waiting and looking decidedly nervous. They hugged her and whispered words of encouragement, then fell quiet as the band struck up.

Patrick walked to his position, clutching his microphone in a damp hand. He glanced into the wings and saw Maggie and Lawrence waving. He was aware of Kenny in a voluminous gown of white and gold sweeping into his line of vision—and then the curtain went up.

"Good evening, ladies and gentlemen!" Patrick strode downstage. "And welcome to An Evening with Kenny LaFontaine!"

As he launched into his opening number, his eyes scanned the audience for a glimpse of the tall man by the bar, but there was no sign of him. To enthusiastic applause, he walked over to stage left while the music shifted to a dreamy introduction and Maggie drifted on stage in her costume of midnight blue chiffon. Even from Patrick's odd vantage point he could see this number was going to be a hit. Lawrence and Albert, looking sleekly muscular, moved gracefully with Maggie, lifting her effortlessly onto their shoulders. A gasp of appreciation came from the female members of the audience when Maggie ripped off both Lawrence's and Albert's pants, revealing their muscular bottoms framed only by the outline of a g-string.

Then it was time for Kenny's entrance and Patrick leaped up the staircase to help him descend. Thunderous applause broke out as the drag star appeared—a vision in white and gold tulle under a blond wig endlessly teased and covered in tiny ringlets. Kenny's hand trembled in Patrick's, but his smile was gracious as he acknowledged the rapturous reception. Patrick stood by his side until, as rehearsed, Kenny said, "You may go... wait for me in my dressing room—but don't start without me!"

Patrick bowed and hurried off stage, the sound of the audience's laughter at a joke they'd heard many times before floating on the air behind him.

✤ ✤ ✤ ✤ ✤

The remainder of the evening went well, with no major mishaps, until Kenny's controversial finale. Patrick had to admit that Kenny looked good in his choice of clothes—a dark brown velvet suit and cream shirt open at the neck—but it wasn't the finale the audience would be expecting. After Kenny had less than wowed them with his mediocre singing and the curtain had rung down, the crowd was restlessly expectant, waiting for Kenny to reappear to finish the show 'properly' in a glamorous gown. When it didn't happen, a discontented buzz went round the club, but was quickly ended by an announcement that Kenny would soon be among them, and the party would commence.

Patrick changed out of his costume quickly, pulling on a pair of black jeans and a new, pale blue Hugo Boss shirt he'd bought at great expense just for this occasion. If the tall man was at the party, Patrick wanted to make sure he had a chance of saying hello before he left. The club seemed even more packed than before as he made his way through the press of people to the bar. *Yes... there he was*—standing alone, a glass of some amber liquid in his hand. His eyes met Patrick's and stayed there. Patrick moved closer.

"Hello. What did you think of the show?"

"I thought *you* were very good," the man said, a small smile on his lips.

"Thank you. I'm Patrick..." He held out his hand and felt it taken in a warm strong grasp.

"I know. I saw your name in the program. I'm Ian Bannister."

"Are you a friend of Kenny's?" Patrick asked, gazing at Ian's full lower lip.

"Not really a friend. I've only known him since the stalker business."

Patrick's eyes grew big. "Oh, so you're..."

"'Fraid so." Ian's smile widened. "Detective Ian Bannister."

"Oh..." Patrick was unsure what to say next. *A policeman,* he thought, *probably straight, although he seems very nice.* And now that Patrick was up close, he could see those rugged good looks were softened somewhat by warm brown eyes, and definitely by that very kissable mouth. "So, the stalker... is he in jail?"

Ian chuckled. "No. The poor blighter just wanted a job, that's all. But that's not why I'm here. Mr. LaFontaine wants to speak to me about something else."

"Oh, yes?"

"Mmhmm." Ian gave Patrick a speculative look. "Are you going to be here for a while?"

"Probably... my friends Maggie and Lawrence haven't even come to join me yet. They're still primping, I expect."

"And of course you don't have to primp."

Ian was smiling at him, and Patrick felt himself blush from the compliment. "Well, I'll be honest and say I hurried because I didn't know how long you'd be staying, and..."

"Why, *Detective...*" Kenny's strident voice interrupted Patrick. "I can see Patrick's entertaining you, as only he can!"

Patrick stared at Kenny, who was wearing a pink silk shirt open to his navel and silver gray trousers that looked as though they had been painted on his legs.

Nothing like advertising the fact you're a queen, Patrick thought. *And what the devil had he meant by 'as only he can'?*

"Such a flirt, aren't you dear?" Kenny gave him a vicious look. "But the big brave detective's here to speak to me." Kenny flicked his fingers at Patrick. "So off you go... shoo!"

Patrick stared at Kenny, appalled, his face pale with shock. As big a bitch as he knew Kenny to be, Patrick hadn't thought he would go this far to humiliate him. He stepped back as Kenny took Ian's arm and started to steer him away.

"Just a minute..." Ian removed Kenny's hand from his arm. "I'd like to have a word with Patrick, if you don't mind."

"Excuse me?" Kenny glared at him through narrowed eyes. "You're here on business, copper, *my* business!"

"I'm here on my own time, Mr. LaFontaine," Ian said, his voice low and deep. "I agreed to listen to you here tonight, *unofficially*—and I'll do that. But first, I have to apologize to Patrick."

"*Apologize?*" Kenny hissed. "What the fuck for?"

"For your bad manners."

For a moment Patrick thought Kenny was going to slap Ian. "Oh, that's okay," he blurted. "No harm done, really." Patrick laughed nervously, and just then a group of very tipsy people descended on Kenny, gushing about how wonderful the show was.

Ian stepped closer to Patrick. "There's a pub called The Hangman on the corner of St. Martin's Lane. Meet me there, if you like, in about an hour."

The Hangman—how appropriate, Patrick thought. *After tonight's little scene, Kenny will probably tie the knot round my neck himself.* Aloud he said, "I'll be there."

Ian smiled and joined Kenny with his group of sycophants. Patrick looked round to see Lawrence and Maggie headed his way. "Thank goodness you're finally here."

"You look shell-shocked," Maggie said. "What happened?"

"You'll never believe it..."

CHAPTER FOUR

Kenny eyed Ian from his position seated at his dressing table. The detective was sitting astride a chair that seemed dwarfed by his tall frame, and, Kenny thought, looking totally delicious.

"Are you always so rough on the people that work for you?" Ian asked.

"Rough—was I rough on poor Patrick?" Kenny crossed his silver clad legs and tried to look demure. "He's a nice enough boy, but a trifle gauche."

"He's got a great voice."

"He's adequate."

Ian sighed impatiently. "So, what is it this time, Mr. LaFontaine, another stalker?"

"A blackmailer," Kenny said. "And I wish you would call me Kenny. Mr. LaFontaine is so formal—so *unfriendly*."

"It's your name, isn't it? So, who's blackmailing you?"

"I don't *know* who it is," Kenny pouted. "That's what I want you to find out."

"D'you have the blackmail letters?"

Kenny handed him two envelopes. "I ignored the first one, thinking it was a joke, then the second one came yesterday."

Ian squinted at the postmark and grunted. "London..." He opened the first envelope and unfolded the letter. "Unless you give me twenty thousand pounds," he read aloud, "I shall tell the police what happened in Madrid two years ago. Put the money in a grocery bag in the used basket stand in Sainsbury's Superstore on Elm's Park Road at 10am tomorrow—Wednesday." He looked up at Kenny. "What happened in Madrid two years ago?"

"Nothing... I mean, I was *there* in a show, but nothing happened. Nothing I could be blackmailed for, anyway."

Ian opened the second letter. "Bitch, I advise you not to ignore me. Now the price is twenty-five thousand pounds. The more you stall, the higher the price. Put the money where I told you before—10am this Saturday. If it's not there, I shall call the police and watch the TV to see the news of your arrest for murder." Ian gave Kenny a long look. "Care to explain some of this?"

"Whoever this person is," Kenny said bitterly, "he's demented. I never killed anyone, in Madrid or anywhere else."

"When were you in Madrid?"

"Two years ago."

"I need the dates."

"September... I can't remember the exact dates."

"Try."

"Oh, for fuck's sake..." Kenny grabbed a book from his dressing table drawer, and flicked through the pages. "...September 12th to the 15th."

Ian pulled his notebook from his inside pocket and wrote down the dates. "You remember the name of the club or theatre?"

"La Fortuna—a dump if ever there was one."

"And the hotel where you stayed?"

"The International—another dump."

"Okay." Ian tapped his notebook with his pen. "First, I'm going to get in touch with the Madrid police and find out what they know about this murder, if there was one."

"There wasn't any murder," Kenny growled. "At least not one I had anything to do with. I have absolutely no idea what this bugger is on about."

"Well, if I don't get any joy from the Spaniards, we might just have to set up a little trap for our blackmailer."

"You mean, put the money there?"

"No money, just a grocery bag stuffed with paper. Ernest and I will be there with a couple of other plain clothes men ready to nab him after you've put the bag where he said."

"*I* have to put it there?"

"For the sake of authenticity, it might be a good idea."

"Well, if *you'll* be there," Kenny said, leering at Ian. "I guess I'll be safe."

"*Very* safe, Mr. LaFontaine," Ian said, standing up. "I'll be in touch after I've spoken with the Spanish authorities."

Kenny sprang to his feet. "Oh, you're not leaving are you? I thought we could have a drink—or something."

"No thanks. I have an early start tomorrow." Ian opened the door and slipped out without another word.

Kenny stood in the centre of his room, a scowl on his face. "Bloody copper," he muttered. "Thinks he's too good for me, does he? Well, I'm not finished with him yet."

But as his mood changed from anger to depression at being turned down by the handsome detective, he wondered if bringing the police into this latest development had perhaps been a very big mistake.

❖ ❖ ❖ ❖ ❖

Patrick sat at a corner table inside the dimly lit Hangman pub, nervously twisting at the glass of beer in front of him. He glanced at his watch. More than an hour since Ian had said to meet him here. What if didn't show up? He'd give him another few minutes, then give it up as a bad idea. He gulped at his beer and wondered if he should get another... He looked up as the door swung open. Ian's tall figure entered and strode directly over to him.

"Sorry," he said, sitting opposite him. "Have you been waiting long?"

"Not really." Patrick smiled at Ian's contrite expression. "I've only had one."

"I'll get you another," Ian stood and went over to the bar to order their drinks, giving Patrick the opportunity to study the detective without appearing to stare. *He really is lovely*, Patrick thought. Not lovely, that was demeaning to a man of Ian's stature and masculine appearance. Handsome, yes, but those eyes were so warm and dark, and slightly mysterious. Patrick shivered at the thought of gazing into those eyes just before Ian kissed him...

"Here you are." Ian placed Patrick's drink in front of him. "What were you daydreaming about?"

"You," Patrick said boldly.

Ian chuckled. "You're not shy, are you?"

"Not when I see someone I like."

Ian took a long drink of his beer, his eyes meeting Patrick's over the rim of his glass. "That makes two of us," he said, putting his glass down and wiping his mouth with the back of his hand.

"I'd like it to be just the two of us," Patrick said, with a meaningful glance around the pub. "Two's company and a pub full of people is definitely a crowd."

Ian chuckled. "Let's go then. You live near here?"

Patrick nodded. "Just off Cambridge Circus."

"That's handier than Ealing."

"I'll say. Come on then. The place is a bit untidy. I wasn't expecting company."

Ian hesitated. "What is it they say about unexpected company?"

"It's the best kind," Patrick said. "Now, come on."

✟✟✟✟✟

"I want to thank you for what you said to Kenny at the club," Patrick said as they climbed the stairs to his flat.

"That man is a total wanker," Ian said, taking Patrick's hand. "Why he thinks he can talk to people that way is beyond me."

Patrick grasped Ian's hand, loving the feel of his warm strong fingers. "He's been told by so many people that he's the best, he believes he can get away with anything. And being rude to his peons is not something he worries about."

"Well, you're nobody's peon, Patrick. You're a talented guy, and deserve to be somewhere better than Kenny LaFontaine's night club."

"Thank you, kind sir." Patrick smiled up at the taller man and gave him a quick peck on the cheek.

"You'll have to do a lot better than that when I get you inside," Ian growled, putting his hand on Patrick's bottom and squeezing gently. Patrick couldn't get the key in the door quick enough.

Once they were in Patrick's flat, Ian pulled him into his arms and planted a scorching kiss on his mouth that had Patrick gasping for air. Ian tugged at Patrick's shirt buttons. He slipped his shirt off over Patrick's shoulders then leaned forward, nuzzling Patrick's armpits. Patrick thought he might just pass out from the sensation of having this total hunk of a policeman holding him in his arms and licking his armpits. Ian's hard arousal pressed against Patrick's thigh and his lips seized one of Patrick's nipples, tugging at it gently, the tip of his tongue teasing the hardening nub and bringing it to attention.

"Jesus," Patrick moaned, thrusting his crotch into Ian's, rubbing their erections together through the material that separated them. He wrapped his arms around Ian's neck, his long, limber legs around Ian's hips and brought their mouths together in a hungry and rapturous kiss. Ian supported Patrick, both hands cupping his bottom, and marched him into the bedroom, where he deposited him on the bed, then proceeded to strip him of his jeans, socks and shoes. Patrick gazed up at the tall man now leaning over him, still fully clothed, his lips and tongue skimming over Patrick's chest and stomach, then lingering over the head of his cock, rock hard and glistening with pre-cum. Ian licked at the slit, gathering up the juice on the tip of his tongue, then took Patrick's mouth again, letting him taste himself in their kiss.

Almost in a frenzy, Patrick tore at Ian's shirt buttons, rolling the detective onto his back and sitting astride his muscular thighs. The shirt gone, Patrick attacked Ian's belt buckle, tearing it from the waistband of his trousers and unzipping his fly, before reaching in to grasp Ian's hard cock through his cotton briefs. Patrick lowered his head to the bulge, tracing the outline of Ian's erection with his lips. Ian groaned, his hips bucked and Patrick practically tore the briefs from him, gasping with delight as Ian's prodigious erection sprang out, slapping against Patrick's lips. Patrick took the burgeoning cock into his mouth, his tongue swirling around the crown, licking up and down the length of the throbbing shaft. Ian's pre-cum spilled onto Patrick's tongue and he lapped at it, loving the sweet and salty taste. He cupped Ian's balls in his hand then scooted down, lying between the detective's legs so that he could take each ball into his mouth, one at a time, gently sucking on it, running his tongue around the soft skin. Ian's body bucked and shuddered from the sensations Patrick's lips and tongue were bringing him, and he groaned his pleasure, his fingers stroking Patrick's hair. Patrick licked his way back up Ian's erection then took the head back into his mouth.

"Jesus, Patrick..." Ian gasped as the moist heat of Patrick's mouth brought him dangerously close to the edge. He sat up slightly and eased Patrick over onto his side, then lay over him, his lips tracing a path over Patrick's slim torso until, with a sigh of pleasure his mouth closed over the prize he sought. Patrick's cock spasmed at the sensation of Ian's lips enclosing his hard hot flesh. Ian's hands, cupping Patrick's bottom, pulled him deeper into his mouth. Patrick swallowed the juice that spilled from Ian's cock, and it sent his senses on fire. He wanted it all in his mouth, to feel Ian come over his tongue, to taste his essence. He sucked harder, stronger as he heard Ian moan, and at the same time felt his own orgasm surge through his balls. Their arms tightened about one another, their hips bucked and thrust and then, with a sudden rush, their semen flooded over each other's tongues. With gasping moans they clung to one another until their convulsing bodies had calmed and they lay still and quiet, save for the occasional gentle caress.

Ian was the first to recover, shifting his position so he could reach and kiss Patrick's lips. "You're terrific," he murmured, resting on one elbow, teasing Patrick's nipples with his free hand. Patrick took the teasing hand in his and raised it to his lips.

"You're fucking fantastic," he said, his eyes glowing as they met Ian's. Their fingers intertwined and for a time they were content to just lie together, trading kisses and smiling into each other's eyes. But their desire for one another was too great to be satisfied with mere flirtation, and soon their kisses deepened with hunger, and their bodies strained together with a rising need and lust.

"I want to fuck you," Ian whispered, his lips fluttering over Patrick's.

"I want you to..." Patrick reached for the lube and condom in the drawer by his bed. Ian sat astride Patrick's thighs and watched as Patrick slid the latex sheath over his throbbing cock. He took the lube from Patrick and slicked it over the condom, then probed between Patrick's buttocks, getting him ready. Patrick sighed with satisfaction as he raised his legs and wound them around Ian's waist, giving him access to his tight hole. Ian pressed forward slowly, the head of his cock pushing past the ring of muscle that guarded Patrick's anus. Patrick gasped as he felt Ian's hard flesh enter him.

"All right, love?" Ian murmured, his lips brushing Patrick's.

"Yes, oh yes," Patrick whispered, raising his hips and tightening his legs around Ian. "You feel wonderful..."

Ian pushed harder, driving himself into Patrick with one long stroke, causing a whimper of pleasure to escape Patrick's lips. Patrick wrapped his arms around Ian's neck, holding their mouths pressed together in a hard, hungry kiss. Their bodies moved in unison to a driving rhythm, Ian's hardness gliding over Patrick's prostate, bringing him ecstasy with every powerful thrust. Patrick felt transported. He'd never been fucked like this before, never experienced such euphoria with any other man. He wanted this to last forever, to keep this wonderful man locked in his embrace and never let him go. But the heat and friction they had generated between them begged for release. Patrick felt his balls tighten as his orgasm built to an almost painful intensity. Ian's muscular body stiffened in Patrick's arms as his climax built inside him.

"Ah, Patrick... Jesus, I'm coming," he groaned, tightening his embrace around Patrick and driving his cock even harder into Patrick's silken heat. Patrick almost sobbed with joy as they came together, his semen coating both their torsos with creamy warmth. He could feel Ian's cock pulse inside him as he came in great wrenching spasms. They clung to one another, their faces buried in each other's necks, their lips searing each other's fevered skin.

For a long time after, they lay wrapped in each other's arms, the sensuality of their coupling giving way to a warm and tender comfort. Patrick had never been happier. He knew he had found someone very special in Ian, and he sent up a little prayer that the detective felt that way too.

Chapter Five

Patrick was expecting quite a lot of flak from Kenny when he got to the club the following night. He couldn't quite forget the venomous look the drag star had thrown at him when he found him talking to Ian. Nor the obvious put down Ian had inflicted on Kenny by taking the time to come back and talk to Patrick. He only hoped that Kenny hadn't realized just what it was Ian had said to him.

But the screaming coming from Kenny's dressing room had nothing to do with Patrick or Ian—Kenny was getting his first look at the newspaper reviews for his show.

"Fucking *peasants*," the drag star was shrilling. "Fucking ignorant arseholes, they wouldn't know talent if it slapped them on their stupid faces!"

Patrick scooted by Kenny's door and made for the boy dancers' dressing room, where he knew he'd find Lawrence. His friend was sharing the reviews with Albert, the two of them giggling as they read what had caused Kenny to have a meltdown.

"That good is it?" Patrick asked as he peeked through the door.

"Oh, come in, Patrick, you have to read this," Lawrence hissed, signaling that Patrick should close the door behind him. "Kenny's going to have a blue fit when he sees this."

"He's already having a blue fit."

"Well, look at his." Lawrence handed Patrick the opened newspaper and the header "**LaFontaine Takes a Nosedive**" greeted his eyes.

"Oh, crikey," he muttered. "The once energetic and vivacious female impersonator, Kenny LaFontaine, should sack the person who persuaded him to sing—or rather croak—two songs at the end of his new show, 'Star Turn.' Presented with a lot of first class dancing and singing, most notably by the fresh new voice and handsome face of Patrick Farland, Mr. LaFontaine sadly failed to rise to the caliber of the other performers. Still, there were the fabulous gowns and the sometimes salty repartee Mr. LaFontaine is famous for, but the finale, where he appears out of drag to sing two songs composed by himself, was nothing short of a disaster. Some changes would benefit the show enormously, principally restaging the finale with Mr. LaFontaine doing what he does best—drag."

Patrick looked at Lawrence and rolled his eyes. "I'm dead," he said quietly. "There's no way Kenny won't cut my songs after reading that."

"Oh, surely he wouldn't be that petty," Lawrence protested.

"Oh yes he would," Patrick sighed. "He's a bitch for all seasons, and that slap in the eye from the critic will rankle like nothing else."

"Patrick's right," Albert said, with some sympathy. "If the critic hadn't mentioned Patrick's name, it wouldn't be so bad."

"But it's great you got a mention, love," Lawrence exclaimed. "The man who wrote this liked you. That's important!"

"It would have been great if he'd liked Kenny too—now all he's going to remember is that I got a better review than he did."

✤ ✤ ✤ ✤ ✤

Amazingly, as far as Patrick was concerned, nothing was said that night, but as he entered the club the following night he couldn't help but notice the narrow-eyed glare he received from the stage door keeper.

He was surprised then, when passing Kenny's dressing room, Kenny called out, "Oh Patrick, would you mind coming in for a moment or two? I thought you might like a glass of bubbly to get you in the mood for tonight's show." He handed Patrick a glass and filled it to the brim with champagne. As they clinked glasses Patrick wondered just what had happened to bring this change in Kenny's attitude. He didn't have to wait long to find out.

"So what d'you think of that dishy detective?" Kenny asked, turning to his mirror to start the transformation from man to glamorous woman. He had already pulled a wig cap over his own hair and was applying a foundation to his face, neck and shoulders.

"Oh... he seems very nice," Patrick said as blandly as he could. Just the thought of what he and Ian had done was enough to make his heart pound with excitement.

"He really wants to get in my pants, you know," Kenny remarked, skillfully drawing in his eyebrows then outlining his eyelids. "I mean, you should have seen him in here the other night," he added with a snide smile. "He was fairly salivating every time I smiled at him."

"Really?" Patrick, watching while Kenny fixed his false eyelashes in place, strove to keep his voice and expression as noncommittal as he could. "You certainly could do worse, Kenny."

"And I have!" Kenny twittered, picking up a contouring brush. "Anyway dear, I have a little favor to ask of you."

"Oh yes?"

"I'm having a little problem with someone who's after me for money."

"You mean blackmail?"

"You're quick, aren't you dear?" Kenny rolled his eyes. "Of course I mean fucking blackmail."

Patrick sighed. Even asking for a favor, Kenny couldn't resist being the bitch he always would be.

"What is it you want me to do?" he asked, biting back the urge to tell the bitch to go to hell.

Kenny didn't answer right away. He was very carefully applying color to highlight his cheekbones and soften his jawline. When it was done to his satisfaction, he threw the brush aside and turned to look at Patrick, who was duly impressed by the amazing change in Kenny's features. Patrick had to admit that even without the wig and gown, Kenny made a very impressive and quite beautiful woman. If only what lurked beneath wasn't quite so disagreeable.

"I'd like you to drop off the money he wants tomorrow, at the place the bastard told me to leave it," Kenny was saying. "There's fifty quid in it for you..."

"Kenny, I don't need paying for doing a favour," Patrick protested. "Do the police know about this?"

"Yes. They'll be there to nab the slimy bugger as soon as he picks up the money." He peered at Patrick from under his ultra-long false eyelashes. "You know, stalking is one thing, sort of flattering in its own little bizarre way, but blackmail? I could wring the bastard's neck myself. So, will you do this for me?"

"Oh, all right." Patrick didn't want to ask if Ian would be there, but felt fairly sure he would be. "So, where do I have to go?"

"Sainsbury's, dear—I mean, how common can you get?" Kenny stood and snapped his fingers. Alfred, his manager and dresser, stepped forward to remove Kenny's dressing gown. "Couldn't have chosen Harrods or Fortnum and Mason's, could he? No, bloody Sainsbury's Superstore on Elm's Park Road. Do you know it?"

"Vaguely... but I can find it, I'm sure"

Patrick felt as though he should avert his eyes as Kenny stood in front of him wearing only tiny bikini underpants, but with the aid of Alfred, the drag star was struggling into the special waspie he'd designed himself. It slimmed down his figure and had an added attachment that pulled his penis and testicles tightly between his legs, fastening at the back with a quick release snap.

"Lovely," Kenny said, panting slightly. "You won't be leaving money of course, just a grocery bag filled with paper." Kenny smirked at Patrick. "I thought I'd tell you that just so you don't get any ideas of running off with the money."

Patrick stared at Kenny, and for a moment was tempted to tell him to take his grocery bag and stick it up his arse—right up. Instead, he smiled and said quietly, "You know, Kenny, your trust in humankind is something of a marvel."

Kenny frowned, unsure of how to respond. "Well, anyway... thanks for doing this for me. You sure you don't want the fifty quid?"

"Absolutely sure. Your money is the last thing I want." He stood up. "Now, I better start getting ready for the show. I'll stop by later for the package."

✥ ✥ ✥ ✥ ✥

Kenny's club did two shows nightly with an hour in between each show. Patrick was hoping Ian might phone or even stop by, but as they started the second show that particular hope gave way to a small niggling fear that perhaps the detective was not as interested as he'd seemed.

"What's wrong?" Lawrence asked as they stood together in the wings watching Kenny do his shtick.

"Nothing…"

"Don't tell fibs. You look upset." Lawrence put his arm round Patrick's waist and squeezed. "Come on, tell Mother."

"Oh, I'm just being silly," Patrick said with a sigh. "That guy I told you about, he came home with me the other night…"

"Lucky you…"

"I thought so, but I haven't heard from him since."

"Maybe he's in recovery," Lawrence said, chuckling.

"Smarty pants. It was lovely though, Lawrence. I hope it wasn't just a one night thing."

"He might have got very busy or something. What does he do?"

"He's a detective—the one that arrested Kenny's stalker."

"A *copper*…?" Lawrence giggled. "Did he use his handcuffs?"

"Lawrence, I thought you were trying to make me feel better."

"Sorry… oops, there's my cue. See you later." Lawrence ran onstage to play the valet to Kenny, helping him off with part of his costume as he transformed himself into Marlene Dietrich. Kenny did a series of impersonations, Mae West, Marlene, and Greta Garbo—all the old movie stars. Trouble was, Patrick noticed, no matter who Kenny impersonated he still sounded like Kenny LaFontaine. The wig and the dress might change, he might look fabulous, but the lack of talent was evident as he spouted the famous divas' famous one-liners and generally messed them up. *He's one lucky bastard*, Patrick mused, watching the drag star regale his audience with what were no more than old end-of-the-pier jokes and tawdry theatrics. What had once seemed like a great gig to Patrick now smacked of the cheapest entertainment.

Feeling thoroughly depressed, Patrick walked slowly back to this dressing room to wait for his cue for the finale.

Kenny summoned him to his dressing room at the end of the show. "Here you are dear," he said, handing Patrick a tacky grocery bag stuffed with paper scraps. "Now, you're to march in there, drop this in the used basket area, and clear out immediately. Don't go hanging around looking for the stupid arsehole. Let the police do the rest."

Patrick nodded and took the bag from Kenny.

"What's wrong dear?" Kenny looked at him through narrowed eyes. "Cat got your tongue?"

"No, I'm fine."

Kenny laughed lightly. "You're still pissed at me for interrupting your little talk with the lovely detective opening night, aren't you?"

"No…"

"Yes you are," Kenny said spitefully. "I could tell you were hoping to get in his pants—but, I mean, what chance d'you think you'd have when it's me he *really* wants."

Patrick swallowed his laughter. "Oh, is he gay then?"

"As a goose, dear. Couldn't keep his hands off me right here in this very room…"

"Amazing," Patrick murmured.

"What's so bloody amazing about it?" Kenny's face flushed under his makeup. "You really think he'd want you over me?"

"I never gave it a second thought," Patrick said straight-faced. "Well, if that's all, I'll be heading home."

"Yeah, that's all," Kenny growled, turning away. "Just make sure you don't cock it up tomorrow."

"I'll do my best."

As he approached the entrance to his flat Patrick slowed his steps on seeing a tall man leaning on the wall by the doorway, his back to Patrick.

"Damn," he muttered.

This was a problem living in the heart of London. Convenient as it was in many ways, vagrants and homeless people made a habit of loitering in doorways and asking for money. He'd been roughed up a couple of times in the past when he'd asked them to move on, and although he wouldn't let himself be intimidated by a stranger's presence, he maintained a wary alertness as he neared the door. His heart jumped into his mouth as the man turned and stepped out in front of him.

"Patrick, it's me—sorry, did I scare you?"

"Ian…" Patrick gasped. "No, but I think my heart just stopped…"

Ian put his arms round Patrick and kissed his cheek. "Sorry, I should've phoned. It's been a bugger of a day at the station. I just got off duty, and I wondered if maybe you might just be getting home, so I thought I'd wait around for a bit."

"A bit of what?" Patrick teased him, suddenly happy as a sand boy.

"Of you, of course." Ian nuzzled Patrick's nose. "You going to ask me in?"

"Silly question…" He took Ian by the hand and led him upstairs to his flat. "By the way," he said, mischievously, "Kenny told me you have the hots for him."

"What?" Ian almost choked. "Let me tell you something, *nothing* could be further from the truth. I can't stand the blighter, if you want to know."

"That's not what he told me," Patrick said, laughing as he unlocked the door to his flat.

"Well, the bloke's delusional if he thinks I'm in any way interested in him." Ian looked around and smiled. "You've tidied up," he remarked.

"Just in case of unexpected visitors," Patrick said, moving into Ian's arms. "So…" His smile teased Ian. "I don't have to worry about Kenny being a rival for your affection?"

"No bloody way," Ian muttered, tightening his arms about Patrick.

Their kiss was deep and hungry, and as Patrick slipped his arms inside Ian's jacket and felt the warm strength of his body he shivered with anticipation and lust. When they came up for air, Patrick gasped, "I also changed the sheets…"

"Then what are we waiting for?" Ian murmured, removing Patrick's jacket and throwing it onto a nearby chair.

Patrick brushed Ian's lips with his. "Can't think of a thing," he murmured, letting himself be picked up and carried into the bedroom. "You always this butch?" he asked, smiling into Ian's eyes.

"Always," Ian assured him.

"Lovely," Patrick sighed as Ian set him down on the bed and started to strip him of his jeans, socks and shoes. When they were both naked, Ian lay over Patrick and smiled into his eyes.

"Can I tell you that the other night with you was the best I've ever had in my life?"

Patrick stroked Ian's cheek gently. "The feeling, Detective, is entirely mutual."

He slid his hand behind Ian's head and pulled him in for a long kiss. As their tongues meshed and hands roamed over each other's body, Patrick felt an almost overwhelming surge of joy. What Ian had just said felt like some kind of a commitment. *Yes, it was too soon to be falling in love,* Patrick told himself, but all the elements were there in place. He loved every part of Ian's body, loved the way he kissed and held him—but even more important, he loved Ian's nature, the sweetness that lay just below his gruff exterior, and the fun that lurked in his eyes even when he was being 'official.' But what was wonderful was that he felt Ian had the same feelings for him.

It was so easy for Patrick to lose himself in the kiss they now shared. Ian's lips, so warm and moist, brought Patrick rapture and a hunger he couldn't remember ever having experienced before. If this wasn't being in love, it was the next best thing. Patrick gave himself up to the sensual sensations Ian's hands and lips brought him. He writhed under Ian, lifting his hips and winding his legs around Ian's slim hips.

"Fuck me, Ian," he murmured, licking Ian's nipples, slowly, deliberately. "I want to feel all of you inside me." He could already feel the hard throbbing flesh between his thighs and the slickness of Ian's pre-cum as he guided his hot erection towards Patrick's waiting hole. For a moment Patrick was tempted to forgo the condom. He wanted more than anything to experience the thrill of having Ian deep within him without the layer of latex getting in the way. The thought of having Ian explode inside him, searing his insides with his hot semen, made Patrick's cock jump with excitement, but then Ian reached past him and opened the drawer to retrieve the lube and a condom, and Patrick's common sense returned. He was glad he hadn't suggested going bareback. He had a feeling Ian wouldn't agree to it anyway after the short time they'd known one another. Maybe later he'd suggest they both get tested… He shivered as Ian's fingers, coated with lube, probed inside him, stretching him gently, preparing him for what they both longed for. Ian smiled down at him, then brushed his lips with a tender kiss as he pushed his way past Patrick's brief resistance.

Ian sighed with satisfaction as Patrick raised his hips to draw him into the depths of his sweet core. He hadn't ever thought of going without protection—'til now. To feel the moist, silken heat inside Patrick was something he found himself aching for. As he gazed down upon Patrick's beautiful and trusting face, he felt his heart twist with desire... and something else... love? Had he really found the one to whom he could give his heart, without fear of it being broken, like before? But was this the time to think of such a thing? Every fiber in his body cried out for release, for fulfillment. Every touch, every sensation that passed between them seemed to urge him on, to bring Patrick to a gut wrenching climax, for them both to reach the heights of ecstasy together. Patrick's cock was hot and throbbing in Ian's hand, and he pumped it slowly, matching the rhythm he moved to inside Patrick. Ian lost himself in the sweet sensations that enveloped his senses—the touch, the scent, the smoothness of Patrick's skin under his hands, the soft, demanding insistence of his lips. He heard himself moan, felt his body stiffen as his orgasm built inside his balls, bringing his blood to a slow boil.

Ian could feel Patrick's cock grow even harder, pulsing in his hand as he too drowned in the sensations they shared. Just before they came in shattering waves of rapture, Patrick raised himself up into Ian's arms, impaling himself even deeper on Ian's cock, clinging to the man as though his life depended on it. Guttural cries of delirious joy escaped their lips, then were muffled as their mouths met and meshed, tongues swirling inside each other's moist heat.

Later, as they lay contented in each other's arms, Patrick, his head on Ian's chest, said, "By the way, Kenny asked me to drop off some blackmail money tomorrow."

Ian sat bolt upright, causing Patrick to slide off him with a thump. Ian glared at him. "And I hope you told him to fucking do it himself!"

"Well, no actually..."

"Patrick, you're not to do this. I don't want you getting mixed up in this kind of sleazy operation."

"You'll be there, won't you? I honestly don't see that it's such a big deal."

Ian gripped Patrick by the arms. "Listen, any time there's a crime involved it's a big deal. I don't want you anywhere near that supermarket tomorrow."

"But I already told Kenny I'd do it. He offered me fifty quid."

"You're doing it for the money?" Ian gasped.

"No, of course not," Patrick said, annoyed. "And stop cutting off the circulation in my arms, will you?"

"Sorry," Ian mumbled, releasing Patrick from his iron grip. "But you're not doing it."

"Ian, for heaven's sake, what difference will it make if I do it, or Kenny does it?"

"It's Kenny's problem, not yours. And the man blackmailing him is alluding to some pretty hairy stuff, if you must know."

"Like what?"

"I can't tell you right now."

"Well, I'll just ask Kenny," Patrick huffed. "*After* I deliver the package tomorrow."

"*Patrick*," Ian groaned.

"Look..." Patrick cozied up to the detective and kissed his chin. "What can go wrong? All I'm doing is putting the package in a basket and leaving. You'll be there to nab the blighter and put him away—and I'll give you a big kiss for being so brave!"

Ian chuckled. "That'd raise a few eyebrows. But Patrick..."

Patrick slipped his arms round Ian's hard torso. "What if I give you that big kiss now?"

"I'd like that..." Ian slipped his hand round the nape of Patrick's neck. "And Patrick..."

"Yes?"

"This might sound a bit overly dramatic, but I have to say it." He kissed Patrick's lips tenderly. "You've become very important to me. I know we've only known each other such a short time, but... well... I think I love you, Patrick."

Patrick's eyes widened as he gazed at the sincerity in Ian's expression. "Oh," he murmured.

"Too soon? Am I rushing things?" Ian's eyes did not leave Patrick's. "You don't have to say anything. It's a tendency of mine to say how I feel..."

Patrick smiled. "A very nice tendency," he said, kissing Ian. "And just so you know, I love you too, Ian. I think I have since that first moment we spoke at the bar in Kenny's club."

"Really?" Ian chuckled softly. "I think it took me at least ten of those moments."

Their kiss was long and sweet and left them hot and breathless, and ready for round two.

CHAPTER SIX

Patrick felt a twinge of nerves as he jumped off the bus on Elm's Park Road and walked across the street to the giant supermarket. He kept looking around for any sign of Ian, or anyone else resembling a policeman, but saw only a crowd of men and women pushing shopping carts up and down the dozens of aisles. They could be anywhere... He saw the sign that read RETURN CARTS AND BASKETS HERE, and made his way toward it. His heart began to hammer in his chest as he neared the sign, and he looked furtively out of the corner of his eye in case he spotted the blackmailer.

No sign of him either...

Following Ian's admonition that he should not loiter in the store but get in and out quickly, he threw the package into the nearest basket then turned on his heel to leave. Next thing, he was knocked flat on his back by a man in a long black coat who grabbed the package and dashed for the emergency exit, setting off every alarm in the building. As startled shoppers milled around in confusion, four men broke from the crowd in hot pursuit—one of them Patrick recognized as Ian. Winded from his fall he got to his feet and followed the four detectives as cries of "Stop thief," and "Where's the fire?" broke out around him.

Outside, Patrick saw the man in the black coat cut across the car park, still pursued by the police, Ian in the lead. Suddenly, he heard the sound of screeching tires, and a car, driven at a high speed, struck the man, sending him hurtling through the air. He landed with a sickening thud on the concrete, the package he'd been carrying spilling its contents of useless scraps of paper on the ground around his body. The car didn't stop, exiting the car park and roaring off down the street.

Patrick watched as Ian knelt by the man then looked up as his fellow officers gathered around. From the look on Ian's face, Patrick could tell the man was either dead or severely injured. He shuddered as he relived what had just taken place.

What could go wrong? he'd asked Ian last night, well, there was his answer. Just about bloody everything.

"Are you all right?" Ian asked Patrick as they waited for the ambulance to arrive

Patrick nodded then mumbled, "I'm sorry."

"For what?"

"For not listening to you—for acting so damned cavalier about this. You were right… crime is a big deal, Ian." After a pause he asked, "Is the man dead?"

Ian nodded, but said nothing. Patrick wanted to take his hand and feel the comfort those strong warm fingers would bring him. He sighed, knowing such a move would not be a particularly good one at that moment.

Ian gave him a small smile. "I know what you're thinking, love. Go home. I'll call you later."

"Promise?"

"Promise." Ian gripped Patrick's shoulder. "You're off tonight, right?"

"Yes, no shows on Sundays."

"I'd like to see you when I get off duty."

"I'll be at home…" Patrick's eyes shone and he had to stop himself from throwing his arms about Ian and giving him that big kiss.

Ian watched him go, jogging across the car park toward the bus stop.

"Friend of yours?" Ernest, too, was watching Patrick leave.

"He's a singer in Kenny LaFontaine's show," Ian said. "Kenny coerced him into delivering the package."

Ernest nodded toward where the dead man still lay awaiting the ambulance. "Witness over there said it was a woman driving the car, blonde, in her thirties maybe."

"So," Ian muttered. "We've got a black Ford Escort of which there are thousands in London, no number plate, and a blonde in her thirties, of which there are tens of thousands in London. Not a bad start, eh Ernest?"

✤✤✤✤✤

Kenny was none too happy when Ian showed up at his flat with Ernest in tow. *Bloody hell,* he thought, trying to keep the scowl from his face. *Does he have to drag this twit around with him?* Aloud he asked, "So, did you get him?"

"Somebody got 'im," Ernest said, making himself at home on an armchair. "Woman ran him over."

"Good for her," Kenny exclaimed with some relish. "Is he in hospital? I think I might visit him and finish him off."

"He's dead, Mr. LaFontaine," Ian said, watching the expression on Kenny's face carefully. "We believe the woman ran him over deliberately."

Kenny faltered for a moment. "Dead..?" He shuddered then asked, "Who is this woman?"

"Don't know yet, all we have for description from the eye witness is a woman, age indeterminate, with a lot of blond hair. Her car had no license number."

"That'll get you far, won't it?" Kenny giggled, raising the hackles on the back of Ian's neck. "So, who was *he?*"

"No positive identification yet," Ian told him. "He wasn't carrying a personal ID, so unless someone comes forward to identify him it might take some time before we know who he was. Tell me, Mr. LaFontaine," Ian leaned forward in his chair. "Where were you this morning, around nine o'clock?"

Kenny's eyebrows hit his hairline. "*Excuse* me?" He gave a high-pitched laugh. "Surely you don't think I had anything to do with this. Why, I've never been so insulted!"

Oh, I'm sure you have, Ian thought. Aloud he said, "We have to check on everyone involved in this..."

"And no one's more involved than you," Ernest said, bluntly, interrupting. "You're the one being blackmailed."

"*Honestly!*" Kenny rose to his feet, hands on hips. "I go to you blokes for help and this is what I get—accusations?"

"We're not accusing you of anything," Ian said. "Like I said, we have to check on everyone involved in this."

"Well, I was here all morning if you must know—in bed, asleep. I didn't get up until close to ten."

"You got anyone to corroborate that?" Ernest asked.

"No..." Kenny batted his eyelashes at Ian. "I was quite alone."

"So, you were sound asleep while the man you asked to take your place dropped off the package?" Ian gave Kenny a cold look. "Weren't you just a bit curious to know how Patrick Farland got on doing what we asked *you* to do?"

"Oh, I knew he'd manage all right," Kenny replied with a dismissive wave of his hand. "I mean, what did he have to do that was so difficult? Throw a shopping bag in a basket." He giggled again. "I mean any fool could do that."

Ian resisted saying, *But the fool we asked to do it, didn't.* Instead he said, "Mr. LaFontaine, involving someone else in this was not a good idea."

"What d'you mean?"

"He means," Ernest interrupted, "that there might have been a problem with the man you sent to do what you should've been doing. The blackmailer knocked Mr. Farland over. It could have resulted in injury, or even a hostage situation. We've had that happen before. You put someone's life in danger because you couldn't be bothered to do what we asked."

"Oh, but Patrick's all right isn't he?"

"Yes, he is…"

"Well then, what's all the bloody fuss about? You're acting like I'm the criminal here—not the fucking victim!"

"The victim is the dead man," Ian said. "We're reasonably sure he was run over deliberately, and if that's the case, then someone else knew about the pickup."

"Well they didn't hear about it from me, I can assure you," Kenny shouted, an edge of hysteria creeping into his voice. "*Patrick* knew about it…"

"Patrick Farland knew about it because *you* involved him in it. He also knew there was no money in the bag. Who else did you tell about what we had arranged?"

"No one, you told me not to tell anyone."

Ian sat back and crossed his arms. "Yet you *involved* Patrick Farland."

"Well, yes…"

"So, might you have mentioned it to someone else—a close friend, someone in the cast?"

"No." Kenny glared at him. "Only Patrick… oh, and Alfred."

"Who the bloody hell is Alfred?" Ernest all but exploded.

"My dresser—well actually, he's a bit more than that. You might call him my manager. He's been with me for years."

"Anyone else?" Ian asked dryly.

"No."

"You're sure?" Ernest pressed.

Kenny heaved a huge sigh. "Yes, I'm bloody sure. Patrick and Alfred, that's it!"

"Okay." Ian stood up. "We're going to ask you to accompany us to take a look at the dead man. See if you know him."

Kenny looked shocked. "Know him? Of course I don't know him."

"He knew *you*," Ernest said, also standing. "Stands to reason you might just know *him*."

"Oh, but I can't stand looking at dead people." Kenny shivered dramatically. "I couldn't even look at my own father when he passed."

"Nevertheless, we need you to do this," Ian said. "So far you're the only one with a direct lead to him. We'll drive you down to the morgue, and I'll have a car bring you home afterwards."

"You mean *now*?"

Ian sighed. "Yes, now, Mr. LaFontaine."

"But this is outrageous—I have a ton of things to do…"

"We can get a court order," Ernest said, his impatience showing. "Just delay the inevitable, that's all."

"Oh, all *right*!" Kenny flounced toward his bedroom. "I'll just be a minute!"

Ian and Ernest exchanged glances, Ernest trying not to laugh too loudly. "Oh, all *right*," he mimicked, flapping a limp hand. "Men are such *brutes*."

✞ ✞ ✞ ✞ ✞

Kenny was as ungracious as he could be as he swept through the dreary corridors on the way to the morgue. He retained a stony silence as Ian opened the door to the room where the dead blackmailer's body was being kept.

He must be over me, Ian thought, hiding a smile. *Well that saves me the awkward moment of having to turn him down.*

"Do I really have to do this?" Kenny's nervous yet still strident voice echoed through the morgue as he stopped in his tracks, looking around him with distaste. "This is just so unnecessary!"

"It won't take a minute," Ian muttered, drawing back the sheet that covered the man's body. He heard Kenny take a sharp intake of breath, and it was quite obvious from his widening eyes that Kenny knew exactly who the man was.

"Who is he?" Ian asked.

"I have no idea," Kenny replied.

"I think you do." Ian dropped the sheet back over the man's face. "I must warn you, it's not a good idea to withhold information, Mr. LaFontaine."

"Oh, all right," Kenny snapped. "He's a trick I had in Spain a couple of years ago."

"He doesn't look Spanish," Ernest said.

"He's not. He's from fucking Blackpool, isn't he? Common little sheister that tried to bleed me dry."

"He was blackmailing you then?"

"Not so much blackmail…" Kenny looked away as if ashamed. "He wanted money for sex…"

"And you paid him?" Ian asked, masking his surprise.

"Not at first." Kenny's laugh was hollow and abrasive. "I thought the fucker loved me… but he showed his true colors soon enough, little bastard." He shivered and looked up at Ian, a plaintive look in his eyes. "Can we get out of here? I'm feeling unwell."

"What's his name?"

"George Osbourne."

"And the last time you saw him?"

"Let's get out of here, then I'll tell you everything you need to know."

Kenny was quiet as he accompanied Ian and Ernest to the police station cafeteria, but Ian had the distinct impression that Kenny's mind was working overtime. Whatever he was going to divulge, Ian would bet it was not going to be the whole truth and nothing but the truth.

As Ernest went to get them coffee, Kenny gazed at Ian with limpid eyes. "I'd feel so much better if it was just you and me, without, you know…" He gave a desultory wave in Ernest's direction. "You give the impression of being so much more, well you know, sympathetic."

Shit. So he's not over me. Ian forced a smile to his lips. "Ernest's a professional, Mr. LaFontaine. He understands the predicament you're in."

"Why won't you call me Kenny?" Kenny whined. "It would make me feel so much more relaxed. My nerves are fairly chewed to bits over this whole thing."

"All right… Kenny." Ian had to push the name through his teeth. "So, how long had George Osbourne been blackmailing you?"

"Ever since Madrid…"

"You've been paying him for two years?"

"Well… let's say paying in kind, so to speak."

"You mean sex."

"Yes."

"So, what went wrong?"

"The blighter wanted me to come out and acknowledge him as my boyfriend." Kenny shuddered. "I told him it would ruin me if the public knew I was gay. He laughed in my face at that, but Ian, honestly, all those old ladies—who are the majority of my fans—don't know. Yes, I know the press calls it the worst kept secret in show business, but I'm telling you, those old biddies would have heart attacks if they thought I sucked cock! They see me as this big blond woman who just happens to be a man—they don't see farther than the paint and the wigs. What's important to them is the illusion I create, and the laughs I bring them. They sure as hell don't want to know that when I strip all of that off, I like to take it up the bum."

Ian was somewhat surprised that Kenny had opened up to him in this way, and he began to feel some sympathy for the drag star. He knew from personal experience how hard it was to maintain the image his friends and associates expected from him, but to have your personal life scrutinized in public by the press and anyone who wanted to sling mud at a celebrity had to be more than just stressful.

He looked up as Ernest returned with their coffees. "What we got then?" Ernest asked as he plunked himself down at the table.

"A disenchanted boyfriend on the make for some easy money," Ian said.

"And what about the murder in Madrid?" Ernest took a loud sip of his coffee. "Was the boyfriend involved in that?"

Kenny glared at Ernest and shook his head. "There was no murder that either of us was involved in."

"Well, that's not exactly true, now is it?" Ernest returned Kenny's sour look with a wide-eyed expression. "We have a report from the Madrid police that a murder took place at the club you were appearing at—one of the waiters, uh… Alfonso Gomez… ended up strangled. All of you were questioned and gave statements. So you see, you were involved, now weren't you? Plus you told Detective Bannister here that you didn't know who the blackmailer was, and now we find out you knew him very well."

Ian had sat back in his seat while Ernest got aggressive with Kenny. It wouldn't do any harm for Kenny to feel unsettled by Ernest's tactics. Ian was certain Kenny was still holding back some information.

"But I didn't kill anyone," Kenny said. "It was most likely George who did it. He was insanely jealous of anyone I tarried with."

"Oh, so you tarried with the waiter?"

"I didn't say that…"

"There's a lot you're not saying," Ernest snapped. "And if you're not careful we might have to take you in and charge you with withholding information pertinent to this case."

Kenny gasped and planted his hands on his hips. "Well I like that!" he snapped, sarcastically. "I came here *voluntarily* to help you out. I'm beginning to think I should have my solicitor here for my protection."

"There's no need for that, Kenny," Ian said mildly. "Detective Holloway and I are just trying to put all the facts together." He ignored the look of surprise on Ernest's face when he'd called the drag star by his first name. He'd explain later. "Anything that you can remember is going to help us put this to rest."

"Well, I thought it was put to rest now that George's a goner. It's over, isn't it?"

"Not really. We still have to find out why George Osbourne was killed—and by whom."

"Bugger that," Kenny snarled. "I could give a toss about that wanker—and whoever did him in, is a friend of mine."

"Is she?"

"Is who what?"

"The woman who ran Osbourne over," Ian said. "Is she a friend of yours?"

"How the hell should I know?" Kenny blurted. "I know dozens of blondes—natural and not—male and female, and everything in between."

"Anyone of them drive a black Ford escort?" Ernest asked.

Kenny sniffed. "I sincerely hope not!"

Ian chuckled as Ernest rolled his eyes. "You do know that they're the choice of London's Metro police force, don't you?"

"More to the point," Kenny said tartly, "Do I care?" He pushed his chair back from the table. "Now I really must insist you drive me home. I've wasted enough of my day already with you blokes. I have shows to do."

"I thought the club was closed on Sundays," Ian said, thinking of Patrick and how much he wanted to see him later.

"It is, but I have guest appearances on other shows." Kenny smiled sweetly at Ian. "Would *you* drive me home, please?"

"Yeah, go on, Ian." Ernest was trying not to laugh. "I've got some paperwork to catch up on, otherwise I'd volunteer."

This was the last thing Ian wanted, to be alone in a car with Kenny LaFontaine. *Damn.* "Oh, okay Kenny," he said, looking daggers at his partner. "See you later then, Ernest."

Ernest grinned at him. "Don't do anything I would."

CHAPTER SEVEN

Kenny was quieter than Ian had expected him to be on the ride back to his flat. He'd also expected him to be flirty and obnoxious, but for most of the journey, Kenny stared out the passenger window, saying nothing.

Then, out of the blue, he said, "Well, I hope you're going to come upstairs and take care of me, Ian."

Ian almost choked. "Excuse me?"

"Oh, you don't fool me, copper. I know you're gay, and I know you fancy Patrick. I saw the way you were looking at one another the other night. Well, Patrick's all wrong for you—he's nobody. I can take you places, introduce you to people you'd never get a chance to meet ordinarily. I'm a star in the West End of London, with all the prestige that entails!"

"That's very nice of you Kenny," Ian said carefully, hiding his amazement at Kenny's crassness. "But you must understand that in my position it's impossible for me to fraternize with you. My job would be out the window if anyone got a clue about it."

"They don't know you're gay?"

"That's not the issue, Kenny. This case would be tainted if word got out that you and I were... well, you know."

"Well, what about after it's all settled?" Kenny pressed.

"Probably not..."

"What? You don't fancy me, is that what you're saying?"

"You're a very handsome man, Kenny, but..."

"You've done it with Patrick, haven't you? That's the fucking reason, isn't it?" Kenny's expression became ugly. "You'd rather screw a no-name tuppence ha'penny singer than me?"

Ian pulled up in front of Kenny's flat and slammed on the brakes. "Mr. LaFontaine," he said, his voice curt and cold. "You are way out of line. What I am and who I see in my private time is no concern of yours. I am a police officer investigating a case you are involved in, and that's all. The fact that you seem to think I'm seeing someone in your show has no bearing on the case whatsoever. If, however, I allowed myself to become involved with you, it would cause both yourself and me immeasurable problems."

"I wasn't suggesting we get involved," Kenny tittered, regaining his composure. "Just a quick blow job would do."

Ian sighed. "I'll phone you later if we have any news for you, Mr. LaFontaine."

"Ooh, back to that are we?" Kenny threw him a malicious smile. "I'll give Patrick your love, shall I?"

"He's not working at the club tonight, remember?"

"Oh, I remember, all right. And when I see him tomorrow night, he won't be working at the club ever again!"

"You must be joking!" Ian stared at Kenny incredulously. "You'd give him the sack because I won't give you the time of day?"

"Well…" Kenny's smile was challenging. "Now you know how to save poor Patrick's job for him."

"Get out," Ian growled.

"Suit yourself, copper." Kenny pushed the car door open. "I hope when you're screwing Patrick next time you can explain to him why he's out of work." He laughed like a wicked witch. "Oh, oh, Patrick, I'm coming, I'm coming—but you're *going*!"

"Fuck you."

"No," Kenny snarled. "Fuck you, Detective fucking Bannister, fuck *you*!"

✥ ✥ ✥ ✥ ✥

Ian called Patrick when he got back to the station. He smiled as he heard the genuine pleasure in Patrick's voice, and hated himself for the news he had to give him.

"Are you busy tonight?" Ian asked.

"Not if you have something else in mind," Patrick replied, teasingly.

"I'd love to see you."

"Then come over when you're ready. I'll make us some dinner." Patrick paused, then said, "You sound a bit serious. Is anything wrong?"

"I'll tell you when I see you."

"Does it have something to do with what happened today?"

"I'll tell you later," Ian hedged. "I have a couple more calls to make. I'll see you around seven."

"Okay... looking forward to it."

"Me too... Bye, Patrick." Ian put the phone down, sighing heavily. He wished this was something he could talk to Ernest about. Ernest knew he was gay, but like most straight blokes didn't really want to hear about Ian's love life. He'd get a laugh out of Kenny LaFontaine's obvious liking for Ian, but anything more serious than that Ernest wouldn't want to know.

"Damn," he muttered, picking up the file he'd started on Kenny's case. He still had to update this with the information Ernest and he had learned from Kenny that afternoon. He looked up as Ernest walked in.

"Just got through talking with the Superintendent about our hit and run victim," Ernest told him. "They're running a background check on the blighter, see what they can come up with."

"We should find out who else was in the show in Madrid," Ian said. "Dancers, singers... They might remember what our unfriendly drag queen seems loath to tell us."

Ernest snickered. "I thought he was very friendly with you. Didn't I hear you call him *Kenny*?"

"That was before the carry-on in the car just now."

"What'd he do?" Ernest was wide-eyed with gleeful interest. "Grab your prick?"

"Not quite, but I had to make it very clear I wasn't interested—and of course, he got nasty."

"He would, bloody nasty type that one." Ernest frowned at Ian. "I wouldn't be surprised if he's not in this deeper than he's letting on."

Ian nodded. "You must be reading my mind, Ernest. That's exactly what I think."

✛✛✛✛✛

Patrick took a look round his living room lit with many a candle. He hoped Ian would find it as romantic as he'd tried to make it. Soft music played on the stereo, and he'd prepared a chicken curry with which to tempt his detective. They'd eat either before or after the main event. Whatever, it would keep warm in the oven. He'd dressed down for the occasion in a pair of soft denim jeans and a sleeveless mock tee shirt. A knock at the door had him rushing to answer it.

"Ian..." He stepped into the taller man's embrace and kissed him ardently, loving the fresh scent from Ian's skin, and the feel of his hard body pressed to his own. "Mmm, it's good to see you again."

"Likewise," Ian said, his voice husky as he kissed his way round Patrick's jaw. "You look nice... feel nice too." He rubbed his hands over Patrick's bare arms then pulled him in tightly against his crotch. Patrick slipped his hands inside Ian's shirt, stroking the warm skin.

"Uh... I've got something to tell you," Ian said quietly. "We should probably get it out of the way, first."

"Sounds serious..." Patrick gazed at Ian's concerned expression. "Did I do something wrong?"

"No, not you..."

"Let me get you a drink while you tell me," Patrick said. "I've a feeling I'm going to need one. Glass of wine?"

Ian nodded. "I had a run in with the star of your show today."

Patrick grimaced as he poured the wine. "Sorry about that. He is a wanker, isn't he?"

"More than a wanker, he tried to put the make on me, and when I turned him down he went ballistic, accused me of having an affair with you and... well, this part is really bad, Patrick."

Patrick handed Ian his glass. "He's going to give me the sack?"

"God, how did you guess that?"

"Because he's nothing if not predictable, and that's just the kind of petty bullshit he'd come up with." Patrick leaned in to kiss Ian's cheek. "Don't worry Ian, it's not the end of the world. In fact, I've become disenchanted with the show if you must know. Watching Kenny's crappy performance night after night is a giant chore, I can tell you." He took a sip of his wine. "There's an audition for a new West End musical on Thursday that I intend going to. Who knows? I just may get lucky." He smiled and kissed Ian again. "Or should I say, *luckier*?"

"I think I'm the lucky one," Ian said gruffly, putting an arm around Patrick. "But I must say I'd feel better if you weren't near that spiteful bitch. He's a mean spirited individual."

"And not very nice, either," Patrick added, laughing. He nuzzled Ian's neck. "I have dinner in the oven, would you like to eat that first, or me?"

"What do *you* think?"

"Me?"

"Right."

CHAPTER EIGHT

Patrick had called his friends Lawrence and Maggie to apprise them of the fact that when he went into the club Monday night, he expected to be fired. They gathered in Patrick's dressing room to commiserate with him, but Patrick wasn't in the mood to be depressed.

"I'm far too happy right now to let a twit like Kenny get me down," he told his friends, pouring each of them a glass of wine. "I'm in love, as the song goes, with a wonderful guy, and Kenny's fit to be tied about it. Just between us, he tried to get it on with Ian and was turned down flat."

"So *that's* why he wants to give you the sack?" Maggie asked, wide-eyed.

Lawrence snorted his derision as Patrick nodded. "The nerve of him... He's old enough to be Ian's father, isn't he—or should I say, *mother?*"

Patrick laughed. "Not *quite* old enough. Anyway, Ian felt responsible for Kenny being a pratt, but I told him not to worry, I'm over this job anyway."

"We all are," Lawrence agreed, his face gloomy. "If it wasn't for the money..."

"I know," Patrick said quickly. "You'd leave with me, but don't worry, we're friends no matter what."

At that moment, Ralph barged in without knocking. "Oh, little confab going on, eh?" He gave Patrick a supercilious look. "Kenny wants to see you in his dressing room, *tout suite,* ducks."

"Here we go," Patrick murmured, straightening his evening jacket. He smiled at Maggie and Lawrence. "I'll see you later."

With the help of his dresser, Alfred, Kenny was tucking 'it' away as Patrick knocked on his half open dressing room door and peeked in. The drag star was wearing his special waspie he'd designed himself. Patrick avoided smiling at the strange spectacle Kenny presented. His face was completely made up to mimic a woman's, he was wearing hose and high heeled shoes, but his body was still that of a man's, giving him a weird hermaphrodite look that was completely asexual. Patrick was sure that was not something Kenny would have wanted to hear.

"You wanted to see me, Kenny?"

"Yes, come in, sit down, Patrick." Alfred took a large blond wig down from the shelf over the dressing table and started teasing it in preparation for the show.

"Can you take that next door, dear?" Kenny said, waving at Alfred. "I need a private word with Patrick."

Alfred shot Patrick a sympathetic look as he left the dressing room, but Patrick was already over it.

"No need to worry about my feelings, Kenny," he said. "I know you're getting rid of me, and I know why."

"Do you now?" Kenny's smile was pure evil. "Do you also know that I've put out the word in the West End that you're trouble, and shouldn't be hired?"

Patrick stared at Kenny for a moment without saying anything. He'd wondered if Kenny would try to badmouth him around town. It was his style after all, once a bitch, always a bitch, but he also wondered just how much influence Kenny had among West End producers.

"That shut you up, didn't it?" Kenny sneered.

Patrick shrugged. "It's no more than I expected from you, Kenny. You play the evil queen so well I'm not surprised that's all you ever want to be in life."

Kenny's lips twisted in anger. "Cheeky sod," he hissed. "Aren't you forgetting who I am?"

"Who are you?" Patrick wasn't about to let Kenny have the final word on this. "Just a drag queen, who by some amazing stroke of luck made it big, but then started believing in his own publicity. You're not invulnerable, Kenny. I would have thought that what has happened would have opened your eyes to just how easily all this could come crashing down around you."

"What are you talking about?"

"I'm talking about the man who was blackmailing you. Haven't you realized yet that when the media gets a hold of this you'll be up for scrutiny every day for the rest of your career? Every time your name is mentioned it will be in conjunction with blackmail and murder. Not the kind of reputation a 'household name' can usually survive."

"Well, I can survive it," Kenny rasped. "I've survived for years on my wits and my talent, and I'll survive this. You, and the likes of you, don't know what grit and graft are all about. I came up the hard way, and I'll not let some blackmailing sheister take it all away from me!"

"Good luck then." Patrick stood and headed for the door. "I hope you have someone rehearsed into my place."

"Who's going to miss *you*?" Kenny gave a sneering laugh. "I'm the star—I'm the one they come to see. No one but me!"

Patrick chuckled. "Maybe, but an audience likes to see some continuity in a show, no matter how *grand* the star is."

He closed the door quietly behind him and winked at Alfred, who had been outside listening to every word.

"See you, Alf," he said, walking quickly to his dressing room. Instead of the depression being fired should have brought him, Patrick felt strangely exhilarated. As he stripped off his opening costume and dressed in his own clothes, his thoughts were of Ian and how super it would be to tell him he was free to see him this evening. Listening to the band strike up the spirited overture to the show, Patrick realized he wouldn't be able to tell Lawrence and Maggie he was leaving, but he would phone them later and tell them what had happened.

✥ ✥ ✥ ✥ ✥

Kenny was in a vile mood as he sat in front of his dressing table mirror at the end of the show and removed his makeup. He had festered all evening as, just as he had suspected, Ian and Patrick were doing one another—after he, Kenny, had made it quite obvious to the detective that he was interested in getting to know him better. Well, he'd fixed Patrick for sure. Out of work singers were ten a penny in London and good jobs few and far between. A word or two in the 'right' ears and pretty Patrick would be out of work for a long time to come.

Kenny sighed and threw a balled up clump of tissue aside. He only wished that he could feel some sense of satisfaction in firing Patrick. It would have been much more to his liking if the kid had burst into tears and begged Kenny not to give him the sack, but the cheeky sod hadn't even seemed *upset*.

Of course, he was gloating because he'd snagged what I wanted, Kenny seethed. *Smug bastard.*

He looked up as Alfred came into the room. "Pour me some bubbly, dear," he said. "What's the word backstage?"

"You're a fucking bitch," Alfred replied. Kenny spun round on his seat and glared at his manager. "I *beg* your pardon?"

Alfred chuckled. "That's what they're saying about you for giving Patrick the sack."

"I want names!"

"No, you don't, ducks." Alfred handed Kenny his champagne and poured one for himself. "You got over being called names like that a long time ago, Kenny. The kids are upset, that's all. Patrick was a popular lad, but they'll get over it, eventually."

"He's bonking that dishy detective," Kenny pouted.

"Oh, so that's what's got your knickers in a twist, eh?" Alfred took a long sip of his champagne then grinned at Kenny. "You'll get over that too, knowing you."

Kenny threw Alfred a sour look. "It just pisses me off that the copper chose some nobody over me."

"Well, let's face it, love..." Alfred threw back the rest of his champagne. "Youth does have its allure."

"*Meaning?*"

"Meaning that Patrick's twenty-something and you're not."

"I should give *you* the sack, you cheeky sod."

Alfred sighed and refilled their glasses. "I wish I had a fiver for every time you've said that to me."

Kenny narrowed his eyes speculatively. "Maybe I could still stick a spanner in their works—I mean, how would the Chief Inspector like it if he found out one of his detectives has been bonking a kid in my show? Not very good publicity for London's finest, is it?"

"And it would be worse publicity for you, dear." Alfred took Kenny's hand and leaned close to the drag star. "Listen to me, my darling. Forget the copper, you've got enough on your plate what with George showing up and getting himself killed. Whoever did him in must know what happened in Madrid."

"But the police said it was a woman, a blond woman," Kenny exclaimed. "Who the hell is she?"

"Maybe George was Betty Bothways."

Kenny snorted. "Not on your life, George was queer—didn't like women at all. He told me that many times. Real women that is... Of course, he did like me to wear my hose and heels sometimes."

"Kinky bugger," Alfred muttered. He sat back and polished off another glass of champagne. "I don't know why you had to involve the police in the first place. Why didn't you just pay George off and be done with it?"

"Because I wasn't about to give him any more of my hard earned cash, at least, not without something in return." Kenny glared as Alfred. "The bastard laughed at me when I said I'd pay him if he came back. Said he had someone else in his life, someone *young*, damn him!"

"Well, if it's any consolation, it didn't get him very far, now did it? The blighter's dead, and you've still got your money."

A knock at the door made them both jump. Ralph poked his head in. "Any notes for me?" he asked, looking at a place somewhere over Kenny's head.

"Notes?" Kenny stared at him blankly for a moment. "Oh... *notes*. No, nothing tonight Ralph. The show went well. Just see that you have a replacement for Patrick quick as you can. I need a leading man for the females in the audience."

Ralph nodded. "Why'd you give him the sack, anyway?" he asked.

Kenny laughed bitterly. "Oh please, Ralph. Don't act the naïf with me. You bloody well know why—everyone knows why by this time—so don't stand there looking like butter wouldn't melt up your arse." He waved a dismissive hand. "Just go do your bloody job."

Ralph left without another word, slamming the door behind him.

"That pratt is getting on my fucking nerves," Kenny growled. "He thinks he's God's gift to the world of dance, when the truth is he wouldn't have a job at all if it wasn't for me."

"You're making an enemy of him, Kenny dear," Alfred said. "It doesn't do to have too many enemies in this business. Remember, he was in Madrid..."

"Fuck 'im. He's just a miserable old queen that can't get laid. He could have the choice of any of the boy dancers if he played his cards right, but they all hated him at the end of the first day of rehearsals. He's nothing more than a bitter and twisted old queen!"

"He's younger than..." Alfred bit off what he was about to say, but Kenny's mean stare told him the drag star knew he'd almost said, 'than you.'

"You've had quite enough to drink Alfred," Kenny said, icicles forming on every word. "Now totter off home before I really do give you the sack!"

❦❦❦❦❦

The following morning, Ian and Ernest had an unexpected break in the case. A black Ford Escort with no license plate, presumed to be the one used to kill George Osbourne, had been found abandoned on a piece of wasteland in South London.

Ernest whistled through his teeth as he read the report. "Well, I'll be... Guess what they found on the passenger seat."

Ian looked at him over his coffee cup. "What?"

"A blond wig, Ian my boy. A *blond wig*."

Chapter Nine

Kenny muttered some nasty expletives under his breath as he looked out of his living room window and saw Bert Halford standing on the other side of the street. Kenny couldn't quite see Bert's face, but he was sure it was the silly twit.

His eyes widened as he saw Bert look into the traffic then take off at a fast clip. The reason became obvious as a police car pulled up in front of Kenny's flat and Ian climbed out, along with Ernest.

"What do *they* want?" he groused, running into his bedroom to comb his hair and throw on a silk dressing gown. Well, at least the looker was there. He might be another bastard, but at least he was easy on the eyes.

He let them ring the doorbell several times before he deigned to answer, receiving an irritated glare from the one called Ernest.

"What a surprise," Kenny cooed, stepping back to usher in the detectives. "To what do I owe the pleasure?"

"The car used to run George Osbourne over has been found," Ian told him without ceremony.

"That's nice." Kenny smiled sweetly at Ian. "Like a cuppa?"

"No thanks."

"They also found this." Ernest pulled the blond wig from the plastic bag in his hand. "Recognize it?"

"It's a wig," Kenny said.

"We know what it is, but is it yours?"

"How the hell should I know?" Kenny growled. "I've got dozens of those. Does it have my name sewn into it?"

"No, it doesn't."

"Then it's not mine. I have a name label sewn into everything I own."

"It does have the maker's name inside," Ian said. "We showed it to them, and they told us it had been made for you, Mr. LaFontaine. And if you look closely here..." He pointed to the netting on the inside of the wig, "You can see that a label had been sewn there at one time."

Kenny gave him a long lethal look. "Just what the fuck is it you're insinuating here? Are you saying that I wore that wig and drove the car that killed George?"

"Well, did you?" Ernest asked bluntly.

Kenny gave a loud and raucous laugh. "Oh, you pair of giant *twits*! Sherlock Holmes must be turning in his grave right about now!"

"Sherlock Holmes was a fictional character," Ian said mildly. "Now, how d'you explain this wig being in the car that killed George Osbourne?"

"I suppose someone stole it—if it's mine," Kenny seethed. "Listen, if you're going to continue with this charade, I'm phoning my solicitor. You pair of dicks are getting on my nerves, and on top of everything else, that bleeding stalker was here a few minutes ago, staring up at me. Fucking coppers— you're all worthless!"

"All right, calm down," Ernest said in a placating tone. "All we wanted to know is if the wig is yours and how it got in the car. Would you know if it was stolen from you? D'you have an inventory or something?"

"I suppose Alfred would know," Kenny muttered sullenly. "You can ask him..."

"You have his phone number handy?"

"Yes." Kenny recited the number then swung round and stalked to the window. "What're you going to do about that pervert that's hanging around me all the time?"

"He's harmless."

Kenny glared at Ian. "I don't *care*," he hissed. "I don't want him anywhere near me, d'you understand? My fucking nerves are shot to pieces with all of this. I'm a performer!"

I'll say you are, Ian thought.

"...And as such I need a calm mind to go on in front of my audience," Kenny ranted. "All of these... these *accusations* and... and *annoyances* will drive me to drink if you don't do something about them. I did not kill George Osbourne, and I don't know who did. I'll admit I'm not exactly grieving over the bastard's demise, but I wouldn't kill him. We were friends once..."

"More than friends," Ernest said.

"Well, lovers then," Kenny snapped.

"He was with you in Madrid," Ian remarked.

"Yes, he was. Did he kill the waiter? No, he did not. Neither did I. We were together the night it happened."

Ernest gave a dry chuckle. "That's convenient."

Kenny threw his hands up. "That's it, I'm phoning my solicitor. You two can go to hell. I've tried to be cooperative, but I'm tired of the snide remarks. Get out, and next time, make an appointment—through my solicitor!"

Ernest grinned at Ian as they left Kenny's flat. "And all this time, I thought he liked you—that he was cooperating in the hope of getting in your pants."

"Shut up, Ernest," Ian growled, scowling. "You don't know how close you are to the truth!"

"Blimey. Bit old for you isn't he?"

"*Ernest*. Give it up, mate!"

Ernest chuckled and clapped Ian on his back. "Sorry. Not often you get a laugh on this job."

"Well, one thing we know about the person that ran George Osbourne down," Ian said, opening the car door and climbing in. "It wasn't necessarily a woman."

❦❦❦❦❦

"It's not the same, is it?" Lawrence was sitting next to Maggie backstage, tackling some stretching exercises.

"You mean without Patrick?"

"Right. I miss him already, and it's been less than a week since he left." He looked up as he saw Albert walking toward them. "Hello, Albert."

"Hi." Albert sat next to him. "You look fed up."

"He's missing Patrick," Maggie said.

"Oh." Albert looked a trifle crestfallen. "I didn't know you two were... uh..."

"We're not," Lawrence said quickly. "He's my best friend."

Albert smiled and Lawrence's heart turned over. *God, but he is so cute*, he thought. *Why don't I have the nerve to ask him out?*

"We're going to the cinema tomorrow afternoon," Maggie said. "Why don't you come with us, Albert?"

"Oh, I don't want to intrude."

"You wouldn't be intruding, would he, Lawrence?"

"Of course not." He looked at Albert hopefully. "Would you like to come? Er... to the cinema, I mean."

"That'd be nice."

Later, Maggie grinned at Lawrence. "I might have a dreadful headache tomorrow afternoon, Lawrence. Will you manage without me?"

"You are a sweetheart, Maggie. I think I might be okay with just Albert sitting next to me in a dark cinema."

"Just make sure you don't make any more of those horrible remarks."

"Like what?"

"Would you like to *come*—to the cinema?"

Lawrence giggled. "It went right over his head."

"There you go again. Honestly, Lawrence..."

They laughed together then sobered as they saw Ralph bearing down on them, a face like thunder.

"What's wrong, Ralph?" Maggie asked.

"That fucking Kenny," Ralph seethed. "He's had me auditioning singers all bloody week, and every single one I've recommended he's turned down."

"He shouldn't have given Patrick the sack," Lawrence said, with some vehemence.

"You might be right," Ralph conceded, with reluctance. "At least he could hold a tune."

"At least he could hold a tune," Lawrence mimicked when Ralph had swept off. "What a wanker. Patrick's one of the best singers around."

"Too good for this place," Maggie agreed. "Didn't he have an audition this week?"

"Today, I think. We should phone him and see how he got on."

Patrick was at that moment leaving the theatre where the audition had been held. He glanced at his watch and smiled. Ten minutes before he met Ian at the Hangman Pub. Ian had insisted they get together after the audition so he could either help him drown his sorrows, or celebrate his new job in the West End. Despite all the nastiness with Kenny, the week had turned out to be a happy one for Patrick, with Ian and his relationship growing stronger with each passing day. They had seen each other every night, with Ian staying over most nights. Patrick had started to wonder if he should talk about them moving in together, but he didn't want to rush things, nor did he want to present Ian with any problems. Ian had told him Ernest knew he was gay, but there was still some form of stigma attached to a policeman being gay. Outing people in responsible positions was a favourite pastime for some British tabloids masquerading as newspapers, and Patrick would never forgive himself if Ian came up on their radar screens.

Trying to push that grim thought to the back of his mind, he made his way across the busy streets to the Hangman Pub. As he rounded the corner he saw Ian's tall figure hurrying toward the pub from the opposite direction. Before he called out Ian's name, Patrick took a moment to savor the sight of the man he'd fallen in love with. *God, but he is beautiful,* he thought, feeling a sensual heat gather in his groin. The knowledge of what lay beneath the dark conservative suit Ian was wearing—the solid lean muscle under smooth skin, the manhood that could so easily be brought to rigid attention—was enough to bring Patrick to his knees, right there on the street. *Well, that wouldn't do Ian's reputation any good.* Patrick chuckled at his wild thoughts and waved at Ian.

"Going my way?" he teased as they met outside the pub door.

Ian grinned at him. "If you'll make it worth my while, young man."

"You're on."

Laughing together they entered the pub. "All right," Ian said as they approached the bar. "What'll it be?"

"Pint of lager, please."

"Two pints of lager," Ian told the bartender, then turned and stared at Patrick. "Well?" he demanded. "Haven't you got something to tell me?"

"Wait 'til we sit down, over there..." Patrick pointed to a quiet corner table away from the main part of the bar.

"Oh, oh... am I going to have a wet shoulder?" Ian's expression was filled with concern. He paid for the beer then they made their way over to the corner table. "Come on, don't keep me in suspense," Ian coaxed as they sat down.

Patrick took a look around the bar to make sure everyone was too busy to notice them then he leaned forward and kissed Ian's cheek. "I got it," he whispered.

"Fantastic!" Ian beamed at him, seemingly unfazed by Patrick's public display of affection. "When d'you start rehearsals?"

"Next month. Only thing is we have an out of town tryout for two weeks. Bournemouth and Nottingham they said. Will you miss me?"

"Silly question, of course I will." He raised his glass. "But here's to you, Patrick, and one in the eye for Kenny LaFontaine!"

"How's that investigation going?" Patrick asked after they'd clinked glasses and downed half their beer in one swallow.

"Oh, he's all pissed at Ernest and me—won't talk to us anymore without his solicitor in attendance. He pulled a real tantrum in front of us this afternoon." Ian shook his head, remembering. "And his stalker's back again, which didn't help matters."

"But you said he's harmless."

"He is, but Kenny's got his falsies in a twist over it."

Patrick chuckled. "I wish I could feel sorry for him."

"It's hard to feel sorry for someone like him. Anyway," Ian's smile returned. "Enough of that, tell me about your new show…"

✟✟✟✟✟

One week later

Ralph glared at Kenny as the drag star poured himself a glass of champagne without offering one to his choreographer.

"I don't know what to tell you Kenny," he said, ignoring Alfred's quiet snigger. "I've listened to dozens of terrible voices all week, and the ones I've had you listen to, you turn up your nose at. Maybe we should just restage the show without a singer."

"I have to have someone introduce me." Kenny stared at Ralph's reflection in his makeup mirror. "The dancing boys are just too nelly to give me the grand entrance like Patrick did."

"Well, you shouldn't have given him the sack then, should you?" Ralph asked tartly. "Then we wouldn't have this problem."

"So phone him and tell him he's got his job back," Kenny said, applying his lip gloss. "I think he might have learned his lesson by this time."

"Lesson?"

"Not to fuck with me, or what I want. He's on the dole isn't he?"

"Not for long," Alfred said dryly.

Kenny gave him a sharp look. "What's that mean?"

"I heard his friends talking backstage. Got himself a part in a new musical was what they said."

"Well... I can soon put a stop to that."

Ralph and Alfred exchanged looks then Alfred said, "Kenny... that might not be a good idea..."

Kenny cast him an evil look. "Why not?"

"Because you'll come off sounding like a fucking bitch," Alfred said, bluntly. "These new West End producers aren't going to be interested in listening to you, Kenny. Most likely, they don't even know who you are."

"Excuse me?" Kenny spun round on his seat and fixed Alfred with a cold stare. "Just who in the hell do you think you're talking to? You might have been with me for longer than I care to remember, Alf, but you are definitely treading on thin ice right now. Everyone knows who I am—*everyone*—and don't you forget it!" He switched his glare to Ralph. "Phone that git Patrick now, and tell him to get his arse back here tonight, and make it sound like we're doing him the favour of a lifetime."

Kenny watched Ralph leave then leveled a spiteful look at Alfred. "Sometimes, I wonder whose side you're on."

"I just don't want to see you look stupid, Kenny. These new producers..."

"Oh, shut up about these new producers, like you know anything about it." He narrowed his eyes as Alfred picked up the blond wig he wore for his opening routine. "Which reminds me... that business about one of my wigs being found in the car that ran over George, what have you done to prevent that from happening again?"

"Nothing." Alfred shrugged his stooped shoulders. "Why would I?"

"Because you're the only one, apart from me, that has a bleeding key to my wigs and costumes," Kenny snapped, glaring at Alfred as he positioned the wig on Kenny's head. "Did you even notice that one of them was missing?"

"Can't say I did."

"*Can't say I did,*" Kenny mimicked. "That's what you told the police, is it? 'Can't say I did'? Christ, they must have thought you were a right twerp. But what the fuck, I'm surrounded by twerps and idiots!"

✞ ✞ ✞ ✞ ✞

Patrick listened to the message from Ralph on his voice mail with disbelief. *Kenny wants me back in his show? He must think I'm a glutton for punishment.*

He picked up his phone and dialed Ian's number. "You'll never guess what's happened," he said, laughing lightly when the detective answered. "Kenny wants me back in his show."

Ian's deep chuckle made Patrick smile. "Couldn't find anyone as good as you, eh?"

"Well, I don't know about that, but he must be pretty desperate to phone me."

"Are you going to accept his offer?"

"I don't know... but I do have some time before rehearsals for the new show, and I could use the money..."

"Tell him you'll need a raise to compensate for being out of work."

Patrick laughed. "I might just do that."

"Does this mean I won't have dinner with you tonight?"

"'Fraid so, if I decide to take him up on his offer."

"Well, like you said, the money would be handy. And besides..." Ian hesitated for a second.

"Besides what?"

"Well, I really shouldn't ask you to do this, but if you see or hear anything backstage pertaining to the blackmail case, I'd appreciate it if you'd let me know."

"Oh, you mean like I'd be working undercover for you? That's exciting!"

"Wait a minute, Patrick. I don't want you poking about or asking questions. Just if you happen to hear anything…"

"Don't worry, Ian, I'll be the soul of tact." He smiled as he heard Ian groan. "Promise."

"*Patrick*. Why did I mention any of this? I just know you're going to be snooping around, listening at Kenny's door, getting yourself into trouble."

"Well, he can only sack me again," Patrick chuckled.

"Just be careful. Kenny LaFontaine's been mixed up with a bloody rum lot over the years."

"Like the one that got run over?"

"Exactly. Listen, I'll meet you at The Hangman after your show, okay?"

"Okay. Shall I give Kenny your love?" Patrick teased.

"That's going to earn you a spanked bottom, young man."

Patrick giggled. "Promises, promises!"

✟✟✟✟✟

Lawrence and Maggie were waiting in his dressing room when Patrick arrived at the club that night.

"Ralph told us you were coming back," Maggie said, hugging him tightly while Lawrence beamed at him.

Patrick hugged his two friends. "You could've knocked me over with a feather when I got the message that Kenny wanted me back in the show."

"Ralph said they couldn't find anyone to replace you," Lawrence said. "Gosh, but I'm so glad to see you back here. It hasn't been the same."

"Any luck with Albert yet?" Patrick asked.

"We went to the cinema together the other day."

"Well, that's a step in the right direction, at least."

"They held hands in the dark," Maggie said, her eyes bright with mischief.

Patrick chuckled. "Only hands?"

"*Please…*" Lawrence tried to look offended. "My mother raised me proper!"

Their laughter was interrupted by Ralph, who, true to form, barged into Patrick's dressing room without knocking.

"Kenny wants you," he said abruptly then shot out again. The three friends looked at each other with varying expressions of dislike.

"What a wanker," Lawrence muttered. "Well, good luck, love." He kissed Patrick's cheek before leaving with Maggie.

Patrick sighed. If Kenny was going to act the big bitch again, Patrick vowed he wouldn't do the show. He'd just walk out— but then, he wouldn't be able to help Ian, and he really wanted to do that.

He knocked on Kenny's door and peeked in. "You wanted to see me?"

"Oh yes, Patrick, come on in." Kenny had his full makeup and wig on, but was wearing a silk dressing gown and drinking from a champagne glass. "Like some?" he asked, pointing at the champagne bottle.

"No thanks, not before the show."

"Really... makes it easier for me sometimes." He fixed Patrick with an unreadable expression. "So, I hear you've got yourself another job."

"Yes, but we don't start rehearsals for another month or so."

"Better than this, is it?"

Oh, oh, Patrick could sense a putdown. "Well, it's quite different," he said carefully.

"Not better, then," Kenny pressed, his lips pursed as he stared at Patrick.

"I have no way of knowing until I start rehearsals."

"Well..." Kenny threw back the last of his champagne. "The grass is always greener, of course, as they say. You remember everything you did for me, your lines and all that?"

"Oh, yes."

"Good. Well, I won't keep you. Better get yourself ready."

Patrick turned to go, then paused, deciding to do what Ian had said not to do. "Uh, Kenny... you all right after that blackmail situation?"

"Not really." Kenny looked up at him and sneered slightly. "What? You want me to thank you for taking that package to the supermarket?"

"No, of course not..." *What a bitch.* "I was just concerned about the stress it must have put you under."

Kenny raised an eyebrow. "Well, *of course* it was stressful, and the *police* are bloody useless as always. Couldn't find a fiver in a bag of 'em. That boyfriend of yours—he is your *boyfriend*, right? He's more useless than all of them put together, can't even get that fucking stalker to go away. Harmless, he says he is…"

Patrick acted surprised. "And he's not?"

"Oh, I don't know what he is. He's just always fucking *there*." He glared at Patrick. "You still seeing that prick then?"

"I'm still seeing Ian, if that's who you mean."

"That's who I mean."

"Kenny…" Patrick decided strangling the drag star right there and then wouldn't be a good idea if he was going to get any information from him. "All this going on must be really upsetting for you—blackmail, stalkers, the police coming and going. I mean, you have enough to think about without all of this added stress."

Kenny sighed dramatically. "You have no idea." He waved Patrick back into a seat and poured him a glass of champagne after refilling his own glass. "No one seems to care that the man that woman ran over was an ex lover of mine." He sighed again. "A very well *endowed* ex lover of mine."

"I'm sorry," Patrick said, hoping he sounded sincere.

"Yes, I thought George was one in a million." His expression turned dark. "Too bad he couldn't keep it in his trousers."

"Well…" Patrick thought he'd go for some humour. "You wouldn't have wanted that, would you?"

"I meant when he was around *other* young men!"

"Oh, right… *other* young men."

"There was that waiter in Madrid…" Kenny swayed in his seat, his eyes slightly out of focus as he continued. "Beautiful he was. George brought him back to our room one night… Oh, but that was a long time ago." His eyes seemed to refocus as he blinked at Patrick. "Bloody hell, why am I telling *you* this shit? Alfred!" he shrieked. "Get your arse in here and get me ready." He flicked his fingers at Patrick. "Off you go, I have a show to do!"

Hiding his smile, Patrick finished his champagne and left without a word. Now he knew how to get Kenny talking. Feed him champagne.

Chapter Ten

Patrick's first night back at Kenny's show was an eye opener. He'd realized Kenny was tipsy while they'd been talking, but to what extent became obvious when the drag star started forgetting lines and cues.

A restless audience and a noisy heckler only made matters worse, with Kenny telling the heckler to 'Fuck off out of my club before I come over there and fuck you.' Some nervous laughter followed that remark, but the heckler took offence, calling Kenny a 'nelly poufter' and demanding his money back.

Backstage, after the curtain rang down, Kenny put on another show for the benefit of anyone within earshot, screaming at the top of his voice about how he was completely over having to play to 'rude gits' who shouldn't have been allowed into his club in the first place.

"I'm trying to run a sophisticated theatre club here," he ranted at Alfred, "and those stupid bitches at the box office let any fucking worthless *git* into my club—*my* club. I will not be insulted like that again in my club."

"Oh, you've been through worse, dear," Alfred said, hanging up the evening suit Kenny had thrown on the ground in a temper tantrum. "Remember that time in Guernsey…"

"Shut your cakehole Alf, for God's sake. Guernsey was a million years ago—I'm a star now, and will be treated like one."

Alfred let out a long weary sigh. *Here we go again.* "Well, what do you want the box office girls to do? Ask a potential punter for a reference?"

"Don't try to be smart, Alf," Kenny sneered. "It doesn't suit you. In future, when some arsehole wants to get into a slanging match with me, I want security to throw him or her out. Make sure they know that, because if it happens again and it's left to me to take care of it, I'll bloody smash the bastard's face in."

"That'd go down well with the press, I must say," Alfred chuckled. "And I don't think the producers of 'Mame' would take too kindly to it, dear."

"Oh, shut up," Kenny muttered, but Alfred's warning served to cool his temper. Right, the offer to be the first female impersonator ever to portray the legendary character of Mame in a West End musical was far too tempting—to screw it up with a display of unseemly rage would be tantamount to professional suicide. He pouted at Alfred's reflection in the mirror.

"Just make sure it doesn't happen again." His turned his head sharply as he saw Patrick pass his door. "Oh, Patrick, a word please."

"Yes, Kenny?"

"You were a bit slow taking my hand on the stairs, you know, when you lead me down. I almost stumbled…"

"Sorry…"

"Yes, well don't let it happen again. It wouldn't do to let the star of the show break an ankle because you're off cue."

"Quite right, Kenny," Patrick said, straining to keep a smile from his face. "I'll make sure it won't happen again." He paused then asked. "Are you feeling all right? You look tense."

"Well, what d'you expect with all I have to put up with," Kenny groused. "Rude punters, stalkers, threats, blackmail." He shuddered dramatically. "No one knows, or cares, how shot my nerves are, and then I have to go one every night as though nothing was wrong. And you wonder why I look tense!"

Patrick tried to ignore Alfred's loud snigger, but Kenny turned on him, eyes flashing. "That's quite enough out of you, Alf," he snapped.

"Sorry, but you do go on, ducks." Alfred winked at Patrick. "Young Patrick was just being thoughtful, weren't you, dear?"

"Um… yes. Sorry about earlier," he said, turning to go. "Goodnight, Kenny… Alf."

"Yes, off you go," Kenny sneered. "Give that arsehole boyfriend of yours a nice blowjob from me, won't you?"

"*Kenny…*" Patrick heard Alfred say in a warning tone as he slipped from the room.

Patrick shook his head as he strode toward the stage door. There was no doubt in his mind that Kenny LaFontaine was the nastiest person he'd ever met—and deserved every bit of bad luck that came his way.

✞ ✞ ✞ ✞ ✞

Ian put a call through to Madrid the following morning. Based on what Patrick had told him about Kenny and George Osbourne having the murdered waiter in their room for a night of frolic and pleasure, it was obvious Kenny was still withholding evidence.

"First he denied that there ever was a murder," he told Ernest while he was kept on hold, "then he denied knowing who was blackmailing him right up until the time we showed him the body. Now it appears that both he and George knew the murdered man quite intimately."

"Makes you wonder what else he's not telling us," Ernest said grimly. "And that Alfred—manager cum dresser chappie—he knows a lot more than he's letting onto, if you ask me. He was in Madrid with Kenny, Ralph was too. They could all be in this, covering each other's arses."

"Right. It might be time to haul them all in for questioning," Ian remarked. "Let Kenny bring his solicitor, but we need some straight answers. Oh, hello..." He nodded at Ernest to let him know he'd been connected with the Madrid police office. "*Si...* this is Detective Ian Bannister, London Metro Police Force. Is Detective Pablo Lopez there? Gracias... Detective Lopez? Ian Bannister. I'm following up on the case of the murdered waiter at the Club La Fortuna, Alfonso Gomez."

"Ah, yes, Detective. That case is still open. Let me get the file."

"You have any suspects?" Ian asked when Lopez picked up again.

"Many suspects, but unfortunately Senor Gomez was a man who, shall we say, spread his favours far and wide."

"Meaning?"

"Meaning he was a male prostitute as well as a waiter, and the night he was murdered he was seen at a party in the company of several men, any one of whom could have been his killer."

"I understand you questioned some Englishmen with regard to what happened to Gomez."

"*Si*, that is correct. Some members of a transvestite show..."

"Kenny LaFontaine?"

"Correct, plus his boyfriend, George Osbourne."

"What about Alfred Manning and Ralph Murray?" He listened to what sounded like many papers being shuffled about.

"Yes. They were part of Kenny LaFontaine's show—his manager and his choreographer, but they were not with Gomez that night."

"So all your suspects had alibis?"

"Everyone vouched for one another, swearing that when the party was over, Gomez was very much alive."

"And after the party…?"

"He was found dead in his apartment the following morning. Do you have some new information, Detective Bannister?"

"Well, George Osbourne was the victim of a hit and run— we think it was a deliberate act. He was blackmailing Mr. LaFontaine…"

"Ah, the love affair was over."

"Looks that way. I'm looking for an involvement between Kenny LaFontaine, George Osbourne and Alfonso Gomez."

"Well, of course they could have been seeing each other before the party. We would have no way of knowing that."

"Unless one of your suspects knew about it."

"Possible," Lopez said. "Gomez has a brother, also a prostitute. He's in jail as we speak for soliciting in the Retiro. I will have a word with him about it."

"Thanks, let me know what you find out."

"I will. *Adios*, Detective."

"Anything?" Ernest asked as Ian put the phone down.

"Gomez was a male prostitute with many clients, according to Lopez. Anyone of them could be the killer. He was found dead after some big party that Kenny and George Osbourne attended."

"Something else our drag queen friend forgot to tell us," Ernest remarked sourly.

"He also neglected to tell us that he, Osbourne and Gomez got it on together in Kenny's room."

"How'd you know that?"

"I have eyes and ears backstage at Kenny's club."

"Ah, eyes and ears belonging to one Patrick Farland?" Ernest asked archly.

"You should be a detective, Detective," Ian chuckled.

Ernest smiled and tapped the side of his nose. "That's what my mother says too."

✞✞✞✞✞

Kenny bristled as he listened to what the two detectives had learned from the Spanish police.

"I can assure you that I had nothing to do with Alfonso's murder," he said between gritted teeth. "And I'm getting a little sick and tired of your innuendos. I have told you the truth from day one…"

"No you haven't," Ernest interjected. "We've had to wheedle it out of you bit by bit. You said there was no murder, you didn't know the victim, you didn't know the blackmailer—but now you know everything, so tell us, who killed Alfonso Gomez and George Osbourne?"

Kenny's face turned all shades of purple before he jumped to his feet and screamed at the top of his voice, "I don't fucking know! It wasn't me, that's all I know. Now get out of my home. I'm calling my solicitor and I'm going to file a very serious complaint about the pair of you. This is nothing less than harassment and trying to drag my name through the dirt. Well I won't have it, I tell you!"

Kenny fell back into his chair, his face pale. "Oh, I think I'm having a heart attack," he moaned. "Something else you'll have to explain to my solicitor."

Ian and Ernest exchanged glances then Ernest shrugged. "Call an ambulance, Ian," he said.

"Forget that," Kenny snarled, recovering quickly. "I have a show to do tonight. Just get the fuck out of here and leave me alone."

As they exited Kenny's flat, Ernest asked, "Do we have the fingerprint results back from the car yet?"

"Not yet. I'll check it out when we get back to the station. Oh, oh… look who's lurking on the other side of the street."

"That bloody Bert," Ernest muttered. "What is he, besotted with that drag queen or what?"

"Besotted's a good word I'd say," Ian chuckled. "Hey, Bert!" he yelled across the street. "Go on, clear off before you get in trouble again."

Bert threw them a forlorn look, then slouched off, his hands deep in his pockets.

"What a character," Ernest remarked. "He must be bloody barmy to want to have anything to do with that nasty piece of work upstairs."

"Love knows no barriers," Ian said, laughing lightly.

Ernest rolled his eyes. "I don't wish to know that!"

Later, after he got the fingerprint results from the Ford Escort, Ian called Patrick. "I need a favor from you, love. It's a bit unorthodox, and of course you can refuse to do it…"

"Have I ever refused you anything?" Patrick teased.

"No, but this isn't about us, Patrick. What I need are Kenny LaFontaine's fingerprints, from something he handles a lot, a comb or a brush…" He listened to Patrick's sharp intake of breath. "But like I said, you don't have to do this."

"No, I'll do it. You think Kenny's a suspect?"

"He's hiding something from us, that's for certain, and I don't think it's because he's trying to protect anyone. Somehow I just don't see him in the role of the protector."

"Definitely not," Patrick chuckled. "Okay, I'll see if I can get in there tonight."

"Make sure you handle whatever you choose carefully, try not to smudge the surface. And Patrick, please be very careful. I don't want you in any trouble because of this."

"Don't worry. I'll be careful. I'll see you after the show?"

"I'll be at our usual place."

"See you, then… and Ian, I love you."

"Love you too, Patrick."

✟ ✟ ✟ ✟ ✟

Patrick knew he'd have lots of opportunities after the show started to get inside Kenny's dressing room, as the star was onstage a great deal of the time, doing most of his changes backstage. He would just have to be careful that Alfred or one of the other dressers didn't see him go in, or wander in while he was there. He had ten minutes after he presented Kenny before he was onstage again, and didn't have a costume change. As he made his way toward the dressing room, he saw Ralph and a stagehand talking right outside the door.

Damn. He walked past them, nodding an acknowledgement, but received only a frosty glance from Ralph. He seemed to be far more interested in whatever the young stagehand was telling him. From his own dressing room he watched as the two men strolled off together towards Ralph's office.

Hmm... bit of hanky-panky going on there?

Patrick slipped out of his room and walked quickly to Kenny's door. No one inside... With one more glance behind him he entered the dressing room, his eyes scanning the array of makeup brushes, lipstick cases and eyeliner pencils that lay strewn across the dressing table.

What to choose? Better not take too long to decide.

He reached out to grab a contouring brush that had a particularly thick handle, then, remembering Ian's warning, picked it up by the bristles and smartly left the room. No one about, he noticed, suddenly realizing he'd been holding his breath the whole time he'd been in Kenny's dressing room.

"Whew!" He breathed a sigh of relief as he closed the door to his room behind him. *How do spies do this for a living?* he wondered, laying the brush on his dressing table. He'd be a nervous wreck in a week. *What to wrap it in?* Oh yes, a piece of plastic wrap off the dry cleaning bag his clean shirts were hanging in. Now he just had to hope Kenny didn't miss that one brush from all the others lying all over the table.

CHAPTER ELEVEN

Ian and Ernest stared at the fingerprint report they'd just received back from the lab.

"Blimey," Ernest muttered. "He's going to come unglued when we charge him with killing George Osbourne."

"And everything else we might find out from his statement," Ian commented. "Funny though, nasty bugger that he is, I didn't see him going this far."

"Really? I can absolutely see him doing someone in with that temper of his," Ernest said. "I wouldn't be surprised if we can tie him to that murder in Madrid."

"Maybe..."

Ernest gave Ian an impatient look. "That's Kenny LaFontaine's fingerprints on the door handle and the steering wheel of the car. And he had motive, what more d'you want?"

"You're right." Ian stood up and clapped Ernest on the shoulder. "Let's go tell the Inspector what we've got."

The newspaper banner headlines screamed the story in the evening edition. **'Kenny LaFontaine Arrested For Murder!'**

Patrick had asked Lawrence and Maggie over to his flat to commiserate with one another over the closing of Kenny's show due to the absence of the star, now remanded pending payment of bail. Patrick had told Lawrence to bring Albert along too as the pair seemed to be getting on very well together.

"You think he actually did this?" Lawrence asked the group as they sat around Patrick's living room devouring a pizza.

"Seems like he did," Maggie said. "Fingerprints don't get there by themselves, do they?"

"No wonder he asked me to deliver the phony parcel," Patrick remarked, tucking in to a slice of pizza. "He had to be somewhere else, waiting. And yet..." Patrick paused, munching thoughtfully.

"What?" Lawrence asked, putting his arm around Albert's shoulders.

"Kenny told me George Osbourne and he were lovers," Patrick said slowly. "He sounded genuinely upset that George had been killed."

"Bit of acting, maybe?" Albert suggested, leaning against Lawrence. "I mean, if you actually do the deed, wouldn't you try to cover up with the right kind of sob story?"

"Yes, but we've all seen Kenny's acting," Maggie said, chuckling. "He couldn't come across as convincing enough to fool any of us."

"So what are you saying?" Lawrence looked at his friends expectantly. "Kenny's a lousy actor, so he couldn't be a murderer?"

Maggie shook her head. "Or he's a lousy actor, *and* a murderer."

✤ ✤ ✤ ✤ ✤

"I have told you, a thousand times, I did not kill George Osbourne!" Kenny's voice, raised to a plaintive, whining cry, rebounded stridently off the concrete walls of the interrogation room. He looked hatefully at Ian. "How could you do this to me? After I let you into my innermost personal secrets, even showing that I was attracted to you, letting my guard down because I believed as a *gay man* you would have some sympathy for me!"

There was an awkward silence as Kenny's solicitor, Inspector Harris and the police officer guarding the door, all looked at Ian, who leaned forward in his chair and stared back at Kenny calmly.

"As I told you before, Mr. LaFontaine," he said, his voice firm and steady, "my sexual orientation has no bearing on whether I think you committed the crime you have been arrested for. If you would just explain to us exactly where you were at the time George Osbourne was murdered…"

"I've told you I was in bed asleep!" Kenny screamed, fresh tears forming in his eyes. "I didn't kill George—I told you, I loved him!"

Ernest snorted. "You told us you didn't know who George Osbourne was, you denied any knowledge of the murder in

Madrid, you lied to us about your association with Osbourne, you lied about every bloody thing until we had you by the short and curlys!"

"Please, Detective, that will be enough badgering of my client like that!" Peter Anderson, Kenny's solicitor, puffed out his chest as he spoke.

"Well, it's the truth," Ernest muttered.

Anderson glared at Inspector Harris. "Inspector, I must protest…"

"Yes, yes…" Harris waved a dismissive hand at the solicitor. "We're just trying to get to the truth here. As it stands, Mr. LaFontaine could save himself a lot of grief if he would just throw some light on the situation."

"I've told you all I know," Kenny whimpered. "I didn't drive the car that killed George, *honest*."

Over a cup of tea, Ernest vented his frustration on Ian. "Don't you want to cut that git's balls off for how he outed you in there?"

"He didn't out me, Ernest… well, maybe PC Huggins at the door and the solicitor fella didn't know, but you know and Harris knows, so what's the deal?"

"It'll be all over the station before you can say 'Well, I never'!"

"I can handle it, Ernest. But thanks for being there for me."

"You're my best mate," Ernest muttered, his face colouring. "I never think of you any other way. You still seeing that singer bloke then?"

"Patrick. Yes, I'm still seeing him."

"Good, seems like a decent chap."

"He is… Listen, Ernest, let me run something by you. Call me barmy if you like, but I don't think Kenny LaFontaine's our man."

Ernest raised his eyebrows. "*What?*"

"Doesn't it strike you as a bit too pat that first we find a blond wig in the car that just happens to belong to Kenny, and then his fingerprints show up? I mean, if he did this, why leave the wig there in the first place?"

"Maybe he was in a hurry to get out of the car and forgot about it."

"Possible. But why didn't he wear gloves, or wipe down the steering wheel? There's something strange about this, Ernest…"

"Blimey." Ernest stared hard at Ian. "And here I was thinking you'd be over the moon about him being the culprit."

Ian smiled wryly. "Believe me I'm not saying these things because I love Kenny LaFontaine. I just smell a rat somewhere. I think we need to talk to his manager, Alfred."

"You think *he* did it?"

"I think someone associated with LaFontaine did it, and Alfred just might be able to tell us a thing or two we don't know. Now that his star is in the clink, he just might be mouthier than before. I've got his number here…" Ian pulled his mobile from his pocket and dialed Alfred's number. After a couple of rings a depressed voice answered.

"Alfred Manning?"

"That's me."

"Detective Bannister here, Mr. Manning. My partner and I would like to have a word or two with you regarding Mr. LaFontaine's arrest."

"Oh yes? Want to gloat do you?"

"Not at all. There are one or two things we'd like to clear up."

"Well, I suppose. If it'll help Kenny."

"Where are you?"

"At the theatre, cleaning up Kenny's dressing room. He won't be using it for a while from the looks of things."

"We'll be right there, Mr. Manning."

Alfred chuckled wryly. "Be still my throbbing heart, I'm sure."

♥♥♥♥♥

Alfred sat down and stared up at the two detectives. "Won't you sit down? Makes me nervous when people tower over me… and you're both so tall."

Ernest grimaced but sat, while Ian leaned against Kenny's dressing table. "So Alfred, can you tell us a bit more about what happened in Madrid?" Ian asked, while Ernest pulled out his notebook and waited, pen poised at the ready.

"Oh, it was all terrible really," Alfred said, his voice quavering slightly. "I warned Kenny that it was all getting out of hand."

"What was getting out of hand?"

"The party—wild it was. Everyone was so drunk and out of control."

"Mr. LaFontaine was out of control?"

"Oh, no... but George and that waiter, Alfonso something-or-other... unbelievable really what they put away—and drugs too." Alfred shook his head, remembering. "Terrible it was..."

"So Ken... Mr. LaFontaine, George Osbourne and Alfonso Gomez all went back to a room after the party?"

"Oh, no. Not Kenny, not that night at any rate... It was just George and the waiter. Had a proper go around from what I heard later from George."

"What d'you mean?"

"Oh, dangerous stuff, you know... where they strangle each other as they come. It's supposed to prolong the orgasm."

"Jesus Christ," Ernest muttered.

"Is that how Alfonso Gomez died?" Ian asked quietly.

"I really don't know." Alfred shook his head sadly. "Nice boy, he was. Lovely eyes... He really liked Kenny, you know, but my Kenny couldn't see past George—more's the pity."

Ernest tapped his notebook impatiently. "Well, let me ask you this Alfred, who d'you think killed George Osbourne?"

"Someone who stole one of Kenny's wigs, I suppose."

"And who apart from you and your boss has access to those wigs?"

"No one..." Alfred's eyes widened. "So you're saying it was either me or Kenny that did George in? You're barking up the wrong tree if you think that. I didn't do it—I can't even drive if you must know—and I'm dead certain Kenny didn't do it. He wanted George back, if you can believe it."

"*Really?*" Ernest didn't even try to hide his sarcasm. "Every time he mentions Osbourne's name it's like he wanted to kill him. Said he was glad he'd got what was coming to him."

"He didn't mean it..."

Ernest chuckled nastily. "Yeah, well we've only got your word for that. According to the man himself, he was well rid of Osbourne."

Alfred sighed. "Kenny's temper makes him say things he doesn't really mean."

"And do things he doesn't really mean?" Ian asked.

Alfred's expression darkened. "Not kill anyone, if that's what you mean. Besides, George's killing seems very deliberate to me—lying in wait for him, so to speak. Kenny would never do that, never."

✟✟✟✟✟

After his friends had left, Patrick started to tidy up his flat, expecting that Ian would most likely call round on his way home to Ealing. He threw out the empty pizza boxes and washed up the glasses and cups they'd used. Maybe he'd have a bath…

Now when he thought about it, he hadn't seen his toilet bag since he'd packed his things up in the dressing room after they'd been told the show had been cancelled. He frowned as he walked into the bedroom and rummaged through the overnight bag he'd brought home from the club.

Damn, it wasn't there. He must have left it in the dressing room. He glanced at his watch—plenty of time to get over there and back before Ian showed up. He threw on his coat and hurried from the flat, jogging the half mile or so that would take him to Kenny's club.

The stage door keeper gave him a baleful glare as he pushed the door open. "We're closed!" the old curmudgeon snapped at Patrick.

"I know," Patrick snapped back. "I left something in my dressing room. I'll just get it and be gone before you can rattle your false teeth."

"Cheeky devil!"

"That's me," Patrick laughed as he ran down the corridor that led backstage. *Crabby old wanker.* As he approached his room he could hear voices coming from Kenny's dressing room. Voices raised in anger.

Sounds like Alfred, he thought, pausing outside his door. He listened for a few seconds more. *And Ralph*. He could only make out a few words, "Trusted you… Madrid… fucking behind his back…"

This could be important, Patrick thought, inching his way toward Kenny's dressing room. He could hear Ralph ask, "What did you tell those coppers that just left?"

"Nothing about you…" Alfred's voice sounded scared and quivery.

That bastard, Ralph, Patrick seethed, *scaring the old man like that.* Patrick felt he should break this up, but his curiosity got the better of him.

"You better not have," Ralph was saying hatefully. "Kenny's where he belongs, the bitch."

"How can you say that, after all he's done for you?" Alfred asked. "Without him, you'd be out of a job for a long time, believe me."

"I don't need him. My work speaks for itself. He was on his way out anyway. People are tired of drag queens—especially *talentless* drag queens!"

"Oh, you wouldn't dare say that to his face, Ralph," Alfred protested. "And besides, no one looks better in drag than Kenny, no one. He might not have the best singing voice, but he always looks incredible."

Ralph snorted with derision. "Yeah, well he won't look so good in prison drag, now will he? And by the time he gets out—if he ever does—he'll be too fucking old to stagger around in heels."

"You're really showing your true self, aren't you?" Alfred exclaimed. "I always knew you were a jealous bitch, but I never thought you'd stand by and see the man you owe everything to go to jail. I know Kenny didn't kill George any more than he killed Alfonso. I didn't tell the coppers you were keen on that boy too. Maybe I should have told them about you and George—maybe I still should…"

"You do and I'll break your scrawny neck, you old fart," Ralph hissed.

"I'm not scared of you." But the quaver in Alfred's voice betrayed him. "It wouldn't surprise me if you killed George. You took that wig, didn't you…?"

Patrick heard the sound of a slap and Alfred's startled cry of pain. *Right, time to break this up*! He pushed the door open and gasped as he saw Ralph with his hands round Alfred's throat.

"Hey! Stop that," he yelled, running into the room and pulling Ralph away from Alfred. "What the hell d'you think you're doing?"

With a surprising show of strength, Ralph flung Patrick aside and ran from the dressing room.

"You all right, Alfred?" Patrick asked, pulling his mobile phone from his pocket.

"Yes, yes," the older man gasped. "He's gone bonkers, that one…"

"You got him rattled," Patrick said dialing Ian's mobile number. "Ian? It's Patrick. Listen, Ralph just attacked Alfred then ran off when I got between them. They were talking about the murder in Madrid, and looks like Alfred got too close to the truth…"

Ian snapped his mobile shut and gave Ernest, who was driving, a sideways glance. "It looks like we've been barking up the wrong tree, Ernest. That was Patrick. Seems like Ralph Murray, the choreographer, just tried to off old Alfred."

"*What?*"

"We better bring him in for questioning."

"Too bloody right," Ernest muttered. "We have an address for him?"

"Mm…" Ian consulted his notepad. "Seventy-six Harlow Road… not far from here, actually. Take the next right to Baker Street."

"You think he'll be at home?"

"We'll find out, won't we? If not, we can have an officer detailed to watch out for him."

"So what did Patrick say exactly?"

"Only that he overheard Alfred accuse Murray of stealing the wig and killing George Osbourne."

"Blimey…" Ernest stared intently through the windscreen. "Isn't that him? Look, the bloke running up the steps there…"

"That's him, all right. Pull over quick, Ern!" Ian jumped out of the car as it came to a screeching halt outside the building Ralph had just entered. Ian put his shoulder to the locked door but the solid wood didn't budge an inch. He rang every doorbell, including the one marked 'RALPH MURRAY FLAT SIX,' holding his palm pressed to the buttons until the door was opened by a little old lady who glared up at him with annoyance.

"What's all this then?" she demanded.

"Police," Ian barked, brushing past her. "Hold the door for my partner..."

"Ooh, fancy that," the old biddy gasped, watching Ian take the stairs two at a time. "Better than the telly, this is!"

Ian rapped on Ralph's door. "Police, Mr. Murray. Open up, please."

The door was flung open, and a terrified Ralph tried to push his way past Ian, who promptly grabbed him and pinned him against the wall.

"I haven't done anything," Ralph shrieked at the top of his voice. "Help, help. Police brutality!"

"Shut it," Ernest growled, heaving himself up the last of the stairs. "If you haven't done anything, where were you going in such a hurry?"

"You can answer our questions at the station, Mr. Murray," Ian told Ralph through clenched teeth. "We have an eye witness who saw you attack Alfred Manning," he added as he pulled Ralph down the stairs.

"Fucking Patrick," Ralph spat.

"Nice of you not to deny it," Ernest said, winking at Ian.

"Oh, Mr. Murray..." The old woman still holding the door open gaped at Ralph. "Whatever did you do?"

"Mind your own business, you nosy bitch," Ralph hissed at her.

"Oh... well." She bristled, and for a moment Ernest thought she was going to kick Ralph as they hustled him past her. "Whatever it was, I hope you're gone for a long time. None of us here like you, you know!"

⚜ ⚜ ⚜ ⚜ ⚜

Kenny LaFontaine Innocent! Choreographer's Confession Clears Drag Star!

Kenny LaFontaine, famed female impersonator, was released from custody today after Ralph Murray, a choreographer in LaFonataine's employ for several years, admitted to the murder of George Osbourne, LaFontaine's ex-lover. Murray also confessed to the murder, in Madrid, of Alfonso Gomez, a male prostitute…

✤✤✤✤✤

"So, Ralph and George were lovers?" Patrick asked drowsily, raising his head from the warmth of Ian's chest. The two were slowly recovering from a bout of passionate lovemaking that had, not surprisingly, taken precedence over any conversation about the Ralph Murray situation.

"If you can call it that," Ian replied, stroking Patrick's hair. "George Osbourne apparently couldn't keep his dick in his pants, and Ralph hated Kenny enough to want to take his boyfriend from him—except that Ralph wasn't enough for Osbourne."

"Enter Alfonso, the waiter."

"Right… I guess Alfonso Gomez was everyone's wet dream. Everyone wanted him, including Kenny and Osbourne—and Ralph. The night Gomez was murdered, Osbourne and Ralph were with him, but Osbourne left, completely zonked on drugs and booze. He didn't remember until later that Ralph had even been there. When he did remember, and found out that Gomez had been murdered, he told Ralph he'd be quiet if Ralph made it worth his while."

"Blackmail…"

"Yes, but it wasn't enough to support his drug habit, so he decided to squeeze Kenny for more. Ralph overheard Kenny and Alfred talking about it, and how Osbourne was going to be at the supermarket to pick up the money. He figured it was just a matter of time before Osbourne forgot his 'promise' to stay quiet about what happened in Madrid and implicated him in Gomez' murder."

"So Ralph was the blond driver?"

"Uh, huh. Alfred had left the storage cabinet unlocked while he was helping Kenny with a quick change on the side of the stage. Ralph stole the wig, lifted some prints of Kenny's from his champagne glass, then transferred them to the car's steering wheel and door handle."

"Clever."

"Very... though I felt it was all just too much of a coincidence. You know, finding the wig that just happened to belong to Kenny, and then his fingerprints all over the place."

Patrick chuckled. "Yeah, like there was a big red arrow pointing right at the top of Kenny's head."

"Exactly. It looked bad for Kenny right then, but when I started to think about it, it just didn't make sense. Why hadn't he worn gloves, or wiped the car down?"

Patrick let his fingers stray across the smooth warm flesh of Ian's torso, and sighed. "I should feel guilty at being so happy, I suppose."

Ian kissed Patrick's forehead. "Why on earth should you feel guilty?"

"Because I've got you, the best looking copper in the land, we've just had some lovely sex, and will most likely have some more once you get your strength back..."

"Hey..."

Patrick laughed and tweaked Ian's nipple. "Just kidding... but that's why I think I should feel guilty. I'm just so happy."

"So am I." Ian tilted Patrick's face to his and gave him a long, loaded kiss. "And I feel no guilt whatsoever."

✦✦✦✦✦

Kenny sat back in his dressing room chair and eyed Patrick up and down. "Alfred told me if it hadn't been for you, he might have been a goner," he said, somewhat stiffly. "I have to thank you for that."

Patrick shrugged. "I just happened to be there picking up some stuff I'd left behind."

"Nevertheless, it was good you were there." Kenny tried to smile. "You and I haven't always got along, but now the show's opening again—with unprecedented advance booking I might add—I'd like to offer you a permanent job as my lead singer."

"Thanks, Kenny. I appreciate that," Patrick said as sincerely as he could. "But I have accepted a part in a new West End musical, so..."

"Oh, musicals come and go," Kenny interrupted with a slight sneer. "This job would have a lot more longevity, I can assure you."

Would it? Patrick thought. Kenny's quicksilver mood changes might close it very quickly. "That's a really nice offer, but I've signed the contract."

"Oh, well then…" Kenny sighed and resumed attending to his makeup. Patrick hid the smile that threatened to play on his lips. He could tell his refusal had afforded Kenny a certain amount of relief. No doubt Alfred had insisted Kenny make the offer.

"Pity about Ralph," Patrick said.

Kenny gave him a narrow-eyed look. "Pity? That ungrateful swine wanted to see me locked away. The bastard was doing George and that Spanish waiter behind my back—he and George had been up each other's arses for years from the sounds of it." Kenny shuddered. "When I think of the times they both swanned around me like butter wouldn't melt… Oh, it just makes me want to throw up. Alfred always said I was too trusting, always too ready to give to those who least deserved it—and how right he was." He wagged a finger at Patrick. "There's a lesson for all of us there—you can't trust anyone, not *anyone.*"

Patrick left Kenny's room, smiling ruefully. He hadn't missed Kenny's insinuation about not trusting anyone, and he hadn't wanted to argue the point just then. He was obviously still pissed off that Ian didn't fancy him. He peeked into Lawrence and Albert's dressing room but didn't go in. They were far too busy exploring each other's lips to need company at that moment.

"Hello, Patrick," He turned to find Maggie waving at him from her dressing room door. "Come on in. The other girls aren't here yet." She gave him a hug and kiss. "Quite a revelation, eh?"

"I'll say." Patrick grinned at her. "As much as I disliked Ralph, I never saw him as a murderer."

"Oh, I don't know," Maggie said giggling. "He looked like he could kill Kenny a couple of times—and you, even—during rehearsals.

"You're right. All that rage seething underneath all the time. What a creep."

"How's your copper?"

"Lovely. I'm seeing him later after the show."

"And Lawrence finally got the nerve up to put a move on Albert."

"Tell me," Patrick laughed. "I just caught the two of them going at it in their dressing room."

"Lawrence is over the moon, bless him," Maggie said, smiling. "Well, now my two best gay friends are all hooked up, I don't feel so guilty about being a happily married woman."

Patrick frowned. "You feel guilty about being married to Tom?"

"Not really, but it sounded good, didn't it?"

Kenny's return to the stage was a tumultuous triumph. His audience greeted his appearance, shimmering in a gown of ice blue and gold, with a standing rapturous ovation. Wisely, he had cut his unpopular finale where he appeared out of drag singing two self-composed ditties. He had replaced it with a stunning fashion parade of practically every gown he owned as the dancers leaped about and Patrick sang, 'Isn't He Lovely?' As the curtain rang down after his twelfth bow, Kenny felt a sense of triumph mixed with some bitterness. Shedding his costume and makeup in his dressing room, he sighed as he watched Alfred pour them both a glass of champagne.

"Why don't I feel on top of the world, Alfred?" he asked, unable to keep the whine out of his voice.

"You will, love, you will," Alfred said soothingly. "Time takes care of everything, and let's face it, you've got bigger audiences now than you ever had. That has to count for something."

"I suppose... but I can't take the audience home with me." He stared sulkily at his reflection in the mirror. "Why can't I find a fella? I mean, that Patrick waltzed off with that dishy detective from right under my nose, and just a minute ago I saw those two boy dancers canoodling in the corner, hands all over each other. Shit. Everyone's got someone, except me!"

"You'll find someone, darling, don't worry." Alfred turned away so Kenny couldn't see him rolling his eyes. "Just when you least expect it, your knight in shining armor will jump right out in front of you."

"Bollocks," Kenny muttered.

He was still in a foul mood when his cab dropped him off in front of his flat. As he fumbled with his key, he caught the shadow of a man standing nearby.

"You again!" he snapped. "What d'you want, following me about at this time of the night?"

Bert Halford stepped forward eagerly. "Just to meet you, Kenny. I think you're so wonderful!"

"Oh, you do, do you?" Kenny squinted at Bert. In the light from the street lamp above the door, Kenny took in the fresh, youthful face that smiled shyly at him. *Blimey, I never noticed he's quite the looker. And he seems more put together, smarter...*

"Yes, you're ever so talented, Kenny—beautiful and funny. And..." Bert paused and looked into Kenny's eyes. "I never for one moment believed you did those terrible things. I knew the police had it all wrong."

"Did you now? Well, well..." Kenny gave Bert a long look from under his lashes. "Bert, isn't it? You still need a job?"

"Well, I actually just started working at the post office, but..."

Kenny gave Bert a dazzling smile. "I think we should go upstairs so you can tell me more about yourself. We'll have a glass of bubbly to celebrate your new job, and then we'll see what comes up, shall we?"

Kenny took the smiling Bert's arm, unlocked the door, and together they entered the building. *Well*, he thought as they climbed the stairs side by side, *sometimes life's not such a drag.* He let his hand slide over Bert's round bottom. *You just have to take what it gives out—with both hands, if you're lucky.*

Women's Weeds

Kimberly Gardner

CHAPTER ONE

"When you read Shakespeare's *Twelfth Night*, keep in mind that the roles are all being played by men."

David scanned the students' faces. Was anybody even still listening? He glanced at the clock. Five minutes to go and fully half the class had already closed their notebooks. A girl in the first row appeared to be text messaging on her cell. And a kid in the back of the room had already plugged in the earbuds for his iPod. His head bopped back and forth in time with whatever he was listening to instead of David's lecture.

Suppressing a sigh, David glanced down at his notes and continued as if he hadn't noticed he'd already lost them.

"When we see Cesario in *Twelfth Night*, we see a woman playing a man. When Shakespeare's audiences saw this play, they saw in Cesario, not a girl in boy's clothing, but a youth of twelve to fourteen working through romantic involvements with two older men. Can somebody name those two characters for me?"

Nothing. Not even a glimmer.

"Those would be the Captain and Orsino." He wrote Captain and Orsino on the board. Then drew a circle around the two names.

Still nothing.

"I'll probably ask this on the test so..."

There was an instant flurry of activity. Pens appeared. Notebooks and laptops opened.

David waited while they wrote it down.

In the back row a hand appeared. It was Mr. iPod. He tugged an earbud from one ear.

"What did you say?"

⚜⚜⚜⚜⚜

Clutching his scarred leather satchel and keeping his head down, David made his way across campus toward the faculty parking lot. The ends of his jacket flapped in the frigid February wind. Just as he reached his car, his cell phone began to vibrate against his hip. He plucked it from its clip on his belt and glanced at the display. It was his sister, Bethany.

Opening the car door, he dropped his bag on the back seat then slid behind the wheel, flipped open the phone and held it to his ear.

"Hey, Beth, what's going on?" David stuck the key in the ignition and started the engine. Freezing air blew from the vents and he hurriedly shut off the blower.

"Nothing much. How was class?"

"Horrendous."

She chuckled.

"Sure, laugh all you want. You never got stuck teaching Intro to a bunch of kids who couldn't care less about theater in general or Shakespeare in particular."

"Well, what did you expect, being low man on the faculty totem-pole? And those so-called kids aren't that much younger than you, little brother."

"Maybe not, but they make me feel about a hundred." David clicked the seatbelt in place. "And they completely ignore me until I say the magic words."

"What are the magic words?"

"This is going to be on the test."

They both laughed and David put the car in gear.

"Poor baby."

"Thanks for all the sympathy."

"Oh c'mon Davie. Most of those kids are there just to fulfill a fine arts requirement, not because they have a burning desire to be great Shakespearean actors."

"Who do you think you're telling?" David eased the car out of the parking lot and into traffic. Only one semester under his belt and he already knew that teaching, even teaching Shakespeare in the theater department of his alma mater, was not his cup of tea. It was just a means to an end, a way to earn a living until he could write and direct in his own theater company, not only for love but for actual money.

"David, are you even listening to me?"

"No. Sorry, I was thinking… and driving. What did you say?"

She blew out a breath. "I asked if you could possibly pick up a bottle of wine on your way. Brent was supposed to stop at the liquor store on his way home but he forgot."

"On my way…"

There was a moment of silence.

"To my house? For dinner? You forgot, didn't you?"

Shit. And it was Bethany's birthday dinner too. Double shit.

"No. In fact, I'm in the car right now."

Okay, it was only half a lie. He had completely forgotten about going to his sister's for dinner, true, but he was in the car. Which made the statement at least as much true as false.

Bethany sighed. "You lie like a dog, Davie. But I think I can forgive you for forgetting my birthday dinner if you stop and pick up some wine. We're having Brent's famous chicken marsala so why don't you get a nice red." She paused. "You are still coming, aren't you?"

"Of course I'm coming. I wouldn't miss your birthday for anything."

David watched his plans for the evening evaporate like so much smoke on a windy day. Not that he had anything, or anyone, especially compelling to rush home to. Hell, he hadn't even had a real date in… Well, longer than he cared to remember. No, the only real 'plans' he had for the evening included nothing more exciting than takeout Chinese, his laptop, and the final revisions on act two of the play he was writing. But that wasn't happening either, not tonight, because his only sister was turning twenty-nine tomorrow and they never missed seeing each other for their birthdays.

He made the next left, which took him away from the city and toward his sister's four bedroom colonial in Wynmore. He glanced at his watch. He should have just enough time to make a quick stop at the booze store and…

Crap. He didn't have a present for Bethany either. Just one more thing he'd meant to do that had fallen through the cracks. Looked like he'd be swinging by the mall on his way to dinner. Hopefully, the marsala would keep an extra fifteen or twenty minutes.

Ten minutes later with two bottles of a good merlot safely tucked in behind the driver's seat, David made a beeline for the mall, parked his car and walked to the nearest entrance, which, conveniently, took him directly into Macy's, Bethany's favorite store.

Now how fast could he grab a bottle of perfume or a pair of earrings or—

"Excuse me. Would you like to try a new fragrance today?"

"Thanks, but I don't think—" David stopped, the old mental train derailing right in mid-thought.

In front of him, only feet away, well within touching distance, stood the most beautiful man he'd ever seen.

Hair so black it looked blue fell in glossy waves around a pale heart-shaped face. Cheekbones sharp enough to chip ice, a full, soft mouth and delicately pointed chin completed the picture.

God, he was gorgeous.

"Yes," David said, suddenly regaining his power of speech.

The bluest eyes David had ever seen gazed up at him. "Yes, what?"

Yes, anything you say.

"Yes, I'll take some of that... What is it?"

The vision laughed. "It's called Frisson. It's a new unisex cologne. But don't you want to smell it before you buy it?"

"Sure." David leaned close and inhaled. "I think it's perfect. Just what I'm looking for."

A slight blush stained those amazing cheeks. "I'm not wearing it. In fact, I'm not wearing any cologne." He held up the atomizer and shook it. "Give me your hand."

David held out his hand. The inside of his wrist was spritzed. Long elegant fingers massaged the spot.

David's pulse jumped.

"You have to rub it in before you smell it." The angel continued to stroke David's wrist, the tips of his fingers lingering over the pale tracing of veins. "Here, now smell."

David sniffed. The fragrance was light and spicy with a hint of citrus. It was nice, but nothing compared to the intoxicating scent of the beautiful man with the big blue eyes and the perfume atomizer.

"So what do you think?" The angel blinked impossibly long lashes. And was he really wearing mascara and eyeliner?

"I'll take it."

"Great." The smile that blossomed felt to him like a ray of sunshine on an otherwise cloudy day.

He found himself leaning, if ever so slightly, toward that warmth the way a flower grows toward the sunlight.

"If you'll step over to the counter, Ginger will ring you up."

David's heart skipped a beat. He glanced toward the checkout where the girl, Ginger, was assisting an older woman who was slowly making her way through each and every sample bottle on the counter.

"Can't you ring me up? She looks a little busy."

"I'm not really supposed to."

"I'm in kind of a hurry."

Even white teeth worried a plump lower lip. At last he nodded and set down the atomizer. "Okay. I guess it'll be all right just this once. Follow me, please?"

Anywhere you want, baby.

David followed the few steps to the checkout. As the young man slipped behind the counter, he let his gaze slide down the lithe body clad in dark chinos and white button-down shirt. The cut of the pants was loose but not so much that David couldn't see the tempting swell of a very pert, very round little ass.

David's mouth watered and his cock twitched. Oh, how he wanted to grab a double handful of that adorable ass and crush their bodies together as he devoured the kid in three quick bites.

"Will this be on your Macy's charge?"

David shook his head. Pulling out his wallet, he extracted his credit card and held it out. "Visa."

He took the card. Their fingers brushed.

Thank God he was wearing a long shirt because David was getting hard, right here in the middle of Macy's fragrance department, for God's sake!

"Could you possibly gift wrap that for me?"

"It's not for you?" He handed David a pen and the slip to sign.

"No, it's a birthday present." David signed his name.

A slight frown appeared between finely arched dark brows. "Girlfriend?"

"Um, no." David handed the slip and the pen back across the counter.

"Boyfriend?" The lashes lowered and a smile flirted with the corners of those pretty lips.

Was this angel flirting with him?

"Not currently." David swallowed. "What about you?"

Crouching down, the salesboy—he couldn't be more than twenty—retrieved some wrapping paper from under the counter and set it down beside the box.

"I don't have a boyfriend either."

Oh. My. God. He is flirting with me.

Dropping his gaze, David focused on the slim hands. The paper was neatly folded around the box. A piece of tape was torn from the roll and affixed to the white and gold wrapping.

"Do you think maybe I could take you out some time?"

The hands stilled.

Please, let him say yes. David sent up a brief prayer to the patron saint of lonely, overworked gay directors.

"I get off in ten minutes. Maybe we could have coffee or something."

Yes!

No!

Damnit!

He lifted his gaze and met those melt-you-on-the-spot blue eyes. "I'm really sorry, but I have to go to my sister's for dinner." He gestured at the box on the counter. "It's her birthday and I promised—"

"No problem." Ribbon was wrapped around the box and a fluffy bow fashioned. "Maybe tomorrow then."

Clearly Saint Fabulous was not hearing him. At this rate he'd never get his hands, or mouth, or anything else for that matter on this oh so sizzling example of male hotness.

"I have auditions tomorrow."

"Oh? Are you an actor?"

"Director, Sort of. I mean I am a director, but it's just a little, nonprofit community theater, nothing major." When his angel said nothing, David ploughed ahead. He was so not going to blow this, not if he could help it. "I'm directing a production of *Twelfth Night* at the Hartwell Community Theatre. It's a company called Fresh Voices and we're just getting off the ground. I'm one of the founding members so…"

David forced himself to stop. He could go on for hours talking about the theater company he and Bethany had started a year ago with all the money they each had in the world. He occasionally had to remind himself that not everyone was as enamored with nonprofit community theater as he was. And the last thing he wanted to do was bore the most promising potential hook-up he'd had in months.

"Really? *Twelfth Night*? I love that play."

"Yeah. We're holding auditions tomorrow night. But I'd really like to—"

"Excuse me." A heavyset blonde in a fuzzy pink sweater and black sweat pants nudged David aside and plunked a box down on the counter. "I'd like to buy this and I've been waiting for the last ten minutes."

Pushy bitch.

David opened his mouth to tell her to wait her turn and the phone behind the counter rang.

With an apologetic smile, his angel picked up the receiver. "Hello? Fragrance counter."

Maybe he should look for a new patron saint.

Chapter Two

"How easy is it for the proper-false in women's waxen hearts to set their forms! Alas, our frailty is the cause, not we! For such as we are made of, such we be. How will this fadge? My master loves her dearly, and I, poor monster, fond as much on him, and she, mistaken, seems to dote on me."

A pause, the first one since Julie had begun reading. Did she have any clue at all what the lines meant? Probably not, and her next question only confirmed it.

She lifted her gaze from the sheaf of pages in her hand. "Um, David, what does fadge mean anyway?"

Which was, David thought, why Intro to Shakespeare was such a necessary part of a fine arts curriculum. Too bad the students didn't see it that way.

Sitting beside David in the first row of the small theatre, Bethany stifled a chuckle behind her hand.

Before David could reply, Fred, the actor on stage with her, chimed in. "It means work out."

"Oh. Really?" She pulled a pen from her pocket and wrote something on her script. "I'll have to remember that."

David got to his feet. "Thanks, Julie. You too Fred. We'll give you a call in a day or two."

"Don't you want me to read the scene with Olivia?"

God no!

David smiled. "That won't be necessary."

"But that's my favorite scene. It's the one I practiced. And that's the one you had Erin read."

"I think I've heard enough." Someone snorted a laugh. David ignored them.

For a moment he was sure she was going to argue, then she smiled and started flipping through her script. "My mom loves this play. She's just going to freak when she hears I'm playing Viola."

"I won't be making up my mind until the end of the week." David took the pages from her as she reached the bottom of the steps that led off the stage. "We'll be meeting again on Thursday and I'll finalize the casting then."

"Why don't you just give it to me now?" She tossed her mane of blond hair over one shoulder. "There's no one else young enough to play Viola." She stepped off the bottom step and walked to where she'd left her stuff on a chair in the second row.

"There's Erin. She could play Viola."

Julie rolled her eyes. "She's just a high school kid."

Oh, and like you're so experienced Miss What-Does-Fadge-Mean-Anyway.

She picked up her jacket and slipped it on. "You know my dad is all excited that we're doing Shakespeare. And don't forget he owns this building."

David's smile never tipped even as he prayed for patience. "Whether he does or not really doesn't play into my decision."

"I was just teasing you, David. God! If I can't get the part on my own..." She sent him an indecipherable look and slung her backpack over one shoulder. As she made her way toward the back of the theatre David thought he heard her mutter something about getting a sense of humor.

The door at the back opened, letting in a blast of cold air. Halfway up the center aisle, Julie squealed and bounded forward.

"Daddy! What are you doing here? Mom said you were in Pittsburgh." She threw her arms around a middle-aged man in a gray tweed overcoat. She hugged him hard and he pecked a kiss on the top of her head.

Greg Redman said something to his daughter that David couldn't hear then inclined his head toward the rear of the theater.

Julie shook her head and, sliding her arm through her father's, led him up the center aisle toward where David and Bethany stood.

Smiling broadly, the man held out his hand as he reached them. "David, how've you been?" They shook. "Bethany, you look well." He produced a ring of keys from his coat pocket. "I brought by the other set of keys for this building."

David took them. "You didn't have to do that, Greg. I told you I would come by your office and pick them up."

Or he could have given them to Julie to drop off.

"That's quite all right. I didn't want Julie walking home in the dark so I thought I'd come by and pick her up." He cast a fond look on his daughter, who preened. "And I wanted to see if we could arrange a meeting, maybe Thursday late afternoon at my office, so we could talk about that grant proposal you submitted. I had a few questions before I take it to the board of directors."

"I have class until two on Thursday," David said. "But I'm free after that."

They arranged to meet Thursday at four-thirty and Greg Redman turned to go.

"C'mon Fred," Julie called over her shoulder as she and her father headed toward the door at the back. "We'll give you a ride home." She held up the keys and jingled them. "I'm driving."

Fred, who was still hanging around even though auditions were done for the night, shook his head. "No thanks, Jules. I want to talk to David a minute and I have to stop somewhere on the way home."

"Okay. Whatever."

As the door swung shut behind Greg and Julie Redman, Bethany let out a sigh. "So what do you think is up with Greg? You don't think there's a problem with the proposal, do you?"

With a slight shake of his head, David indicated Fred seated on the edge of the stage and flipping through his script. David wasn't about to discuss their financial situation in front of the other man.

What the hell had ever made him think Fred was hot anyway? Good looking in that bland sort of all-American way maybe, but hot? He liked to think that the two dates Fred had talked him into had been simply lapses of judgment on his part and not a total lack of sense. Still, he hated being reminded that he'd actually considered, no matter how briefly, having sex with this guy.

David walked over and stood next to Fred. Not too close, but near enough that the other man had to be aware of his presence.

"You wanted to talk to me?"

As usual Fred wouldn't quite meet David's eyes. "Yeah." He licked his lips.

His gaze slid sideways toward Bethany. "I was thinking maybe we could get together and talk about your vision for Orsino."

Crap. He so did not want to get together with Fred. Not now. Not ever. Of course, if he intended to cast him as Orsino and coax a decent performance out of him, he couldn't say so.

It seemed diplomacy was the word of the night.

"Didn't you hear me tell Julie I haven't made up my mind about casting yet?"

"I'm the best actor you've got. Who else are you going to cast as Orsino? Evan?"

"I might," David said, already knowing he would be casting Fred as the duke of Illyria. Damn if he'd tell him that though.

Fred snorted and slid off the edge of the stage. "Yeah right. We'll talk Friday then, if you insist."

David watched him walk up the center aisle, noting the extra little swivel he put in his hips.

What a jerk.

"I told you we should have done Moliere." Bethany got to her feet. "Shakespeare is hell."

"Shakespeare is heaven," David countered. "Community theatre is hell."

"No, just the actors."

"Yeah well, we couldn't do it without them."

"Too bad that." They both laughed. "Viola is such a great role." She stretched, one hand pressed to the small of her back. "It's a shame we don't have anyone besides Julie who can play her."

"Is your back hurting?" David slipped his clipboard into his bag and zipped it closed.

Bethany nodded. "A little. Must be from sitting in these crappy seats." She rubbed a hand over her belly. "I thought I'd have to be a lot more pregnant than this before my back would really start aching."

"Maybe you should call the doctor."

She shook her head. "I just need to go home and put my feet up." She paused. "What about Viola? What are you going to do?"

David shrugged. "Unfortunately, Julie is right. I really don't have anyone else who can even come close to a convincing Viola. Unless you want to give it a try."

Bethany rolled her eyes. "Oh please, David. I haven't acted in years. Besides, I don't think a pregnant Viola is quite what you're looking for. And we won't even talk about a pregnant Cesario."

David suppressed a smile. Bethany was right, of course.

"I guess I can always work with her."

"That's the spirit. As long as she can learn the lines, she'll do all right. And if anyone can manage to get a decent performance out of her, it's you."

The outside door banged open, admitting a rush of frigid air.

David and Bethany both turned to look, and David's breath caught. Coming toward them down the center aisle was the beautiful young man from the Macy's fragrance counter. Their gazes met and he smiled. "Am I too late?"

David opened his mouth but found he had forgotten how to form words.

"Too late for what?" Bethany stepped forward.

"To audition." The young man glanced at Bethany then his gaze turned back toward David. He bit his lip. "Do you remember me? From Macy's—"

David nodded and found his voice. "Of course I remember you. No, you're not too late, but how did you know—"

"You said you were a director. And you told me the name of your theatre company. So I Googled it and," he made a little voila gesture, "here I am."

Bethany cleared her throat.

Blue eyes looked from David to his sister and back. "The website said the auditions were open, but if—"

"They are." Suddenly remembering his manners, David tore his gaze from the vision and turned to his sister. "Beth, this is... God, I don't even know your name."

"It's Kieran. Kieran Reilly." He held out his hand.

David took it. The hand was warm. The grip strong and sure. He imagined that hand on more intimate parts of his body and a frisson of lust shivered through him. "I'm David Sullivan."

He couldn't believe it. This angel had taken the trouble not only to look him up but to come here in search of him. Stuff like this just didn't happen to him.

There was another throat clearing from Bethany.

Self-consciously David released Kieran's hand. "This is Bethany Anderson. She's the set designer and she also does the costumes."

"I'm also David's sister and when I'm not pregnant I hang the lights and work the sound board and do whatever else needs doing."

"Yeah, Beth is my Girl-Friday for most of our productions."

Bethany shook Kieran's hand. "We were just about finished for the night." She eyed David. "But I'm sure we could hear you read."

"I don't want to keep you."

"It's no trouble." Bethany turned to David. "You're not in any rush, are you?"

David shook his head. "Me? No, no rush." He set his bag down on a nearby chair and dug inside for a script. He held it out. "We're doing *Twelfth Night*."

Kieran nodded. "You told me." He flipped pages. "This is my favorite Shakespeare play."

"Have you acted before, Kieran?" Bethany slipped out of her coat and tossed it over the back of a chair.

"I got my bachelors in acting last year from Arcadia University."

"Wow, a real actor. We're not going to know how to act."

"No pun intended," David said. He opened his script. "Which part were you interested in?"

Kieran's cheeks flushed and David felt his heart do a funny little back flip in his chest. God, he so needed to get a grip. He was acting like he'd never auditioned, maybe never even seen, a good looking guy before.

"I'd like to read for Viola, if that's all right."

"That would be great," Bethany said. "It'll be just like in Shakespeare's time with a male actor playing a female role." She nudged David. "Won't that be great, director man?"

"I hadn't really thought of having a man play Viola." But his brain had begun to spin through the possibilities. Kieran was slight, probably no more than five-six or so, and he was certainly as pretty as any girl David had ever seen. And wasn't the whole premise built around the switching of gender roles? So wouldn't it be perfect to have a man play a woman playing a man?

And suddenly David knew he'd found his Viola. Now if only, by some miracle, Kieran could actually act.

He offered a script to Bethany. "Feel like being an Illyrian count for a few minutes?"

"I can do that." She took the script. "Same scene the others read?"

David nodded.

Kieran and Bethany began to read the same lines Julie and Fred had crashed through only moments before.

David took a seat in the front row. He fought to keep his mind on the audition where it belonged rather than on how hot Kieran Reilly looked in his ripped and faded jeans and his white button-down shirt with the tails hanging to mid-thigh. He could almost see himself on his knees at Kieran's feet, those long fingers fisted in his hair, and how the unbuttoned shirt would frame that slim torso as he mouthed Kieran's prick through his jeans. David loved sucking cock, and he was good at it too. He would have Kieran trembling with need in no time.

Shutting his eyes, David inhaled. He imagined he could practically smell the other man's desire as he pictured himself nuzzling the hard, hot length through the snug denim.

"...My state is desperate for my master's love. As I am woman—now alas the day!—what thriftless sighs shall poor Olivia breathe! O time! Thou must untangle this, not I, it is too hard a knot for me to untie!"

There was a moment of silence.

"Kieran, do you already know this play?" Bethany was studying Kieran, who flushed and bit his lip.

"Sort of. I played Viola when I was in school. It was a long time ago but I guess the lines stuck with me."

"It can't have been that long ago."

He shrugged. "Three or four years."

"Wow, that's great. Isn't that great, David?"

David jumped. His copy of the script slid to the floor in a flurry of pages.

Shit. He'd completely lost track of the action on stage, he was so taken with the action in his head.

"What? Yeah, terrific." David caught the look his sister sent him and felt his cheeks grow hot.

"Well, that's one less person we have to worry about getting off book." Bethany descended the steps from the stage, her hand once more pressed to her lower back. "He's so cute," she mouthed then grinned at her brother as she passed him her script. "I'm out of here, if you don't need me for anything else." She looked back to where Kieran stood at the top of the stairs. "It was nice meeting you, Kieran."

She sent David another meaningful look as she put on her coat.

He turned away from his sister's too-perceptive gaze. Even at twenty-five, she still had the uncanny knack for making him feel like an awkward adolescent.

Of course no one knew him better than she did. It was just the two of them and they had always been close. He adored her and the feeling was totally mutual. So given all that, it was no stretch to think that she could see his attraction for Kieran.

And not more than two minutes later, David found himself alone in the theater with the object of his little fantasy.

Oh yeah, no doubt about it. His sister saw how much he wanted Kieran Reilly, and not just to play Viola either.

David tugged ever so nonchalantly at the hem of his sweatshirt. His dick was a steel fencepost behind his zipper. Thank goodness for long shirts since he couldn't seem to control his body's reaction around Kieran. And what would he say if he knew what David had been thinking only minutes before?

Kieran descended the steps, reaching the bottom just as David did. He paused on the last step, bringing them eye to eye. And, David couldn't help noticing, cock to cock.

God help him.

For what felt like forever they just stared at each other, neither one speaking. Kieran's eyes were so blue he could happily drown in them.

He searched his brain for something to say, some witty comment or compliment that wouldn't sound too trite. But before he came up with anything, Kieran reached up and plucked David's glasses right off his face.

"What are you doing?"

"I wanted to see your eyes without the lenses." He leaned forward. "You have beautiful eyes. So dark. So sexy."

Knowing he had a tendency to squint without his glasses, David fought the urge. He let out a short laugh. "Thank you. Except I can't see a damn thing without them."

"That's all right. We can do this by touch. Here, let me guide you." Holding the glasses by one earpiece, Kieran closed the remaining distance between them and touched their lips together.

The kiss was soft, just the lightest brush of lips and not a hint of tongue. And it was over entirely too soon.

No! David's brain screamed when Kieran drew back. Somehow he managed to keep from seizing the man and dragging him to the floor in a fit of wild passion.

Kieran smiled. "I've been wanting to do that ever since I saw you in Macy's." He paused, a hint of uncertainty coloring his voice. "I hope that was all right."

"No," David blurted. Kieran's eyes widened and he rushed on. "I mean, it was great just... way too short."

"Oh God, for a minute I thought you meant—" He shook his head. "Well, you are the director. If you say it was too short..." His words trailed away. His gaze dropped to David's mouth and lingered. "I don't guess you'd let me try again? I know I could do better now that I've had a chance to rehearse."

He could feel the blood pounding through every single vein and artery in his body.

David licked his lips. "I think we should absolutely try it again. Let me share my director's vision for how this should go."

This time when their lips met Kieran's parted almost immediately, his tongue sliding along David's lower lip before dipping inside.

Mmm. Their tongues began a sensuous dance, slipping and sliding, over and around. Little licks and nips, sips and tastes.

Kieran's flavor flooded through him, filling David's senses until he couldn't feel or taste or see or smell anything else. The warm, wet heat of his mouth. The soft, full lips that clung to his. The silky slide of tongue. It was everything and nearly too much.

Dropping the script he held, David slid his hands around Kieran's waist and drew him close. That slim, strong body molded against him, the hard length of Kieran's cock pressing against David's own.

Kieran's arms wrapped around him. His fingers slid into David's hair, angling his head for a deeper kiss. He rocked his hips, their cocks sliding together, the friction so delicious even through their clothes.

David skimmed his hands down to Kieran's ass and squeezed.

Kieran moaned into his mouth. The kiss broke. The smaller man leaned back, cheeks flushed, eyes glazed with lust. "God, you feel good." He tugged on David's hair. "And you're a great kisser. I could go on kissing you all night. Kiss me again, David."

Their mouths came together. One of Kieran's legs came up and wrapped around David's waist. He began to rock, the tempo of his hips increasing until David thought he might just blow in his pants.

Drawing back just enough, David slipped his hand between their bodies. "Kieran, God, let me touch you." He fumbled for Kieran's zipper, suddenly desperate to hold that hot, hard flesh in his hand. "Let me—"

"Don't. Just kiss me for right now. Please?" Kieran's hips shifted and he tugged on David's hair, trying to fuse their mouths once more.

"But why? I want to touch you. I want to make you come in my hand."

"I have a better idea." Clever fingers tugged at the zipper of David's chinos then slipped inside to wrap around his cock. Kieran's thumb brushed over the head where a wet spot marred the cotton of his boxer briefs.

He rubbed his cheek against David's. "I want to suck your cock, Mr. Director. Please, may I suck it?"

Kieran punctuated his request with a light squeeze.

David's eyes just about rolled back in his head and he let out a breathless little laugh. "God, Kieran, you're killing me here."

"Please?" Kieran's breath was warm in David's ear. "Please, let me taste you, David. Make you come in my mouth."

Easing him back, Kieran stepped down from the bottom step. As if in a dance, he turned them and walked David backward until his butt rested against the stage.

He made short work of David's belt then flipped open the button of his pants and spread the material wide.

David shut his eyes. He should stop this right now. Anybody might come in and see them, him with his pants around his ankles and this beautiful, wicked angel on his knees with his mouth full of David's cock. A perverse little thrill raced through him, raising goosebumps all over his body.

Kieran hooked his fingers in David's waistband and tugged. As he slid to his knees, down went the chinos and briefs underneath, down to the tops of David's thighs but no further. His cock sprang free. It slapped against his belly, leaving a wet trail behind.

Kieran licked up the pre-cum, his warm wet tongue making David's muscles tremble. He pressed his cheek against David's cock and hummed quietly. Soft warm lips trailed down his length then nuzzled his balls. He lapped at David's sack before drawing first one then both globes into his mouth. He sucked very gently, tongue working, driving every last thought from David's head.

Releasing him, Kieran looked up and smiled. "Mmm, you smell so good. Bet you're going to taste good too. Touch me, David. Fuck my mouth."

David realized he had a death grip on the edge of the stage. He let go and slid one hand into Kieran's hair. With the other he stroked his cheek as he gazed down into those gorgeous eyes. He couldn't speak.

"Cat got your tongue, Mr. Director?" Lips slid oh so slowly over the head of David's cock. Kieran's tongue probed the slit then he took him deep.

"Ah, God." David had to close his eyes again. The sight of this beautiful man on his knees, his nose buried in David's pubes, was very nearly enough to undo him. He began to count backwards from a hundred just to keep from blowing too soon. His fingers flexed then fisted in the wild mass of Kieran's hair. His hips shifted. Kieran's hands gripped him. The man was surprisingly strong, holding David tight enough that he'd probably have bruises tomorrow. He bobbed his head, sucking and slurping. He set an excruciating rhythm, slow then fast, fast then slow, teeth and tongue and lips working together to drive David out of his mind.

Desire coiled tight low in his belly and snaked clever fingers down around his balls.

Eighty. Seventy-nine. Seventy-eight.

David counted and Kieran sucked. Slowing down then speeding up, Kieran swirled his tongue around the shaft, teased the big vein, then took David deep again and swallowed around the head.

David's hips snapped forward as fire raced up his spine and down his legs. He gripped Kieran's hair and pulled out just in time. He shot, cum splashing over Kieran's lips and cheeks and chin. It was the hottest thing he'd ever seen.

Kieran's tongue slipped out and licked his lips. He smiled up at David. "Mmm. You taste amazing. I knew you would."

David helped him to his feet. Glancing down he noted the spreading wet spot on the front of Kieran's jeans. He chuckled. "See, you should have let me take care of that for you."

Kieran looked down at himself. His answering laugh was rueful. "Yeah well, stuff happens."

Grabbing the hem of his own shirt, David wiped the cum from Kieran's cheeks and chin then leaned in and brought their lips together. He tasted his own spunk and the flavor had his cock twitching and trying to rise again.

"You're so sexy," David murmured into Kieran's mouth.

Kieran leaned back and met David's gaze. "You didn't have to pull out." Before David could think of a reply, Kieran pecked a quick kiss at the corner of his mouth. "Maybe next time, hmm?"

Did that mean there would be a next time?

David nodded as he tucked himself away. "Maybe."

Kieran caught David's hand and lifted it to his cheek. "I'd like there to be a next time." Lips grazed the backs of David's fingers. "If you want."

"I'd like that too." David curled his fingers around Kieran's and squeezed. "I'd like that a lot."

Chapter Three

"I appreciate you making the time to meet on such short notice, David." Greg Redman pushed his chair back from the conference room's enormous oak table and stood.

Taking his cue from Greg, David did likewise. He knew when he was being dismissed. Their meeting was over and he had no clue how it had gone.

"I appreciate you taking the time to go through the proposal with me. Grant writing is not my tour de force. But I guess you figured that out by now."

Greg chuckled. "No one I know enjoys asking for money." He sighed. "It's a pity there isn't more support for the arts in this community, especially from the local businesses. It's why Sheryl and I started this foundation in the first place, to lend a hand to projects like yours."

"Mmm." David searched for something more to say. He was horrible at this kind of chitchat. If only they had the money to hire someone to do fundraising. Of course the first step was raising the funds to hire the person to raise funds. It was a vicious circle and he was caught in the middle of it.

If Greg noticed David's lack of response he gave no sign. Walking to the door of the conference room, he paused with his hand on the knob.

"Julie is so excited about this play. It's her first acting experience outside of school productions. Sheryl and I are very proud of her. She wants to make her career in the arts, you know?"

Very white teeth flashed in Greg's tanned face. He was one of those men, the outdoorsy, sportsman type, who kept his tan all year round. Unlike David himself who had been a burner and peeler all his life.

"She's a great kid," David said. "And I'm sure she'll be a wonderful actress one day."

A little wave of guilt washed over him at the lie. He wasn't at all sure of any such thing. But given that Greg was Julie's father and that he very well might hold the future of the theater company in his hands...

Greg's smile broadened. He opened the door. "I hope you're right." He ushered David into the lobby and walked with him to the elevator. "She played the nurse in Romeo and Juliet last year at her school, and I have to say, it was unlike any performance of that role that I've ever seen."

David suddenly felt like he was standing in the middle of a minefield. What the hell was he supposed to say to that? He took a breath.

"Every actor puts his or her own interpretation on any role they're given."

Greg studied him for a moment then nodded. "I suppose you're right."

The elevator dinged.

Thank God.

The doors slid open. They shook hands and, with no small sense of relief, David got in.

"Oh, one more thing." Greg caught the doors just before they closed and held them open. "Before you go, I nearly forgot to mention, I invited several of the foundation's board members to attend the play on opening night. They were interested in seeing one of your productions for themselves before they make a decision on your proposal." Greg smiled, showing lots of teeth. "Not to put any undue pressure on you, of course." He released the doors. "Have a good evening, David."

"You too," David managed, somehow forcing a smile in return just before the doors slid shut and he was left alone in the elevator.

※ ※ ※ ※ ※

"I didn't say having Kieran play Viola was a horrible idea. Stop putting words in my mouth, Davy." Bethany lowered the passenger side window an inch, letting in a rush of icy air. "Mmm, smells like snow, doesn't it?"

"Snow doesn't have a scent, Beth." David shivered and cranked up the heat. "Okay, you didn't exactly say that, but you can't be serious about giving Viola to Julie Redman. I mean, there's no comparison between the two actors. Give the role to her and we might as well do the play with sock puppets." David turned the car off Germantown Avenue and slowed as he searched for a parking space.

"Snow does too have a scent. Here. Smell." She lowered the window all the way. "You said yourself, Julie isn't that bad and that you could work with her. Now why all of a sudden are you so set on having Kieran Reilly anyway?"

"Why are you so set on Julie Redman? Will you please shut the window? I'm freezing my ass off over here."

She closed the window but didn't answer his question, so David continued.

"I thought you liked Kieran. You sure pretended to like him the other night."

"I was not pretending. I do like him. He seems like a nice kid and a decent actor."

"So what's the problem?"

"You know very well what the problem is, David." An edge crept into her voice. "Do I have to paint you a damn picture?"

Of course he knew what the problem was. They both did. And they'd been going back and forth about it ever since that afternoon, first via email and now in person as they drove to the theater for the cast meeting.

David said nothing and the silence between them stretched out, growing heavier by the minute. He found a space and edged the car into it. Shutting off the engine, he glanced over at his sister. She was staring straight ahead through the windshield. He could see by the set of her jaw that she was pissed with him. That and by the way she had her hands clenched together in her lap.

Reaching over he pried her icy fingers apart. "Where are your gloves, little girl?"

"Don't try to jolly me along, David. It's not going to work." She pulled her hand away and opened the car door.

She only called him David in that tone when she was really mad.

Sighing, he got out of the car and followed her. She was practically running up the street and he had to lengthen his stride to catch her, which he did easily.

He fell into step beside her. "Beth."

She ignored him.

"Will you stop and listen for a minute?"

She walked faster.

So did he.

They reached the entrance of the theater at the same time. But when Bethany tried to open the door, David slapped a palm against it.

"Bethany let's talk about this."

"There's nothing to talk about. Now stop being a jerk and let's get inside. I'm freezing."

Guilt washed through him. It was freezing out here on the street corner and she didn't have gloves. But, damn it, they couldn't do this, not inside in front of everyone.

She yanked on the door handle.

He didn't budge.

"David!"

"Bethany! We are not going in there until you tell me why you're so pissed off."

"It doesn't matter. You're the director. If you want Kieran Reilly for Viola, then Kieran's getting Viola."

"It does matter. You're my DA, and more importantly my sister, and if you have a reason you think Julie would be better than Kieran then I want to hear it."

The breath she blew out appeared as a plume of steam in the glow of the streetlight. "If we don't give Viola to Julie, it could hurt the theater and you don't even care."

"How is that going to hurt the theater?"

Bethany rolled her eyes in that oh please expression David knew so well.

"Have you forgotten how much the Redmans do for us? Sheryl Redman does all of our printing at her shop."

"And we pay for it too."

"Oh David, how many times have we not had the cash for advertising or playbills or whatever and she's floated us until we got the money together?" David opened his mouth but Bethany talked right over him. "And what about Greg Redman? What about the grant, David?"

"What about the show, Beth? If we give Viola to Julie it's going to hurt the show."

"And are you going to be the one to tell Greg Redman the reason his precious little Julie didn't get to play Viola?" Her voice rose on each word. "Are you?"

He would not get into a screaming fight with her standing here outside the theater. He. Would. Not.

David spoke very quietly. "And what is the reason, Bethany?"

"The only reason you want to give Viola to Kieran Reilly is so you can get into his pants. Do you think I can't see that? I'm not blind, David. And you're doing it at the expense of the theater and that's just wrong. So don't give me that it's all for the show BS. Now open the damn door and let's go in and get this over with."

Was he? No, she was wrong. Kieran would make a fantastic Viola. David knew it in his bones. Still, the accusation stung. And it hurt all the more coming from his sister. She knew how much he loved this company. He worked his ass off as did she. Hell, they all busted their asses to keep it going. He would never do anything to jeopardize that and Bethany of all people should know it.

David opened the door and held it for her. She went inside without another word or even a glance.

Bethany removed her coat and dropped it on a seat at the end of the second row and placed her bag on top.

"What are you doing back there? You always sit up front." David tossed his own jacket and bag on a seat in the front row. "Come up here and sit with me."

"I'm good right here." Her tone was cool, icy even.

"Beth—" David broke off as the door at the back opened and a whole group of people piled in.

That pretty much killed the argument, not that it was over because they hadn't settled anything between them.

David looked down at his cast list. Bethany was wrong. He was not making his decision based on sex.

And what would his sister say if she knew about that little scene between Kieran and him the other night? That second, more personal audition of Kieran's other talents?

David shoved that particular thought well away. That BJ had nothing to do with his choice. And his choice would have no ill repercussions on the theater. He wouldn't let it.

Over the next ten minutes, people arrived in twos and threes.

"Why don't we just sit in the theater seats?" Fred unfolded another chair and set it in place, completing the circle on the stage.

"Because I like to be able to see everyone and this arrangement works better for that." David glanced at his watch then around at the members of the group. "Okay, I guess we'll get started."

"Julie isn't here yet." Joan MacTavish unwrapped a mint and popped it in her mouth. She was the owner of a local bar that was extremely popular with the college crowd for its dollar pitcher Thursdays. She and Julie seemed to have become fast friends in a very short time.

"Do you know for sure she's coming?" David took the pile of scripts from his bag and tapped the edges together.

"Of course she'll be here. She's very excited about doing this play."

David handed half the stack to Bethany, seated next to him in the circle of chairs. She got slowly to her feet and winced.

"You okay?" David touched his sister's arm.

"Fine. It's just my back."

"Sit down, Beth. Let me do that." He reached for the scripted but she held them out of his reach.

"I said I'm fine. I'm pregnant, not an invalid." She gave him one of her don't make a fuss looks, quickly stepped away and began handing out scripts.

The door at the back of the tiny theatre banged open and Julie rushed in, blond hair flying as she ran down the center aisle and up onto the stage.

"Sorry I'm late." Her backpack thudded to the stage. Unzipping her puffy pink jacket, she dropped it next to the backpack. "My stupid astronomy class ran overtime and—" She broke off in mid-explanation, the thought ending on a squeal as she launched herself across the circle and pounced on Kieran. "Oh my God, Kieran! What are you doing here?"

Kieran caught her. They hugged and Julie kissed his cheek.

David was awash in jealousy before he even saw it coming.

Kieran was gay, wasn't he? Of course he was. They had nearly made a date and David was sure Kieran had been flirting with him in Macy's. So what the hell was this? Maybe Kieran was bi. But Julie, of all people?

Don't think about that.

"Fred, let me sit here." Still clinging to Kieran, Julie nudged Fred Sellick's knee with hers.

"Why? There's a seat over there." He gestured to an empty chair beside Joan, a chair the other woman had been saving since her arrival.

"You can sit there. I want to sit next to Kieran." She beamed at Kieran. "God, I haven't seen you since graduation day."

"Will you just sit somewhere so we can get on with this?" Evan, an older man who, David had discerned, fancied himself a Shakespearean great on par with Richard Burton, stood up. "I'll sit next to Joan and you can have my seat."

At last everyone finished moving around and got settled.

David stepped into the center of the circle. "I'm giving everyone a list of the assigned parts along with your script. Some of you, you'll notice, are playing more than one part because we just don't have enough people. I know you've all done this before so it shouldn't be a problem. If anyone has two roles that conflict, let me know right away."

"What do you mean by conflict?" A petite redhead named Erin cracked her gum.

David forced himself not to wince.

The girl was a student in his Intro to Shakespeare class. She was new to theater and he had assigned two minor roles to her. Once he saw how she did...

"It means you're playing two people who are on stage at the same time." Julie spoke with authority. She flipped her bangs out of her eyes and gave the other girl a keen look. "And get rid of the gum. You can't possibly speak clearly with gum in your mouth."

Erin shot Julie a mutinous look. But she took the gum out, wrapped it in a tissue and stuck it in her pocket.

As he handed Julie her part, David gave her a smile then turned to Kieran. When he took the copy of the script David had marked up for him their fingers brushed. Kieran's gaze dropped to David's mouth and lingered there for just a moment and he licked his lips.

David's cock stirred.

Down boy.

Turning quickly away, David resumed his seat in the center of the semicircle.

"Okay, as you'll see I've marked up the scripts with everyone's parts highlighted so—"

"David, you gave me the wrong script." Julie glanced around the circle.

"Here we go," Bethany murmured beside David, pitching her voice so only he would hear.

"Who's got Viola, because I need to switch with you."

"I gave you the right script," David said. "You're playing Maria."

Julie's gaze snapped to David. "No I'm not. You told me I would be playing Viola."

"No I didn't." David kept his tone even. Of course he had known deep down, whether he admitted it to his sister or not, that there would be trouble over his decision.

"You did so. Remember the other night when I read? You said there was no one else young enough to play Viola."

"You said that, Julie. I said I would let you know in a day or two what I had decided."

A chair creaked, someone coughed and David stopped himself from saying any more. He wasn't going to let her drag him into a discussion right in front of everyone.

"Look, Julie, if you want to discuss this, we can—"

"Who's playing Viola?" She flipped through her pages until she found her character list. "Oh my God, Kieran?" She laughed and turned to Kieran sitting next to her. "Kieran, switch with me. You don't mind, do you?"

There was a half-beat of silence.

"Um, actually…"

"I mind," David cut in. "This is how I assigned the roles and there won't be any switching."

Julie's eyes widened and her mouth opened then closed. A flush began at the collar of her shirt and crept up into her cheeks.

"You can't do this to me. I already told everyone I was going to be Viola. My dad—" Her voice hitched and she swallowed. "My dad thinks I'm playing Viola."

"I'm sorry." Guilt niggled at David. Why should he be guilty? This was his decision and he was making the right one. Still, she looked like someone had kicked her puppy.

Julie turned to Bethany. "You think I should play Viola, don't you?"

Bethany shook her head, cutting off Julie's protest. "Julie, it doesn't matter what I think. David is the director. What he says, goes."

Some unidentifiable emotion passed over Julie's lovely face turning it momentarily ugly.

She said nothing.

"Julie," Bethany began.

Julie stood up. The chair she'd been sitting in crashed backward.

"Julie." David took a step toward her.

"No!" She stormed up to David and jabbed a finger into his chest. "You can't do this to me. I know why you gave him Viola. And you're not getting away with it."

Joan held out her script. "Honey, you can play Olivia if you want. I don't mind switching."

Julie whirled to face her. "I don't want to play Olivia. Olivia is old. I want to play Viola."

Joan looked like Julie had slapped her. She subsided, pressing her lips together like she wanted to cry.

David took a long breath before he spoke. He could handle tantrums. It wasn't his favorite part of directing, but it came with the job and he thought he was pretty good at defusing tension. But this little prima dona was getting on his last nerve.

"Julie, you're out of line." David kept his voice even. He would not let her see how much she was getting to him. "Either you play Maria like I've assigned you, or you can leave the show."

"Fuck you." Julie flung her script to the floor and stomped on it. "And fuck this stupid theater company. I'm not playing stupid Maria."

Shoving her way out of the circle, Julie grabbed her jacket and backpack from the floor and stormed up the aisle. The door slammed behind her, leaving everyone in stunned silence.

Chapter Four

"Therefore, good youth, address thy gait unto her," Fred, playing Orsino, leaned into Kieran, looking as if he were about to kiss him. *"Be not denied access, stand at her doors, and tell them, there thy fixed foot shall grow till thou have audience."*

Kieran leaned back, clearly uncomfortable. *"Sure, my noble lord, if she be so abandon'd to her sorrow as it is spoke, she never will admit me."*

"Be clamorous and—"

"Cut." David stood up. The action was not working at all, the chemistry all wrong between his two leads. "Orsino, what are you doing?"

"What do you mean?" Fred's brows drew together and he sent David a perplexed look.

"I mean, what are you doing in this scene? What's happening?"

"Um, I'm asking Viola to go talk to Olivia for me?"

"No." Taking the steps two at a time, David joined Fred and Kieran on stage. "You aren't asking Viola anything. You're asking—no, that's wrong too, you're compelling Cesario to go to Olivia, the woman you love, and make your case. So when you cross to him and say… Go on, say the line."

"Address thy gait unto her—"

"Be not denied access," David picked up the line, exaggerating his delivery so Fred could hear what he wanted. When Kieran opened his mouth to give his line, David gestured him to silence. "Hold that a minute." He turned his attention back to Fred. "You're passionate about this woman. Do you have someone you're passionate about, Fred?"

"You just said I was passionate about Olivia."

"No, I mean you. Do you have someone you're passionate about right now in your life?"

Several of the cast members giggled.

David ignored them. "Do you?"

Fred's cheeks flushed crimson. "Well, yeah, I guess so."

"Then when you say the line, think about that person and let me hear that passion. Can you do that?"

Fred nodded. "Yeah, I can do that."

"Let's try it again. And this time let me hear your conviction. And not just hear it, I want to see it. Now go off stage and come back on just the way we blocked it."

Fred exited and re-entered. Pausing down stage left, he delivered his line. *"Who saw Cesario, ho?"*

"On your attendance, my lord; here."

"Stand you a while aloof, Cesario, thou know'st no less but all; I have unclasp'd to thee the book even of my secret soul." Fred crossed to Kieran and laid his hands on his shoulders. *"Therefore, good youth, address thy gait unto her; be not denied access, stand at her doors—"*

"Cut." David returned to the stage. "Orsino, you're compelling him to go to your beloved on your behalf, not thinking about kissing him. So quit looking at him like you want to eat him up."

"But am I not already attracted to him? On a subconscious level, I mean? That's how I'm playing it."

"No, in this scene you're in love with Olivia. You're head over heels about her and she won't give you the time of day. You are not even thinking about anyone else. Not Cesario. Not Viola. Hell, you don't even know about Viola yet. It's Olivia you **want**, only Olivia."

"But I mean subconsciously."

"No, not even subconsciously. Forget about the subconscious for right now." David blew out a breath. There had to be a way to show Fred what he wanted. It should not be this hard. "Okay, let's do this. Go and stand down there where I was before and watch me. Watch how I touch Cesario, how I look at him. Listen to how I deliver the lines." Seeing Fred's features begin to harden into that stubborn mask, the one that meant he wasn't hearing anything, David hurried on. "I'm not saying you should play it exactly this way, I just want you to see how I'm seeing Orsino. I'm not explaining myself well, so let's try it this way. Okay?"

Fred nodded and left the stage and David turned to Kieran. "One more time?"

Kieran nodded. "Fine with me."

David walked off stage right and re-entered just as Fred had done. "*Who saw Cesario, ho?*"

They both crossed to center stage as Kieran spoke his line. "*On your attendance, my lord; here.*"

David turned to Kieran as if just seeing him. He was struck once again by the man's beauty and felt his lips curve. "*Stand you a while aloof, Cesario, thou know'st no less but all; I have unclasp'd to thee the book even of my secret soul.*" He went to Kieran and laid his hands on his slender shoulders. "Therefore, good youth, address thy gait unto her," He gazed into Kieran's eyes. "*Be not denied access, stand at her doors, and tell them, there thy fixed foot shall grow till thou have audience.*"

"*Sure, my noble lord, if she be so abandon'd to her sorrow as it is spoke, she never will admit me.*"

They continued with the scene, David's world narrowing until it was just the lights and the lines and the two of them, everyone and everything fading away.

"*That say thou art a man: Diana's lip is not more smooth and rubious; thy small pipe is as the maiden's organ, shrill and sound, and all is semblative a woman's part.*"

David's gaze dropped to Kieran's mouth and lingered. Kieran licked his lips and David was suddenly swept by the memory of how those lips felt wrapped around his cock. Some expression flickered over Kieran's face that told David he was remembering precisely the same thing.

And his mind blanked. He had no clue what the next line was or even whether it was his.

Heat flooded his face and he did the unforgivable, the very thing he told his actors never to do. He glanced over at Bethany who was holding book.

"Um, line?"

"I think I get it," Fred said. He mounted the steps, walked up to David and clapped him on the shoulder. "Yeah man, I think I get it all right."

David ignored the asshole. "Let's take ten, shall we? When you come back, I want Cesario and Olivia on stage."

"You're being a little hard on Fred, don't you think?" Bethany met David at the foot of the steps that led from the stage.

"Yeah, well, I'm just trying to show him what I want."

She made a face. "Actors don't like to be told how to play a scene like that. You of all people should know that."

"I just want him to follow direction."

A shrug was her only response before she turned and headed toward the back of the theater.

David shoved a hand through his hair. She was probably right. He'd gotten carried away playing that scene with Kieran. And what was worse, now Fred thought he had something on him, which he very well might. Not that it mattered. He was fine with the other cast members knowing he and Kieran were... What were they anyway?

From the corner of his eye, David caught sight of Bethany. She was waving at him, calling him back to the rear of the theater. He had yet to tell her about the foundation's board of directors' plan to attend opening night. Ever since their argument the night of the casting, things had been strained between his sister and him. And despite repeated attempts on his part to normalize the situation, she'd held on to her mad. He felt bad about that.

"What's up?" David asked as he reached her side.

She hooked her arm through his. "Come outside with me."

"Why?" David stopped walking at studied her. "You going to kick my ass then leave me out there face down in a snowbank?"

He could see that she tried not to smile and failed. The fact that he'd succeeded in making her smile, even a little, lifted his mood.

"There's someone outside who wants to talk to you."

"Who is it? And why don't they just come in?"

"You ask too many questions." Bethany tugged him out the door into the frigid night air.

Under the glow of a streetlight stood Julie Redman. She smiled shyly as they approached. "Hi David."

"Hey Julie. What are you doing out here?" David tugged down the sleeves of his sweatshirt and shivered.

"I wanted to talk to you."

"I'll leave you two alone," Bethany said.

"No," David and Julie said at once.

Bethany sighed. "All right but make it quick. I'm freezing."

Julie looked up at David at bit her lip. "I'm sorry for how I acted before. It was very unprofessional and I hope you aren't still mad at me."

David's jaw dropped. An apology was the last thing he would have expected from her. Still, a part of him wondered what her motivation was. She must want something, otherwise why was she here.

"No, I'm not still mad."

"Good, I'm glad." She hesitated and glanced at Bethany who smiled and gave a slight nod. "Um, do you think I could maybe come back to the show?" Before he could answer, she rushed on. "I know all the parts are assigned and I wouldn't expect one anyway after what I did. But I was hoping maybe there was some other job I could do like props mistress, or holding book, or I could even build sets. If you'll take me back."

Julie dropped her gaze. Her mittened hands clasped and unclasped in front of her.

David glanced at Bethany. She watched him intently, waiting to see what he would do. She was putting him on the spot, testing him.

"I think we could find something for you to do, if you really want to come back." He paused. "There might even be one or two small parts I could give you."

"Really?" She lifted her gaze. It shone with hope. "You'd really give me another chance?"

"No lines, of course. Just as an attendant or something."

"That's okay. I don't care. I just want to come back to the show."

"Okay, then you're welcome to come back."

She thanked him so profusely that David had to stop her. It was getting embarrassing, for God's sake.

Julie led the way back inside with David and Bethany following.

Just inside the door, Bethany pulled him to a stop. She gave his arm a quick squeeze. "You did good, Davie. I'm proud of you. And I'm sorry for those things I said. That was uncalled for and—"

"Forget it, Beth. It's over." David smiled. "Now let's figure out what kind of job we're going to give Julie."

Chapter Five

Kieran perched on a stool near the end of the bar. He kept his gaze fixed on the club's entrance while he sipped his drink and waited.

Sipped. Hah. More like guzzled.

He forced himself to set his glass down on the bar. He even turned his attention to the dance floor and tried to ignore the sick feeling of dread that was trying to climb up his throat.

What if David didn't show? Or worse, what if he did show, took one look at Kieran and bolted?

It wouldn't be the first time something like that had happened to him.

Kieran smoothed a hand down over his skirt and reached once again for his vodka and cranberry. Placing his lips to the straw, he took a long sip and heard the rattle of air and ice cubes as the last of the drink disappeared.

Almost immediately, the bartender materialized with another drink. He slid the glass in front of Kieran. He pushed bills across the bar but the man shook his head.

"From that guy over there at the end of the bar."

Kieran glanced in the direction the man indicated and locked gazes with a big, dark skinned guy seated at the other side of the long mahogany horseshoe bar. The guy smiled, white teeth flashing in his dark face, and stood up.

Clearly he'd been watching for a reaction.

And now he was headed in Kieran's direction.

The guy moved like a big cat, all predatory grace in tight black jeans and a cutaway vest that showed off his smooth chest. Kieran looked back at the door, desperate to see David's shaggy blond head making its way through the crowd. Nothing.

But if he doesn't show, a little voice in Kieran's head whispered, this guy wouldn't be a bad substitute. He shut that voice down without a second thought. He was not looking for a stranger fuck. He was here for David.

Tall dark and catlike reached him. A big warm hand settled on Kieran's spine just above the low-cut back of his dress. The guy leaned in close, invading Kieran's personal space. Or maybe he just wanted to be heard over the music.

"My name's Tre." His voice was deep, his breath scented with whiskey. "You want to dance, gorgeous?" His other hand came to rest on Kieran's thigh just below the hem of his skirt. "Or we could go in the back and you could show me what you've got under that dress. What do you say?"

Kieran was turned sideways on the barstool, one spiked heel hooked over the rail at the bottom. He shook his head. "I'm waiting for someone."

Tre stepped in close and pressed himself against Kieran's side. "You sure?"

The move was quick, but it lasted long enough that he felt the substantial bulge in the man's jeans. Kieran's anus clenched in an involuntary response and his cock stiffened.

God, he was feeling slutty tonight.

It must be the clothes. He'd dressed carefully, choosing a snug red dress cut low in back and with a flippy, flirty little skirt that hit him about mid-thigh, just below the tops of the patterned black stockings he wore. On his feet he wore pumps with four inch spiked heels that exactly matched the red of his dress. It was his come-on-and-fuck-me outfit. Flashy and slutty and it made him feel totally glamorous, and tonight he needed that.

Tre opened his mouth and started to say something. But just then Kieran spotted David. He stood on the opposite side of the dance floor, clearly out of his element. He scanned the crowd.

He's looking for me. Kieran's belly fluttered with nervous excitement and his heart took up a steady gallop that competed with the driving beat of the music.

He stood up a little too quickly and teetered on his heels. His head spun. He was a little tipsy and steadied himself with a hand on the bar.

"Excuse me, I see my date."

A hand closed on his arm. "Hey, if you change your mind..."

Keeping all his attention on David, Kieran tugged his arm free. "Thanks, but I don't think so."

He cut across the dance floor, weaving in and out between gyrating bodies, blinking against the flashing lights.

David didn't see him. Or didn't recognize him, one or the other. Kieran took full advantage of the time it gave him to enjoy the look of the man.

David wore dark pants and a dark shirt open at the throat. The clothes hugged his lanky frame. He looked good, if completely out of place amid the glitzy ragged chic of the patrons and club kids that surrounded him. Lights reflected off the lenses of his glasses, making it impossible to see his eyes.

Kieran reached him and laid a hand on his arm. Even in heels, the top of his head came only to David's chin. David looked down at him, the lack of recognition clear on his face.

Kieran leaned in close, placing his mouth right next to David's ear to be heard. "David, it's me." He gave David's arm a light squeeze and let his lips brush David's cheek.

Mmm, he loved the feel of freshly shaven skin.

David's dark eyes widened behind the lenses of his glasses, magnifying his surprise. "Oh shit! Kieran? It really is you." David laughed. "You look incredible."

Relief flooded through Kieran weakening his knees. Until that moment he hadn't fully admitted to himself how much David's reaction was worrying him. It looked like he'd had nothing to worry about after all.

David drew Kieran in close to him with an arm around his waist. He bent his head so their faces were close. "Want to dance?"

Kieran nodded and let himself be guided in among the writhing bodies and flashing lights. The heat from David's hand penetrated the thin material of his dress. It felt wonderfully strong and possessive at the small of Kieran's back.

They reached an empty space and David turned to him; settling his hands on Kieran's hips, he began to gyrate to the music.

One of Kieran's hands rested on David's waist, the leather of his belt smooth under Kieran's fingers. The other hand he placed on David's shoulder. As they moved together he let his fingertips play with the ends of David's hair that fell just over his collar. They started out with some space between their bodies, easier to dance that way, the floor was crowded. Someone jostled Kieran from behind, knocking him forward and into his partner.

"Sorry," the guy behind him yelled as his partner danced him away.

David's arm came around Kieran's waist. Warm breath wafted against his temple. "Are you okay, baby?"

Kieran nodded, a little thrill racing through him at the small endearment, or maybe it was the protective way David held him.

Kieran leaned in closer and rested his cheek against the silky material of David's shirt. He loved the feel of a hard male body against his, the intimacy of being so close in a crowd, had loved that feeling ever since the first time he'd ever danced with a boy. He'd had lots of dancing partners since that long ago night in his freshman year of high school. But this felt different somehow, better, more intimate.

Kieran closed his eyes as David turned them in a slow circle, his hand sliding down and coming to rest on the curve of Kieran's ass.

Under his short skirt, Kieran's cock stirred. He angled his body so David couldn't miss the feel of his growing erection. He sensed more than heard David's hum of approval as his legs were nudged apart. David's leg slid between Kieran's and he rocked a little against the hard muscle of David's thigh, blending the dancing with his need to be just a little slutty, just enough to let his partner know that anything he might want to do was okay with Kieran.

The arm around his waist tightened and now both David's hands were on his ass, gently kneading, a fingertip dipped suggestively into Kieran's crease, pressed and them was gone.

Kieran whimpered. He let one hand slide between their bodies and palmed David's erection through his pants.

He recalled the taste and texture of David's cock as it slid past his lips and over his tongue, the warm splash of semen as David came on his face, marking him. Kieran wanted to feel that pulsing heat in his ass, to have this man claim him in that most intimate way. He wanted this man, this virtual stranger, to fill and fuck him and make him his.

God, he really was a slut.

David flicked his tongue in Kieran's ear, sending a shockwave of sensation straight to Kieran's dick, already straining against the lace of his panties. "If you don't quit rubbing my cock like that, I'm going to have to pull your skirt up and have you right here on the dance floor."

The words ignited something in Kieran, some fiery need he'd never known he had. The thought of being taken in the middle of a crowded dance floor, having his skirt yanked up and his panties ripped and being fucked out here where anyone could watch—it was thrilling beyond anything he could have imagined.

"Do it." Kieran nipped David's earlobe. "Fuck me."

David faltered, his rhythm lost. His fingers flexed on Kieran's ass. "Okay," he breathed, "let's get out of here."

"No." Kieran squeezed David's cock, swiping his thumb over the head. "Do it here, in the club, where anybody can see."

David gaped at him. Clearly shocked. His hips shifted and he gave a little thrust into Kieran's grip. "I don't think—" He broke off in mid-sentence but his gaze darted around the club as if he might really be considering it.

Taking this for encouragement, Kieran grabbed David's hand and tugged him through the dancers. He'd been here before and knew right where they could go.

Giddy on the thought of what they were about to do, Kieran didn't glance back at his date as he pulled David past the tables and the bar and back into a small hallway. The tiled floor was slippery and Kieran's heels slid on the slickness.

David caught and steadied him. "Kieran, where the hell are we going?"

"Right back here." Kieran got David moving again, past the bathrooms, past other couples in various phases of sexual intimacy, on back to the emergency exit.

Without stopping to consider, he hit the emergency bar. An alarm shrieked. Yanking David through and into the alley he slammed the door, cutting off the sound.

Shoving David against the wall, Kieran plastered his body against the other man's, capturing David's lips in a hungry kiss. He was starving for contact, ravenous to have David's hands on him, David's gorgeous cock inside him. It seemed like forever since he'd had a lover who accepted him for who he was and wasn't trying to change him into someone or something else. That knowledge alone would have been enough, but David was so much more. Smart and funny and sexy as hell and Kieran just knew he would be a fantastic lover. He couldn't wait to find out.

David tore his mouth away. "You're crazy."

But he was laughing and the words came out a little breathless. His hands were everywhere at once, Kieran's back, his hips, his ass. David stroked and squeezed and explored as if he too couldn't get enough or soon enough.

Hands burrowed under Kieran's skirt, bunching it up around his hips, finding his bare ass. David groaned. "Jesus, you aren't wearing any—" His words died on another groan as his fingers found the string of the sheer, black thong Kieran wore under his dress. "Jesus fuck."

Kieran laughed, thrilled by his lover's reaction. The laugh ended on a squeak as the tip of one finger penetrated his hole. Just a little. Just far enough to tease, like a promise.

Kieran whimpered and shifted his hips, trying to push back on that tantalizing fingertip.

The finger disappeared and a kiss was pressed to Kieran's temple. "Come home with me, baby."

Kieran started to protest. "But I want—"

"Please? I want you in my bed. I want to see all of you. Peel you out of this dress and lay you out on my bed." David kissed him again. "I want to see you all rumpled and freshly fucked in my sheets. I want to smell you on my pillow. Please, Kieran? Come home with me."

How could he say no to a plea like that?

Kieran stepped back out of David's arms, smiled up at him and reached for his hand, lacing their fingers together. "Where are you parked?"

✦✦✦✦✦

They reached David's apartment in record time. Thank God there was little to no traffic on the streets at that hour, because David couldn't concentrate on anything other than Kieran; beautiful, sexy Kieran in the passenger seat, well within touching distance. Kissing distance. Fucking distance. He could hardly wait to get Kieran home and out of that slinky red dress.

David thought of the thong panties under Kieran's skirt, the firm round ass, the rock hard dick and heavy balls barely contained by the silky scrap of material.

David's own dick pressed painfully against his zipper. He imagined thrusting into Kieran's tight little hole, plunging in balls deep. Maybe he'd leave the underwear on while they fucked. David wasn't sure he'd have the nerve to ask, but you never knew.

Kieran's heels clicked on the hardwood as they mounted the stairs to David's third floor apartment. Such an unfamiliar sound. He'd never had a woman up here. Hell, he'd never had a woman anywhere, ever. And Kieran certainly was not a woman. David thought again of the long, thick cock under that skirt, and smiled to himself.

"What are you grinning about?"

Kieran pressed close behind him on the landing as David picked through his keys for the right one. His erection rubbed along the crease of David's ass, reminding him again, as if he needed it, of Kieran's maleness.

David dropped his keys. Kieran bent swiftly and picked them up. He pressed them into David's hand and molded their bodies together.

"Hurry." His breath wafted warm against the side of David's neck. "I can't wait to get your cock up my ass."

David slid an arm around Kieran's slender waist and fitted the key into the lock with the other hand. "What do you mean? I thought you were going to fuck me."

Kieran's eyes widened and his jaw dropped.

Shoving open the door, David laughed and pulled him inside. "I'm just teasing you, sweetheart. I can't wait to get my cock up your ass either."

What the hell was wrong with him? He didn't talk like that. He thought those things, sure. Who didn't? But to say them out loud was just... well, not him. But Kieran made him do things he'd never done before, want things he'd never wanted before.

Like fucking a guy in a dress maybe? That little voice in David's head prodded him again. Is that what you mean?

Shut up. He's doing this for the role. He's an actor. They did stuff like this to get into a role.

But that voice would not be so easily silenced.

Seems he's awfully comfortable dressed like that. Those heels. That dress.

Shut. Up.

Kieran was looking at him, a frown creasing his brow. He touched David's arm. "Something wrong?"

"No, of course not. Everything's perfect. You're perfect." Impulsively David scooped Kieran up into his arms—another thing he'd never done before—and carried him down the narrow hall to his bedroom.

Kieran let out a little breathless laugh and wrapped his arms around David's neck. "God, nobody ever carried me to bed before." He rubbed his cheek against David's. "It's so romantic."

"That's me, just a diehard romantic." He kept it light though his heart was pounding so hard he was sure Kieran must be able to hear it.

As they passed through the doorway David turned sideways so as not to knock Kieran against the doorjamb. Once inside the bedroom, he set Kieran gently on his feet.

A shaft of moonlight spilled through the window. It bathed Kieran in its silvery glow, turning his pale skin nearly translucent. The vision was ethereal.

"You are so fucking beautiful," David breathed. He went to his knees at Kieran's feet like a supplicant and rested his hands on the other man's legs. Slowly he ran his palms up Kieran's calves, skimming his fingers lightly over the tiny dots on the sheer black stockings like a blind man reading Braille, enjoying the contours of the long lean muscles, firm rounded calves and slim thighs.

David leaned forward and pressed his cheek against Kieran's crotch. Shutting his eyes, he breathed in, inhaling the musky scent of Kieran's desire. He nuzzled the thick erection through the skirt and heard his lover's soft gasp.

David's fingers found the silky skin at the tops of Kieran's stockings. He traced the elastic bands holding them up, following the lacy trim around until his knuckles brushed the heavy weight of Kieran's balls. Now it was David's turn to whimper.

Unable to wait another moment, he shoved the skirt up around Kieran's hips, baring the cock which, until now, he had only dreamed of. The skimpy thong was too small and the head of Kieran's cock poked above the band at the top. A pearlescent drop of pre-cum gathered at the slit. David collected it with his tongue, savoring the salty sweet flavor of his new lover. Mmm, so good. He rubbed his cheek along the shaft encased in sheer black fabric and mouthed the swell of Kieran's balls at the base. He sucked them into his mouth thong and all.

Still in his heels, Kieran teetered. He clutched at David's shoulders. "David, shit. That feels amazing. Oh my God. I can't…"

Releasing Kieran's sack, David licked a long wet trail up the length of his dick. When he reached the head he slid his lips over it as best he could with the thong still in place. He sucked. The silky heat and familiar yet unfamiliar shape in his mouth, against his tongue, the taste of this new and exciting man, it was all too much and David was positively drunk with it.

David palmed his own dick through his pants. It wasn't enough. Sliding the zipper down, he reached in and drew it out. He grasped his shaft and stroked.

The fingers still gripping his shoulders flexed. "David, please, I need you."

David pulled off of Kieran's cock with a soft pop. Rising to his feet, he pulled Kieran close, found the zipper at the back of Kieran's dress and tugged.

"I need to see you, baby." He brushed feather soft kisses over Kieran's eyes, his cheeks, the tip of his nose and along his jaw. "Can I see you, my beautiful Kieran? All of you?"

Kieran moaned and shifted restlessly in David's arms but he didn't object.

David trailed kisses down Kieran's throat and along his mostly bare shoulder until he reached the thin strap holding up the dress. Still using his lips, David nudged the strap off Kieran's shoulder then did the same on the other side. With a soft sigh the silky material slid down Kieran's body and puddled around his feet.

Kieran stood by David's bed, bathed in moonlight, clad in nothing more than that tiny thong, a lacy black strapless bra, those amazingly sexy stockings and heels. His dark hair fell in loose curls around his face. His eyes were huge in his pale face, the makeup smudged and blurry, the irises gone a deeper darker shade of blue. His lips were bruised and puffy from David's kisses, the lipstick entirely worn off. On one shoulder a love-bite was just beginning to purple.

That was his mark on Kieran's skin. Something elemental shot through David at that thought, some primitive possessiveness. It was caveman and thrilling at once and he reveled in it.

"You're the sexiest thing I've ever seen." With the tip of one finger, David traced the lightest dusting of dark hair that bisected Kieran's flat belly. Really no more than a shadow, it disappeared under the thong and ended at the neatly trimmed triangle of curls at Kieran's crotch.

Kieran plucked at the buttons of David's shirt. "Now let me see you."

Normally shy about undressing in front of anyone, even a soon-to-be lover, David shucked his clothes without self-consciousness or even a thought to modesty. Not until he was down to just his boxer-briefs and socks did he pause.

Suddenly very aware, not only of his own body but of the intensity of Kieran's gaze, David felt the heat rise to his face.

"Oh, I should have got my socks off first, I guess." He laughed, feeling the blush begin to crawl down his neck. "Let me just—"

"Wait." Kieran stopped him with a light touch on his arm. "Let me."

Kieran went to his knees in front of David. With his face on level with David's throbbing cock, he looked up and, meeting David's eyes, licked his lips and smiled.

Oh. My. Fucking. God.

David closed his eyes, afraid he might blow on the spot just from the sight of Kieran, beautiful sexy Kieran, no more than a breath away from his dick.

Hooking his fingers in the waistband of David's underwear, Kieran drew them down. He leaned in and kissed the tip of

David's prick before he tapped David's foot. "Lift up so I can get these off."

David obeyed, resting a hand on Kieran's smooth shoulder. He raised one foot then the other, allowing his lover to finish undressing him. Once he was naked, David caught Kieran's hands and drew him to his feet then into his arms. Kieran's trapped cock slid silkily against David's bare one, drawing twin gasps from both men.

Finding Kieran's lips, David traced them with the tip of his tongue before dipping inside. Kieran sucked the tip of David's tongue as he rocked their hips together. His fingers fisted in David's hair, holding him still, sucking and swirling, teasing and tasting, until David was ready to beg.

Kieran drew back slightly, heavy-lidded eyes focused on David's face. "I want you to fuck me so bad, David." Reaching between them he grasped David's cock and caressed the head with his thumb. "Don't make me wait anymore."

David nodded. "Anything you want, baby."

With both hands on Kieran's waist, David backed him toward the bed. Just as the backs of his knees hit the edge of the mattress, Kieran released David and, sliding a hand around to his back, he unhooked his bra and cast it aside before he tumbled back on the bed. Shoving the thong down his hips, Kieran dragged it off and tossed it to the floor.

David caught Kieran's ankle and held it. "Leave the stockings on?"

Kieran's eyes widened ever so briefly then he smiled. "You want the heels on too?"

"Yes," David breathed. His cock strained against his belly and he raked his gaze down Kieran's body then back up to his face. "Leave them on too."

Kieran nodded. He held out his arms and spread his thighs wide in silent invitation.

David crawled up the mattress on all fours. His heart galloped in his chest. The blood rushing through his veins, throbbing in his dick. He lay down alongside his lover, Kieran's arms and one leg winding around him and pulling him close.

He found Kieran's mouth at the same moment their dicks slid together. David groaned and thrust his tongue between Kieran's parted lips.

They rolled over, David ending on top of Kieran. Now both legs wrapped around his waist, the light scratch of the patterned stockings adding another thrilling sensation to the mix.

"David. God. Please?" Kieran thrust against David's belly. The heel of one shoe dug into David's ass, the small bite of pain nearly sending him over the edge.

David hugged Kieran tight and showered kisses over his face. He traced the full lower lips with the tip of his tongue and fed on the needy little sounds Kieran made.

"Where's your stuff, baby?" Kieran nipped at David's tongue. "Let me get you ready."

"Nightstand. I'll get it." Rolling over, David yanked open the drawer and rummaged inside. He dropped a bottle of lube and a condom on the bed, slammed the drawer and turned back in time to see Kieran, knees pulled up to his chest and lube in hand.

Their eyes met and held. Distantly David heard the click of the lube cap and the soft squirting sound.

Kieran smiled. "Watch me."

David's gaze followed Kieran's hand, fingers slick with lube, as he reached between his legs. He stroked along his crease then teased at the small puckered rosebud of his opening. One finger slipped inside, then two. Kieran's breath quickened and he pumped the fingers in and out, in and out, hips rocking just a little with each thrust.

He wrapped his fingers around his prick and pumped in time with the fingers in his ass. "Get yourself ready, David. I need your cock in my ass right now."

Unwilling to look away from Kieran, David felt around blindly for the condom. His fingers closed on it and with shaking hands he tore the packet then smoothed the latex down his shaft.

Kieran had three fingers in his ass now and his eyes had drifted closed. He bit his lower lip and seemed to be lost in a haze of pleasure.

David dripped additional lube over his sheathed cock then crawled up between Kieran's legs and lightly touched his thigh, once more tracing the top of the sexy stockings Kieran still wore.

Kieran pulled his fingers from his ass and let go of his cock. He hugged his knees up even further. "Do it."

David lined up, the head of his dick just touching Kieran's entrance. "Kieran, look at me."

Obediently, Kieran's eyes opened.

Their gazes locked.

David pressed forward. Kieran's body resisted but only for a moment, then the head slipped in.

Kieran gasped and David went still. So hot. So tight. David squeezed his eyes shut and struggled to control the urge to push, to bury himself in that silky heat and claim this man for his own.

When he thought he could move without blowing his load, David opened his eyes and found Kieran watching him. "Okay, baby?"

His lover nodded. "Yeah. Good. More."

Slowly David pushed, filling Kieran's channel inch by inch until his balls rested against the other man's ass.

Kieran linked his ankles behind David's neck then grasped David's arms with both hands. "Kiss me."

He raised up and David leaned forward, fusing their mouths for one searing, needy kiss before they broke apart and David began to move.

He pulled nearly all the way out then thrust in deep. Kieran's muscles gripped him in a silky vise, sucking him in, holding him like they would never let go. David repeated the motion, setting up a smooth rhythm, angling his cock to hit Kieran's gland.

"Ah fuck." Releasing David's arm, Kieran gripped his own cock. "Not yet. Don't make me come yet."

David did it again, loving the way Kieran thrashed under him, the pleading tone of his request.

The heels scraped along David's back as Kieran fought for leverage and David increased the speed and depth of his thrusts. He fucked Kieran like their lives depended on it. Everything in David's world shrank down to this moment, this man, this claiming and coming together. The scrape of Kieran's heels, the silky scratchy slide of his stockings, the hand still gripping his arm hard enough to bruise, all mingled with the smells of sweat and sex and the unbearable need to come and take Kieran with him.

Kieran thrashed his head from side to side, his eyes squeezed shut; a single tear leaked from one corner and caught the light, sparkling like a jewel before sliding back and disappearing into his hair.

"David," Kieran whimpered, "I'm gonna come. Oh God!"

David's hips snapped backward and forward, his cock pistoning in and out of Kieran's ass, his orgasm sparking along his spine before bursting into flame.

He shoved in deep just as Kieran cried wordlessly and hot cum splashed up and over his lean torso.

David held himself at the peak of his thrust, cock throbbing as he pumped jets of cum into the condom and he imagined instead that he was filling Kieran's ass with his spunk.

All at once his arms gave out and he slumped forward onto Kieran's chest. Slim, strong arms encircled him and held him tight as they both gasped for breath, their hearts thundering together, their skin slick with sweat and cum.

Shifting slightly so Kieran could unfold his legs, David's cock slipped free of his lover's ass. David dealt with the condom then pulled Kieran into his arms. He stroked sweat-soaked hair back from his face. "That was incredible." He kissed him. "You're amazing. So hot." Another kiss. "So sexy. I swear, I could fuck you all night."

Kieran laughed, the sound still a little breathless. "You won't see me complaining. Besides, you did all the work."

"If that was work you can sign me up for overtime." David licked a drop of sweat from Kieran's temple.

Long fingers tangled in the hair on David's chest. "Mind if I stay?"

"Of course I don't mind." He laid a hand atop Kieran's over his heart. "I'd like that."

The truth was he'd hoped Kieran would stay. Though they were virtual strangers, there was something that felt undeniably right about it. Maybe it was the way Kieran fit against him, or the way that slim strong body felt in his arms.

David said none of this however. He didn't want Kieran to think he was a romantic sap, not even if he actually was one.

"Great." Kieran cuddled closer and rubbed his cheek against David's bare shoulder. Despite the late hour, he had only the lightest rasp of beard stubble. "I guess we should get up and clean up."

"Mmm." David touched his lips to the corner of Kieran's mouth. "Stay right here. I'll get you a towel."

Sliding out of bed, David padded to the bathroom. He ran the water till it warmed up and wet a washcloth for Kieran. Then grabbing a towel from the rack, he returned to the bedroom.

Kieran was propped on one elbow, a sheaf of papers in his hand.

At first David had no idea what the pages were, then it dawned on him. It was the printout of his play. He'd been reading it over and making notes in the margins as he lay in bed just the previous night, and now Kieran was reading it along with all his scribbles and comments, the stuff meant for no one's eyes but his own. And he wasn't sure how he felt about that. But there was no time to make up his mind because just then Kieran's gaze lifted and met David's.

"You wrote this?"

David's face went hot and it had nothing to do with the fact that he was standing there naked. He nodded.

"It's terrific." He must have seen something odd in David's expression because he quickly laid the pages aside. "I'm sorry. I guess I shouldn't have been reading it. I was just reaching for a tissue and I saw it lying there and..." He shrugged and looked away. "I'm sorry."

"No, don't be sorry. It's fine. I guess I'm just not used to anybody being here and I leave stuff lying around." He walked to the bed and sat down on the edge of the mattress. "It's okay. Really."

Kieran looked doubtful. "I guess your other... " He seemed to search for a word. "...your other dates aren't so rude as me."

David laughed. "What other dates?" Taking the cloth, he cleaned Kieran up, wiping away the cum and lube before gently drying him with the towel.

"Yeah right, like you don't have other guys up here." Kieran's lips curved and he reached up and touched David's cheek. "I don't believe it."

"Believe it or not. It's been a while since I brought anyone home like this." Dropping the towel and washcloth on the floor, David slipped under the covers and stretched out on his back alongside Kieran. When had he taken off the shoes and stockings, David wondered. Not that it really mattered. He sighed. The sheets were so warm, the man beside him even warmer. He could get used to this.

Kieran turned on his side, his arm sliding around David's middle. A thigh rested atop David's and a knee nestled between his.

With a fingertip, Kieran circled first one nipple then the other. "Tell me about the play?"

"Mine?"

"Of course yours." Kieran chuckled. "Who's the main character?"

"His name is Damon Childress. He's a gay guy from a small town in Oregon."

"Mmm. What else? How does it start?"

"You read the beginning." Catching Kieran's hand in his, David raised it to his lips and took the index finger in his mouth.

"Only like the first page and a half before you came back from the bathroom." Kieran pulled his finger from David's mouth and traced his lips. "Are you going to let me read the rest?"

Unaccountably shy all of a sudden, David hesitated. What if Kieran thought his play was sentimental drivel? If he said so David knew he would be crushed, which would probably ruin any chance they might have at something more than a one-night hookup. Not that he really thought Kieran might say that, but still... He smiled to himself, remembering how he'd felt back when he'd first begun writing.

"What's so funny?" Kieran nuzzled the corner of David's jaw.

"I was just remembering how, when I was in play writing class in college, we used to do this thing we called ugly baby night. We would all read from our works in progress then comment on each other's stuff. It was totally nerve racking because you were always afraid the others would see how bad you sucked and say so. That they would call your baby ugly."

"I doubt yours was ever ugly." Kieran brushed a soft kiss under David's ear.

"See, your expectations are already too high." Turning on his side, David pulled Kieran close. He found Kieran's lips with his and kissed him long and slow.

"Mmm." Kieran hummed into David's mouth, molding their bodies close, mashing their groins together. Kieran wiggled his hips, making David's cock twitch with renewed interest.

David trailed his fingers down Kieran's spine, articulating each vertebra on the way to the tempting swell of Kieran's ass. Cupping the firm round globe he thrust, encouraging his own and his lover's growing erections.

"Ooo, yeah." Kieran thrust back. "Feels good. I could get used to this." He paused. "I mean—"

"It's all right. I know what you mean." He did too. And David thought once again that he too could definitely get used to this.

CHAPTER SIX

"Thank you so much, hon." The woman with the gray-streaked ponytail zipped her purse and beamed at Kieran.

He tucked her receipt in the gift-bag and handed it to her. Seeing as she'd just racked up a two hundred dollar sale for him, the smile he sent her was totally genuine. And given that he'd only just that week been promoted from fragrance tester to sales associate, that just freakin' rocked, didn't it?

"You're quite welcome, miss. I hope your daughter enjoys everything."

"Oh, I know she will." She added the bag to her already overflowing collection of purchases, gave Kieran another happy smile and left.

"Nice going." Ginger studied her reflection in the makeup mirror sitting atop the counter. "She comes in here for a bottle of perfume and you get her to buy the whole store." She laughed and reapplied her lip gloss then recapped the tube and dropped it back in her bag. "No wonder they promoted you already. I don't know how you do it."

Kieran shrugged. "I'm an actor. It's my job to make people believe." Idly he picked up first one then another of the little sample bottles of perfume and began rearranging them on the tray.

"What does that have to do with selling perfume?" Ginger pulled out a comb and ran it through her shoulder-length red hair.

"I just try to make the customer believe that her life won't be complete without whatever it is I'm selling. It's not so different from going on an audition and trying to sell yourself to the guy who's doing the casting. It's all a matter of marketing."

Like he'd done with David.

"Hmm, I guess. But I still don't know how you do it." She eyed him. "I think it's just you and those dimples. You smile and those middle-aged women go all fluttery." She pressed a hand to her chest and pretended to swoon.

Kieran laughed even as he felt the heat rise to his cheeks.

From the corner of his eye he saw a familiar figure approaching the fragrance counter. It was Orsino—Fred—Kieran corrected himself. What was Fred doing here anyway? Probably just shopping, doofus. That was what people did at the mall. And why did the guy creep him out so much?

Plastering on his professional smile Kieran greeted his fellow cast member. "Hey Fred, how's it going?"

"Hey man, I wasn't sure I'd catch you here." Fred rested his elbows on the counter and smiled at Kieran. "I came by yesterday and you weren't here. Glad my timing was better today."

"Yesterday was my day off. But how did you know I worked here?" He tried to remember if he'd mentioned his job the other night at rehearsal. He didn't think so. No, in fact he was sure he hadn't. And even if he had mentioned it, he and Fred hadn't exchanged more than a passing hello. In fact they'd hardly spoken outside the lines they had in the play.

"I'm psychic." Fred winked and his grin broadened, showing off his perfectly straight, perfectly white teeth.

"Psychic, huh?" He tried to keep it light though his gut churned with nerves. Something about the dude felt off somehow. The theater was full of posers and people who just got carried away with themselves, but he didn't think that was it, not in this case.

The memory of the other night came back with unwelcome vividness. The way Fred kept touching him as he talked. Or how he kept inadvertently brushing against him as they moved around the stage in response to David's directions. The guy was a close talker too, getting right up in Kieran's personal space even now, even with the counter separating them.

Kieran suppressed a shudder. He wasn't imagining it, of that he was certain. But neither could he afford to alienate a fellow cast member, especially one with whom he was going to have to work so closely in order to make it a good show. He tried to shake off his uneasiness, or at least conceal it.

Act like you're friends. You're an actor. You can make Fred believe that.

"So you're here to buy some perfume?" He turned the statement into a question by adding a little lift at the end of the line. He could totally do this, and maybe in doing it he could get the transaction over and hurry the creep on his way.

Fred glanced sideways at Ginger. "Um, I kind of wanted to talk to you. Can you take a break?"

"I really can't leave the counter, not until—"

Ginger waved him off. "Go on. I'll be okay."

"But what if we get busy?" Kieran stared hard, willing her to see how much he did not want to go anywhere with Fred, and in seeing for her to give him an out.

"It's fine, really. Just don't forget to come back." She lowered her lashes and sent him a knowing smile.

God, she thinks I'm interested in him. FSM, help me.

"Great." Fred straightened up. "Let's get some coffee or something. I want to talk to you about the play."

With no other choice, Kieran fell into step beside Fred. As they headed for the store exit into the mall, Kieran checked out his fellow actor and tried to see what Ginger saw. He was half a head taller than Kieran. His wavy chestnut hair was tousled just so and still touched with summer-blond at the tips. His shoulders were broad, his waist slim and his hips narrow. With a complete personality transplant, the prospect of coffee with the man might even have been appealing. But as it was, he planned on ordering the shortest possible espresso and drinking it as quickly as possible so he could get this encounter over with.

"So what about the play?"

They walked along the mall, the hiss and splash of the fountain mingled with the piped in elevator music, creating a kind of white noise that Kieran usually found very soothing. Today it annoyed him and made his head hurt.

It was probably far too much to hope that Fred was here to say he was dropping out, that he'd changed his mind and wouldn't be playing Orsino after all. Still, just for a moment Kieran let himself imagine what it might be like if David were playing Orsino instead of Fred.

It wouldn't take much acting to have the audience believing their attraction. Hell, he'd been attracted to David ever since that first glimpse of him at the fragrance counter two weeks earlier, and now that they were lovers... Kieran smiled recalling how his stomach had fluttered when he'd taken David's hand and sprayed the inside of his wrist with the cologne sample.

Maybe someday he'd even tell David that he'd made up that stuff about how you had to rub it in before you smelled it just so he could hold the hand of the tall, bespectacled blond for just a little longer.

And David's pulse had jumped under his fingertips. The memory was so vivid he could almost still feel it. Such a simple touch yet so exciting. Kieran's dick had gotten hard as granite right there in the middle of Macy's fragrance department.

"What are you smiling about?" Fred bumped Kieran's shoulder. The back of his hand brushed Kieran's and he too smiled.

"Nothing. I was just remembering something." As nonchalantly as he could manage, Kieran eased away, just a half a step, not so much Fred was likely to notice, at least he hoped not.

"This way." Fred caught Kieran's hand and tugged him toward the outside door.

"Where are you going? I only have a couple minutes."

"Just outside here. I want a cigarette and you can't smoke in the mall."

"Fred—"

"My name's Stephen."

Kieran stopped and pulled Fred to a stop with him. "Why do they call you Fred if your name's Stephen?"

"My last name is Fredericksdorf. When I was in like second or third grade the kids started calling me Fred and it stuck." He gave Kieran's hand a little tug. "C'mon. I don't want to dick around if you've only got a couple minutes."

Outside the sun shone bright and warm but the air was freezing. Kieran shivered and hugged himself against the chill.

Fred pulled a pack of cigarettes and a lighter from the pocket of his down vest and held them out. "Want one?"

"I don't smoke."

Fred lit up, pulled in a drag and let it out, studying Kieran through the smoke. "You were totally awesome the other night, you know." He blew smoke through his nose and laughed. "Not many guys would have the balls to play a girl the way you are."

Kieran shrugged. He couldn't help feeling pleased by the compliment, even considering the source. "Viola's a great part. I'm glad David's willing to take a chance on me."

The wind gusted and Kieran shivered.

"Shit, man, you're freezing." Fred held out the hand not holding the cigarette. "Let's go sit in my car."

"I'm okay," Kieran said through chattering teeth. He was freezing his ass off but he did not want to go sit in Fred's car.

"Bullshit. C'mon, you're freezing." Fred tossed his cigarette to the blacktop and ground it out under his shoe. He pulled keys from his pocket and gestured. "I'm parked right over there in the handicapped spot."

He started for the car, glanced back, saw that Kieran wasn't following and held out his hand.

An awkward moment ensued as Kieran stared at the hand but made no move to take it. He should just go back inside. He did not like Fred and he did not like what was going on here.

"What's the matter?" Fred wiggled his fingers. "I don't bite, you know." There was that smile again.

What was the matter anyway? The guy just wanted to talk. They were in the play together after all. They would be spending a lot of time in each other's company throughout the run of the show. Lots of opportunity to act friendly. So just suck it up and start now.

Inside the car it was much warmer and just getting out of the wind helped a lot. Fred turned the heater on. "I was thinking about our scenes, you know? Orsino and Cesario?"

"What about them?" Kieran's fingers began to thaw out and he held his hands up to the vent.

"About how you're supposed to be in love with me. About how we could really generate some chemistry onstage if we got to know each other better."

Alarm bells began to ring in Kieran's head. He'd thought the actor playing Orsino was straight, would have sworn to it. But the hand now resting on his thigh told another story.

He reached for the door handle and shifted his leg, trying to dislodge the hand without making a huge hairy deal out of it. "I don't think—"

"C'mon Kieran. I saw the way you kept looking at me. You were giving me those come on eyes all night."

"It's called acting. My character is attracted to your character. It's pretend. It has nothing to do with me and you, Fred."

"Stephen. I want you to call me Stephen. Acting my ass. Nobody's that good. You want me."

He couldn't believe this was happening. What the hell was this asshole on anyway?

"I am that good." Kieran reached once more for the door handle. But just as his fingers closed around the handle he heard the locks click. He tugged on it but nothing happened. "Dude, that's not funny. Now open the door and let me out. I have to go back to work."

"In a minute." Fred didn't move, just sat there and watched him. Then he shifted and unzipped his jacket. The bulge of his dick was clearly outlined under the snug denim of his jeans. He gave his length a long, leisurely stroke. "See something you like?"

Jerking his gaze back to Fred's face, Kieran tried to sound bored rather than panicky. "Man, you're making a huge mistake." He forced a laugh. "I'm not interested, okay? I'm not sure how to make it any plainer."

Fred's hand quit stroking his erection and he stared hard at Kieran. "You're gay, aren't you?"

For a moment, only a moment, he considered denying it. Fuck that. He was not going to lie just to save this asshole's ego.

"Yeah, I'm gay, just not interested."

"Just in the director, huh?" Fred's mouth twisted into an ugly sneer. "Why do you look so surprised? It isn't like we don't all know why he cast you instead of Julie. Not as if he's likely to want what she's got to offer."

"I don't know what you mean."

"I think you do. C'mon, Kieran, I know you and David are fucking. He fucks all the pretty boys. It's not like you're the first, or the only." Fred laughed. It was an ugly sound. "All I know is you better be worth it, considering everything he's giving up."

"What do you mean, giving up?"

"Ask David. Let him tell you." The locks clicked. "Now you run along before your little friend gets the wrong idea about us."

Kieran yanked the door handle and practically fell out of the car in his rush to escape.

❦❦❦❦❦

"So I told her when we do *Our Town* next season, I was going to dress everyone in pvc and leather. She got this horrified look on her face and said something about how expensive that was going to be." David laughed.

Kieran didn't join him, not right away, not like it was a spontaneous reaction. Only after a moment did he smile and even that looked like a forced effort.

Something was definitely up. But what? And why didn't Kieran want to tell him?

Despite their short acquaintance, David had known as soon as he saw Kieran waiting for him outside Macy's entrance that something was wrong. It was all over his face though he'd denied it more than once.

David finished the last of his half of the pizza and dropped the crust on his plate. Pulling another of the skimpy paper napkins from the holder on the table, he wiped his mouth then his fingers.

Kieran was still toying with the first piece of pizza he'd taken. The rest of his half sat, untouched, on the serving plate.

"Should we get that to go?" David reached for his wallet and extracted some bills.

Kieran shook his head then shrugged. "If you want, but I've had enough."

He pulled a wad of crumpled bills from his pocket, but when he held them out David waved them away. "Don't worry about it. I've got it."

Silently Kieran returned the money to his pocket and slid to the end of the booth. "You ready to go?"

With a final glance at the remaining pizza, David nodded and stood too.

They left the restaurant in silence. As they crossed the parking lot Kieran didn't speak. He seemed lost in his own thoughts.

David took his hand and laced their fingers together. "Did I do something?"

Kieran's eyes widened. "No, of course not."

But the answer had come too quickly for David's comfort. Something about it felt off. In fact, something about this whole evening felt off.

Maybe he should forget about asking Kieran if he could stay at his place tonight. He should probably just go to Bethany's and crash on her couch.

Except he didn't want to go to Bethany's. He wanted to spend the night with his new lover.

In the car, the silence pressed in on David like a physical weight. He turned on the radio and punched the preprogrammed buttons until he found music. A searing Eddie Vedder guitar riff poured from the speakers.

"David, listen—"

"Kieran, I was—"

They both stopped speaking at once.

"You first," David said.

"No, you go ahead."

He thought about arguing. Pushing Kieran to say what was on his mind, then discarded the idea. What did he have to lose?

"I was wondering if I could maybe stay at your place tonight." Before Kieran could answer, David rushed on. "I had a little—well, not really so little—plumbing disaster in my apartment."

"Oh no. What happened?"

David went on to explain how the soil pipe had cracked and leaked filthy, disgusting water through the ceiling of the downstairs apartment where his landlord lived.

"Even though they got a plumber to come out right away, my bathroom is sort of nonexistent at this point and I have no running water in the whole apartment ,so…"

The hesitation was no longer than a single breath. In fact he might have imagined it. Maybe Kieran hadn't hesitated at all and he was just hyper-aware tonight.

A hand covered David's on the shifter and squeezed. "Of course you can stay with me." Another squeeze. "I'd like that."

⚜ ⚜ ⚜ ⚜ ⚜

"Turn left at the stop sign." Unnecessarily Kieran pointed. His stomach jittered with nerves. David was coming home with him and would see where he lived for the first time.

Had he cleaned up this morning before he left for work? Put away his girlie clothes and his makeup? He couldn't remember but probably not, since he hadn't expected David to be coming over.

It didn't matter. He wouldn't let it. After all David knew he dressed up occasionally. So what if he thought it was just for the role? So what if Kieran had found it simpler to just let him believe that?

Because if David saw the contents of Kieran's closet and dresser, the lie would be revealed for what it was. And what was infinitely worse, Kieran would be revealed as a liar who regularly danced back and forth over the gender identity line, which very well could cost him his relationship with David. It wouldn't be the first time his gender fluidity had cost him someone he cared for.

Don't think about that. David isn't like that. He's nothing like that. Not that Kieran knew anyway.

"Which way?"

Kieran started. They were stopped at a red light and David was looking at him.

"Straight. It's in the middle of the next block, the house on the left side, right after the stop ahead sign."

"Can I pull into the driveway or is it better to park on the street?"

"The street's probably better." Kieran leaned forward and pointed through the windshield. "You can take that space right out front."

The empty parking space told Kieran that Jon, one of his three housemates, wasn't home. Like Kieran, Ronnie and Matt didn't have cars, so there was no telling whether or not they were there.

All his housemates knew Kieran wore dresses and all were okay with that. They were so okay with it in fact, that any one of them might mention it or not in front of David, which presented an entirely new anxiety that Kieran hadn't previously thought of.

Great.

Nothing he could do about it now except hope for an empty house.

As soon as he opened the door, he knew that was too much to hope. The stereo blared out some heavy metal hair band from the eighties and the TV competed at top volume. The smell of Chinese takeout from the place down the street filled the first floor.

David leaned close and yelled into Kieran's ear to be heard over the din. "How many people did you say live here?"

"Just four of us." Kieran walked to the stereo and turned down the volume.

"Yo, what the hell?"

"Yo Matt," Kieran yelled back.

Matt appeared in the living room doorway. He was shirtless and barefoot, wearing his customary gray track pants and his hair stuck up in all directions. "Dude, I have a huge test tomorrow and I'm trying to study."

"We're just passing through," Kieran promised. He turned to David. "This is Matt. Matt, this is David."

Mat's gaze drifted down David's body and he nodded.

Jealousy flared sudden and hot in Kieran's chest. Maybe leaving David in Matt's company, even for a few minutes while he ran upstairs, was an even bigger risk than he'd thought. Matt would screw anything in pants and Kieran saw by the way his housemate was looking at his lover that David was Matt's type du jour.

"You guys want some Chinese?" Matt propped his long lean self against the doorjam and sent David a dazzling smile.

David glanced at Kieran.

"We just ate." Kieran took David's hand and tugged him toward the stairs. "And we don't want to disturb your studying."

As they started up the stairs, the volume on the stereo increased as, presumably, his housemate went back to his books.

"Is he always like that?" David asked as they climbed the steps to the third floor.

"Pretty much. Matt flirts with everybody. It's just his way. He doesn't mean anything by it."

They reached the top landing and David paused. "Can I use your bathroom?"

"Sure." Kieran pointed. "On the left."

The door had hardly closed behind David before Kieran dashed into his room. He ignored the makeup scattered across the top of the dresser. Lots of guys wore makeup and David already knew he did. Quickly he picked up the clothes, both men's and women's, scattered over the bed and floor. If only he wasn't such a slob.

Balling everything up, he shoved the whole mess into the bag that served as his clothes hamper then stuffed it in the closet. Just as he was shutting the door, he spotted a pair of lacy black panties on the floor near the foot of the bed. He grabbed them and tossed them into the closet with the rest of his laundry. There. He was good to go.

Had to be since he had no time to do much else. Taking one final look around, he relaxed a little. He crouched down and peered under the bed. His favorite pair of red high-heels peered flirtatiously back at him.

They were the same heels he'd worn that first night he and David had gone dancing. Kieran recalled how he'd kept them on while David fucked him. His cock twitched and began to fill at the memory.

Hearing the telltale squeak of the bathroom door, Kieran shoved the heels further under the bed and straightened up. Sooner or later he was going to have to tell David that the women's clothes were not just an actor's way of getting into the role, that there were days when he felt more girl than boy and the clothes were just part of that. Yes, at some point David would have to be told. Some day. But not today.

"Hey, I was hoping I'd find you naked and waiting for me in bed." David's lips curved in that slow, shy smile.

Kieran's heart flipped over and something tightened low in his belly. He flicked open the button of his jeans. "Shut the door and we'll see what we can do about that."

"Sounds like a plan." David closed the door.

Kieran saw the one thing he'd forgotten and froze. On a hook, on the back of his bedroom door, hung the beautiful, silk nightgown his sister had given him for his last birthday. The gown had long sleeves and a low neck. It was simple and elegant and Kieran loved the feel of the silk against his skin. But just then he wished he'd never seen the thing. Maybe David wouldn't notice.

"What's wrong?" David paused, his shirt half unbuttoned, the tails already pulled free of his jeans.

"Nothing." Kieran shoved his own jeans down, leaving the lace-trimmed blue panties on. The distraction worked.

"Wow, you really are into this cross-dressing for the role thing, aren't you?" David slipped the last button on his shirt and shrugged it off.

"Hey, anything for my art." Kieran stepped free of his jeans and pulled his shirt over his head. Wearing only the bikini panties, he advanced on his lover. "See something you like?"

"I like everything I'm seeing right now." David caught him around the waist and yanked Kieran against him before crushing their mouths together.

The kiss stole Kieran's breath. Sliding his arms around David's neck, he pressed even closer, rubbing himself against his lover like a cat begging to be petted.

David groaned into Kieran's mouth. His hands slid down and squeezed his ass through the slippery material of his panties.

"God, you're so sexy. You make me so hard."

Kieran laughed. He loved that look in David's eyes. It made him feel beautiful and sexy and desirable.

Sliding his fingers inside David's waistband he gave it a tug. "Get these jeans off and let me see how hard you are for me."

Shoving his pants down, David stepped out of them. He picked them up and turned, laying them over the back of the desk chair and stopped. He went very still.

Already knowing what David was looking at, Kieran followed the direction of his gaze. A cold chill crept through him, followed almost immediately by a panicky need to explain. He scrambled off the bed.

"David, I can explain."

Saying nothing, David walked to the door. For one horrible moment, Kieran was sure he was leaving. But he stopped and took the nightgown from its hook and held it up.

With no idea what he meant to say, Kieran went to him and touched his arm. "David, I—"

David held out the nightgown. "Give me thy hand and let me see thee in thy woman's weeds."

Kieran swallowed. He knew the next lines were Viola's but for his life he couldn't remember what they were. Nor could he seem to move. But he had to say or do something.

"It's not just for the play," he whispered.

David nodded. "It's all right." He took Kieran's hand and pressed the nightgown into it, folding his numb fingers around the silk. "Wear it for me."

Kieran's heart began to beat so hard he thought it might just pop out of his chest and flop on the floor at David's feet. He searched the other man's face for any sign, even the slightest indication, that David was not okay with this. But he saw only desire.

He took the nightgown and lifted it to slip it over his head. A light touch on his arm stopped him.

"Lose the underwear." David's lips curved. "As much as I like them, I want you naked under that silk. It is silk, isn't it?"

Kieran nodded, unable to speak past the lump formed of emotion in his throat. Shoving the underwear down, he stepped free of them and slipped the nightgown over his head.

He loved the feel of the silk sliding over his skin, like a lover's caress, like David's caress. The gown was long, to his ankles, the feel exquisite and sensual as it slid down his body. It brushed over his cock and Kieran's breath caught.

"Kieran baby, look at me."

Unaware until that moment that he'd closed his eyes, Kieran opened them. David reached for him and Kieran stepped into his arms. He rested his cheek against David's chest, the soft crisp hairs tickled his lips and once more Kieran closed his eyes.

David's hands moved over him. His shoulders, his back, his hips and his ass, they stroked and caressed as if he couldn't get enough.

"You feel so good," David whispered into Kieran's hair. "I could touch you all night like this."

You could touch me forever, Kieran thought but didn't say. Instead he molded his body against David's and reveled in the heat of his skin through the silk, the unbearably sensual sliding of their cocks separated by only the thinnest breath of fabric.

Kieran rose on tiptoe and lightly touched their lips together. "Let's go to bed."

Without letting him go, David walked him backward until the backs of his knees bumped the edge of the mattress. He prepared for David to tumble him backward as he had done once before. But instead, supported by his lover's arms, Kieran found himself slowly lowered onto his back on the bed. David leaned over him, their gazes locked, lips no more than a breath apart.

I love you, Kieran thought, and only just kept himself from saying aloud. It was true. He could love David Sullivan, already did love him. And now that he knew he could trust David with who he was, maybe it was time to tell him.

"What are you thinking so hard about?" David touched his nose to Kieran's.

"Nothing." Kieran shoved his worry aside and tightened his arms around his new lover, tugging David down on top of him. He rubbed his cheek against his lover's, enjoying the light scrape of beard stubble.

"Liar." David pressed a kiss to the corner of Kieran's mouth. "If you can still think at all, then I must be doing something wrong." He moved his hips, the silk creating a deliciously slippery barrier between their bodies.

Kieran moaned. He ran his palms over the smooth skin of David's back and down to his ass. Gripping his hips, Kieran bucked up against him.

"No way, you're perfect. Ah God, feels so good." He squirmed and thrust against David, their cocks sliding together, the silk growing damp with pre-cum.

"I want to fuck you so bad, Kieran."

"Yeah. Do it now. I want it. I need it."

David rolled over and tapped Kieran's hip. "Turn over."

Kieran turned on to his stomach. But when he started to pull off the nightgown, David stopped him.

"Leave it on."

Kieran glanced over his shoulder. Had he heard right?

David's cheeks colored. His eyes shone with lust. "I like the way it feels. I want to feel it while I'm fucking you. Is that all right?"

Kieran nodded and adjusted his position, raising up on his knees and presenting his silk-covered ass.

Hands slipped under Kieran's gown, palms slid up the backs of his thighs. The silk was pushed up and bunched around his hips. The hard, hot length of David's prick pressed against Kieran's ass.

He whimpered and pushed back.

David leaned over his back. Lips brushed his nape. David's hips shifted, his bare cock rubbing along Kieran's crease.

So hot. So good.

"Fuck me." Kieran wiggled his hips, pushing back against that lovely hard length.

"Condoms and lube?"

"Top dresser drawer. Hurry up, will you?"

"You need a nightstand, babe." The mattress shifted as David got up.

"I know it." Kieran turned his head and rested his cheek on his forearm. He heard the familiar squeak of the floorboard in front of his dresser and the slide of wood against wood as David opened the drawer. Then silence.

"Did you find them?" Raising his head, Kieran craned to see over his shoulder. "David?" When still David didn't respond, Kieran rolled over.

Oh shit!

Kieran scrambled off the bed and went to David, who stood absolutely still. He stared down into the open drawer, the wrong drawer, the drawer that held Kieran's lingerie. Piles of silky, sheer and lace-trimmed underwear, panties, padded bras, garters and stockings were all neatly laid out and on display for David to see.

Kieran tried to speak, to say David's name, something, anything to fill the awful silence and found he could not. He swallowed and tried again, this time finding his voice, if not the words that would make this all right.

"That's the wrong drawer." He opened the top drawer on the other side of the dresser, produced a box of condoms and a bottle of lube and set both on top.

David still said nothing, still didn't move.

"David." Kieran touched his arm. "I told you it wasn't just for the play."

At last David looked up, his expression unreadable and that scared Kieran more than the silence.

"How often?" The question came out hardly above a whisper.

"A lot. Nearly every day, I guess. Even under my... " he had to swallowed and moisten his lips. "My boy clothes, I wear them."

"That's why you wouldn't let me unzip you that first night in the theater, isn't it?"

Kieran nodded. "I was afraid."

"Of what? Of me?" Hurt filled David's dark eyes.

"No, not of you, not exactly. I was afraid you'd think I was a freak and I wanted you to like me. And want me."

"Why did you dress up when we went dancing?"

Kieran shoved a hand through his hair and blew out a breath. "Because I needed to know how you felt about it." He averted his eyes. "I liked you and I need to know if, knowing everything, you could still like me back."

"I do like you." A pause. "And I like this, all of it." He gestured at Kieran's nightgown then at the drawer full of lingerie. He shoved both hands into the drawer, burying them in the heaps of silk and lace as if meaning to drag out fistfuls of the stuff. Closing his eyes he let his head fall forward and laughed a little. "God, it makes me so hard." Pulling his hands from the drawer, he reached for Kieran and drew him close. "You make me so hard."

Through the silk, David's hard hot prick pressed against Kieran's belly, the evidence of his words.

Winding his arms around David's neck, Kieran rested his head on his lover's shoulder as his heart slipped away and into this man's keeping.

CHAPTER SEVEN

Kieran sat at a small table by the front window of Starbucks. He had an excellent view of the street and he saw Bethany before she saw him. Of course he had planned it that way, reaching the shop ten minutes earlier than the agreed time so he could prepare himself. Even so, his pulse accelerated as he watched her get out of her car and put money in the parking meter. The wind blew a flurry of dry leaves along the sidewalk and she shrugged deeper into her coat.

He sat back, sipped his latté and waited. Moments later the door opened and Bethany entered. She paused, scanned the tables and spotted him. She lifted a hand in greeting then tilted her head toward the counter.

Because he was sitting, she hadn't really seen him, or not what he was wearing anyway. Kieran wondered what she'd say, or more to the point, what her expression would say when she did.

For their meeting he'd chosen a long black skirt and matched it with a black and red sweater that had leather patches on the elbows and shoulders. His makeup was careful and subtle and he wore low-heeled black suede boots. He thought he looked pretty good. But it was her opinion that counted, because if he and David had any chance at a future then he needed to know why Bethany didn't like him and if there was anything he could do to win her over.

A little voice in his head whispered that dressing in a skirt was maybe not the best way to do that, but Kieran ignored it. If there was one thing he'd never been able to do, it was pretend to be someone he was not. And if David accepted him for who and what he was, then Bethany too needed to see the whole picture.

She came toward him, her drink in one hand, a tentative smile playing around her mouth. "Kieran, hi."

Pulse pounding, Kieran pushed back his chair and stood up. He held out his hand. "Hi. I'm glad you could come."

"It sounded important so—" Her eyes widened and she paused, her coat still dangling from one arm.

At least she didn't look utterly horrified.

Kieran said nothing and for a long time neither did she. Then she laughed a little and shook her head.

"Wow, you look better in a skirt than I do." She took her coat off the rest of the way and hung it on the back of her chair. "I guess David was right to give you Viola. If I didn't know I might think you really were a woman."

She sat and so did he.

"So you thought he shouldn't have cast me as Viola?"

She shrugged. "My brother and I often have differences of opinion where casting is concerned." She sipped her tea. "But obviously you're very serious about the role."

Kieran took a breath. "I don't dress this way just for the role."

"Really."

The woman gave excellent bland-face.

"Yes. Really."

"Does David know?"

Kieran nodded.

"And he's okay with it." She lifted the cup to her lips, sipped and studied him over the rim. "You know, Kieran, David's been gay... Well, always, I guess, but he came out to our family when he was just a young teen. I was the first one he told." A softness entered her voice and she smiled at the memory.

"What does that have to do with me?" Kieran traced a fingertip around the rim of his cup.

"He's never been interested in women, never even dated a girl that I know of."

"I'm not a girl, Bethany." It wasn't the whole truth, not exactly, because there were days, plenty of them, when he felt more female than male. But that discussion was far too complex for a Tuesday afternoon at Starbucks so he let it go at that.

"Then why the women's clothes? If you're not planning to change—"

"I'm not planning to change my sex. I like being a man. I like men. I like them a lot. I like David a lot."

She nodded. "I can see that."

"What do you mean?"

She pinched the bridge of her nose and seemed to think about her answer for a moment. "It's how you look at each other, I suppose. The way you relate to each other at rehearsals. Sometimes I catch David watching you when you don't know it and vise versa. And I can see that there's something there." She sipped her tea. "Are you and my brother dating?"

Kieran nodded. "We've gone out a few times."

"Is it serious?"

"Maybe. I don't know. It might be."

"Why did you ask me to come here today?"

Kieran moistened his lips. "I care about him. And I wanted... I feel like you don't like me, don't approve of me, something."

"And you thought showing up looking better than me in a skirt would win me over?" She laughed and covered his hand with hers. "Oh Kieran."

Kieran felt the heat rise to his cheeks. "I don't—"

"It isn't that I don't like you or don't approve of you. It's that I love my brother and sometimes I get a little overprotective of him. If I think he might get hurt, if I even suspect that the possibility is there, it makes me very defensive. I can't help that and I won't apologize for it. But it's nothing personal against you."

"I'm not going to hurt him." Kieran tried to pull his hand away but Bethany held it tight.

"I know you're not, or not intentionally anyway." She squeezed his hand. "But there's something else you should probably know."

Kieran's whole body tensed. "What?"

"Your instinct was right. I didn't want David to cast you as Viola. When he told me who he'd chosen we argued about it. And I still think he could have chosen smarter."

Now Kieran did tug his hand free. He wrapped both hands around his nearly empty cup. What was he supposed to say to that anyway?

"Now I've offended you."

"No."

"Yes, I have. It's not that you're not a good actor. You're a wonderful Viola."

"Then what is it?"

She hesitated. When she answered she spoke slowly and with great care, choosing her words very deliberately. "My brother and I started Fresh Voices just over year ago so we could bring the kind of theater we both love to our community. I'm a teacher—I don't know if you knew that—and I want to do workshops with young people in this area. I want to pass on my love of the theater. David is teaching now too. But it's not what he loves. He's a writer and a director. He has a graduate degree in directing. Did you know he's writing a play?"

Kieran nodded. "He told me."

Her pale brows lifted. "Did he?"

"Why is that so surprising?"

"Because he doesn't talk to many people about his work. I didn't realize he'd told anyone about his play other than me." She paused. Sipped. "You must be important to him if he told you that."

"I asked if I could read it and he said I could."

"And have you?"

"Not yet."

"You'll see, it's very good. Sensitive and compelling and—" She laughed. "Well, I am his sister, but that is my unbiased opinion. Anyway, my point is, we'd like to bring his work to our stage sometime in the next couple of seasons. But that means our company has to survive. And for right now that means money."

Kieran listened as she explained about the Redmans' foundation and the grant proposal she and David had submitted. Gradually it all became clear. So that was what Fred had been talking about.

"So you wanted Julie Redman to play Viola."

She nodded. "It might have given us a little leg up in the evaluation process, if you know what I mean?" She looked a little embarrassed. "I'm a bit more mercenary than my brother and I thought… well, it doesn't really matter now, I guess."

"Of course it matters. Do you really think you won't get the grant because Julie wasn't cast as Viola?"

She shrugged. "Who knows? I hope not but, I guess if we did know, maybe David would have chosen differently. And maybe he wouldn't. He's always been very independent where his work is concerned." She blushed. "No offense, Kieran."

He shook his head. "None taken. What can I do to help? What if I tell David I think he should give Viola to Julie?"

"You can't. He would kill me if he knew I told you about this. And besides, he wouldn't listen anyway. Promise me you won't tell him."

"I won't say anything about it."

Kieran didn't tell her about Fred or what he'd said. That story might get a little complicated and, in any case she probably didn't need to know that.

Bethany glanced at her watch. "I really need to get going. I have a doctor's appointment and if I don't leave now, I'll be late." She smiled apologetically. "I guess I don't really understand the cross-dressing thing, but if David is okay with it, then who am I to judge?" Getting slowly to her feet, she slipped into her coat and buttoned it up. "I'm glad we had this chance to talk, Kieran."

"Me too." He stood. They shook hands then Bethany hugged him. It was a quick, impulsive squeeze, over almost before he had time to be surprised.

"Be good to my brother or I will have to hurt you." Giving him one last smile she turned and left.

He watched her go. On a personal level, that had gone better than he'd dared to hope. As far as the show went, he had no clue what to do about that.

Chapter Eight

As Kieran walked to rehearsal that evening, he still wasn't sure what he should do about what Bethany had told him. The one thing he did know was that somehow he had to find a way to talk to David about it. The question was how to do that without betraying Bethany's confidence or breaking his promise to her.

Opening the door to the theater, Kieran stepped inside.

He was greeted by chaos. There were people everywhere and they all seemed to be talking at once. Some, like him, still wore their jackets while others were already in costume. A half-dressed Olivia charged across the stage and disappeared through the curtains at the back. A crowd had gathered downstage-left, all staring at something Kieran couldn't make out because they blocked his view. In the auditorium people rushed this way and that and everyone talked at once. Above it all someone yelled, "Call an ambulance! I can't tell if she's breathing."

Julie Redman rushed up the center aisle. She nearly collided with Kieran, who caught her arm and steadied her as she teetered on her heels. She stared at him like she had no clue who he was. "You're not David. Where's David?"

"I don't know. What happened?"

"I don't know. Why are you asking me? I didn't do it. God, where's David?" She turned.

Before she could rush off, Kieran grabbed her shoulders and shook her. "Julie, what happened? Who got hurt?"

"Bethany! Oh Kieran!" she burst into tears and flung herself at him.

He caught her, staggered back two or three steps but somehow remained standing. "Tell me what happened."

Through her sobs she was barely coherent. He had to stop her twice and ask her to repeat herself before he discerned that one of the sets, Olivia's garden wall it seemed, had fallen over and that Bethany had been knocked unconscious. No one seemed to know where David was or even if he had arrived yet. The rest of the story was lost in Julie's hysteria, but he supposed it didn't really matter.

Still supporting her with one arm, Kieran pulled out his cell and dialed the emergency services number. This much at least he could do.

"Hello, I have an emergency and I need an ambulance."

✞✞✞✞✞

Fatigue and worry dragged at David like physical weights around his ankles as he left the hospital. A thin covering of snow coated the cars in the parking lot as well as the narrow strip of grass bordering the blacktop. Tiny flakes fell fast and furious. They clung to David's lashes and stung his cheeks but he hardly felt them.

Now where the hell were they parked?

"Are you okay?" Kieran slipped his hand into David's and laced their fingers as they crossed the parking lot. "Sure you don't want me to drive?"

"I'm okay. Just a little tired is all." He scanned the rows of parked cars. "Do you remember—"

"It's over there." Kieran pointed.

At last David spotted his Volkswagen two aisles over. Fumbling in his jacket pocket, he trudged toward it. "Goddamn it! My keys—"

"Are right here." Kieran held them up. "I drove us down here, remember?"

David nodded. "Yeah, I remember. Now." He blew out a breath, a cloud of steam forming in the freezing air. "Maybe you should drive, if you don't mind?"

"I told you I don't mind."

They reached the car and stopped. Kieran wrapped his arms around David and hugged him tight. "It's going to be okay. She's going to be okay."

"I know, just..." David held on. He rested his cheek against Kieran's hair, the tiny ice crystals caught there melted against his skin and ran like tears.

They stayed like that, neither speaking, for what felt like a long time. Kieran rubbed David's back in slow circles. The snow fell all around them, coating their hair and clothes. But he didn't want to let go of Kieran, couldn't let go.

Now that he knew the crisis was past and he knew Bethany and the baby would be okay, David felt as if he might fly apart. He felt fragile and shaky and like at any moment he might throw up.

But Kieran was here, thank God, and Kieran was holding him together. He would be fine as long as he didn't let go.

He'd been late getting to the theater, held up at school by a student in need of extra help with his midterm project. He had rushed directly from his office on campus to the theater, not even stopping at home to change his clothes. As he'd turned his car onto Hartwell Avenue, David had seen the flashing lights and his heart had leaped into his throat.

He hadn't even taken the time to park his car, just stopped in the middle of the street and jumped out. Just as he did, the ambulance attendants emerged from the theater carrying his sister on a stretcher.

David was unclear on what happened next. He knew only that Kieran had been there, taking charge and doing what David himself had been unable to pull himself together enough to do. Kieran had gone with him to the hospital and stayed with him and held his hand through the endless wait before the doc had come out and told him that Bethany and the baby would be okay, that she had a relatively minor concussion and would need to spend the night in the hospital, just to be sure. Of course Bethany's husband Brent had been there, worrying right alongside him. But he couldn't lean on Brent. The poor guy had enough to deal with just holding himself together. But Kieran had been with him.

And Kieran was still with him.

Someone cleared their throat. "Um, David, I need to talk to you."

David and Kieran both looked up and reluctantly David let his lover go. Julie Redman stood on the other side of the car, her white knit hat pulled low on her head, her hands shoved deep in the pockets of her jacket.

What the hell was she doing here? But before David could get himself together, Kieran once more took charge.

"Julie, what are you doing here? It's nearly eleven o'clock."

"I needed to talk to David." She joined them by the driver's door. "How's Bethany?"

"She's going to be okay," David said. Though he had released Kieran, David still clung to his hand. He couldn't stand to break the contact altogether. "They're keeping her overnight for observation."

"What about the baby?"

"The baby's going to be okay too."

"Julie, what's so important it couldn't wait?" Kieran asked.

"I told you, I need to talk to David. Alone."

Kieran glanced at David, his eyebrows raised.

"Whatever it is, you can say it in front of Kieran."

She hesitated for a long time.

He was too tired to play her silly game. David reached for the car door.

"David, wait. Don't go. What happened tonight, I'm not sure it was an accident."

David went very still. Beside him he heard Kieran gasp. "What are you talking about?"

In the glow of the parking lot lights she bit her lip. "I don't know exactly. I mean, I don't like to say…"

"Julie, you can't make a statement like that and just leave it," Kieran said.

Her gaze dropped and she studied her mittens. "I think it might have been on purpose."

"Why do you say that?" Suddenly David felt an icy chill that had nothing to do with the snow.

"You need to talk to Fred about it." Her voice was hardly more than a whisper and David had to lean close even to hear. "I can't say exactly. We were moving the sets around, getting things ready, you know? And Fred was acting weird, saying stuff… I don't know."

"Julie—"

"I have to go."

"Wait." Kieran and David said together. David caught her arm and tried to turn her so he could see her face.

"I don't know anything else, David. You have to ask Fred." She pulled free of him, spun around, slipped and nearly fell.

"Julie!" Kieran made a grab as she regained her footing and rushed off.

"Let her go." David scrubbed a hand down his face.

"But—"

"Let's get in the car."

"What are you going to do?"

"I'm going to call Fred." David flipped open his phone. "Of course he probably won't want to tell me anything either. I might have to kick his ass. And I'm just about in the right mood for that too."

"Wait." Kieran stopped him with a hand on his arm. "I have another idea."

Chapter Nine

Alone in the empty theater, Kieran waited for Fred. He glanced at his watch for at least the tenth time in the last five minutes. Fred was late. Maybe he wouldn't come at all. Not likely though.

When Kieran had called him an hour earlier, his fellow actor had sounded at first disbelieving then downright suspicious when Kieran asked him to meet at the theater. He'd had to really lay on the flirting and flattery to convince Fred of his sincere desire to meet. Funny that as he'd become less and less sincere, Fred had become more and more amenable to the idea of getting together.

"Vanity thy name is Fred."

Kieran smiled to himself, though the thought of letting the creep anywhere near him, let alone actually touching him, was almost enough to cause him to rethink the wisdom of the plan. But when he heard the door bang open, he knew it was too late to back out now.

He rose from his seat in the first row and stepped into the aisle, giving Fred the full impact of his costume. Not the one he wore as Viola in the show, but the one he had chosen for the part he would play tonight.

The open-toes of his black stiletto heels peeked out from under his ankle-length skirt. As he walked up the aisle, the long slit flashed appealing glimpses of leg, sometimes even showing the lacy top of one sheer black stocking. He'd finished the outfit with a blousy white shirt, cinched in at the waist with lacings up the front and low-cut enough to give tantalizing glimpses of his smooth chest. The effect was at once feminine and piratical with a hint of the tart tossed in for good measure.

"Jesus shit!" Fred laughed. He advance toward Kieran, one hand held out. "You really do look like a chick, a really hot chick."

Kieran smiled and licked his red-painted lips. "I'm not one. Want to see?"

Breathless at his own daring, Kieran lifted his skirt, opening the slit wide enough so Fred could see the tiny black panties, barely enough to hold in place his cock and balls.

Fred groaned. "Oh man, fuck me."

Kieran twitched the slinky fabric back into place.

"Show me again."

Kieran shook his head. "Later. First, you promised to run lines with me, remember?" Fred opened his mouth, probably to argue, but Kieran laid a finger against his lips cutting off the words. "I said later, okay?"

Fred sucked the finger into his mouth and stroked it with his tongue before letting go.

Kieran suppressed a shudder. He forced himself not to wipe his finger on his clothes.

"All right," Fred graciously conceded. "But later I am so having you in that dress." He grinned. "You really do make a hot chick."

"I thought you didn't like girls." Kieran caught Fred's hand and led him toward the stage.

"As you pointed out before, honey, you ain't no girl." He laughed at his own crudeness. "No wonder David likes you so much."

Kieran winced at the mention of David. "That's all over."

"Yeah? Since when?"

He led Fred up the steps and onto the stage. "You were right about him, you know. All he wanted was to fuck me. I think it's the main reason he cast me as Viola."

"I told you. Some guys will do anything to get laid." Fred walked to center stage, faced the empty seats and struck a pose. When he glanced at Kieran and smiled, Kieran dropped him a wink. "What scene did you want to work on?"

"Let's try act five. Is that okay?"

"Sure, except we don't have the other characters."

"We'll just skip their lines. You know all your cues, right?"

Fred nodded.

"Okay, let's start with, Be not amazed; right noble is his blood."

They took their places. Kieran's heart beat wildly and his knees felt like Jell-O.

"Aren't you supposed to be standing over there by the wall?" Fred pointed. "Isn't that how David has it blocked?"

Kieran grimaced. "After what happened the other night, that wall makes me nervous. Somebody could really get hurt by that thing falling on them."

Fred dismissed this with a wave of his hand. "It'll be fine."

Kieran looked doubtfully at the large fake wall. "I don't know."

"Look." Fred walked over to the wall and shook it. "See? Solid as a rock."

Kieran hung back, playing it for all he could. "If it had happened a few minutes later it would have been me under there when it fell." He pouted just a little. "Can't I stand somewhere else?"

Fred crossed to him. Sliding his arms around Kieran's waist, he pulled him close and leaned in, stopping with their mouths only a breath apart. "You can stand anywhere you want to, baby."

Oh Christ, Fred was going to kiss him. Blech!

Fred brought their mouths together. Kieran shut his eyes and tried to think happy thoughts as Fred's tongue thrust between his lips. He was a mushy, slobbery kisser, not at all like the mind-melting experience of lip-locking with David.

At last Fred broke the contact. "Man, you're an awesome kisser." He slid his hands down to Kieran's ass. "Can I tell you a secret?"

"Sure." God, but he wanted to wipe his mouth with his hand or sleeve or something.

"Only if you promise not to tell anyone, especially not that prick David."

"I won't."

Fred rubbed his lips over Kieran's once, briefly. "I fixed that wall so it would fall down the other night."

"You did? Why?"

A shrug. "I was pissed."

"At who?"

"At you. At David. At this whole stupid fucking show. I don't know. I just wanted to fuck with you guys." He shook his head. "But I fixed it later. I just loosened the ropes that were holding it up. It fell before it was supposed to but that was all right. Anyway, it's okay now, so you don't have anything to worry about, sweetheart. But why don't we just say fuck this shit and go somewhere just the two of us?"

Kieran opened his mouth to say, what he had no clue, but he never got the chance.

"Get your hands off my boyfriend, you fucking prick, before I break your neck."

Fred jumped and released Kieran so fast he nearly fell over." What the fuck are you doing here?"

David came striding out from back stage, his face a frozen mask of fury. He seized Fred by the front of his shirt, yanked him up to his toes and shook him. "What the hell is wrong with you? You could have killed someone with your stupid bullshit. You did hurt someone. You're goddamn lucky my sister's going to be okay or I'd have ripped your fucking head off. I still might."

"Crazy bastard, let me go. You can't prove anything."

"You just admitted it. We both heard you say it," Kieran said.

Fred turned to Kieran.

"Don't say a word to him." David shoved Fred away. "Get the hell out of here before I call the cops and have you arrested."

"You can't prove anything." But Fred retreated, his attention never leaving David, like he was not quite sure David still wouldn't come after him and kick his ass.

As the door slammed behind Fred, David turned to Kieran. He blew out a breath. "Are you okay?"

"Yeah." He scrubbed the back of one hand over his mouth as if he could wipe away the memory of Fred's kiss.

David walked to Kieran and slipped his arms around him. "I hated seeing him touching you. Fucking bastard's crazy. I should call the cops on him. Get his ass arrested." He laid his cheek against Kieran's hair. "Are you sure you're okay?"

He nodded and pressed close. "Did you mean what you said before?"

"About what?"

"About me being your boyfriend."

David laughed, his arms going tight around Kieran. "Yeah, I guess I did. Is that okay with you?"

"That is totally okay with me."

David kissed him, just a soft sweet brush of lips. "Okay, so, one problem solved. Now, who the hell are we going to get to play Orsino?"

CHAPTER TEN

Viola's face gazed back at Kieran from the dressing table mirror. The thunder of applause still echoed in his head as he removed the lid from the cold cream. With two fingers he dug out a generous glob and coated his cheeks with it. Pulling a tissue from the box on the table, he began the laborious task of removing the heavy stage makeup that covered him from his hairline down to his fake cleavage.

They had packed the house tonight, every seat in the theater sold. And they'd brought the audience to its feet at the close of the last act. A freakin' standing O! And when he took his bow they had cheered for him. For him! Whistling and shouting out his name. In Kieran's opinion it was just about the coolest thing ever. He doubted he would ever tire of that rush.

He wiped away the last of the makeup from his chest then dropped the wad of tissues in the trashcan and began to work at the laces on his bodice. He needed to change his clothes, fix his makeup and get himself together for the party being held at Julie Redman's house. There were rumors of Dom Perignon circulating among the cast, started, he suspected, by Julie herself. He wasn't a big drinker and didn't like champagne much. Still, the idea of clinking glasses with David had a certain appeal to Kieran's romantic heart.

Stepping out of his skirt, Kieran reached for the purple sweater-dress he'd chosen for the party. He'd just finished pulling it over his head when the dressing room door burst open.

Orsino bounded across the room and tackled Kieran, almost knocking him off his feet.

"Whoa Jules, take it easy." Kieran laughed. He caught Julie around the waist and hugged her back.

"You were totally awesome tonight!" She kissed both his cheeks and her wide-brimmed hat fell off. "We were both awesome, weren't we?"

"Yeah we were." Kieran picked up Julie's hat and set it on the table. He still couldn't quite believe she'd cut her nearly waist-length hair just so she could play a more convincing Orsino.

"Your hair looks great like that."

She ran her fingers through the boyishly short cut and smiled. "You really think so? It still feels a little weird, but I think I like it." She checked her reflection in the mirror and nodded. "I'm so glad David gave Fred the boot. Otherwise I might never have found out how much fun it is to play the guy's part. Know what I mean?"

"Probably better than most."

They both laughed.

"Hey, do you want a ride with me to the party? Dad brought the SUV and we have plenty of room."

"Aren't you going to change first?"

She looked down at the knee-britches, short jacket and boots that made up her costume. "Nah, I like this outfit. I think it makes me look sort of butch-sexy, don't you?" She gave him no chance to reply and didn't even seem to notice. "Hey, listen. I heard my dad talking to his friends from the foundation and they freaking loved us. Isn't that awesome? I think he's planning to announce at the party that we're getting the grant." Her eyes widened like she hadn't meant to say that last bit. "Oh, but don't tell David, okay? I think Daddy wants it to be like a big surprise."

Kieran promised to keep her secret. Inside his heart swelled with happiness and relief. He and David had talked about the grant and, as Bethany had predicted, David had refused to even acknowledge the possibility that having Kieran play Viola could hurt their chances at getting the money. Thank FSM David had been right.

"So, do you want a ride?" Julie asked.

Kieran dragged his attention back to the conversation and shook his head. "Thanks, but I was planning to go with David."

"David already left, I think. I saw him going to his car just a few minutes ago."

"Oh, he did?"

There was a knock on the door. "Julie, are you in there?"

"Yeah Mom, I'll be right out." She turned back to Kieran. "We'll probably be leaving in a couple minutes, as soon as my dad gets done yacking it up with his friends. So if you do want a ride…" She went to the door, opened it and left the dressing room.

Kieran listened to her voice and that of her mother as they faded. He turned back to the mirror and reached for his makeup bag.

Why had David left without him? Not that they'd discussed going to the party together, but Kieran had just assumed that, like him, David would want to share this night and their mutual success. Evidently not.

Uncapping his mascara, Kieran leaned in close to the mirror and widened his eyes.

Behind him the door opened. In the mirror he saw the enormous bouquet of roses come through the door first then behind it, David, his face still glowing with the excitement of the night.

"There's my star." David crossed the room and stopped in front of the dressing table. "Can you make space for these?"

Kieran's heart did a little flip in his chest. "I think so. Who are they for?" He shoved aside tubes and bottles, brushes and jars.

"They're for my star. Who do you think?"

"From you?" Kieran whispered, already overwhelmed by the romance of the gesture. Of course he'd received opening night flowers before, but these were from David.

"They better be." David grinned. "If there's another guy sending you roses I'm going to have to go kick his ass."

Kieran laughed even as his heart did another one of those funny little back flips. "Not necessary. I don't have anybody but you bringing me roses."

But as he reached for David his lover stepped back. He plucked the small white envelope out of the bouquet and held it out. "Read the card."

"I'll read it later. C'mere."

"Read it now."

Kieran took the envelope, opened it and read: *Love sought is good, but given unsought is better. Love, David.*

About the Authors

JET MYKLES'S been writing sex stories back as far as junior high. Back then, the stories involved her favorite pop icons of the time but she soon extended beyond that realm into making up characters of her own. To this day, she hasn't stopped writing sex, although her knowledge on the subject has vastly improved.

An ardent fan of fantasy and science fiction sagas, Jet prefers to live in a world of imagination where dragons are real, elves are commonplace, vampires are just people with special diets and lycanthropes live next door. In her own mind, she's the spunky heroine who gets the best of everyone and always attracts the lean, muscular lads.

In real life, Jet is a self-proclaimed hermit, living in southern California with her life partner. She has a bachelor's degree in acting, but her loathing of auditions has kept her out of the limelight.

You can find Jet on the web at: http://www.jetmykles.com

J.P. BOWIE was born and raised in Aberdeen, Scotland. He wrote his first (unpublished) novel at the age of 14 - a science fiction tale of brawny men and brawnier women that made him a little suspect in the eyes of his family for a while.

J.P. wrote his first gay mystery in 2000, and after having it rejected by every publisher in the universe, he opted to put his money where his mouth is and self published *A Portrait of Phillip*. Now several books, short stories and novellas later, he is writing m/m erotica almost exclusively. J.P.'s favorite singer is Ella Fitzgerald, and his favorite man is Phil, his partner of 15 years.

Visit J.P. on the internet at http://www.jpbowie.com.

KIMBERLY GARDNER has been making up stories for as long as she can remember. As early as the seventh grade, she recalls slashing her favorite rockstars for her own and her friends' enjoyment. It was also around that time that she began a lifelong love affair with the romance genre, devouring category romances as fast as she could smuggle them into the house. So it's not all that surprising that her two passions, romance and putting pretty boys with other pretty boys, would ultimately come together in her writing.

Moliere says, "Writing is like prostitution. First you do it for love, then for a few close friends, then for money."

Kimberly is delighted at long last to be doing it for money. She can be found on the internet at:

http://www.kimberlygardner.com

THE TREVOR PROJECT

The Trevor Project operates the only nationwide, around-the-clock crisis and suicide prevention helpline for lesbian, gay, bisexual, transgender and questioning youth. Every day, The Trevor Project saves lives though its free and confidential helpline, its website and its educational services. If you or a friend are feeling lost or alone call The Trevor Helpline. If you or a friend are feeling lost, alone, confused or in crisis, please call The Trevor Helpline. You'll be able to speak confidentially with a trained counselor 24/7.
The Trevor Helpline: 866-488-7386
On the Web: http://www.thetrevorproject.org/

THE GLBT NATIONAL HELP CENTER

The GLBT National Help Center is a nonprofit, tax-exempt organization that is dedicated to meeting the needs of the gay, lesbian, bisexual and transgender community and those questioning their sexual orientation and gender identity. It is an outgrowth of the Gay & Lesbian National Hotline, which began in 1996 and now is a primary program of The GLBT National Help Center. It offers several different programs including two national hotlines that help members of the GLBT community talk about the important issues that they are facing in their lives. It helps end the isolation that many people feel, by providing a safe environment on the phone or via the internet to discuss issues that people can't talk about anywhere else. The GLBT National Help Center also helps other organizations build the infrastructure they need to provide strong support to our community at the local level.
National Hotline: 1-888-THE-GLNH (1-888-843-4564)
National Youth Talkline 1-800-246-PRIDE (1-800-246-7743)
On the Web: http://www.glnh.org/
e-mail: info@glbtnationalhelpcenter.org

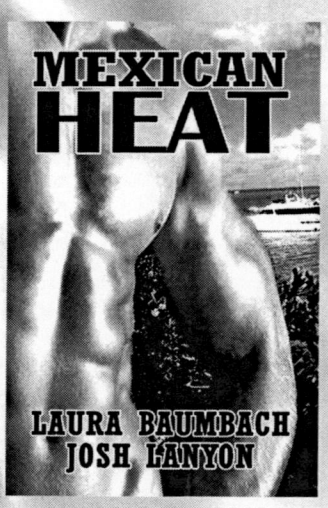

Stimulate yourself.
READ.
www.manloveromance.com
THE HOTTEST M/M EROTIC AUTHORS & WEBSITES ON THE NET

Printed in the United States
151831LV00001B/5/P